RELENTLESS

VANESSA VALE

Relentless

ISBN: 978-1-7959-0036-2

Copyright © 2014 Vanessa Vale

This is a work of fiction. Names, characters, places and incidents are the products of the author's imagination and used fictitiously. Any resemblance to actual persons, living or dead, businesses, companies, events or locales is entirely coincidental.

All rights reserved.

No part of this book may be reproduced in any form or by any electronic or mechanical means, including information storage and retrieval systems, without written permission from both authors, except for the use of brief quotations in a book review.

Cover Design: RomCon

Cover Photo: I-Stock, © Zastavkin

GET A FREE BOOK!

JOIN MY MAILING LIST TO BE THE FIRST TO KNOW OF NEW RELEASES, FREE BOOKS, SPECIAL PRICES AND OTHER AUTHOR GIVEAWAYS.

http://freeromanceread.com

GET A FREE BOOK!

JOIN MY MAILING LIST TO BE THE FIRST TO KNOW OF NEW RELEASES, FREE BOOKS, SPECIAL PRICES AND OTHER AUTHOR GIVEAWAYS.

http://freeromanceread.com

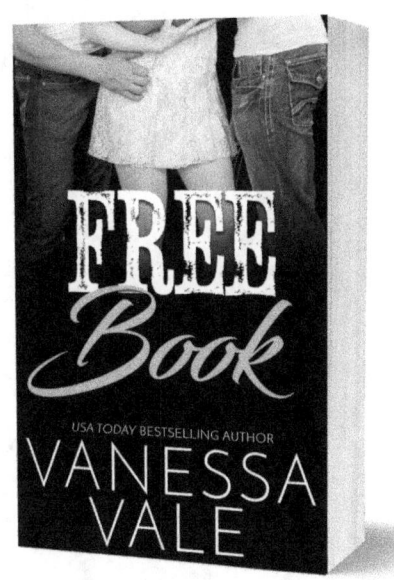

1

nna

If I had known how much fun it was to drive, how exhilarating it would feel, I would have done it sooner. Living in New York City didn't require a car, but life required a government ID, so years ago I'd borrowed a Prius long enough to take the driving test and obtain a license. I hadn't been behind the wheel since.

Until now. My dark sunglasses shielded against the bright Denver sun, the lowered window caused my long hair to whip around my face, forcing me to tuck it behind my ear to keep it out of the way. The air was hot, but the unaccustomed lack of humidity made it easily tolerable in comparison to the mugginess of Manhattan. The radio pumped out some local rock station and the highway was wide open; everyone was at work at eleven in the morning. Everyone but me, and surprisingly, it felt good to take a break. It was Friday and, for once, I wasn't sheltered in my little home office designing away. Safe.

It had taken my friend, Zach, weeks of cajoling to talk me into being his date for his sister's wedding. He needed a date—a female one—to keep his family in the dark about his not-out-of-the-closet status. Cruising down the highway with the Rocky Mountains, snow-capped even in July, as a backdrop, I was glad he'd been persistent. Tentative when we'd first arrived late last night, afraid I'd made a mistake about going away, I told myself over and over this was Denver. Like New York, it was safe. No one would know me.

I tapped my just dry nails on the steering wheel to the beat of the music. The subdued French manicure I'd gotten—at the small shop suggested by the hotel concierge—would be perfect for the rehearsal dinner later and the wedding reception tomorrow. With most of the day until I had to be dressed and ready to meet Zach in the hotel lobby before me, I felt carefree. I had no doubt he felt the same way, spending the day with other men in the wedding party playing golf. Glancing at the speedometer, I gave my rental a little more gas and laughed to myself as I maneuvered around a slow-moving semi.

The sound of a siren startled me out of my carefree moment and I darted a glance in the rearview mirror. Glaring red and blue lights, almost throbbing in their intensity, confirmed the police were directly behind my car. What had I done? Checking my speed, I wasn't going much over the speed limit to warrant a ticket. Was I? A sick hit of panic shot through me, making my palms slippery on the wheel. My heart hammered against my ribs as if trying to escape.

It wasn't twelve years ago. I wasn't eighteen anymore. I wasn't even in the same state. But what, then? What could they want with me? My foot tapped the brake and I jerked against the seat belt, unfamiliar with the sensitive car. Trying to find the blinker, I accidentally turned on the wipers. The back and forth rub of the blade against dry glass was loud once they turned off the siren. Flustered, I fumbled then switched the wipers off and maneuvered over toward the shoulder.

Coming to a stop, I put the car in park. The radio's once fun tunes were now jarring and annoying. I jammed the button with my palm and the car went silent, leaving only the sound of passing cars and trucks. I watched as the cruiser slid in behind me, angled toward my far bumper, with the strobe lights continuing to pulse. I watched in the mirror for the police officer to get out as I focused on breathing. *In. Out. In. Out.* Now was not the time to panic. To let them see I was scared. What was he doing back there? Why was he making me wait? My fingers were in a death grip around the steering wheel and I tried to relax them, to relax my shoulders that had crept up toward my ears. The overwhelming need to put the car back in *Drive* and make my escape was all-consuming. I didn't trust the police, didn't like them, but knew not to make the situation—whatever it was—worse by making them angry.

After long minutes, the man got out of his car. His uniform was dark and crisp, all sharp creases and starched collar. Walkie-talkie, pager and mace circled the utility belt. And then there was the very large gun in its holster. The man's hand was positioned just above it as he approached, as if ready to shoot with the least provocation. His hair was cut high and tight, his eyes obscured by reflective sunglasses. I could see through the side mirror he wore a bulletproof vest beneath his shirt, giving him an appearance of a veteran linebacker. Positioning himself by the rear door behind me, he leaned in so his body was shielded by the car. He hadn't moved his hand away from his gun.

"Ma'am, license and registration please." His voice was deep and his tone serious. I didn't recognize him. He wasn't one of them. He couldn't be. I was being silly. A tail light was out or something. No one had found me.

"It's…it's in my purse." I licked my lips as I fumbled in my small bag on the passenger seat, only large enough for my wallet, my cell and a few other essentials. "Here."

He took it from me, looked at it. Looked at me. "Registration."

"Oh." Right, registration. I shook my head to clear it as I reached over to open the glove box, pulled out a packet of papers, then handed them to the man. I pushed my hair back behind my ear with my fingers. Knowing they shook, I put them in my lap and clasped my palms together. *Breathe.*

"This is a rental car," he stated.

"Yes." I didn't know why I was pulled over, but I knew to answer their questions succinctly and only provide the information they requested. I had firsthand knowledge of how they could use any babbling against me.

While he was looking at the documents, a second police cruiser pulled up and parked in front of my car. Oh God. Why would two police cars be needed for a broken tail light? This time a female officer emerged, similarly garbed and talking into the receiver of a walkie-talkie strapped to her shoulder.

I swallowed down the bile that inched its way up my throat. It was hard to be calm when my heart beat so fast, as if I were given a shot of epinephrine. The sun blazed through the window and my shirt was damp against the seat back. "Turn off the ignition and step out of the car, please, ma'am," the policeman said.

The female officer watched me from her position by the hood of my car, her hand poised on her service weapon.

With fumbling fingers, I did as requested, disconnected my seat belt and opened the door. The man moved back to make room, but once I stepped from the car, he loomed over me, blocking the sun, and I had to tilt my head back to look up at him.

"Please follow me around to the other side of the car."

I had no choice but to follow, thankful to be away from traffic. I took a peek at the tail lights. Not broken.

The female officer joined us, looked me over in my sleeveless white blouse, floral skirt and strappy sandals. "Please take off your sunglasses."

Their words may have been polite, but they were all business.

I complied, squinted in the sunlight.

"Do you have any weapons on you, any knives or drug paraphernalia?" she asked.

I shook my head as I looked her in the eye. "No."

"I'm going to frisk you. Please put your arms up and out."

"Am I...am I under arrest?" I asked, my fingers fiddling with my sunglasses. I knew they had to have reason and I had to know what it was.

"No, ma'am," she replied.

The other officer watched passively as I lifted my arms to stand in the shape of a T. When the woman efficiently confirmed I wasn't concealing anything dangerous, he said, "We have reason to believe you have a dead body in the trunk of your car."

My arms fell back to my sides.

"A...a dead body?" I had imagined many things he might say, but that was not one of them. Sweat dotted my brow, my upper lip. I used the back of my hand to wipe at it. I knew they were both gauging my reaction to their words, assessing my threat of being dangerous and even guilty in my every move and body gesture. "My car?"

"Yes, ma'am. The description matches the vehicle we're looking for. We are going to need to search the car."

I glanced over my shoulder and stared at the bland, maroon four-door sedan. As with most rentals, it was American-made, newer model and boring. It didn't look like a car that would have a dead body in it, but then again, what one did?

I recognized my coping mechanism: humor. I needed to squelch that down so they didn't think I was being blasé about something so serious. They had no idea how serious this was to me. I couldn't panic, couldn't get upset. I'd learned to hide my emotions, shield them so they couldn't be used against me.

When I was seven, I'd learned quickly that it would bring me nothing but trouble. When I was eighteen, I'd refined the skill even more. Now, I had to override the panic, focus on something else besides what was happening to me. That's when I noticed little yellow wildflowers in the dirt shoulder. I stared at them as they shifted in the soft breeze.

It was happening again. It was like twelve years ago. Someone was up to something. Out to hurt me. This couldn't be a joke. Nothing was ever a joke.

I stared at the yellow flowers as I replied, "Search warrant?"

"Don't need one. Probable cause," the police officer shouted above the roar of a passing eighteen-wheeler. He didn't offer explanation. I didn't need one.

They must have a credible enough source to eliminate the need for a search warrant. Time was obviously of the essence. No doubt they couldn't wait all weekend for a judge to sign one with the vehicle in question being a rental. Obviously, the owner—me—would be considered a flight risk.

It was time to switch my mind off. I needed to put the mental walls up, to remember how it felt to shelter my mind behind them, protecting myself from whatever was happening to me. I could only nod and watch the stupid flower.

The woman remained by my side while the man went around the car to the driver's door, leaned in and popped the trunk. At the sound, I turned around. Watched him walk to the back, lift the lid and stood. Staring.

Giving a little shift of his head, the woman joined him. So did I.

"Oh my God," I whispered, my throat closing up at the sight. There, in the trunk of my full-sized rental, was a dead man. Forty-something, receding hairline, overweight, suit and tie. Glazed eyes stared up at me. There was a bullet hole in his forehead. And he was starting to smell. God, the horrific scent lifted up in the breeze. It wasn't powerful, yet. I assumed the only way I hadn't noticed it was that the windows had been open.

I felt the blood rush out of my head. Little black dots danced in front of eyes, making it look like flies were crawling on the body. I pivoted on my heel as I felt my stomach revolt, vomiting all over the concrete. Once the dry heaves subsided, I stayed bent over, one hand on my knee, trying to catch my breath. I wiped the back of my hand over my mouth, wishing I had some water to wash away the acidic taste in my mouth. All this time neither officer hadn't moved, the woman's black work shoes and creased pants in my periphery.

The police probably thought I'd thrown up because of seeing the dead body. I hadn't. I'd thrown up because I knew I was in big trouble. *It was happening again.* All my fears, all my worries over the past twelve years had come to life. Or death, like the body in the trunk. God, I knew I shouldn't have left New York, shouldn't have left the safe structure I'd made of my life for a little *fun*. I didn't *do* fun. I wasn't allowed. Because the moment I had some fun, just a tiny little bit, this was what happened.

Slowly, I stood back up and discovered other police cars had pulled up. Three additional men were staring at me, two more in uniform, one in plainclothes with a badge attached to a chain dangling from his neck.

I tucked my hair behind my ears, lifted my chin. The walls were completely fortified now. I was on my own once again. I couldn't get Zach involved; he had a family wedding to contend with. He couldn't tell everyone his date was an accused murderer. He didn't need to deal with this. I could do it on my own. I *always* did it on my own.

The female officer looked me in the eye, probably assessing whether I was going to throw up again. "You're going to have to come with us," she told me, taking my forearm in a strong grip. I was going to jail. Again. Going to be accused of murder. Again. I'd lived through the nightmare once. I wasn't sure if I could do it again.

Protect yourself. You're smarter this time. You know game. You know the rules. "I want a lawyer." My voice was as dead as the man in the trunk.

2

rif

"Okay, you got me in here. Now, what the hell do you want?" I asked, rubbing my five o'clock shadow that had gone around the clock an extra day. It itched and it was hot, but it had to stay to help me be Nick Malone. I considered it a prop in my act. "You said you had something interesting to show me. I don't have time to be dragged back into the station about something that you thought I'd find *interesting*."

"You've been undercover too long, Grif. You've lost all your manners." Peters, a homicide detective I'd known for a decade, gave me the once-over. "Nice outfit. You look like shit."

Grif. I hadn't heard my real name used in a while. Jake Griffin. Who the hell was he again? I couldn't remember anymore. I'd been undercover too fucking long.

"I just woke up and this—" I plucked at the black T-shirt one size too small, "—is what you wear when you run a nightclub. I don't suppose there's any fresh coffee around here?" The room was loud, the usual hustle of the homicide division. Phones rang, voices carried and the clack of fingers on keyboards was incessant.

Peters looked at his watch. "It's one thirty."

"Do you really want to know what I do with Moretti and his goons? Because this assignment's not all fucking rainbows and sunshine." My voice had an edge I couldn't help. I was exhausted and more than ready to see the end of this never-ending assignment. I saw a full pot of coffee across the room in the little mini-kitchen area and veered over to it. When Peters followed, I added, "I was up all night dealing with employee issues at the bar. I'm a cop, not Human Resources."

I poured a cup, took a sip of the coffee, winced, then gulped down the scalding swallow, hoping the caffeine would give me the jolt I needed to have patience for whatever Peters wanted.

"Yeah, I can see how being in *the* hottest nightclub in town with twenty-two-year-old women giving you their phone numbers written on their panties would be rough."

I leaned against the counter, remembering that situation, and the shit I'd gotten from Peters and the others at the station for sharing that little gem. What was her name? Cathy? Karla? "Jesus, that was one time and I swear she had more plastic parts and oversized headlights than a Ford." I took another swig of coffee, winced, and watched Peters chuckle. "God, I'm getting old, aren't I?"

Undercover work was miserable at best. You had to give up everything to take on a role, a persona, for the duration of the assignment. In this case, I'd been infiltrating the Moretti crime family for over six months, getting in deep enough to be given the role of running Scorch, Denver's newest nightclub—and Moretti's latest purchase. It was where I needed to be, at the supposed pulse of the man's money laundering. I just had to prove it. That meant going to bed at dawn and sleeping the day away like a fucking vampire.

"Bobby Lane. Name ring a bell?"

I perked up. "Moretti's son-in-law. A mean little shit that handles the prostitution aspect of the family business. Not a believer in women's rights, and I'm pretty sure that his wife knows that firsthand."

"That's the one."

I just stared at him, waiting. He was enjoying this *way* too much. I circled my hand around in a circle to get him talking.

"He's dead."

I kept from spitting out the coffee across my friend's shirt. Barely.

"When? How?"

Peters gave a little shrug. "Appears to have been late last night. Bullet to the brain."

I grinned. "Bobby Lane was a fucking asshole and deserved whatever he got. I would have heard this through Moretti soon enough." I took a sip of coffee, looked at him over the rim of the cup. "That's not the only reason why I'm here."

He pointed at me, smiled. "That's why you made detective. His body was found in the trunk of a car."

I shrugged. This wasn't news. "So? Aren't they usually?"

"This car got pulled over because of an anonymous tip. It was driven by a woman named Anna Scott. Heard of her?"

I shook my head. "Where is she?"

"Room four."

I took my bad coffee and headed to the back where the interrogation rooms were located. I waved at a familiar face or two but didn't stop to talk. It was quieter past all the desks of the bullpen, but the smell of stale coffee and Chinese takeout lingered.

"You're sure this isn't the hooker trick? I'm not falling for the hooker trick," I mumbled, thinking back to the many pranks we'd all pulled on each other to keep the tension and stress levels down when dealing with harsh cases. I hadn't heard about Bobby Lane's murder so it could have been a ruse Peters used to have a little fun at my expense.

"This one's not a hooker." He opened the door to the dark viewing room. It was obvious when I looked through the large window into the next room that Peters was right.

There was no way in hell the woman sitting there, all prim and proper with her hands in her lap, was a hooker. Through the one-way glass she looked like Happy Suzy Homemaker, not a pro pulled off the street. "She killed Bobby Lane? No fucking way."

The room was soundproofed, so she didn't know she was being observed.

"She was driving the car."

"Yeah, on the way to the PTA."

"Whatever. Give me your first impression," Peters said.

I assessed the woman with my detective eye. "Close to thirty and beautiful."

Peters cocked an eyebrow but remained silent.

Shit, had I said the last out loud? What the hell, she was beautiful.

Her skin was so pale next to her straight, dark hair. It was long, loose over her shoulders. "Her hair's nicely cut, which means she has money." She had dark eyes fringed by even darker lashes, sculpted brows and minimal makeup. "Not overly vain. Her lipstick's gone or she never wore any."

Her clothes fit her slim frame perfectly; a skirt that was mostly orange with flowers all over it. "She's modest." I pointed at her. "Her skirt comes to her knees, even sitting down. It's not skin tight." I leaned in to get a closer look, even though she was only ten feet away. "Her blouse has buttons all down the front, but none are open to reveal cleavage. In fact, is that a tank top or something she's wearing underneath? She's not flaunting her assets." She had assets all right. I couldn't miss the lush curve of her breasts, even beneath her white blouse. "Moretti's ladies flash a little more skin than that."

"Go on," Peters prompted.

"By the look of her arms, I'd say she stays in shape."

"She's not what I'd call a bodybuilder," Peters added.

"No, but I bet she does more pushups than you to get triceps like that."

We both stared at her in silence for a moment. I had no doubt Peters was considering his fitness regime.

"Strappy sandals. She's a girly girl," I continued. "But low heels indicate she's practical. No stilettos for her."

"I'm impressed. What about the toe polish?" Peters asked.

"Hidden vixen?" I asked, half joking, taking in the fire-engine red. There was more to this woman than met the eye—and she wasn't showing much. She was *too* perfect. The real woman was hidden beneath the façade she had in place and I had to wonder what she was like. This façade, it was well fortified, well practiced, as if she was used to it being up around her like a castle wall. What would I have to do to pull it down, and what would I find once I did? I was getting a hard-on looking at her. And she was a suspect. One hell of a suspect. Jesus, it had been too long.

There had to be something wrong with me. The college girls in skimpy clothes with skimpy morals at Scorch every night didn't even make my dick twitch. I never looked twice at any of them. This woman, and she was *all* woman, had me pressing uncomfortably against the zipper of my pants, even knowing she might have killed a guy. A total asshole who wouldn't be missed by many, but still. My dick didn't seem to really care.

"If hidden vixen is code word for murderer, then you might be right."

"Self-defense maybe?" She didn't look like a woman who'd been assaulted, especially by a misogynist like Bobby Lane. There wasn't a mark or blemish on her creamy skin and Bobby didn't play nice. Just the thought of her being touched by that bastard made me clench my fists. A bullet to the brain wouldn't be enough.

"Doubtful, since she flew in last night," Peters told me.

A surprising wave of relief washed over me. *Shit, I'm in trouble here.*

"Record?" Had she been in jail before? Arrested? Convicted of a crime? Speeding? Unpaid parking ticket? Unlicensed dog?

"Clean," Peters replied.

I set my paper cup down on the table, leaned back against it and crossed my arms, my eyes never leaving her face. "There's more to her than I've just said." I stared at her for another moment. "She hasn't moved since we came in. She's staring at some spot on the wall in front of her. That crack or something. She's too relaxed. She's not sweating, she's not panicked, she's not fidgeting. And look. She's got goose bumps on her arms. The AC's cranked. She's got to be cold and she doesn't even realize it."

Even in our small room I could feel the cool breeze from the ceiling vent. The HVAC system in the old building had two settings: too hot or too cold.

Her face was devoid of any type of emotion. I wondered how a smile would change her appearance, bring her to life. She might have a beating heart, but she didn't really seem alive. She seemed closed off.

"Shock, maybe?" Peters leaned back against the table as well. "She lawyered up first thing when the traffic cop found the body. Hasn't said a word since. Hasn't taken her hands out of her lap. Refused the soda we offered. Doesn't seem like she's on drugs, either."

The can was in front of her, the condensation a small pool of liquid on the table indicated it had been there a while.

"Did she call anyone?"

Peters shook his head. "She didn't want her one phone call."

I raised my eyebrows. "Pretty girl like her with no one to call. Afraid of her husband?"

"Single."

"It looks like she's...thinking," I considered.

"Maybe." Peters didn't seem to buy that idea. "She's from New York City and was driving a rental car," he added. "A public defender met with her for about twenty minutes, is off conferring with someone or taking a bathroom break. Whatever. Told us she's ready to talk. Here they come now."

We watched as a woman dressed in a suit that screamed lawyer came and took a seat next to the suspect. This woman, Anna Scott, followed the lawyer with her eyes, but otherwise remained devoid of emotion. She didn't look like she was on drugs—she definitely wasn't amped up on meth, and if she was on some kind of downer or hooked on pain meds, she'd be unconscious or glazed over, not quiet and focused. I didn't think she was in shock, even if Peters wondered just that. She just looked...in control.

I recognized the two detectives, Gossing and Werbler, who took seats on the other side of the table. They were good men and good detectives. If this woman had shot Bobby Lane, they would wheedle it from her.

Werbler began. "Do you know Bobby Lane?"

The public defender nodded at the woman. Anna Scott cleared her throat. "No."

"Paul Moretti?"

"No. You know I'm from New York. I don't know anyone here." Her voice was soft, but deep with intent even though the speakers in the wall.

"Ever been to Denver before?"

"No."

"Ever been to Scorch?"

"If it's in Denver, then obviously I haven't."

"Come on, Ms. Scott, give us something to work with here, because otherwise I'm willing to believe you killed Bobby Lane."

Anna Scott looked between the detectives. "You're the good cop and you've drawn the short straw for bad cop. It's not going to work. You know my name and all the other information about me you've been able to pull up on the computer in the past two hours I've been sitting here. You no doubt know I'm in town for the weekend with a friend for his sister's wedding by seeing our hotel rooms were reserved for the wedding party." She swallowed deeply, licked her lips. Why did I find that really hot?

"Boyfriend?" I asked Peters, keeping my eyes on the other room.

He shook his head. "Two hotel rooms, so I don't think so."

"Are you sure you don't want some soda?" Werbler asked, pointing to the can.

"I'm not touching that can so you can get my fingerprints."

Werbler's mouth fell open, but he shut it quickly.

I lifted an eyebrow at her knowledge. She was a surprise. And a delight. I watched as the detectives shifted in their seats.

"Is she a lawyer?" I asked Peters.

"Records say architect. Runs her own business. Works from home."

An architect that knew about the law.

"I flew in last night at eleven thirty, which I'm sure you know. Passenger records are easy enough to obtain, which I'm sure you've done. So being on a plane somewhere over Nebraska at the time of death with over one hundred other people is a pretty solid alibi."

"Are you saying you know when he was killed?" Gossing asked. "Does that mean that you were involved, but maybe didn't pull the trigger? Getaway driver, perhaps?"

The detectives were trying to fluster her. They'd made grown men cry before, but their attempts didn't appear to be working now. Her hands hadn't moved, her skin wasn't flushed in anger. Nothing.

"I saw the man, you said Bobby Lane was his name? I saw him in the trunk of the car with the two traffic officers for about ten seconds. Rigor had set in because he was curled up in the fetal position. I don't have to be an ME to know that means he'd been dead for at least twelve hours." Anna tucked her hair behind her ear. Her first sign of movement. Her nails were short with a simple manicure. No wedding ring.

"Not a doctor? Parents? Anyone a doctor?" I asked Peters, my eyes focused on Anna.

I saw Peters look at a folder on the desk out of the corner of my eye. "Says her mother died when she was six, father when she was eighteen. No record of how. No siblings. No living relatives."

I saw a small smile play at the corner of the public defender's mouth. I could tell she was enjoying this. So was I. Holy hell, it was like watching a teacher scold two recalcitrant school boys. But I never had a teacher who looked like Anna Scott.

"Even if I had somehow shot him," she continued, "I couldn't have lifted him up from wherever I'd done it to place him in the trunk. I'm not big, or strong enough, to do it."

I couldn't tell with her sitting down, but she wasn't more than five-five. Bobby Lane was a big man, well over six feet and hadn't exercised in his life. The extra fifty pounds he'd carried around his middle was proof.

"Maybe you killed him when he was standing in front of the trunk and he collapsed into it after you shot him."

"No blood. No bullet hole in the trunk. No GSR on my hands."

"So you're willing to test for gunshot residue?"

"I am."

I had to know more. She was like a puzzle I had to solve. "Any information on IQ, medical records, being institutionalized?"

"What, you think she's a psychopath? Sociopath? Schizo?"

"Doubtful, but she's very smart, very knowledgeable...familiar with all this." I waved my hand at the room around us. "How can she look so innocent and wholesome and be so...well versed in police proceedings? In death?"

"Ted Bundy looked pretty wholesome back in his day." Peters shrugged. Not all answers were available. Some detectives had to dig for it. Sometimes they never learned all the answers. Peters was well aware of this. "All I know is that she acts like she's got a stick up her butt."

I cocked my head, watched her closely. "She acts like it. *Act* being the key word." I looked at her eyes. Flat. Unfeeling, but focused. "She's...scared. She's hiding behind, what's the word?" I snapped my fingers. "Aloofness. As if this isn't affecting her. I bet she's shitting a brick on the inside."

Anna took a deep breath and I enjoyed watching her breasts rise and fall. Calm as can be, she continued. "As for the *car*, I put my rental agreement in my carry-on when I left the lot at the airport last night. I assume you checked with the company and know that car isn't mine. Since I have an alibi, and the car isn't mine, the only explanation is that my car is still in the lot at the hotel."

It was the detectives' turn to take a deep breath. The public defender tapped her pen on the table.

The answer clicked into place for me. She was right. She'd been in the wrong car.

"Valet," I said.

"What?" Peters asked.

"The valet." I pointed at her. "No way this woman parks her car in a dark hotel lot after midnight when she got in. She's too smart to do something as dangerous as that. She flew in with a friend. I'm guessing he has his own rental since he's part of the wedding party. Probably has wedding stuff she doesn't have to do. A different schedule. He's not her boyfriend. You said two rooms." I paused, considered her through the glass. "She doesn't trust him enough to drive her—definitely not a boyfriend or anyone close then. If he drove his own rental and they got separated from the airport to the hotel, she wouldn't chance being alone in the lot. So she valets the car. She's in complete control of everything. She has to be. She's handling Gossing and Werbler like it's their first day at the Academy." I stood and paced in front of the window. "Fuck, it's so simple. The valet gave her the wrong car. What kind is it?"

"Ford Taurus."

I gave a quick bark of laughter, turned to look at Peters. "There are a million of them out there. I'm right, aren't I?"

Before Peters could answer, Werbler spoke up. "Miss Scott, your rental is indeed in the parking lot of your hotel. It seems when you gave your ticket to the valet this morning he brought you the wrong car. They said you had a burgundy Taurus."

"Maroon."

"Excuse me?" Gossing asked, leaning his elbows on the table.

"My rental car is maroon, not burgundy."

"You couldn't tell the difference when the valet gave it to you?" Werbler wondered.

She arched one elegant eyebrow. "I'm not suggesting the car in question and my rental car are two different colors. What I'm stating is that the valet you questioned is clearly color blind since he doesn't know the difference between the two. Perhaps he isn't the most reliable of sources of information. How many cars did he valet this morning? How many were a Taurus like mine? You're just wasting my time with this line of talk as you're both smart enough to have already validated everything by my rental agreement with the car company."

Maroon and burgundy were the same to me, but I was no artist, so what did I know? I couldn't help but grin at her don't-fuck-with-me tone and glanced over at Peters. The way she looked, all fresh and innocent, the way she dressed, all tame and soft, screamed *prissy*. But she wasn't, because that type of woman did nothing for me. Annoyed the shit out of me. Anna Scott was…an anomaly. I read people. I was good at it. It was my job to be good at it. Saved my life a time or two. But I couldn't get a bead on her. Which made her a challenge, and I loved a good challenge. And if said challenge happened to make me wonder what she was wearing beneath her prim little outfit, all the better.

I'd wager her appearance was all for show. Some kind of outward shell she showed to the world. Beneath, she'd wear soft lace and satin. Would her skin be as silky soft as it looked? Would her nipples be as pale pink as I imagined? I shifted against the table. "You're right, this is *interesting*."

"You're telling me I'm sitting here in a Denver police station being questioned for murder because a valet didn't look at his ticket and gave me a supposed burgundy Taurus instead of maroon," Anna Scott stated matter-of-factly.

Werbler and Gossing shifted once again, embarrassment keen on their faces. "Yes, ma'am."

"Then I'm free to go." It wasn't a question.

She glanced at her lawyer who gave a quick nod. The woman hadn't said a word. It seemed Anna Scott didn't really need legal council, just the protection one afforded her by law. The protection of keeping her mouth shut until she'd gotten her ducks in a row to defend herself.

"Yes, you are," Gossing told her. "After you submit to a GSR test."

"All right." Anna Scott shifted her seat back, the metal scraping against the linoleum floor and stood. I was right, about five-five. Standing, without the table to shield her, she looked...fragile. Even with her shoulders back, her dark hair like a waterfall, her chin tilted in a way to make her look like she had a stick up her ass, she was lovely. Almost innocent of the world, which was the strangest statement since she'd obviously had a run-in with cops before, regardless of what her record said. My mouth went dry just taking in my fill. I took a sip of my now cold coffee. Winced at the miserable taste.

Her thumbs brushed slightly against her skirt, but other than that she was still. No smile, no sparkle in her eyes at her victory over the police. I'd be dancing a jig after getting myself out of a possible murder charge. That, or I'd need new pair of pants. I moved closer to the glass for a better look. She was damaged. Something had happened to her, but I didn't know what. Hadn't we all? Anyone who made it to adulthood had to have something happen to them. It's how you survived that mattered. And it appeared to me that Anna Scott was surviving. And that was it.

A strange emotion settled in my chest, one I hadn't felt in a long time. I tamped it down. No way was I going to feel something, anything, for this woman. The fact that she looked so alone—so aloof surrounded by so many—made me want to pull her into my arms and tell her everything was going to be okay. To protect her. I shook my head at my crazy thoughts. Women like her and those protective feelings only brought me trouble I didn't want.

"Who is...was Bobby Lane?" she asked.

The detectives had stood when she did. "Worked for Paul Moretti," Werbler shared, watching her closely. So was I. "Head of a crime syndicate, gang, whatever, that deals in drugs, money laundering, prostitution, gun running and other sideline activities."

She wasn't giving away anything. It appeared she didn't know Bobby Lane, but I couldn't tell for sure. She was innocent of the crime against Bobby Lane. Her alibi was solid. The mixup was certainly plausible. Slightly ridiculous, but definitely plausible. But it was just as obvious she'd been interrogated by the cops before, which meant she wasn't as innocent as she seemed.

"Bobby Lane was Moretti's son-in-law and it was rumored he was being groomed to take over for him. Lane was last seen at Scorch, a nightclub downtown, owned by Moretti," Werbler added.

I'd been at Scorch all night and hadn't seen Lane, but that didn't mean shit. It had been crowded and I'd had to deal with fucking pain-in-the-ass employees all night. If he'd been there, it wasn't to see me. Thank Christ.

Anna nodded. "Thank you for sharing, but it all means nothing to me. I'd like my things and if you can please call me a cab, I have a wedding rehearsal to go to."

Werbler opened the door for her. "We'll have one of the officers give you a ride back to your hotel after the GSR test."

Anna arched a brow at him. "I think I'm done with the police for today. Thank you."

Once they left the room to have her hands tested for gunshot residue, I just looked at Peters. "Well?"

"There's something not quite right about that woman," he said, picking her folder up off the table.

"What? The fact that she knows police interrogation methods, that she knows about rigor mortis, that she doesn't want her fingerprints checked?"

"Yeah, that."

"She didn't kill him. You know that as well as I. She was set up. Whoever the killer is must've panicked when they found out the car was missing. Shit, I would've loved to see that. They must have realized they'd been given the opportunity to offload the body—and the lengthy prison term that goes with one—onto someone else. They're probably celebrating over drinks right now."

Peters nodded, so I continued. "But they didn't expect Anna Scott. She got her neck out of the noose on her own. The way she handled the interview, when Werbler told her Bobby's name, she didn't appear to know him, but she's one cool lady. The only thing I know for sure is that I don't ever want to play poker with her."

Peters quirked a smile and said, "This is where you come in. If she's innocent, she goes to a wedding and flies out on Sunday. If she's tied into all this somehow, then Gossing dropped Moretti's name, Bobby's name and Scorch. You'll hear about the hit as soon as you go back in tonight, hear about her if she did it. You're our inside man."

"If she's involved with Moretti, I'll know soon enough. If she shows up at Scorch, I'll be waiting." *With fucking bells on.*

I wanted to know more about Anna Scott and whether she was mixed up in all this or not. If she wasn't working for the bastard, then what *was* her secret? She sure as hell had one. She intrigued me, and nothing had intrigued me for a long time. Those warning bells were clanging in my head about not getting involved with a woman like her. It would be stupid, almost suicidal, to do so. She wasn't a simple one-night stand I had falling all over me night after night at the club. The hard-on she'd brought about was only now starting to subside. If my dick reacted just by looking at her through a window, I could only imagine what it would be like when I got her into bed. I was going to find out. She flew out on Sunday. The clock was ticking.

3

nna

I WAS ABLE TO HOLD IT TOGETHER UNTIL I RETURNED TO THE HOTEL, TAXI PAID for with trembling fingers, and into the shower before my legs gave out. I started shaking and couldn't stop, my muscles quivering and spasming, even huddled on the slick tile floor. I couldn't get warm even beneath the hot spray, couldn't get the smell, the *feel*, of the police station out of my head. I bent my knees and hugged my arms around them tightly as if it would keep me from flying apart. No amount of soap and scrubbing was going to wash away the day's events. Nor keep the past from coming back. I could wash the dirt from my body, but never the searing thoughts from my mind.

When I saw the body in the trunk earlier, I'd thought Todd had found me. Had found a way to make me pay. To bring my worst nightmare back to reality.

No one is going to help you. You're going to rot in jail like all of the other murderers. Self-defense? You really think the police will believe you? You're nothing. Nothing.

I forced the words down, forced the feelings of loneliness, desperation and fear that had gripped me. It was the past. Over. They hadn't found me. Just like at the police station earlier, I focused on my breathing. *In. Out. In. Out.* I couldn't stay in the shower forever. I couldn't hide, no matter how much I wanted to just stay in my room until it was time to go to the airport for the return flight. I'd tried getting out, going someplace new, something fun... freedom. It hadn't worked. But Zach needed me and I'd rather go with him to the rehearsal dinner than explain why I wanted to hide. Once I got back to New York on Sunday I could hide again. I was good at hiding.

Tugging the belt on the soft hotel robe tightly about me, I wiped my hand on the mirror to clear the damp fog. My face was pale, dark circles smudged beneath my eyes. My hair hung in wet clumps around my face and down my back. I plugged in the straightening iron for it to warm, picked up my brush and began to comb the tangles from my hair.

Thirty minutes later, I zipped up my pale blue silk dress. It had a slim bodice with a high, straight neckline, sleeveless, with satin ribbons in the same soft color tied at each shoulder that held the front and back together. The skirt was a slight A-line, flaring at the hips and falling to mid-knee. Slingback pumps gave me a few inches of lift. My makeup was soft, my lips a pale pink. The top of my hair was pulled back in a clip, leaving the bottom long and sleek down my back. Small diamonds glinted at my ears.

Picking up my slim watch on the counter, I saw I had twenty minutes before meeting Zach in the lobby. I clipped it on my wrist as I walked over to check my email on my tablet while I waited. I clicked through and deleted the spam, sent a quick note to a client before I pulled up my news feed. I'd set my browser to pull up any information, updates or news with the keywords Todd Lawton and Grayson Edwards. Every time I checked, my nerves fluttered in tense and unpleasant anticipation. I usually received a few bits of news a week, mostly about their attending a dinner, a philanthropic donation or a boost in Edwards Enterprises stock shares. I didn't expect the news that came through this time from the San Francisco paper, however.

Elizabeth Edwards, daughter of Mr. Grayson Edwards and his wife Victoria, became engaged to Mr. Todd Lawton over the weekend. Elizabeth recently graduated from the prestigious Montworth Academy and Mr. Lawton is Vice President of Operations with Edwards Enterprises. A Christmas wedding is planned.

Along with the text was a photo of the happy couple. I'd never seen a picture of my half-sister before, my father and his second wife sheltered her, and took a moment to stare at her. We looked nothing alike. While my hair was dark, hers was blond. She appeared to have a taller, slimmer build, similar to her mother's. It had been over twenty years since I'd seen my stepmother in person, but I remembered her well. I only hoped Elizabeth inherited her good looks, not her personality. On the surface, she was really lovely. Young. Innocent.

Todd looked the same. Attractive in a tanned, tennis player sort of way. Groomed impeccably, indicative of his wealth and power handed to him by my father. At forty-five, his hair had receded a little, although I had no doubt that was a battle fought hard with medical intervention. He wore a blue suit and a tie that matched Elizabeth's pale yellow dress. His hand rested on her shoulder. The background was out of focus, but appeared to have been taken outdoors. To anyone else, they looked like a happy couple, much in love. To me, knowing the real Todd, I could see the cold gleam in his eye, hidden until after the nuptials.

I remember posing for a similar photo, Todd's hand placed identically on my shoulder, too. A chill ran through me remembering the feel of it. My dress had been a soft pink. Floral. I'd worn my hair differently then, letting the natural curl have its way across my shoulders, the color a few shades lighter. I'd been so excited, so enchanted that a man had been interested in me, found me desirable. Wanted me. I'd been shamefully wrong. Naïve.

I'd been so silly to consider Todd had anything to do with the dead body in the trunk of the rental car. While I'd been thinking he'd hatched a plan to ruin my life once again, he'd been busy in San Francisco becoming engaged to my half-sister. Why would he waste his time on me? He had a new victim.

I knew all too well what that meant. A loveless marriage, abuse, unhappiness, solely for money. Money for Todd. I'd survived his plans with my father, barely. I was older and wiser now because of it. But so were they. Elizabeth, the half-sister I'd never met, who probably hadn't even been told of my existence, wasn't as well versed in deceit. She was going to be the unwitting pawn and would be crushed. Ruined, then tossed away. Or worse, trapped. I'd managed to escape, but I had no doubt Todd and my father had learned from the experience and wouldn't let it happen again.

I had to help Elizabeth, had to warn her. Save her. But how? The very idea of going back to San Francisco made me feel panicked, my heart beating frantically, my palms damp. I couldn't do it. I'd gotten away. Changed my name, changed my look, made a new life. In hiding. There was no way I could go back. I'd bested Todd once. He'd kill me before he let me do it again.

Even if I did show up on my father's doorstep and ring the bell, Elizabeth probably didn't know who I was. She wouldn't just go off with a stranger, nor believe one telling evil tales about her father and fiancé. If she'd been told anything about me, whatever she'd heard couldn't have been good. They'd surely invented stories about how bad I was for never coming to the house. Sex, drugs, addiction, felony, prostitution. I didn't doubt they'd used any of those words to describe me in harsh light.

How could I help her? I couldn't just leave her to a similar fate, or worse. This was something I couldn't do alone. I needed help. I just had to figure out who. And fast.

Glancing at my watch, I knew now wasn't the time. I had to be in the lobby. Zach was waiting. *Zach.* Could he help me? No. Too nice, too sweet to deal with men like Todd and my father. I took a deep breath, let it out slowly. It was time to go. To pretend once again.

Grif

It was ten and the nightclub was just starting to fill up. Friday nights were the busiest, the line to get in wrapping down the block and around the corner. The bouncer at the door was selective, letting in only those deemed worthy. To keep the high-profile members of society in, the VIP section full, Scorch made entrance a privilege to the masses, not a guarantee.

With the sleek polished chrome and leather interior, a large dance floor and intimate booths, it epitomized everything the owner, Paul Moretti, was not. He'd come from an impoverished family, a rough life built by the rules of the street, his mother giving up the fight for control in his rearing when he was a boy. Amassing his fortune was done punch by punch as a youth, then hit by bloody hit as an adult, Moretti was known in Denver and throughout the West as a man not to fuck with. Businessmen didn't defy him. Women didn't deny him. He got what he wanted and nothing—or no one—else mattered. The longer I stayed undercover, the more stories I heard. And none of them were good.

I knew it was only a matter of time before I got the call. I'd been waiting for it. Word of Bobby Lane's murder had spread swiftly, as only bad news did. All of the employees of Scorch, from the newly hired server to the seasoned bartender, wondered who'd done it. And why. Had it been a hit? Payback for something, or someone, Bobby had done? He'd been a ladies' man, even married, so if he dipped his wick in the wrong woman, a husband had a right to retribution. That was the way it worked. And that was just one reason among many that I didn't dip my wick at all. Not while undercover. Not with a married woman, or any woman who worked, lived, or breathed near *anything* that belonged to Moretti. That kind of woman was dangerous beneath the covers. One slip-up and pillow talk could turn deadly. If I was going to be shot in the head and left in the trunk of a car, I wanted to be found by my colleagues on the force with my pants on.

That was why, when the bartender gave me the phone call hand sign from across the jammed dance floor, I knew who'd be on the line.

After battling my way through the throng to my office at the back of the building and shutting the door on the techno music—the beat still strumming along the floor—I picked up the line.

"You've heard, I'm sure," Moretti said, his voice deep and gravelly like only a pack-a-day smoker could manage. He didn't do social niceties like hello.

"Who hasn't?" I dropped down into the desk chair, swiveled it so I could put my leather boots up on the cluttered surface. It would most likely be the only time I'd sit before closing. I rested my head against the high back, closed my eyes. "Should I offer my condolences?"

"I don't know what my daughter Ginny ever saw in that bastard. He did good on the job, the girls have brought in more money since my son-in-law took over that racket." He coughed. "But he sampled the merchandise more than he should've. I'm surprised his dick didn't fall off."

I didn't want to even guess what Bobby'd shared with Ginny. I knew Moretti would say that was her mother's problem, so I didn't ask.

I gave a noncommittal grunt in reply. There wasn't anything to say. I was just relieved my assignment was to bust the old man on money laundering, not prostitution. No way could I send women out on the streets like Bobby did night after night to line Moretti's pockets.

"Regardless, someone whacked him. I want to know who."

I waited a beat. "And?"

Moretti sighed. "I know your past. I know everything about everybody who works for me. You used to be on the force. Use that angle to find out what's going on."

My cover story was a mixture of fact and fiction. We knew going in Moretti would dig up what he could about me before being let into his inner circle. I had to have the right qualifications—in Moretti's eyes—for the job. That included being dishonorably discharged from the Army for being tried for killing a fellow soldier, but acquitted on lack of evidence. I'd moved from the Army to a stint with the Denver PD where I was again removed from duty because of tampered evidence in a murder trial, although I couldn't officially be pinned for the crime. Moretti looked on these imaginary, and very questionable, acts as a Human Resources department would an MBA from Harvard.

I really had been in the Army, doing two stints in Afghanistan before being medically discharged because of a bullet to the knee. I was still with the force, but making me look rogue, look like I could have accusations and even a murder slide off me like water from a duck's back, made me a prime candidate for hire in Moretti's eyes. It had worked.

"No problem. I have a few favors I can call in."

"Good. Good."

"And the girl?" No way would I let an innocent get hurt. Especially Anna Scott. Why I felt I had to protect her, I had no clue. I just did. And that meant keeping Moretti's hands off her.

He chuckled. "She's certainly a loose thread."

I faked a laugh. "Whoever did the hit better get a lottery ticket. And send the girl some flowers."

Moretti chuckled. "No kidding. They lost their body, then realized they could dump the whole problem on some unwitting schmuck. What are the chances? I couldn't have done it better myself."

"Did you? Did you do it yourself?"

"What the fuck do you think?"

I didn't put it past the man to kill his own son-in-law. He probably did. They hadn't been close. No one was close in this business. Moretti's question was like a live grenade. I needed to put the pin back so it didn't blow up in my face.

"So, the girl?" I repeated. If Moretti had killed Bobby, he might put a hit out on her since she most likely messed up his plans. She might be in danger. She might be heading back to New York on Sunday, but the man's reach easily extended that far. Or, he could just forget about her since the heat was off. It was a toss-up to which way Moretti'd go with her.

"The cops know she's innocent. Wrong place, wrong time. Think she'll be a problem for us?" he wondered. Meaning, would the cops knock on Moretti's door to help some random woman?

The bastard valued my opinion, which meant the months of work were paying off. I paused as if considering. "Bobby Lane is the one wronged here. You're the grieving father-in-law. I doubt the police are going to look at you for this hit. I'd say you're free and clear."

"True. Still, I should have someone check on her. Discreetly. Confirm what we're saying."

"Your goons don't do discreet." It was a fact and Moretti knew it.

Moretti coughed long and hard, forcing me to remove the phone from my ear. "You do it. You've got finesse. A way with the ladies."

My eyebrows went up even though Moretti couldn't see. "I haven't had my *way* with any of the ladies. None that you know about, at least."

"See? Discreet." He paused. "She's yours. Check her out. Do her, fuck her. Whatever. Get her to talk using that finesse. See if she knows more than she's letting on. Just make sure she's not a problem."

"Done."

4

nna

THE NEXT EVENING, I SAT AT THE ASSIGNED ROUND TABLE RESERVED FOR MEMBERS of the wedding party and their guests. White linen covered the table with a centerpiece of pale roses and yellow tulips. Small glass globes filled with water and floating candles were interspersed between the butter dishes and sugar bowls. The room's west wall was floor-to-ceiling windows, and we were able to enjoy the setting sun behind the mountains. The only other mountains I'd seen were the Alps during my time in Switzerland. The view here was so much different, so arid and rugged, yet equally impressive.

The tables were being cleared of the salmon entrée, prior to the toasts by the best man and maid of honor. I was exhausted, my eyes hot and scratchy like sandpaper, having barely slept the night before. As I tossed and turned, my mind had shifted from being questioned by the police to my half-sister's engagement, blurring together into some sinister nightmare that had me waking in a cold sweat at five, sheets tangled about my legs. I'd given up all hope of more rest and went to work off my restless energy on the treadmill in the hotel's gym. Other than that, I'd spent the day in my room watching TV, telling Zach that jet lag had worn me out when he wanted me to join a group going to a brewery tour. I had no intent on doing anything else in Denver except attending the wedding, then going to the airport. I'd learned my lesson. Again.

A server came around pouring coffee and I gratefully took a sip, knowing there was hours to go. Zach clasped my hand, gave it a gentle squeeze. I looked up at him, his groomed blond hair and tanned skin. He was very attractive, a strong jaw, full lips and strikingly blue eyes. It was impossible to miss the ladies in attendance take a second glance at the bride's brother. I was the perfect eye-candy for Zach, keeping him completely heterosexual in the eyes of his parents and the rest of his family, and keeping those other women away. He'd held my hand as he introduced me to those he knew, kept me company as we mingled with those we didn't, even gave me a gentle kiss on the cheek or forehead throughout the weekend as part of our plan. It was easy to play along because Zach was safe. He wasn't going to leap over the invisible line I'd made, a line that I wouldn't allow any man to cross. He had no interest.

Needing a break, I excused myself to the ladies' room, grabbing my clutch off the table. Zach stood as I did, gave me a wink. The restrooms were down a long hall with windows also facing the Rocky Mountains. Small groupings of chairs were placed for quiet conversation. As I rounded a corner, I ran into a wall. A warm, solid wall dressed in a tuxedo. "Oh," I gasped, trying to step back, yet stumbling in my heels. Strong hands gripped my upper arms, steadying me. Rock-hard abs pressed against my breasts, my head against his chest.

I sucked in a breath as my body recognized and responded to a virile male aligned so perfectly to me. My nipples tightened instantly into tight points. I hadn't been touched by a man in this way in over a decade, and the sensations racing through my body weren't remotely the same. Before, it had been with a complete lack of feeling on my part, just two bodies making contact as if for survival on a freezing night. But this...this was utterly new. Utterly incredible. And very scary.

"Are you all right?" a dark voice murmured close to my ear, his warm breath tickling the hair at my nape. His palms were warm on my exposed skin, his touch gentle. He let me pull back enough to look up into dark and brooding eyes, shadowed by a strong brow creased with...concern? Irritation? My gaze roamed over his features. He was tall, well over six feet, forcing me to angle my head back to look my fill. His jaw was square, at least two days growth of dark whiskers made him appear dangerous. His dark hair was cut short on the sides, longer on top. Well groomed for the wedding, I had no doubt the ebony locks would fall over his forehead on less formal occasions.

Women must flock to him. One side of his full mouth was tipped up in a bemused, half smile. Oh God, I was ogling him and he knew it. Small crinkles at the corner of his eyes softened all his hardness, making him seem...wow.

I felt my cheeks flush, my heart pound.

My fingers curled into the lapels of his jacket, crinkling the smooth fabric. "I'm so sorry," I mumbled as I released my hold, smoothed down the material. Confirmed his muscles were indeed impressive. I gave myself a little mental shake and stepped back, although he didn't loosen his grip on me.

"No harm done." His voice was a dark rasp.

I couldn't look him in the eye. Had he felt my nipples harden against his belly? Flustered, I stared at his broad shoulders and nodded. That wasn't helping because I swear I hadn't seen a tuxedo so well filled out before. His scent swirled around me, a slight hint of spicy aftershave.

A finger lifted my chin, forced me to look at him.

"Um..." I couldn't form a proper sentence when his piercing gaze was on me, when they roved over my face as if he wanted to do *something*. He was so attractive, so appealing that my brain had somehow shut off, practically short-circuited. "I really need to go."

He grinned, exposing straight white teeth and a dimple on the right side. Oh, dear Lord, a dimple. I had no idea one little dimple could make my body react so quickly, so easily; my panties were instantly wet, making me squirm. My body was scaring me, reacting like it was. Instinctually, honestly. Unlike my brain which screamed, *Flee!* He was a whole new kind of danger. Danger I knew nothing about, didn't know how to defend against.

"Right, the restrooms."

I was so stupid! I shut my eyes, hoping when I opened them he would be gone. But, he was still there, still smiling at me. If I thought my cheeks were heated before...had I just told the man I had to *go*? Not go as in go away, but go as in—

"Please," I whispered, my voice thready and desperate. This time when I stepped back, he released his hold, my arms chilly where his warm hands had been. My gaze focused solely on the pattern in the hotel's carpeting, I made a hasty retreat to the ladies' room to hide. Forever. I could handle seeing a dead body with a hole in its forehead but couldn't talk to a man. Couldn't have the most basic of conversations. A man who, in the span of twenty seconds, made me flustered like a tongue-tied teenager. My heart continued to pound as I leaned against the wall, dejected. I could talk to Zach, to the guys at the dojo. To clients. This guy? Not a chance.

Thankfully, the room was empty. No one could see the tears that came to my eyes, my feelings scalded not only by his touch, but by mortification. My body had reacted to him in a way I'd never felt before, but really, why would he be interested in me? I wasn't anything special. Anything at all. I was just a silly woman who couldn't watch where she was going.

I angrily wiped at a tear that rolled down my cheek. *Just one more day.* One more day and I could get back to New York and forget this entire trip happened. *Everything* that could go wrong had. Dead body, half-sister's forced marriage, inability to talk to the most attractive man I'd ever seen without sounding like a complete idiot. If it hadn't happened to me, I wouldn't have believed it. I mean, seriously, a dead body?

I sighed. Zach would send out a search party for me if I hid much longer. Touching up my makeup, I ensured there were no visible signs of my little breakdown. After washing my hands with cool water, I retreated from the quiet safety of the ladies' room, hoping to duck back to my seat without running into Mr. Handsome. No such luck. He stood looking out the window at the soft glow behind the mountains that signaled twilight, hands in his pants pockets. Hearing me, he turned around, smiled.

Seeing him from a distance, he was more gorgeous than ever. I'd observed his wide shoulders, felt the expanse of his chest, his solid abs, but now I noticed how his hips were narrow, his legs long. Standing tall, not only his physique but his bearing as well, was of a military man, someone who didn't just work out, but lived strong. Required it.

"I owe you an apology," he said as he stepped closer, his voice still soft, as if he only wanted me to hear even though we were alone in the corridor. I wanted to retreat, but knew I had to hold my ground, hold on to the shreds of dignity I had left. "I was completely inappropriate and made you embarrassed. I'm sorry." He looked contrite, sincere. "I'm just not used to beautiful women running me over. I was fumbling for words and the wrong ones came out."

I lifted a brow. He thought I was beautiful? "I did not *run* you over."

"Beneath this brawny physique"—he ran a hand over his belly, which had zero fat—"I'm actually very tenderhearted." His smile grew and I glimpsed straight, white teeth.

I couldn't help it. I smiled, too. "Right," I replied sarcastically. "A woman like me could never hurt a man like you."

His grin slipped just a little. "You'd be surprised. Let's start over. I'm Nick Malone." He held out his hand. I stared at it a moment before placing mine in his. His grip was again gentle, and my palm was completely engulfed by his large one, making me realize how much bigger he truly was.

"Anna Scott."

"Anna. That's a pretty name." He released my hand only to place his at my lower back, guiding me back toward the reception.

My eyes darted away, then back. He made me nervous. "Thank you."

"Bride or groom?" he asked, taking a quick glance at the party.

I paused. "What?"

"The wedding. Which side are you with?"

"Oh, um...my date is the bride's brother."

"Where is this date of yours?"

We stopped at the edge of the room, giving us the vantage of the entire reception, without being overly noticeable ourselves. I looked toward my table, not seeing Zach, then glanced around. A string quartet played a piece by Beethoven as guests were either still at their tables, mingling in small groups, or at the bar, like Zach.

"Over there," I pointed.

He looked in that direction. "Talking with the woman in the purple dress?"

I nodded. They were too far away for us to hear their conversation, but the woman tilted her head back and laughed at something Zach said.

"Boyfriend?"

I turned to face Nick, licked my lips. If I was going to be Zach's safe date for the weekend, then he could be mine. I didn't know Nick at all and even though I was attracted to him, my mind was screaming *stranger danger!* "Yes."

His eyebrows shot up. "Really?" He darted a glance at Zach, then focused back on me.

I nodded, worried he could see through my lie. The way Nick looked at me, it was as if he could see to the truth. About everything. "It surprises you I have a boyfriend?"

He tilted his head ever so slightly, gave me a bemused smile. "I would be surprised if you didn't."

"But you don't believe me." I lifted my chin. Zach was pretty hot. I could land a guy like him, if he wasn't gay. I just had to try.

"I think you're a naughty girl." He grinned. He was flirting with me. One didn't have to be good at it to know it.

I gulped, cleared my throat and just stared at his dimple. "Um...why do you say that?" I was the least naughty person in the entire world.

"Because you're lying. That's definitely not your boyfriend."

"Oh? How can you tell?" I crossed my arms over my chest, trying to be defiant. I wanted—no, needed—to use Zach as my boyfriend for protection from Nick, to hide these immediate and intense feelings that had my heart beating as if I'd been on a long run, my palms sweaty.

"I like that gleam in your eye when you get angry." When I said nothing more, he continued. "He's gay."

I felt my mouth drop open. "How—"

He shrugged one very broad shoulder. "It's obvious. The woman in purple, she's quite attractive. Even if he was madly in love with you, he's not glancing at her cleavage. Any conscious, straight man would at least glance at it."

He had a point. The woman did have her abundant breasts on display. They were like a car crash; I couldn't help but stare at them. Clearly, she was hoping to get lucky at the reception, maybe even with Zach. As if that would happen. Only a man like Nick, virile and oozing pheromones—and straight, there was no question about that—could get lucky with the woman in purple.

I couldn't blame Nick for wanting her. I couldn't compare and not just in cup size. She could obviously flirt, knew how to play the game. Just the thought of Nick leaving me to go score with another woman made me furious. "Then why don't you go over there and take a peek for yourself?"

Nick raked his gaze down my body, back up again. "I like a woman who's a mystery. That leaves a little bit to the imagination. It builds...anticipation."

I assumed he meant my dress, which didn't offer a hint of décolletage with the severe, high neckline that ran from shoulder to shoulder. Anticipation for... oh. Anticipation to see what's underneath. The room's temperature just went up a few degrees.

Redirecting Nick away from talk about what was beneath my dress, I asked, "What else?"

I eyed Zach from across the room, looking for some obvious sign that said "gay" only Nick had picked up on.

"You're over here talking with me and he doesn't care."

My heart turned cold, recognizing the error in his words. "That doesn't make him gay. That makes him a typical guy." I thought of Todd and his brother, David. He'd *given* me to his brother and hadn't cared.

You're worthless. Go and try to please David. Todd's words haunted me, lingered and reminded me what men were like. I forced a quick, false smile and took a step away, ready to leave him and return to my table. I felt uncomfortable with this man—no matter how attractive he was—or the direction our conversation had taken. I should just get another glass of wine and stick to Zach's side the rest of the night.

I felt Nick's big hand on my shoulder, just like in the picture of Elizabeth with Todd. Just like the almost identical picture of Todd and me from years before. Goose bumps rose on my arms, a tingle of panic raced over my skin. Nick slowly turned me back to face him, but he must have seen the reaction to his touch and dropped his hand. "Easy there." His voice was low. "I just meant that if you were mine, I'd know where you were at all times."

Oh God. Those words. Men were the same. Even the gorgeous ones.

"Jesus, you're going to faint if you don't breathe." He held his hands up. "I won't touch you, but you need to breathe."

I did as he said and forced in a few deep breaths, trying to calm my racing heart, trying to scrub away the memory of Todd's hands, David's hands, on me. *I'd know where you were at all times.*

He leaned in a little, closing the space between us, but didn't crowd me. "You can't go back out there. You're white as a sheet. Walk with me back toward the bathrooms to give yourself a minute. I won't touch you. I won't let anyone touch you."

5

Grif

Holy shit, I'd never seen color drain from a person's face so fast. I'd set her off when I placed my hand on her shoulder. It was innocent enough; we were at a wedding reception, for Christ's sake. I'd barely touched her beyond a handshake and placing my palm against her back. She was the one who'd run into me in the first place. She's the one whose lush body had been plastered against mine. Her nipples had hardened against my chest and I'd had to suppress a groan at her body's reaction. I hadn't done a thing.

I couldn't have fucked up this first meeting any more if I'd tried. I'd stuck my foot in my mouth, embarrassing her. I talked to her like a soldier with his platoon, not a lady. Moretti's idea was for me to make contact with her, get her into bed, pleasure her into giving away her every secret. A little pillow talk. How soft her skin felt, how enticing her curves, it would be no hardship. She had secrets, that was for damn sure, and per Moretti, I was just supposed to fuck them out of her.

That plan was shot to hell the moment her tongue darted out and licked her lower lip. The moment I could see the dark flecks in her eyes. She wasn't just a woman who ended up with Bobby Lane's dead body in her trunk. She wasn't the coolly detached woman who, in a calculated way, decimated Werbler and Gossing, two seasoned detectives. She wasn't just the woman Moretti wanted watched. She was Anna Scott who had secrets. Her own personal demons, and somehow, I'd brought them back to life with just a touch. No way in hell could I do what Moretti ordered. Hell, I wanted her in my bed, what conscious man wouldn't, but not because Moretti said so. I didn't fuck on command.

Now, in a life-changing moment, I wanted, *needed,* to discover what haunted her so I could protect her. During my stint in the Army, with the police, I'd been sworn to protect and serve. The words had meant nothing before. Only another deployment, another assignment. Just one brush of her body against mine, her slim fingers clenching into my jacket, and I was done for. She slayed me with just the feel of her skin beneath my palms. I hadn't felt this *thing* with Nadine in all the time we were married, but I felt it now.

It wasn't about being an undercover agent doing my job anymore. Fuck Moretti. It was about being a man. And she was going to be my woman. She just didn't know it yet.

Without touching her, I steered her to a quiet corner by a potted palm, shielding us a little from prying eyes. The music was muted here, making it easier to talk. I bent down so we were eye to eye.

How could I get her to talk to me, a complete stranger? She definitely knew how to clam up, I'd watched it first hand at the station the day before. She most likely wouldn't talk to me now. Why would she? I was a complete stranger, a guy who'd somehow triggered something that had her panicking. Regardless, I had to try. I couldn't leave her thinking I would hurt her. "Okay, Anna. Tell me what has you so scared. Is it me?"

I waited patiently as she ran her hands over her upper arms, her eyes looking anywhere but at me. Her short, quick breaths had her breasts rising and falling, taunting me. I slid my jacket off and wrapped it around her shoulders, careful to keep my hands from brushing over her. If I covered her lush body, then maybe my need for her would lessen. As if. Seeing her dwarfed in my jacket only ratcheted up my protective instincts. The air stirred and I caught a hint of her scent, lightly floral and very intoxicating. Shampoo? Perfume?

Tugging the lapels together in one small hand, she finally looked up at me, gave me a small smile. "Thanks." Her color looked better at least.

In Afghanistan, I'd waited out insurgents during an ambush for days. One woman with a few secrets shouldn't even try my patience, but I was wrong. I resisted the urge to grab her shoulders and shake her until she talked. Gossing and Werbler had probably felt the same way.

"Do I scare you?" I asked again.

"Not..." She cleared her throat. "Not in the way you think."

I grinned at her honesty. She felt whatever the hell it was between us. Chemistry. It was definitely chemistry. "That's good, love. That's really good." She scared the hell out of me, too.

She tried to look around me, but I blocked her view of the hallway, of her escape. Shifting slightly, I let her see past me and know she wasn't trapped.

Her arched brow rose at the endearment, but said nothing for a moment. Glanced down the hall. "I am a little naïve when it comes to some things, I'll admit. I've been on my own for a long time, but I don't need a keeper. I don't need a man to watch my every move."

I frowned. "I don't want a woman who needs watching." I paused. "This is about what I said?" I saw the answer on her face. "I only meant that if you were mine, I wouldn't be able to take my eyes off you because you're so damn pretty. I'd want to cross the room to be near you, to be able to touch you. Like I want to do right now."

Her eyes lit up with surprise. "Oh." Her plump lower lip was glossy and it was hard not to stare at it, wonder how soft it was, how good she'd taste. She wasn't playing coy to hook and reel a man in like a fish.

Which only meant she didn't know her worth. And that meant— "Some fucker really messed with you. Was it Zach?" I stood up straight, ready to beat the shit out of the guy at her word.

She placed a hand on my arm, then pulled it back as if burned. "No. Not Zach. He's my friend." She must have seen the skeptical look on my face because she added, "Really."

I relaxed, glad to know Zach was decent. *Moretti? Had Moretti done things to her? Forced her into the mess with Lane?* I wanted to ask, but couldn't.

"Who hurt you?"

She straightened her spine, shifted her shoulders back, looked me dead in the eye. Her color had returned and the spark in her gaze showed me she was more mad than sad. "I don't even know you. You can't just go slaying my dragons for me."

"Can't I?" It was my job to protect the innocent—at least when I was Jake Griffin. With Anna, I wanted to do the protecting more with my fist than with the badge I had hidden away.

Anna laughed bitterly. "Who *are* you?"

Instead of answering, I gave her advanced warning. "I'm going to hold your hand." I watched her eyes for any reaction, but she didn't resist when I took her small hand between both of mine.

She inhaled sharply as she looked down at our combined hands.

"You feel it, too," I whispered, absorbing that spark, that awareness that passed between our palms. I stared at the top of her head, her dark hair sleek and shiny. I knew if I touched the soft strands, they would feel like silk.

I felt her tense, ready to tug her hand free. "Don't. I won't hurt you. You have to trust me on that."

She glanced up at me beneath a dark fringe of lashes. "Like I said before, I don't even know you."

I couldn't push her anymore. We weren't in an interrogation room, but I was pumping her for answers. She wasn't going to give them to me. Not right now. She was too good at *not* telling just to give in now. Had I really expected it? Flirting didn't work. I couldn't fuck it out of her. I could barely touch her let alone convince her to go back to my room, let me strip her down and give her an orgasm or two to loosen her tongue.

"I don't want to scare you off like the bastard who's got you spooked, so I'm going to let you get back to the party. I'm sure even Zach is wondering where you are by now. Can I meet you for coffee tomorrow?"

I knew her answer, but I had to play clueless.

She shook her head. "I don't live here. I'm from New York. I'm leaving tomorrow to go home."

I paused, let her think I was considering. I wanted to find out who'd hurt her and beat the shit out of him. But that wasn't why I was standing in front of her. I'd crashed the wedding to make contact for Moretti, the asshole. I had to tell her about Scorch. Expose my connection to Moretti and to Bobby Lane's body. To show her I was somehow related to the fiasco she'd inadvertently fallen into yesterday. To make her see that Moretti was watching and the one way she'd stay alive was to forget what happened and get on that plane. To forget me.

I let go of her hand with an inward sigh. What had I been thinking? I'd let a pretty face blind me to the real world. This attraction—this lightning strike of feeling I had for her—wasn't real. It wasn't love at first sight, but something damn similar. Lust. I'd lived like a monk for so long I'd forgotten what it felt like. Yeah, this was just lust. I couldn't have her. Who the fuck was I kidding? She couldn't be mine, not while I was undercover. Not as Nick Malone. I couldn't do anything for her except stay away. How fucking depressing was that?

So I did my job. I reached into my pants pocket, took out my wallet. "Here. Take my card. If you ever need to talk, call me. Day or night." I handed it to her. It was plain stupid giving her proof to my relationship with Moretti and Bobby Lane in one sentence and then telling her I'd help her with her problems the next. Why the hell would she turn to me when I gave her the proof of my connection to the cluster fuck of her trip? Zach—nice, safe Zach, would be a better bet than me.

Squeezing the lapels tightly, she asked, "Call you?"

She looked so innocent standing there in my tuxedo jacket, dwarfed beneath it so only the very hem of her demure, yet very sexy, dress showed. "If anything, anyone bothers you. Call me. I can help."

Maybe. If it didn't blow my cover. Shit. If she needed help, I'd give it. Fuck Moretti. *Shit.* This was a complete mess because I couldn't do both. Be both Nick Malone and Jake Griffin.

Anna glanced down at the card, her body tensing as if struck by a live wire. The look in her eyes when she lifted her chin was a mixture of panic, fear and confusion. She licked her lips again and my dick got hard.

"I've...um...you're right." She *knew*. Knew I was one of the bad guys who'd fucked up her weekend. "Zach's probably wondering where I am. It was...nice meeting you, Nick."

With those final words, she turned and fled. This time, I let her. I exhaled a deep breath, wishing for a drink. Shit. To think, just for a moment there, I'd forgotten myself, wanting her for my own. To, like she said, slay her dragons. I'd gotten lost in her eyes, so expressive, so secretive. Her scent had practically drugged me into a state of forgetfulness. As if I were a regular guy with a regular job. *As if.*

I was just a thug that worked for Moretti. That's what she now thought anyway. Like I told Peters, it wasn't all sunshine and rainbows. I offered my help but I wouldn't be able to give it, and I sure as hell couldn't tell her the truth. Not undercover. Not when the case against Moretti was almost complete. So I gave her the damn card. Gave up any chance with her. Jesus, this was all kinds of fucked up.

If she were innocent, she'd be back to her life in New York by tomorrow night, definitely safer away from me and the dangerous shit I was involved in. Whatever had happened to her, she was skittish and wary of men in a way I'd only seen in domestic abuse or rape cases. My jaw clenched at the possibility that someone had touched her that way, but I couldn't help unless she was willing to share. The way she'd acted in the interrogation room earlier, she'd learned to build some pretty good defenses. So the guy who would teach her that not every man was bad, that all touches weren't cruel, wasn't going to be me. I ran my hand through my hair as I stared down the empty hallway. Fuck.

"Get a fucking grip, Grif," I whispered to myself.

I pushed those pussy-whipped thoughts aside as I walked to the elevator. My gut screamed there was more to her than fragile waif, and my gut was never wrong. It had saved my neck over and over in Afghanistan and on the streets. The angel in me may have offered her my help, but the devil on my shoulder had given her the card because I knew, deep down, she was too good to be true. God didn't just deliver the woman I'd dreamed about—but just didn't know existed—to a guy like me.

There had to be something wrong with her. She might not have killed Bobby Lane, but she was hiding something, I knew it without a doubt. She had to be. All women had something to hide. With the card, she now knew I worked for Moretti, and most likely she did, too. Now, all she had to do was show up at Scorch and prove it. Prove women were as slick as I'd learned to believe.

6

nna

When I finally made it back to the table, the maid of honor was giving her speech so Zach could only lift a dark eyebrow at me in question. He wanted to ask me where I'd been, I knew, but it wasn't the time to talk. Once we lowered our glasses from the toast, he leaned in, whispered, "Nice jacket." He grinned, raised and lowered his eyebrows.

Oh God. I still had Nick's jacket. I looked around the room, didn't see him. Of course not. He'd left to go back to Scorch. I was wearing a jacket of a guy whose colleague was found dead in the trunk of a car. A bad guy. Why did a bad guy seem like a good guy? He didn't act like a thug. He sure didn't look like one. Were all bad guys drop-dead gorgeous with hair I wanted to touch, a body I wanted to learn and a mouth I so desperately wanted to kiss? As if my luck couldn't get any worse, I was lusting after a guy that worked for—what was the man's name? Morelli? Moretti. The detective from yesterday had said Scorch was one of his businesses.

I glanced at the card in my damp palm. *Nick Malone, Manager, Scorch.* It listed his phone number and the address of the club. I hadn't missed the heat in Nick's eyes. He may not have been very forthcoming, but his interest in me wasn't a lie. I felt it in his touch, in the way he'd gotten angry at the thought of

Zach hurting me. He really wanted to know who'd messed with me. The most amazing thing—Nick was the only person who had ever seen I had something to hide. Then again, he was the only person who made me feel *something*. Anything.

I didn't even know it was possible anymore. That's why, when he'd leaned in and whispered in my ear, my skin prickled, my nipples—and other places—ached to be touched. My body, for once, craved. Nick was the only man to make me feel that way, instantly and irrevocably. Like a drug, I wanted more. I tuned out the best man's speech. I watched, but didn't see the cutting of the cake.

My body might have awakened to Nick, but my brain knew he was bad for me. He worked for Moretti. He wasn't a guest of the party. He'd crashed it. Looking for me. Making sure...making sure what? Had he wanted to hurt me? Had Moretti sent him to lure me to my death? My stomach churned at the idea of a bullet to the brain. After what happened to the dead guy in the trunk, I couldn't ignore that distinct possibility.

Nick hadn't tried to harm me, grab and take me from me from the party to shoot me. In fact, he'd done the opposite, pulling me in close, whispering in my ear, running his thumb over my palm. He wanted to help me, just...wanted me. So when he gave me his business card, he'd made it clear Moretti had made contact, made me aware that the man knew who I was, but Nick also gave me a way to reach him if I really needed it. I felt that part was sincere, but a complete contradiction.

I took a sip of my water, the glass wet with condensation. There was an angle I hadn't considered before. If Nick worked for Scorch, then he knew who *I* was. Knew I was the one who was in the car with Bobby Lane's body in it. That's why he gave me the card. He wasn't hiding who he was or his connection to Moretti. He wasn't hiding what he knew about me and still offered to help.

Did I need his help? He was the only man that had made me feel alive in years. A decade. Longer. He could definitely help me with that, but I doubted that was what he'd had in mind when he offered. He was gorgeous, his eyes piercing and intense, his hands gentle yet persuasive. I had no doubt if I could turn off my mind, my body would melt like butter beneath his skilled hands. But I had bigger problems than reviving my libido.

I needed help saving Elizabeth. Could Nick do that? Would he?

"Want to dance?" Zach asked, breaking into my thoughts. I smiled, nodded, then stood. I couldn't sit at the table and stare at my water glass all night. Since it was far from appropriate to be Zach's date and wear another man's jacket, I shrugged it off and folded it over the back of my chair.

"You okay?" he asked, leading me out onto the floor.

"Fine. I'm sorry, I'm still a little tired. Time difference probably."

He looked down at me as he spun me around the room to a romantic tune. "Altitude, too. Wears you out."

I laughed. "No wonder I could only go a mile on the treadmill this morning before I collapsed. I thought I was getting old."

"Are you going to tell me about the jacket? Should I be jealous?" He winked.

"I'm really sorry. I'm your date for tonight and I go off and get another man's jacket."

"As long as that's all he gave you," he replied, his voice dark.

I rolled my eyes and patted him on the shoulder. "You're a good big brother."

"Someone's got to watch out for you."

I stiffened in his arms momentarily, then tried to relax. Nick had said something very similar.

"I can take care of myself, you know."

He gave my hand a squeeze as he spun us around the dance floor. "Oh, I know it, all right, but a guy's supposed to watch out for his girl."

"I didn't know I was *your girl*."

"Of course, you are. The guys at the dojo think the same. You don't have to be a wife or girlfriend for a guy to have your back. Before you freak, they know you're not interested in any of them, but that doesn't mean they don't care about you and wouldn't do anything to make sure no one messed with you."

I stopped dancing. Zach and I just stood there in the middle of the floor, other couples moving around us. "Really? I didn't realize."

"You'd do the same for me."

I thought for a moment. I would. I'd do anything to help Zach. I was in Denver, wasn't I? Pretending to be his girlfriend. "Yes, I'd kick any guy's ass that messed with you." I grinned.

He did, too, before pulling me in a little closer, started dancing again. For the rest of the night, I thought about Zach's words. Was that what Nick had meant? That he'd protect me, regardless? Was this really what the good guys did? Was Nick one of the good guys? How could he be if he worked for Moretti?

My mind circled and circled, like Zach and I around the dance floor, but I didn't come up with any answers.

After the reception was over, after Zach walked me to my hotel room door and I'd closed it behind me, I realized in a moment of perfect clarity that I *could* ask Nick for help with Elizabeth. Standing there, staring at the fire emergency placard on the back of the door, it came to me. He was the perfect person to do so. Neither my father nor Todd knew him. No one in New York did. If he worked for Moretti, he moved in circles I couldn't fathom. Could work angles I couldn't contemplate.

He'd help, not only out of chivalric duty.

He didn't have a choice.

I took his jacket that I'd carried back to my room, put it back on. In front of the hotel, I asked the doorman for a taxi. When it arrived, I pulled out Nick's business card and gave the driver the address to Scorch.

Grif

Things were in chaos when I returned to the bar. One of the liquor shipments hadn't arrived as scheduled, a bartender had called in sick and a new server had spilled a tray of drinks on a group that was now very unhappy. I yanked off my bow tie and stuffed it in my pocket, undid the top button of my tuxedo shirt and got back to business. Most issues were easy to resolve, but took most of my focus; free drinks and a move to the VIP section fixed ruffled feathers, a call to the distributer brought a shipment of vodka that hadn't been sent to Phoenix by mistake. To resolve the bartender shortage, I took over one end of the bar for the night. Not something I wanted to do, nor got me any closer to arresting Moretti, but the crowd didn't take my feelings into account. They just wanted their drinks.

One a.m. and the club was still crowded. Pouring drinks didn't occupy my mind enough to keep it from wandering to Anna Scott and how sweet she'd been. I swear I was getting a case of blue balls, my dick getting hard every time I thought of her sweet mouth, her pale skin. It was the mystery of her, the secrets she had hidden beneath that dress. *That*, was torture. Good thing the bar was high enough to hide my reaction.

I poured a row of shots for a group of guys, put their money in the till and turned back to find Anna standing there, her manicured fingers on the edge of the sleek bar top. She still wore my black tuxedo jacket like a suit of armor, with the sleeves rolled up. It was as if thinking about her had conjured her up. I froze. She was as beautiful as I remembered, her hair still sleek and perfect, her eyes dark and clear, her lips free of the lipstick she'd worn earlier, now a natural pink, even in the intense blue and white lights pulsing in time to the music.

Holy. Fucking. Shit.

She was *good*.

For once in my career, I had been completely and totally off the mark. Her good looks, hot body and naïveté had blinded me to the truth. She was just like Nadine. A fake. A liar. A cheat. My gut clenched with disappointment; I *really* wanted her to be innocent. I'd hoped she'd get on that plane and then I'd have known she was that sweet little thing, soft and lush, I'd initially pegged her for. To know that someone like that still existed. To be something different than the dregs of society I was stuck with. *I* was the naïve one to fall for her act, even for a little while.

Disney movie over, reality set in. She was a cold, calculating bitch. She'd duped Werbler and Gossing. She got past Peters' radar. Mine, too.

Tonight at the reception? She'd played the innocent waif, damaged and fragile. I'd fallen for her hook, line and sinker. She was really, really *good* at being bad. At least my hard-on was gone.

"What can I get you?" I asked, placing a cocktail napkin down on the gleaming wood in front of her. I was a sucker and I felt it in my gut. Didn't mean I had to show it.

"Club soda."

I took the time filling her drink to cool down. The crowded bar was not a place to yell at a woman, no matter what she'd done. After placing it in front of her, I crossed my arms over my chest. "Here to return the jacket?"

She looked down as if she'd forgotten she had it on. "Oh, um...not the only reason."

"Hey, baby. Let's dance." A twenty-something guy, drunk off his ass, practically licked Anna's ear. He was tall and wide, as if he majored in weight lifting. She had to tilt her head away, no doubt from his foul breath.

"No thanks," she shouted over the music.

"Oh, come on, baby. I know you want to." He placed his hand on her arm, gave it a squeeze. I could see the fabric of my jacket crinkle beneath his grip. "We're going to be good together. I've got just what you need."

"I said no!" she shouted, her voice cutting through the music.

"Hey, get your hands off her," I yelled, but I was on the wrong side of the bar to do anything more than signal a bouncer with a wave of my hand. Just because she was a bitch didn't mean she deserved to be pawed by a dick.

"I'm not taking no for an answer." He switched from fun drunk to belligerent in the blink of an eye and turned toward the dance floor, pulling Anna along.

Before I could make my way around the bar, she grabbed the guy's hand on her arm, gave it a twist while she stepped back and put him in a wrist lock. His elbow bent at an awkward angle and she moved his arm easily behind his back. Just like I learned at the Academy. The guy immediately went up on his tiptoes—I could tell because he went a few inches up in the air—to relieve the pressure of her joint manipulation. He faced me, his belly pressed into the brass edging. I couldn't even see Anna behind him, but she held him pinned in place, the guy's face a weird mix of pain and astonishment. I grabbed his neck and yanked his head down so his cheek was mashed into the bar top.

"The lady said no, asshole."

7

rif

I LOOKED UP AND SHE STILL HAD HER HANDS ON HIS WRIST, PUSHING IT UP HIS back to ensure the most discomfort. Two bouncers appeared on either side of her, grabbed the guy's shoulders. She let go and stepped back, letting them lead him away. I couldn't miss the impressed looks my men gave her. One even winked.

My heart rate started to lower from stroke point. The unnatural instinct to rip the man limb from limb had been overpowering. Knowing Anna was safe lessened that need, but the anger still simmered.

I turned to Vince, the other bartender. "Take over here." I wiped my hands on a clean rag, tossed it down. "I've got to deal with something in the back." Glancing at Anna, I tipped my head in the direction of my office, not waiting to see if she'd follow.

She did. I kicked the door to the office shut behind us, flicked the lock shut so we couldn't be interrupted. The deafening music was muted but the droning beat remained.

Anna faced me, but she glanced around the utilitarian room. There was a desk covered with papers and other crap that filled most of the space, a wheeled desk chair and liquor boxes stacked along one wall. A trash can was beside the desk, filled with empty take-out containers. A calendar of a scantily clad woman from three years ago was the only decoration on the walls. I wasn't planning on staying long at the job, so an interior decorator wasn't needed.

The difference in our height was enough where I had to bend down to look in her eyes. "Did he hurt you?"

She was breathing a little faster than normal, her pupils dilated, but she shook her head. Even with the fluorescent light from the ceiling casting a bluish glow across the room, I could see bright flags of color on her cheeks. Her adrenaline must be pumping. Mine always was after dealing with someone like she had. "No."

"What were you thinking? That guy could have...shit." I tried to get control of myself, but it wasn't fucking easy. I stood up and ran my hand through my hair.

"I know how to defend myself," she countered, putting her hands on her hips. My jacket flared out at her movement, making her seem even smaller.

"*That* is more than obvious." I moved to the desk and leaned my hip against it. I didn't offer her the chair. "Where'd you learn a move like that?" I held my hand up. "Never mind. I don't want to know." Mercenary school? Moretti's School for Felonious Girls?

"Karate," she answered. Credible, but hard to believe considering the thugs and assholes I had to deal with on a daily basis. They learned moves like that on the street. It was either learn, or get the shit kicked out of you.

"Any bodies in the trunk of your car tonight?" Obviously, with her being here she'd made the connection from Bobby Lane's body to me, but I had to be sure.

"I took a taxi. My rental's being taken care of by the hotel."

I just raised an eyebrow in response. Yeah, she'd connected the dots. She wasn't stupid. "So, enough chit chat. I guess Moretti sent you. Let me know the story he wants to give about Bobby and I'll spread the word."

She just stood and stared at me as if I'd sprouted horns from my head. "You think Moretti sent me?"

I shrugged. "Why else would you be here? I mean, if you were innocent, you'd be with your gay boyfriend right now waiting to catch the bouquet. Then, tomorrow, on your way back to the Big Apple." I picked at an imaginary speck of dirt on my sleeve.

She paused as if considering my words. "So, what? I'm the hit man Moretti hired to off his son-in-law? Is that how you say it? Yeah, I'm a real professional." My brows went up at her sarcasm. "Caught with the body in the trunk. Really dumb of me."

"Or smart enough to come up with a story about the whole car rental swap." I spun my finger around in the air. "Word gets around. I have to admit, I fell for it."

She took a deep breath, let it out. Dropped her hands to her sides. "Earlier tonight, at the reception, did you mean it when you offered to help me?"

"A friend of Moretti's is a friend of mine." I wasn't playing nice. Why should I? No one in Moretti's organization would be considered *nice*. I felt like a fucking fool once. What was it with women? First Nadine, now Anna. I thought I'd learned my lesson. A woman was never what she seemed. Never sweet and innocent and wanting the simplicity of a man loving and protecting her. The whole picket fence romance movie. Boy, had I been wrong. At least I hadn't gotten in too deep by marrying this one. I hadn't even kissed her. Then why the hell did her duplicity feel like a jagged sliver beneath my skin?

"You don't believe me. Wow." She shook her head. "You're one to talk. What's your real title, your real job? Thug? Murderer? Because you can't just be a bar manager. I've heard the term wet work before. I guess in your case it doesn't just refer to pouring drinks."

She thought *I* was a hit man? She was a piece of work.

"You were a lot different a few hours ago at the reception when you made me promise to come to you if I had a problem."

"Yeah, well, we're not what we seem, are we?"

She looked at me for long seconds. Just staring. I figured I'd get tears or anger or even a slap across the face for my shitty attitude. What I didn't expect was acceptance.

"Whatever. You're going to believe what you want." She gave a negligent shrug. "Nothing I say is going to sway you."

I picked up a paperclip, unbent one of the wires. "It seems you've been in this situation before."

"Yeah, you'd be surprised."

Something flickered in her eyes, but I couldn't read it. Even if I had, I wouldn't believe what I saw. She was a damn fine actress. Should I be the one to tell Peters and the others they'd been duped or let them figure it out on their own?

"I didn't come here to make you believe me," she continued. "I came for your help. You offered earlier, so here I am. There's a woman who needs rescuing from a bad man and I can't do it by myself."

"You've got the *karate* moves to rescue someone. You don't need anyone else, let alone me." I tossed the straightened clip back on the desk. Grabbed another. I saw her jaw clench. I wasn't making it easy for her. Like I really cared.

"He's a bad man. He's done it before. I've got proof."

"Moretti's a bad man. He's done it before. *You're* the proof." I let that sink in for a minute. "Moretti's not going to let me leave Scorch and go off to New York to save some damsel in distress, sweetheart. It's not like we're in the kind of business that has vacation time and a 401k. Besides, why should either of us help you?"

Her hands clenched at her sides and I saw anger flare in her dark eyes. "Because he owes me."

I laughed. "Owes you?"

"Yes, *owes* me. The police are completely distracted by a dumb woman who got the wrong car at a valet stand and got stuck with a corpse. They're not paying attention to who really killed Bobby Lane. They don't really even care. I take it Bobby wasn't a very nice guy. I wouldn't know since I've only seen him dead."

Anna had a dry sense of humor. She'd seemed so vulnerable and soft at the reception. The woman in front of me now was completely different, all fiery spunk and attitude. She was still soft in all the right places—my gaze roved over her body, completely hidden beneath my jacket. But I couldn't help remembering her earlier, her curves hidden beneath, yet accentuated by the slim bodice of her blue dress. The way she'd looked, surprised by the connection between us. How her eyes had softened when I touched her waist. The way she'd been soothed by my words after her panic attack. So which was the real Anna? Was it even possible to figure out? Hell, was it worth the energy to do so?

"The person who did shoot him got someone to take the heat for him," she continued. "Me. They couldn't have asked for anyone better. I mean, look at me!"

She was the perfect dupe; a woman in from out of state for a wedding, pretty, educated, a spotless record not even tarnished by a parking ticket.

Who'd have considered her for popping Bobby? The police didn't. I hadn't either.

"The murderer is completely off the hook and Moretti looks like the grieving father-in-law," she added. "He *owes* me, and I want him to pay up. With you." She pointed her finger at me.

"I've never been propositioned quite this way before," I murmured, tossing the next unbent paper clip on the desk. "The door's locked. You can have your way with me right here. An orgasm would do you good. You're too tense."

Anna pulled my jacket from her shoulders as if she were allergic, threw it at me. I caught it with loose fingers, felt the warmth from her body, laid it on my desk chair. Her scent rose from the material, like lemons and spring flowers. She still wore the pretty blue dress, still looked innocent and sweet. Still had the right curves. If she offered herself now, I wasn't sure if I could hold back. She'd be just like the bar bunnies. A quick fuck followed by a quick goodbye.

"Get over yourself," she shouted, stomping over to stand right in front of me, the flared hem of her dress brushing my legs. "I don't know what happened to you between when you offered your help, with what I mistook for sincerity, and now. You even made me promise. Coming here was a big mistake." She shook her head in obvious disappointment. "Forget it. No one's going to help me. I'm on my own, like always." She poked her manicured finger in my chest. "I don't need you. I don't need anyone. I learned this lesson when I was six, but I'm glad you reminded me. Thanks, Nick."

She turned on her high heel, flipped the lock with a loud *snick*, then looked back at me over her shoulder, the little blue ribbon on her dress almost brushing her chin. "Earlier, you said, 'Trust me, I would never hurt you.'"

I cocked my head to the side. "You're in one piece, aren't you?"

That's when I saw it. Right then. She let it slip. That guard, that wall she'd had up during the interview at the station. It had been around her now. But it fell. It was like a force field in a sci-fi movie that stopped working. And I caught a glimpse of it, for the merest of moments. Utter disappointment, then acceptance. Acceptance of that disappointment, as if it was something she was used to, something she expected. To her, I was just like every other guy who'd fucked her over.

"Yes. I'm in one piece," she said, her voice hollow, as she opened the door and left. A swirl of her perfume followed in her wake as if trying to keep up.

Shit.

Grif

"What?" I growled into my cell. The hovel I'd been living in since switching from Jake Griffin to Nick Malone had one perk—blackout curtains. Sure, Moretti paid me big bucks to run his club. Now. But my initial cover had me falling far from my job on the force, thus the dumpy apartment. No way in hell was I moving to swanky digs just for Moretti. Maybe the place had been used as a meth lab in the past, maybe the last tenant worked the graveyard shift. I didn't care. I was just glad it was dark in my bedroom at—I opened one eye and looked at the clock on the bedside table—ten thirty.

"Jesus, Grif. Are you always cranky?" Peters tsked me.

"Yes. I went to bed at five. Give me a break." I'd spent the bulk of yesterday sleeping, then working at Scorch all night. I was on my stomach and I refused to open my eyes. Once this call was done, I was shutting the ringer off and getting three more hours of sleep, even if there was a fire in the building. "What do you want?"

"Your lady friend. Got some more information. Or lack of."

"Which is it?" I tried to clear the fog. "Who the hell is my lady friend?"

"Anna Scott."

I perked up a little at her name, as if Peters had given me a cup of coffee to go with his news.

"What about her?" Hearing her name only made me even more surly. The woman had the gall to come to the bar and tell me Moretti owed her. Like I was payment or something. "Didn't she get on her plane yesterday?"

"TSA says she did. Works for me. That's not why I'm calling. We pulled her record for the interview on Friday, but only did a cursory glance. We knew pretty fast we couldn't pin her for Bobby Lane."

"You mean when she cleared herself." I rolled onto my back, tossed an arm over my eyes.

Peters coughed. "Whatever. I did a more thorough search of her, just to close her out as a suspect. Her record is blemish free. Nothing on it. I dug a little deeper out of curiosity. Her background check shows she graduated from Harvard. Her work history starts seven years ago."

"I'm not hearing anything interesting yet." I sighed. "Get to the good stuff. You wouldn't have bothered me otherwise."

"Bought a pretty pricey apartment in New York right before she started Harvard. In cash."

I dropped my arm, stared up at the dark popcorn-textured ceiling. "What else?"

"Where did that kind of money come from? Harvard doesn't come cheap. No student loans. Paid in full. I checked her bank balance. She has checking and a savings account. Not enough dough in there to match a cash real estate purchase. In Manhattan. So I pulled her social." I had an idea what he was going to say, but the man was on a roll and I was wiped, so I let him talk. "No hits on that social security number until Anna was eighteen. No passport, no teenage job, no college fund."

"Parents' tax returns? Kids are a real nice tax credit, but you've got to list the social."

"Nothing. Like I told you on Friday, records say her mother died when she was six, father kicked the bucket when she was eighteen. Bob and Mary Scott. Nothing pops about their deaths. Nothing pops about them, period."

"Bob and Mary?" Those were some pretty bland names. "Maybe just simple, law-abiding citizens who weren't on our radar," I said. I didn't believe it and I knew Peters didn't either. "The money could've come from their wills." I flicked on the bedside lamp, swung my legs over the side of the bed. Sat there in my boxers and considered.

"Even then, and with that amount of money, she'd need a bank and it would be tied to a social security number. It's not like she'd have stacks of cash under her mattress."

"Someone could have paid her college tuition and we'd never know. Maybe a family friend. But her apartment? What about birth certificate?"

"None I've found," Peters replied. "Her license says Anna Louisa Scott. What I've shared matches that name, that home address."

"School records before college? She had to go to high school somewhere. Had to have a very serious transcript to get into Harvard."

"Nothing. I can't pump Harvard admissions for her records without a warrant. We both know that's not going to happen."

Peters and I were both curious about her, more now than ever, but curiosity wouldn't get us a search warrant.

"Fingerprints?"

"Zilch."

"She knew she wasn't in the system and wanted to stay that way. That's why she didn't touch the soda. Without the fingerprints, it's like she doesn't exist," I said, rubbing my whiskers. "If she's not Anna Scott—"

"Then who the hell is she?" Peters finished.

8
———

rif

THERE WAS NO CHANCE I'D GO BACK TO SLEEP AFTER THE CALL, SO I TOOK A shower and tried not to think about Anna and everything Peters had shared. Coffee was needed to get my brain functioning to work through this puzzle. I was drying off when there was a knock on my door. I wrapped a towel around my waist, walked into the living room and looked through the peephole. *Shit.*

I opened the door and stepped back to let Moretti in. He didn't look like the typical made-for-TV mobster. He wasn't short, balding, nor overweight. In fact, he was around six feet, just an inch or two shorter than me. Hair once black was now salt and pepper; I wasn't sure if it was from the stressful lifestyle—always watching his back—or from age. It was far from receding and I had to admit, he wasn't half bad looking. In his early fifties, he was trim, almost fit. If I didn't know he was a pack-a-day smoker, I would think he exercised.

He had good genes on his side, which made him even more dangerous. The ladies looked at him twice, especially since he always dressed impeccably. The men didn't fear him. Not until they got to know him. Mothers herded their daughters in the opposite direction, not wanting them to become his mistress, or worse, married off to one of his many offspring. Men either learned to respect Moretti or they wound up dead. Unfortunately, they learned it by *seeing* their friends end up dead.

Moretti had never showed up at my place before, not because he didn't know where I lived, but because I wasn't important enough to him to use up his time, which suited me just fine. I'd only been worthy enough for a couple of phone calls before. A personal visit was one honor I was not thrilled about.

"Give me a minute. Make yourself at home." I was glad I was naked. It gave me the time to get dressed to figure out why he was here. I slipped on a pair of jeans, white T-shirt, skipped shoes.

When I came back, Moretti still stood directly inside the door, observing my uninspiring living room. The police department had found it for me. It was in a below average part of town, the squat brick building held four units with blue collar, hard-working tenants I never saw. Working at the club made it perfect for me to be the neighbor no one met. The apartment came furnished, but not in a good way. Old, worn-out sofa, a TV that was made before satellite service was invented, a scarred wood dining table with only two chairs. It screamed bachelor pad, a bachelor who wasn't bringing a woman home anytime soon.

"I pay you enough to move out of this dump," he commented.

I shrugged. "Keeps the marrying types and their mothers off my back."

"No doubt." He paused, then got to why he was really here. "I was informed we need to hire the woman as a bouncer," Moretti said, moving to one of the dining chairs and sitting down. He sounded serious, but I knew the only way he'd hire a woman would be by the hour.

I thought about the look on the asshole's face that Anna had wrist locked. Priceless. "It was pretty impressive for someone of her size."

"Mmm." Moretti was quiet, perhaps considering a woman protecting herself, which was probably a novelty for him. He pulled a pack of cigarettes from his shirt pocket, lit one. "Why did she show up?"

I'd had a reprieve from the man yesterday. Moretti, a devout Catholic, didn't believe in working on Sundays. He took the day off to attend Mass, eat the large Sunday dinner his wife prepared and to sit and watch his grandchildren play while the same wife did the dishes. Unless you joined him personally for the eight-a.m. service, you had to work. I might be able to fake being a bad guy, but I figured pretending to be Catholic wouldn't get past Moretti—or God.

Since it was Monday, the man wanted answers. Since he was stinking up my apartment with his cigarette, I knew he wasn't going to be put off. I paused, quickly sorting through the various possibilities here. I had to be on my fucking toes and I wasn't after only a few hours' sleep. Hell, I hadn't gotten that coffee yet. Did Moretti really not know about Anna? Did the bastard send her and he was testing *me*? Was he wondering how I was handling her, if I'd been doing what he'd wanted? It was always like tiptoeing through a minefield with him.

"She was in town for a wedding. I made initial contact with her at the reception like you wanted. We hit it off. Gave her my card. Told her if she wanted a good time before she left town to stop by. She did. End of story."

It was almost the truth; all the parts he could confirm were accurate.

"So she took care of herself, but then you showed her who's boss. Nicely done." If Moretti wanted to think I fucked her, so be it. I wasn't going to tell him otherwise. "And now?"

"Now...what?" I rubbed my chin, my hand rasping over my whiskers. God, I wanted to shave.

"Are you going to fuck her again?"

"She's in New York, for Christ's sake. How can I fuck her in a different time zone?"

"Go there. Have a good time," Moretti said, looking around for a place to drop his ashes. I inwardly rolled my eyes and pulled a small plate from the cabinet, put it down on the table in front of him. If he was looking for the Martha Stewart guest treatment, he was at the wrong place.

"Okay," I said cautiously, scraping back the other dining chair on the linoleum floor, then sitting down. I propped back, let my legs stretch out. Hopefully, I looked way more relaxed than I felt. My gut was telling me this wasn't going to end well.

"A gift to you."

"Huh, didn't know she's one of yours. You had me fooled." I wanted him to tell me so I knew once and for all. "I didn't realize you offered your players up, especially with that type of present."

Moretti laughed. "She's not one of mine. I know nothing about her, except what you tell me."

She wasn't working for Moretti? Had I gotten everything wrong the other night? Was she innocent or working for someone else? Had she really just ended up in the wrong fucking car? Then why had she shown up at Scorch? She'd said she needed my help with a friend. Had that been the truth? What the fuck *was* the truth? My mind was moving at mach one and I couldn't get a handle on it.

"We didn't do much talking the other night, if you know what I mean, so you're going to have to fill me in." I crossed my arms over my chest. "Spell it out for me."

Moretti let out a puff of smoke, tapped his cigarette on the plate. "Go to New York, fuck her brains out. Then finish her."

When I looked in the mirror these days, I barely recognized myself, but I wasn't a killer. "You want me to kill Anna Scott. Why? If she's not working for you, then she was in the wrong place at the wrong time."

"Was she? They may have shot Bobby, but the hit was against me. One of mine. Anna Scott played her role beautifully. Ever heard of Frank Carmichael?" Moretti's blue eyes focused on me.

"The guy who deals with the Ukranians and their drug shipments, other stuff. He's from New—" I stopped, making the connection.

"York. Exactly."

Shit. *Shit.* Anna Scott was a hit man.

Anna

"Tell me about your weekend," Stephanie prodded as she poured herself another beer from the pitcher on the high-top table between us. She took karate with me and was one of a consistent group who went to a bar around the corner from the dojo after class on Thursday nights. There were five of us tonight and we jammed in close, several flat screen TVs showed off the Yankees game, who were winning to the delight of the crowd.

It had taken the group about a year of coaxing to get me to join them, but I'd learned that an hour or two at a bar was fairly string-free. There wasn't a chance of being pulled into bar hopping late into the night since everyone had to be up, and sober, in the morning for work. Even if they did do something after, they knew they'd pushed their limits with a beer and had yet to ask me for more.

I'd spent the entire week trying to block out my insane weekend. People could write a book about it. Who got the wrong car at the valet? Who got pulled over with a dead body in their trunk? Who had the hots for a dangerous felon—most likely a murderer? Who kept it a secret?

Me.

Once I waved goodbye to Zach after our shared taxi had dropped me at my apartment last Sunday, I'd done everything I could to stay busy, to wear myself out to the point of exhaustion so all I could do when I crawled into bed was sleep. I didn't want to think about the dead body. I didn't want to think about Nick. His dark hair, which would be coarse and thick. His strong brow that made him look brooding and very intense. The muscles of his abs that flexed when my fingers had brushed against them. God, I had to stop! Worse than mentally stripping off Nick's clothes, I didn't want to think about his rejection. I'd been stupid to seek out his help and think he was actually a decent guy. He'd gone from kind to cruel as if he had a personality disorder. I just wanted to forget him, forget the entire weekend and be thankful I hadn't wound up dead. Like my newly awakened libido was going to let that happen.

"Well?" Stephanie prodded, when I still hadn't responded. A cheer rose from the rowdy crowd around us when a Yankee hit a home run.

Unfortunately, sitting in a bar watching my karate classmates slowly get buzzed made them want to delve into my personal life more than usual. Or, it could be because I'd actually done something interesting. For once.

"The wedding was great. Zach's sister's dress was gorgeous," I commented, trying to stick to generalities as I cracked open another peanut from the bowl in the middle of the table. It wasn't a fancy bar, but it was familiar. I stuck to peanuts while the others stuck to beer. If I pretended to watch the game, perhaps they'd give up.

"I've already told them everything about the wedding. They want to know the other stuff," Zach said, trying to hide his grin behind a sip of beer. I turned from watching the nearest TV to glare at him. He lifted one brow and looked at me slyly in return. *The jerk.*

"Other stuff?" Paul, the dojo owner asked, curiosity blatantly obvious. "I didn't know you did *other stuff*." His words stung, even though they were true, but his wink took away the sting.

Stephanie grinned at me. "Now, I'm dying to know." She emptied the remainder of the pitcher into her glass.

I wasn't planning on telling them any of the *other stuff* because I had a feeling Zach and I considered them two different things. Zach wasn't referring to dead bodies and rental cars. "I don't know what he's talking about," I responded.

Zach shook his head. "Oh, don't give me that, Miss I've-sworn-off-men. At the reception, you went to the ladies' room and came back wearing a guy's tuxedo jacket." Everyone knew I'd gone with Zach to keep him in the closet, so meeting a man while being Zach's date wasn't considered cheating. "And it wasn't mine."

Ryan, another karate classmate and a guy who'd asked me out once or twice when we first met a few years back, piped up. "Just the tuxedo jacket?" His eyebrows were up under the dark hair that swept over his forehead.

"Seriously?" I rolled my eyes. "Not *just* a tuxedo jacket. I was at a wedding reception," I countered. "I was cold and someone gave it to me."

Ryan sat up straight and was focused on me like a heat-seeking missile on a target. "It's like ninety degrees out. How could you be cold? Did this guy come on to you?" Ever since I shot him down, Ryan had been one of the many guys who took on the role of big brother. If he couldn't have me, he wanted to make sure the guy who would was worthy. He hadn't had much opportunity to screen any of my dates—none, actually—so hearing about a man's tuxedo jacket brought out his caveman qualities.

9

nna

I SHOOK MY HEAD AS I THOUGHT OF NICK. SO TALL, SO DARK—NOT JUST IN coloring, but also in mood—and handsome. Cliché? Absolutely. Had he come on to me that night? Not really. He hadn't given me a cheesy pick-up line; he hadn't needed one. Pheromones practically dripped off him, which I sucked up like a parched man quenching his thirst. I'd been the one to run into him. In fact, he'd barely touched me at all. But when he held my hand, when his palm had been at my lower back as we walked, I'd felt heat. Sparks. Lust. An ache I'd never known existed. A need I still craved even after a week; the only way to solve it was with my bedside vibrator. It was definitely safer than the real thing.
"No. He was a perfect gentleman."

Well, he wasn't quite that. But who wanted one, anyway? If the heat in his dark, brooding eyes was an indicator, he hadn't been thinking gentlemanly thoughts. He'd called me naughty. *Naughty!* Naughty meant dark, delicious secrets that were shared with someone behind closed doors. He'd even been concerned. But that was before...

My thoughts shifted to Nick's harsh words at the bar, Scorch, which canceled out his heated touch, his concerned glances from the reception. It was like he was schizophrenic—two sides to the same man. One pulled me in like a siren and Odysseus' men, the other only validated why I kept everyone at a distance. A schizophrenic jerk. No, worse than that. He was a total asshat. If that wasn't bad enough, he was some kind of criminal for a known crime ring! I'd been able to go online and research Moretti and none of it was good.

"Who was that guy anyway?" Zach interrupted, but paused as the bar erupted in cheers for another home run. "I never even saw him. I can ask Chris about him if you want." Chris was Zach's new brother-in-law and made the obvious assumption since he was at the reception Nick was a friend of his.

"Just someone I ran into in the hallway by the restrooms." I tried to play it low key; telling them he was a hit man wouldn't be good. They probably wouldn't believe me anyway. "How was your blind date last weekend?" I asked Stephanie.

"Oh, no. You're not diverting this conversation off of you." Stephanie waggled a finger in the air. "We've waited years, and I mean *years,* to hear about a guy in your life. It's like you're a nun."

Sadly, it was a true statement, and the only guy that attracted me was certifiable.

"I'm not settling for the *perfect gentleman* crap," she continued.

All eyes were on me.

"You want me to tell you what, then? That I had a one-night stand in Denver? Is that what you want to hear?" I asked, my voice going up slightly from panic. I hated being the center of attention, especially when it came to men. I wasn't an innocent virgin, that was for sure. Todd had robbed me of that once we married. But I wasn't an expert in the dynamics between a man and a woman, the interplay that was part of the attraction, part of dating and falling in love. Or, just the simple attraction and accompanying lust. I knew what lust was, read about it, heard about it from Stephanie and even some of the guys, but never really felt it myself. Not until last weekend and Nick.

Sadly, that fact spoke volumes about my short marriage.

Every night this week I'd dream about Nick taking me back to my hotel room and running those hands over my body. Doing things to me I ached to have fulfilled. Nick had said there was chemistry between us. I had no doubt if I'd given him even the slightest chance we'd have been explosive together. My body didn't care that he worked for the type of people who wound up dead in the back of a trunk. My brain stripped out his assholeish behavior and left the hot man candy behind. My nipples tightened at the thought of his warm, callous-rough hands running over them, not that he was a total jerk who'd been toying with me. I squeezed my thighs together beneath the table, trying to relieve some of the need just thinking about the sexual what-if's, not the deadly ones. "You really want to hear about a guy I picked up at a wedding reception?"

Stephanie nibbled on a peanut. "Only if it's true."

Zach, Paul and Ryan sat there, hyped up, waiting for my answer, ready to go and punch some guy's lights out who was halfway across the country.

Except that...oh my God. He wasn't halfway across the country. Nick was... oh, Nick was right here, in front of me. All six feet plus of him. My heart lurched. I had to get out of here. *Now.*

Why was he here? He'd made it crystal clear he wanted nothing more to do with me. The only thing we had in common was a dead body and an extreme dislike for each other. Now, now—he was standing in a bar in New York, staring at me. It wasn't a coincidence. Not this bar. Not now. This was planned. He wasn't a nice guy, so he was here for a reason.

He was here for...me.

He was going to kill me.

My palms were slick as I stood from my seat, keeping my eyes pinned to the man that hated my guts. I knew who he was and what he did. Did that make me a liability for him? Oh shit, bad guys killed liabilities. The shouts of the bar patrons muted to nothing. He was equally focused on me, his dark gaze piercing beneath his deep brow. His dark hair was tousled, less styled than the formal wedding, his face unshaven.

Shit. I was attracted to him. I hated him, was afraid of him and I wanted to jump his bones. There was something seriously wrong with me. Why did I want to have sex—the first time since I was eighteen—with an asshat who killed for a living? Sure, I'd wanted to conjure him up so I could have my way with him. That was fantasy. The way he looked right now, slightly intimidating and very dangerous—at least to a woman's virtue—I really wanted to follow through with that idea. What woman wouldn't? Reality was different. He wasn't here for sex. He could have any woman at that bar of his in Denver. He didn't need to fly over a thousand miles for that. Then what? I wasn't going to stay here to find out.

There had to be a back door by the bathrooms, but he'd follow me, and I did not want to be in a back alley with the guy. Skirting around the table, I ignored my friends and kept my goal in sight, the front door. He moved fast, catching me by the arm. His hold was surprisingly gentle, considering why he was here. Whatever the reason, it wasn't good, and possibly might include the trunk of a car.

"Sorry I'm late," he murmured, giving me a gentle kiss to my brow. I avoided looking at his full lips because they were exactly like my fantasies. They were soft and warm against my skin. The simple yet deceptive gesture had my friends staring and my panic rising.

With his brooding intensity focused on me, I didn't hear Stephanie until she turned around and tapped me on the shoulder. "Um, Anna. Holy shit. Do you know him?" She blatantly checked him out. With his broad shoulders and tapered waist, Nick made a simple T-shirt look sexy. Low-slung jeans rode low on his lean hips. On his feet were a pair of beat-up sneakers.

"Obviously," Zach countered, eyeing Nick warily. I didn't blame him.

Stephanie seemed to have more brain function, or plenty of curiosity, because she got everyone in motion. "Zach, get a stool. Paul, move over. Ryan, wave down our waitress for another pitcher and extra glass."

"What are you doing here?" I asked, my voice a rough whisper as Zach, prodded into motion, slid a chair between himself and Stephanie.

Instead of answering, Nick pulled out the stool for me. Having no alternative, I sat down. He moved in behind me so my back was pressed against his hard stomach. His left hand moved over the bare skin of my upper arm in a way that indicated a lover's familiarity. Goose bumps skittered across my skin, and I wasn't sure if it was from aversion or arousal.

"So, Anna, going to introduce us?" Zach asked, watching Nick's hand slide up and down my arm.

I gave my head a little shake and faked a smile. "Sorry. Um...everyone, this is Nick."

Nick shook everyone's hands, but didn't move from his position behind me, keeping me wedged between his body and the high-top table. He looked to be an attentive date, sheltering me from the rowdy baseball fans who were bumping into our backs, but I knew otherwise. Where he stood, how he touched me was calculated and said without words he had the upper hand. I wasn't going anywhere without him.

It was difficult not to squirm as I shared everyone's names. I'd never mentioned a guy to this small group of acquaintances before, let alone have one show up out of the blue and being so...*there*. The waitress dropped off the pitcher and a glass for Nick. Paul poured another round for everyone.

"How do you two know each other?" Stephanie pointed between the two of us, brazen interest on her face.

"Anna did a little work for my boss," Nick replied. I'd forgotten how deep his voice was.

I licked my lips, took a sip of my beer, trying to cool my suddenly parched throat, as well as to stall for time. He still thought I worked for Moretti. That I flew all the way to Denver to shoot Bobby Lane, then come back and go to karate class followed by drinks with my friends. Was this what hit men did? Kill someone then return to their regular lives?

"Oh, do you mean that big hotel project?" Stephanie continued.

"Right," Nick said, taking a big swig of his beer. "The hotel project."

I wanted to tear through the bar, taking out people on the way to the door if I had to, to get out into the open air, with viable options for escape. If he'd found me at the bar, he surely knew where I lived. I could run, but couldn't hide.

I dropped the cocktail napkin I'd shredded onto the table. I couldn't have Stephanie grill him further; who knew what she'd ask? Something simple like —*What do you do for a living?*—was a landmine I wanted to dodge. I darted a glance to the guys. From their grim expressions, they were ready to rip Nick limb from limb. I couldn't blame them. The way Nick stood behind me screamed possession. There was no doubt to anyone in the bar that I belonged to him. That idea kicked my panic into high gear. Had it only been about two minutes since he appeared?

If he was going to kill me, he wouldn't have shown up at the bar, introduced himself to my friends where they got a good look at him—especially Stephanie —and could describe him to a police sketch artist. He would have made contact with me at my apartment or any other time of day when I was alone if he wanted to go incognito. The longer I stayed with my friends, the safer I'd be, although the more in danger they became. I didn't know what Nick had planned and it shouldn't involve my karate friends.

"We should go," I said, giving Nick a quick glance over my shoulder.

He nodded and stepped back enough to allow me to stand. I dreaded leaving with him, but I couldn't let my friends continue their questions either, nor make them potential targets. The stool slid easily across the dusty floor littered with broken peanut shells.

"I'd forgotten about meeting up with Nick." I shook my head as if I were an idiot, running a hand over my hair. "Sorry, guys. We've got plans."

I grabbed my gym bag off the floor then hoped to skirt past Nick. He was fast and I was stupid to think he'd let me go anywhere without him. Nick slung his arm round my waist before I made it two feet, in a casual way that indicated familiarity, not like a guy holding me prisoner. His palm felt warm against my side and his fingers gave a little squeeze, as if he could read my mind.

"You sure you're okay?" Zach asked as he stood to block our exit, eyeing Nick carefully.

"Zach, right?" Nick said, his voice casual and relaxed, although I knew he was anything but. His body radiated heat like a furnace in the winter. "Anna told me about your sister's wedding. Congratulations."

Wow. The man had the gall to talk about the wedding he'd crashed. Zach had been right there the whole time and he didn't even know. Of course, the woman in purple had been a distraction. Nick was unbelievably confident in himself, cocky even, knew just what to say to put people at ease, to get them to do what he wanted. Including me. He'd gotten me to do just as he wanted, to leave with him without incident.

Zach gave a small smile, still a little unsure of Nick, but his tense shoulders relaxed. Nick's words must have appeased him somewhat because he sat back down, opening the path for us to leave.

"Nice meeting you all," Nick said to the group, then looked down at me. He slid my bag off my shoulder and tossed the strap over his. Hunh. Who knew thugs could be chivalrous? "Ready?"

Hell no. I didn't want to go off with a virtual stranger whose casual demeanor belied an underlying life of crime. He could easily orchestrate my murder and leave my body in the trunk of a car. Dangerous intent wasn't what I saw when I glanced at him. Instead, his dark look was heated, filled with arousal. When he looked into my eyes, as if he wanted to gobble me up like a tasty dessert, all I could do was nod. My body wanted something only he seemed able to give me. Whether I wound up dead afterward didn't seem to make a difference to my libido.

What I didn't want, no matter what, was the chance of the others ending up dead as well. I gulped down my fear as I gave a little finger wave to my astonished friends and let Nick lead me out of the bar with a hand on the curve of my waist. They'd seen his face so they could describe him to the police and knew I was with him, so there was that thin thread of a lifeline.

The sun hadn't set yet, but the air was cooler in the tall buildings' shadows. Nick casually led me down the block, away from the bar, as if we were just like all the others enjoying the warm night. He kept his pace slow to match mine, even with his long legs.

I stopped us by moving out of his hold and turning to face him, forcing the flow of pedestrians to work their way around us. The honking of horns, the chatter of people talking on cell phones filled the humid air.

"What are you doing here?" I hissed, my eyes narrowed.

Nick grinned and his dimple appeared. "What? You didn't miss me?"

10

nna

I'd missed his dimple, that was for sure, but it was probably best not to share that. I crossed my arms over my chest. "No, I didn't miss you," I said, hoping the acidic tone of my words would make him go away. "I thought you hated my guts."

He shrugged. "Hate's such a strong word." His gaze flicked over me. "I like this look on you."

I looked down at myself. White T-shirt with the karate school name across the chest, tan cargo shorts and flip-flops. My hair was back in a ponytail, my makeup was minimal. I needed a shower. "Is this more in line to what you think a killer should wear?"

Nick glanced around, not bothered by the people moving past us, but I could see anger flare in his eyes along with the heat. He moved in close so I had to tilt my head back. I wouldn't retreat and let him think I was scared of him. "We're not talking about this here." His voice was quiet, but laced with steel. "Your place is only a few blocks away."

He took hold of my arm, his touch gentle, but firm. Warm. I felt the zing all the way to my toes. Nick must have felt it too because I saw a little tick in his jaw and a frown mar his brow as he stared at his hand.

"My place? Are you kidding? I'm not going anywhere with you."

"Why not? We're good together. There's something between us and you know it."

True, but there was more going on than just attraction.

"Yeah, a dead body," I said, my voice only loud enough for him to hear. I rammed my elbow into his stomach. I smiled at Nick's grunt and the release of his hold. I turned and started to walk off, holding my breath, waiting to be grabbed once again.

"I know where you live. I know where you do karate," he called out.

His words made me turn around, made my blood run cold.

"My friends know what you look like," I countered, walking back in front of him.

He stood there so casually with my stupid gym bag over his shoulder. Was he cleaning his fingernails? The rat bastard. "You say that like it's a good thing."

Oh shit. If Stephanie and the guys knew what he looked like, then Nick knew what they looked like, too. It wouldn't be hard to track them from the gym to their homes and kill them. My only witnesses were in danger and didn't even know it, and solely from association with me.

"You wouldn't," I said, my voice flat as Nick turned into an entirely new threat level.

"Look at me and decide if you think I'm the kind of guy that's just going to walk away." His strong brow shadowed his eyes, making him look menacing and deadly serious. Hands on hips, his posture and bearing screamed intense and dominant male. He closed the distance between us. "Let's go to your apartment and talk."

I knew nothing about this man other than his nefarious career choice and that my body responded to him instantly and intensely. Both were disastrous to keeping myself out of danger and out of his bed. Nick was pure, unadulterated trouble, but I really had no choice but to take him home with me.

"Fine, but the doorman will know you're there," I grumbled.

"Do you really think I'm going to take you home and kill you?" he asked, his brows raised.

"Maybe not in my apartment, but why else would you be here?" I eyed him suspiciously, even though he had carried my bag for me. What man took a woman's bag, carried it across town for her just so he could kill her?

He didn't reply, although his teeth ground together. Placing a hand to my waist, he guided me in the direction of my apartment, his body on the street side, keeping me away from the fast-moving traffic.

Of course, he knew where I lived. He knew more about me than I did of him, which was practically nothing, and that made him even more dangerous. I let him lead the way, only to prove he knew where he was going.

Hank, the doorman, held the door to the building, greeted me by name.

"This is my friend, Nick Malone. He just came to town," I told him, making sure he got a good look at Nick so he could describe him to the police, just like my karate friends, if I wound up dead.

Hank shook Nick's hand. Hank looked stunned I had someone with me, especially a man, but tried not to show it. In all the years Hank had worked for the building, I'd never once had a guest.

"Glad to know she's got someone like you watching out for her," Nick told the doorman as he slung his arm over my shoulder once again in a carefree gesture that screamed familiarity. Hank puffed up, pleased by the compliment.

If I wanted to get rid of Nick, now would be the time. I could tell Hank to call the cops, but I didn't know what Nick could, or would, do if I did so. Like Stephanie and the others at the bar, getting Hank involved might endanger the man.

Asking for help wouldn't solve anything. Nick, or someone like him, would be back. A doorman wasn't going to keep Nick away from me. Like Nick had said, he knew where I did karate, probably where I got my dry cleaning and where I got my hair cut. I couldn't stay in my apartment hidden for the rest of my life. I lingered on that depressing thought as I pushed the button for the elevator.

He held the door and let me enter first and remained quiet on the ride up to my floor. "I need to get my keys," I said, gesturing to my bag as we stood in front of my door.

He held it out to me, but kept the strap over his shoulder. I pulled the keys from a side pouch, opened the door with fumbling fingers. Nick was the first person I'd ever had in my apartment. It was my sanctuary, my safe place in the world. I let no one in; there had been no reason to do so. Before now.

When I'd first arrived in New York after fleeing San Francisco, buying the apartment had been the first thing I'd done. The building was safe, on a quiet street, and on the opposite side of the country from my ex-husband, father and problems that haunted me. Until now, no one had found me. My escape had been well planned—I'd had forty-two days in jail to do so—and my identity was still solid after all this time. How had Nick done in one week what they'd been unable to accomplish in twelve years? *He had my name.* Todd and my father didn't have that big clue and that had kept me safe. Until now.

"Holy shit, were you robbed?" Nick asked from behind me, dropping my gym bag to the floor. He moved into my foyer as he pulled a gun tucked in the back of his jeans and pushed me behind him and back into the hallway.

My heart leapt into my throat at the idea of my personal space being violated. Who would want to rob me? I had nothing of substantial value, only basic electronics like my TV and computer.

"Nick—"

"Stay out there." His head darted from side to side, his brow creased with the intensity of his focus, taking in his surroundings and ignoring me. He moved on the balls of his feet, his stance tense, but ready. It screamed military.

My apartment was small. Living room, dining room, kitchen combination, bedroom and bathroom. I didn't need more space; no one came for dinner, no guests slept over to need a spare bedroom. It only took Nick about ten seconds to confirm there weren't any burglars. He exhaled deeply as he put the gun back. Knowing he was armed made me swallow back the lump of fear that had lodged in my throat. If he wanted to kill me, why was he protecting me from a burglar?

"I wasn't robbed," I muttered, stepping through the door. "This is how my place always is."

Glancing around, I looked at my space through Nick's eyes. Since the apartment was small, it looked cluttered. My kitchen was modern with a tiny butcher block island, pots and pans hanging from a rack above it. I made a corner of my living room my home office, with a large drafting table covered with papers on one wall, a lower desk positioned in front of a large window held my computer. We were four floors up, above the trees that lined the sidewalk, so the view looked to the office building across the street.

A comfortable arm chair, my couch and TV were wedged into the space that was the dining area; I didn't need a dining table since it was only me, and I *never* entertained. Plants dotted small tables; the apartment was bright from many windows and they thrived. Laundry was on the floor—my one weakness —where I'd taken clothes off and left them.

It always looked like a bomb went off, but it was my bomb. My mess. He had no right to make fun of it.

"Are you sure? I mean...." He pointed at me.

I looked down at myself. "What?" I looked...unkempt. The T-shirt was one I wore under my gi top to class, the shorts were several years old, but comfortable. The flip-flops were just a cheap pair from the corner store. I hadn't had a chance to shower since class earlier.

"You did an hour of karate and you don't even have one hair out of place. Your makeup is perfect and even your shorts look ironed. Then, I come in here and it looks like a tornado moved through."

I ran a hand over my hair. It was still sleek and smooth. A little hairspray went a long way to keep those annoying wispy hairs from sticking up every which way. While I felt like a total slob, Nick thought I was tidy. The man was blind.

"I'm not a hoarder. The place isn't dirty," I grumbled. "In fact, you'll find it immaculately clean, beneath the clothes on the floor." I kicked the sneakers I wore running this morning out of the way. How dare he question how I kept my apartment? The first person I let in complains about my housekeeping. If this was how guests acted, I hadn't been missing anything all these years.

He held up his hands in defeat, obviously picking up on my *don't fuck with me* vibe. "I'm not judging. You should see my place. I'm just a little surprised, that's all."

I snagged a lavender bra off my armchair and tossed it into my bedroom, glancing at him out of the corner of my eye as I did so. He hadn't missed my personal indulgence in fine lingerie and I felt the heat of embarrassment. "After spending five years in military school, I've earned the right to be messy."

He arched a brow but didn't say anything to that, and was smart enough to ignore the bra.

"What's the deal with .38?" I asked, questioning his gun.

"Part of the job," he answered soberly.

"Moretti hands out firearms as part of new employee orientation?" I asked, one brow raised.

Nick shrugged. "Something like that."

"Are you planning on shooting me? If you are, that one's a little loud to be discreet."

He walked over to my drafting table, casually looked at my work, flipped through some of my sketches, lifted his chocolate gaze to mine. "Maybe I'm going to save you."

"From the bad guys?" I questioned. "Aren't you one of them?"

I started picking up laundry, uncomfortable just standing there. He was invading my personal space and it rankled. He had a gun and that was daunting. I could defend myself, but not from bullets.

Nick's square jaw tightened, but he didn't reply. Instead, he moved next to my desk, checking out the colored sticky notes on my computer monitor, the white cotton drapes at the window. After a minute, he said, "You've done some bad things," he said, looking out the open window. He didn't phrase it as a question.

I clenched the clothes piled in my arms, held my breath, felt my heart skip a beat. *He knew.* Why wouldn't he? He knew where to find me on a Thursday night. He knew where I lived. Did that mean he knew what I did to David?

He turned to face me, his dark gaze pinning me in place. "Haven't you?"

You killed him. You killed David. No one's going to believe your self-defense bullshit. Everyone knows what really happened. The story's out. I can't be tied to you. Sign the divorce papers. I can't be associated with a murderer.

I pushed down Todd's harsh words from the past, swallowed down my fear that they were coming back to haunt me. I could lie, but it wouldn't do me any good. I could only infer by his words that he knew the truth. Somehow. I couldn't escape it. I couldn't escape *Nick*. He'd find me, wherever I went. What did it matter admitting to him I killed David? Nick wasn't a saint himself. I took a deep breath. Oh God, he *knew*.

I bit my lip, nodded.

He closed his eyes for the briefest of moments, exhaled, then said, "We've both done some bad things. We're a lot alike."

"That's why you're here? Because we're both...bad?"

"I'm here because there was something between us last week, regardless of our pasts." He walked toward me with his slow, easy gait. "In my office last week I was a hypocrite, treating you the way I did and making you feel bad about being *bad* when I'm the exact same way. What right did I have to judge?" He shrugged. "I was an asshole and I'm sorry about that. I'm here because I couldn't forget your eyes, the softness of your skin. I couldn't forget *you*."

11

rif

ANNA'S MOUTH FELL OPEN AT MY WORDS, HER LOWER LIP AS SOFT AND LUSH AS I remembered. She wasn't wearing her poker face now. The various emotions that flitted across her face were easy to read: sadness, confusion, surprise. I'd caught her completely off guard, just as I'd wanted. She couldn't shore up her walls of defense that been in place last week. At the police station. In my office at Scorch. She looked more like the Anna I'd met at the wedding reception. Soft, endearing, honest.

To keep those walls down, I needed to distract her, to make her forget about erecting them. I knew just how to do that. I closed the final few feet between us, took the dirty clothes from her hands and dropped them back on the floor at our feet.

The hell of it was, I'd wanted her then, I still wanted her now. Even more so. I surrounded myself with assholes, thugs and criminals all day long. From what she'd just admitted, she fell under the criminal category. Her past was a turn-off—I wanted to avoid entanglements, especially intimate ones, with someone like her—but my dick didn't seem to care.

The woman had no idea how twisted up, how *fucked* up, I was over her.

Ever since I talked with Peters and her mysterious past, ever since Moretti had stirred up the confusion of my thoughts about what she was, she distracted me. Hell, she'd been distracting me since that first glimpse of her in the interrogation room. I couldn't figure her out and that was completely screwing with me.

I'd followed her, watched her since I flew in the other day to learn her routine, to see if she met with Carmichael or anyone else. What I learned was that she ran three miles in the morning. Same route. Spent the day in her apartment, I assumed working, only came out to pick up dry cleaning at the place around the corner. The closest one. She didn't say hi to anyone but the doorman. Didn't smile. She seemed to consistently go to karate for a class that began at seven. That was it. No dates. No men spending the night. No clandestine meetings. No one, period. She stayed in her apartment, went to karate, and ran.

Who lived that way? I wasn't one to talk. I did less socializing that she did. Working undercover meant I had zero life of my own. I, too, escaped by running as often as I could, but that wasn't much when I was supposed to be one of Moretti's lackeys. They didn't exercise.

Anna couldn't figure me out either, that was for sure. She was afraid of me. Of me! She had a cop keeping her safe from whatever ghost haunted her and she didn't even know it. She thought I was going to kill her. Hell, why wouldn't she? I'd given her that impression on the sidewalk in front of the bar. I'd been an asshole to her back in Denver and worked for Moretti who was a known criminal and showed up out of nowhere. With a gun. What else was she to think? Regardless of my words, no matter how sincere I'd said them, she didn't believe me.

She was breathing fast, her eyes widened as I approached. Her adrenaline must be pumping. I'd invaded her personal space—her apartment—which spoke to who she was, her personality, the *real* Anna. It was more than obvious by the look of the place she never had guests. The look of surprise on the doorman's face confirmed that. Hell, when I first walked in, I'd thought Moretti had sent someone else, tossing her place and waiting to kill her off instead of saving that for me. She was a contradiction; worldly enough to be a hired killer, but sheltered to the point where she didn't allow anyone to get close, to invite them to her apartment.

I'd spent the time since Moretti's ultimatum in my shitty apartment, fumbling for an answer. How the hell was I going to save her? I didn't hurt women, let alone kill them, but Anna didn't know that. Sure, I could go undercover and do some bad stuff, but pulling off a hit crossed the line. I couldn't have said no to Moretti. She was as good as dead if I had. He'd send someone else, someone who had no problem putting a bullet in Anna's brain.

She just admitted she did some bad stuff, might even work for Frank Carmichael, like Moretti suspected, but that didn't mean she should die. I may have been tasked with killing her, but my personal objective was to figure out how to keep her alive. The only way to do that was to stay close to her.

The first thing: I had to get her to believe I liked her alive. In fact, I just needed her to like me again. She hated me. Right or wrong, it was true. No woman wanted to be stuck with an asshole, so I had to make amends. Somehow.

I looked down at the front of her T-shirt, checked out the logo and name of her karate school as I tried to ignore the lush curve of her breasts. "Last week, when you said you'd learned to defend yourself by doing karate, you were telling the truth."

Anna licked her lips. "Everything I said was the truth."

I watched her tongue dart out and had a quick mental picture of her tongue running over the head of my cock.

I nodded absently, ran a hand over her dark hair. She flinched, but I had to feel how silky it was. Even pulled back securely, it was sleek and smooth. "Ever done that before? Outside of karate class."

"Take a guy down?" She shook her head as she stepped back, nervous. I was close, too close for comfort for her. She was filled with restless energy with her laundry shield gone. "No, never."

"Felt good, huh?"

She flicked her gaze to me, gifted me with a grin. "Amazing. Absolutely amazing."

That smile, God, that smile. It did things to me, made me feel...just made me *feel*. I had hot women surround me night after night at Scorch. Peters had been right—phone numbers on panties wasn't anything new to me. But Anna, simple, uptight Anna had me craving her smiles. Made me want to do things to her, make her feel things, see things, experience life in a way that made her smile, and often. I was turning into a fucking Hallmark commercial, but I didn't care.

"But you couldn't share it with anyone. Couldn't grin like you are now and feel good about how you handled that guy. Couldn't tell your friends tonight over drinks because you were supposed to be tucked into your bed at the hotel that night, not at a trendy bar, right?"

Her smile dimmed. "No. I couldn't tell anyone. I've never been able to tell anyone anything."

I reached out and gave a gentle tug on her long ponytail. She gave a little gasp in response as I forced her head back so our eyes met. "Until now." Neither of us were referring to karate anymore, but it was too deep, too much for her to delve into now, so I circled back to the guy at Scorch. "I saw what you did. Saw his face. It was really impressive."

There it was again. Her smile. It was back and it was genuine. Color bloomed in her cheeks, her eyes lit up with something akin to happiness. I'd thought her beautiful back in the interrogation room in Denver, had told Peters that. Now, in her casual yet finicky outfit, her hair in a simple tail, only a hint of makeup on her face, she looked lovelier than ever. In my office at Scorch I hadn't been able to see—or wanted to notice—how she had a sprinkling of freckles across the bridge of her nose, how her dark eyes were fringed with equally dark and long lashes.

"I have to admit, it was pretty hot." I couldn't help my husky voice when her scent pulsed toward me with every frantic heartbeat against the soft skin at her neck. I ran a knuckle down her smooth cheek, hoping to soothe her, to appease my need to touch.

She stepped back, held up one hand. "Look, I don't get you. You hated me, I mean you thought I was a total bitch for some reason. Now...now, you show up here all nice and...stuff." She paused. "Saying what, that you're attracted to me? What do you want me to think?"

I didn't blame her. I ran hot and cold like a faucet when around her. Being undercover made me wary of everyone, had me assume the worst. It was how I stayed alive. No woman could just be kind, thoughtful, sexy, brave. Women like that didn't exist in Moretti-land. None had been worth taking the risk.

"At the reception, I pegged you for a woman not mixed up in the life. Sweet, sexy, innocent. Then you showed up at Scorch and I figured you worked for Moretti. I thought you played me."

She stood there, frozen for a moment. "You really thought I worked for Moretti?"

I nodded. She really didn't work for Moretti, which was good because she wouldn't blow my cover, but it was still possible she worked for Carmichael. Right now, I didn't really give a shit who she worked for.

"I'm going to kiss you," I warned. I didn't want her to panic, or worse, put me in a wrist lock. I watched her eyes dilate further, her tongue dart out to run over her lower lip I recognized now as a sign of nerves. "I have to. I have to know what you taste like."

That was the only advanced warning I gave her right before I tugged on her shoulders, pulling her into me.

We were cut from the same cloth. Pasts to hide, secrets to keep. This chemistry, this *intensity* between us was something neither of us could deny. Something we could share with each other when our lives were full of secrets. It was the only real thing between us. This couldn't be faked.

She tasted as sweet as I'd imagined, her lower lip just as plush as I'd hoped. She offered no resistance as my tongue plunged into her mouth, running over hers, learning her every soft, wet inch. She moaned, deep in her throat, and I pulled her closer, used my hand to angle her head just the way I wanted.

"Okay?" I asked, lifting my head only a fraction of an inch so I could feel her hot breath against my skin. I don't know why I asked, she could have denied me.

She licked her lips again, nodded.

I groaned at the sight, at the thought of the other things that tongue could do. Her hair was silky soft beneath my palm. My other hand moved to her hip, holding her close against me, my need for her obvious against her belly. She was soft and round in all the right places and I didn't want to let go.

I had no doubt she was a little unworldly; her touch was tentative and the little erotic sounds she made were more of surprise than seduction. It didn't matter. Everything she did only ratcheted up my thirst for her, my cock literally pulsed with need to be buried deep inside her. If I kept this up, I'd take her, right here in her living room, using her like I would one of the bar bunnies back at the club. That's what Moretti expected, but not what I wanted. The bastard might dictate my life until we had the evidence we needed to arrest him and the bigger fish he worked with, but he didn't dictate what I did with a woman. I didn't fuck on command. He wasn't going to pimp me out like one of his whores. I pulled back, broke our kiss, but kept my hand at her nape.

"Jesus, we have to stop." If I was going to have her, and I was, there was no doubt about that, then it was just going to be about me and Anna. No motives, no reasons for doing so other than the *want* to lose myself in her, to have her right there with me when I did. To see the look on her face when I made her come.

Her eyes fluttered open, awe and arousal made her look at me as if through a fog. A haze of lust. My hips automatically thrust toward her, knowing I'd made her look like that, feel like that, so lost to her surroundings. Overwhelmed, no...flooded with arousal.

I lifted my hand, ran my thumb over her bottom lip as I'd wanted to do all week. To feel its fullness. Now, it was not only delectably soft and kissable, it was red and swollen. I'd done that. It was a heady feeling knowing I could make Anna respond in this way.

"God, you're confusing me," she murmured, her breath ragged. "And that kiss, it's making it worse. Why are you here?"

I stared at her intently, resisting the urge to rip her clothes off and fuck her up against the wall. "You know the reason." My voice was quiet, rough.

"Not because of Moretti. Not because he owes me. I was stupid to think he'd even the score," she said bitterly.

"Then why do you think?" I crossed my arms over my chest to keep from reaching out and grabbing her and pulling her in for another kiss.

"To help my friend?" Hope flared in her eyes.

"Is there really a woman who needs help?" I asked. Had it just been a line to get me to New York?

She cocked her head as if surprised by my question. "Yes."

If I helped her with her friend and the *bad man,* I would have the time I needed to figure out how to get out of killing her. It would also give me a reason to be with her, to keep her safe. Moretti sure as hell would send someone else to do my job if he felt I was taking too long. He told me to fuck her and have fun with her first. I figured I had a week. At the most.

"I'm here to help *you,*" I murmured. It was true. I did want to help her—to help her stay alive. If solving her friend's problem was a means to this end, then that's what I had to do.

"Help me?" She looked at me warily, almost bleak. "Even though I told you I've done some bad things?"

Her expression had me reaching out. I couldn't help it; I ran my knuckles down her cheek. "Like I said before, we all have our reasons for doing stuff. Are you planning on killing me?" I wondered, hoping to tinge my words with a little humor.

"With what?" She gave a little laugh and glanced down at herself. "Are you planning on killing me? You've got the gun." Her hands moved from my biceps, around my back to the where my gun was.

"Jesus, you could shoot yourself." I grabbed it before she did, placed it on her kitchen counter. "That's to keep you safe, not hurt you." Moving to stand in front of her again, I tilted her chin back up with my finger, cupped her face with my hand. "I wouldn't hurt you. I won't let anyone hurt you. At the reception, you panicked when I touched you." I added a little pressure to my hold. "I want you. I want to do more than kiss you, touch more than your shoulder, but doing just that made you freak out. I need to know if that's going to happen again."

She nodded, stepped back, organized a messy pile of papers on her desk. I couldn't tell if she was upset or pissed off; Anna was exceptionally good at hiding her emotions when she wanted. "Usually, when a man touches me, like that guy at the bar, I'm numb. I don't feel it. I don't feel anything."

I wasn't thrilled with the mental picture of some guy's hands on her. Touching her intimately.

"I can think, react, defend myself. Get angry, whatever." She dropped a stray pencil into a glass holder beside her monitor. "But with you..." She turned back to face me, looked me straight in the eye. I could see the truth of her words. There would be truth in what came next, a truth I needed to know. But she changed her mind, gave her head a little shake and turned away to rebuild her walls. That's when I knew.

Anna might want to turn away, to hide, but I didn't. I might want to be gentle with her, but she needed a little nudge out of her safe, protected little world. "So you panicked because I make you feel something."

She ran her hand over her right shoulder. "I panicked because you grabbed me here. It's a trigger for me. Something happened to me, you're right about that. It has nothing to do with you."

She turned away.

"Bullshit, Anna. I make you feel, and it scares the hell out of you." Her words had cut deep, sliced through layers of equally numb feelings I'd felt since I'd found Nadine with her lover. Since the divorce. Anna's words could bring me to my knees. Would she admit I had such an impact on her? Did she know that she could do the same to me? To make me feel in a way I'd forgotten even existed?

I stalked over to her, grabbed her arm and spun her around, forced her to look at me. The *real* me.

"I'm just supposed to believe when you say you're not going to kill me? Why should I?" she shouted. She tugged against my hold, but I wouldn't let her go.

"Because besides being an ass to you in my office, I've done nothing for you to think that."

"You work for some big crime boss!" She pushed at my chest. For all I knew, so did she. And I still wanted her.

This wasn't going as planned. "Do you really think I'm going to hurt you?" When she didn't answer, just looked at the front of my shirt, I continued. "My gun's over there. If I wanted to kill you, I'd have done it by now. Hell, I wouldn't have flown across the country to do it. I'd have killed you in Denver when I had the chance." She stopped trying to work her way out of my grip. Slowly, she looked at me, her dark brown eyes assessing. Wary. I ran my knuckle down her cheek, softened my tone. "Tell me how I make you feel."

12

rif

ANNA TOOK A DEEP BREATH, LET IT OUT. "You—"

"I what?" I prompted when she pinched her mouth closed, as if afraid the words would fall out.

"You're...you're heat and electricity," she admitted. "You make my mind go blank. I feel alive when I'm with you, Nick. I forget myself when I'm with you. Forget the fear."

Yes. She wasn't indifferent, she was affected. *I* affected her. It was almost too much to handle. She'd shared something pretty intense, which no one in our line of work dared to do. She'd given those words to me, how she felt—how I made her feel—to hold and to protect. It was a heady sensation, but also a lot of responsibility. Could I handle it, especially in my—our—line of work? I had to sit down. I moved around her, dropped into her comfortable armchair.

I was still the asshole. She admitted heavy truths while I hid behind lies. My name wasn't Nick. I didn't work for Moretti. She assumed so, and I let her. Was it fair? No. I had no choice. If anyone knew I was a cop, my whole career would be blown, and there'd be a mark out on my head. I couldn't keep Anna safe if I was dead. I met the first woman who deserved honesty from me through a sick twist of fate and I couldn't tell her the truth.

"This—" she waved a hand between us, "—there's something here. I need to know if you think this is real, or if you're just here for sex. Will you use my ache for you like a weapon? Kiss me to get the answers you want, seduce me and remain unaffected?"

I tried not to wince. It was like a kick to the gut to hear her words. To know her questions had been dead-on—before I went to the reception last week. My plan *had* been to seduce her into finding answers, then leave her. But she was wrong on one key point. I hadn't remained unaffected. I felt the same things as she, a connection that scared the hell out of me, too. It changed everything. I couldn't just seduce her. I didn't want that. I wanted it all. Wanted to know that —if everything else around us was a lie—*this* was real.

I didn't want seduction. That was too easy. I wanted connection. Wanted to learn what pleased her, what made her gasp, what made her melt beneath my touch. Yes, it was fucking scary, but for once, maybe it was worth it.

What happened once she found out the truth about me? What happened when I couldn't handle knowing she killed people for a living? Then what? Move to New York and play house with her? Doubtful. We had too much baggage to make this last for the long haul. I needed to forget the guilt, forget everything about what made us all wrong for each other and live in the now. Could we have *now*?

I crooked my finger at her. "Come here," I said, my voice a rough whisper.

She eyed me warily, but followed my instructions. Stood with her legs between my spread knees, looked down at me.

"You're so beautiful. I wouldn't do anything to hurt you. If I touch you in a way you don't like, just say so. I'll never hurt you." I repeated myself, but they were important words. I had to know she understood.

She nodded. Once she was within reach, I tugged her down to me. A gasp of surprise escaped her lips as she fell forward, her hands instinctively going to my shoulders to block her fall, her knees landing awkwardly over mine. I very gently shifted her thighs so she straddled me, my thumbs moving in slow circles over her soft skin below the hem of her shorts.

"Oh," she said, although it came out close to a moan. Her eyes flared with surprise and awe.

I kept my wayward hands on her soft thighs, her shorts and my jeans a barrier between us. "You ache for me, love?" I whispered, my voice rough with need, repeating her earlier words. Needing to see her hair, I gently worked the tie free, let the dark tresses fall like a curtain over her shoulders. So dark, soft and sleek. The scent of her shampoo, tropical and luscious filled the air between us.

She tilted her chin back, exposing the soft curve of her neck, so I continued the caress down to the collar of her simple cotton T-shirt. Nodding, her hair whispered across her back at the movement.

"I ache, too. And, Anna, I'm not unaffected." At those words, I tugged on her hips, pulling her in so her very center pressed up against my cock. Her eyes flew open in stunned desire. "Feel that?"

She rocked her hips into me as she nodded again. I hissed out a breath at the same time she let a little cry of delight escape.

"That's not unaffected."

ANNA

I LEANED INTO NICK, MY CHEEK NEXT TO HIS SCRUFFY ONE, JUST BREATHING. When I shifted my hips, I felt him, hard beneath me, rubbing against a spot that had me gasping in surprise. The move was instinctual, as if my basest needs recognized the opportunity to be fulfilled.

"It's too much. Too fast," I gasped, my breath coming in little pants. *I was straddling the lap of a killer and I didn't care!* The intensity of the pleasure coursing through me was dulling all logic and reason. I hadn't had a man touch me in so long I forgot what it felt like. This wasn't just touching, this was deeper. *More.*

"I know," he murmured, his own breath fanning the hair at my nape. His palms were warm on my thighs, pinning me in place. Not that I had any intention of moving. "And we still have all our clothes on."

"Is it always like this?" I wondered. I hadn't even known it was possible. My nipples were once again pebble hard; it seemed they turned that way whenever I was in Nick's presence. My panties were wet, my clit throbbed, oh God. I never even knew it worked in conjunction with a man. I squeezed my legs into his thighs, hoping to dull the need. It totally didn't work. There was something completely wrong with me if I reacted this way to a probable felon. I knew nothing about the man except he was solid muscle, unbelievably handsome and a *really* good kisser.

He shook his head, his forehead lightly bumping my cheek, his hair soft against my skin while his nose nuzzled behind my ear. "No."

"This is crazy. I shouldn't be doing this because you're…and I'm—this is wrong. God. I barely know you and I'm sitting in your lap and—"

Nick shifted so he could put a finger to my lips, silencing me. His touch was soft, warm. Gentle. Our eyes met, held. His dark gaze narrowed and he murmured, "Crazy feels pretty good."

I smiled against his finger.

"This is probably the only completely honest thing between us. No matter how much I want to take you here and now, I won't. We both need to know, to be completely sure, that this is real. Our first time I don't want you questioning this. Us."

Our first time. I wanted that with Nick so badly. "But—"

"But what?" he asked, his brow creasing. This close I could see dark flecks in his eyes.

"You work for Moretti. You're a—"

"Bad guy?" he finished for me, quirking a brow. He didn't look offended by my words. It didn't seem like much bothered him, not much could ruffle his feathers.

"Killer?" I questioned, my face scrunched up, afraid of the repercussions of uttering that word.

Nick shook his head, dropping down so our eyes met. "No. Not a killer. Bad? Yeah."

I could only nod. So he didn't kill people for a living, or so he said. I was all but riding his lap. The only thing I knew for fact was that he was just as hot for me as I was for him.

"You've admitted you've done bad things, too," he murmured, his thumbs continuing their soothing motion on my thighs.

I nodded again. He'd inferred earlier he knew what I'd done to David. *I was the killer!* If he knew this, why was he here with me? Why would he even want to be? I was completely messed up, wary of the world and everyone in it. There were innocent women who didn't have anywhere near the amount of issues I had that would be a better—safer—choice for Nick.

Thinking that, I climbed off his lap, stood before him, vulnerable.

"We go into this with our eyes open," he added, looking up at me. "For once, we have someone who knows the truth, right?"

Maybe he wanted me because I was just as bad, just as tainted by evil as he was. And he was no saint. I didn't know much about his boss, Moretti, but I'd Googled him and the stories weren't good. He wasn't a philanthropist; he was a thug, a drug dealer, a pimp, a murderer. So what did that make Nick? How bad were the secrets he kept? Was I one to cast stones after what I'd been through? What I'd done? If he'd thought I worked for Moretti, I couldn't blame his attitude in his office. He wasn't going to kill me. He had no reason to do so, as far as I could tell. He wanted me. A guy couldn't fake something like that. I felt *it*.

Maybe he was going to sleep with me, then kill me. Why wouldn't a guy wait to kill the girl until *after* they had sex? It gave a whole new meaning to a happy ending. I mentally rolled my eyes. No, he'd said he wasn't a killer, and at this point, I was inclined to believe him. At least on that. I was being ridiculous, coming up with wild scenarios to avoid getting close.

Was it finally time to let someone in? Having the truth out there meant maybe I could.

The honesty I saw in Nick's eyes was hard to take. He was willing to give this—whatever *this* was—a try. Like it was something simple. Maybe it was; I was definitely over thinking it. I took a deep breath. I couldn't miss his gaze dip for a moment to my breasts. "Eyes open," I agreed, a bit unsteadily.

He stood, closed the little bit of distance between us. "Let's go to bed. I'm wiped."

"Bed? Um, I've...I mean—"

He put a finger over my lips again. He seemed to like to do that. "Just to sleep. That's all. Let me hold you tonight."

I stared at him, considering his words. *Just to sleep.* No chance of that if Nick was lying next to me. I'd never even had a man in my apartment before, let alone in my bed. I'd been married to Todd for six months, but that wasn't the same. We'd had a king-sized bed and there had always been at least three feet between our bodies, except when...I wasn't going to think about that. There was no chance Nick intended any kind of space between us.

I had a choice now. I got to decide. He wouldn't push me or force me to do something I didn't want, that I wasn't ready for. I knew that, deep down. That didn't make it less nerve-racking.

Nick wasn't a monk, I knew. He'd been with women before, women who knew what they were doing, knew how to play the game. I didn't even know the rules. "I've never...I, um." I felt my cheeks flush. I couldn't get the words out, practically clogged on my shame.

"What? You've never what?" He searched my face as if he could see the answer there. "You're a virgin?" His brow went up in surprise. No, he wasn't a mind reader, but I had no doubt he couldn't imagine my answer.

I shook my head. "No." Taking a deep breath, I continued. "I've never...I've never been held."

He stared at me, as if I'd grown horns. "You've never been held. By a lover?"

Lover. Was Nick my lover? Todd hadn't been anything close to one. We'd had sex, but the word *love* had been missing from our marriage, let alone our marriage bed. The very idea of Nick filling that role made my heart speed up. It was impossible to take it back, to hold the secret close again. It was out, like this little bomb had exploded between us and he needed time to recover. I needed time to deal with the possibility that he might laugh in my face. I stepped back, walked around him and into the bedroom. I started straightening the sheets and blankets on the unmade bed. "By...by anyone. Not in the way you mean."

Nick recovered fairly quickly, reverting back to his usual laid-back, nothing-can-faze-me state, and stood in the doorway and just watched me as I smoothed out the light blanket. "You've been with a man before, obviously."

"Obviously," I repeated sarcastically, tossing a decorative pillow into the center by the headboard. Why was I remaking the bed when we were supposed to be getting in it? "I was married for six months. Didn't mean we were close."

"No, it meant your husband was an asshole. What about your mother?" He moved up behind me, gently turned me around to face him, took the second pillow from my grip, dropped it back on the floor. "No scraped knees?"

I wasn't going to cry at the pity in his voice. He was more surprised I'd never been hugged than by the fact I'd killed a man. He didn't care that I was a murderer, but was bothered that I hadn't had much comfort in my life. I was quickly learning that Nick was a man unlike any other. "My mother died when I was little. My father," I sighed, continued, "was...indifferent."

Indifferent was definitely the word for it, but it didn't give the depth of his lack of interest in me. There wasn't an adjective in the English language for that. He wasn't neglectful, that's for sure. The finest boarding schools in the world would agree he hadn't neglected me.

He lifted up my hand, kissed my knuckles tenderly. "It's time I showed you how then."

I stood there and blinked at him. He wasn't laughing, he wasn't leaving. He was serious.

Not knowing what to do, I went to the linen closet and offered him a clean towel and new toothbrush. While he took a shower I picked up my bedroom, tossed my dirty laundry into the hamper. I put my shoes back on the floor of the closet and just puttered, trying not to think about the fact that there was a naked man in my bathroom. Quickly enough, he came out.

In just his boxers.

Oh my God. I thought he was unbelievably attractive with his clothes on, but...wow. His dark hair was slicked back from his face, still damp from the shower, his equally dark scruff on his jaw made him look rugged and dangerous. Which he was, in more ways than one. His shoulders were wide, his torso muscular and lean, a smattering of dark hair led from his chest down over his to-die-for abs and into a line that disappeared into the waistband of his dark blue boxers. His long legs were sprinkled with equally black hair. This wasn't a man who sat around all day. Whatever he did for Moretti was more than just work behind a bar.

Don't think about that! I didn't want to know what he did for Moretti. I looked up at him and forgot my whole train of thought. Nick's chocolate-brown eyes were heated, intense and focused solely and completely on me. "Your turn," he said, his lip quirked up at catching me.

I was ogling him. Ogling that damn dimple. Shamelessly. I averted my gaze, felt my cheeks burn. My bedroom hadn't ever seemed small before. Now, with six plus feet of Nick watching me in just his underwear, it felt tiny, like there wasn't enough room for both of us. Unless we were in bed. I fled into the bathroom, not sure what else to do.

I didn't linger in the shower, didn't wash my hair. I didn't have time to straighten it, not without him wondering what was taking me so dang long. He'd probably think I was afraid to come out. *Which I was.* Staring at the closed door, I took a deep breath. Could I do this? Once I opened the door, I'd be sharing more than just my past. Rejection wasn't something I handled well. What if I wasn't appealing? What if I couldn't please him? I didn't want to please him too much, because that meant that we'd—

Get a grip! I could face Nick or spend the night in the bathroom.

I turned off the light behind me, wearing pajamas, a black short-sleeved shirt and matching shorts. They were soft cotton, edged in white lace and were as modest as I could manage without pulling out my winter fleece. The bedside lamp was on, the room cast in soft shadows. Nick was on one side of my queen-sized bed, the white sheet pulled up to his waist, hands folded behind his head. Watching me. He took in my outfit, but his eyes lingered on my breasts. I felt hot all over when he looked at me like that. He didn't say anything, just reached over and pulled back the sheet for me.

Okay, he didn't laugh. I was so nervous, my heart was pumping in my ears. Could he hear it? My fingers played with the hem of my shirt. What was I supposed to do? I didn't know how to just lie in bed with a man. Where did my hands go? On his chest? What if I did it wrong? I was going to mess this up! This was a bad idea. I could sleep on the couch. Move to Kansas. I could—

"Anna."

My gaze darted up to his. My tongue flicked out to lick my lower lip.

"Breathe."

A slow, reassuring smile spread across his face and I took a deep breath. How did a guy, who was so *bad,* seem so good? Why did I want to trust him? Why did he get me to do things, albeit not crazy to most people, like share my bed with him? Guys at the karate school had asked me out, given me very obvious indication that they were attracted to me, but not one of them had gotten behind my defenses as quickly as Nick had. I'd never let them. Never wanted them to. With Nick, I did. I *so* did.

He held out his tanned hand and I just looked at it. His long fingers, the rough calluses on his palms, the close-cut nails. Nick was offering something to me, something simple and new and special. I just had to reach out and take it. I might be climbing in bed with the devil, or maybe the devil's underling for all I knew.

"Stop thinking. I can practically see smoke coming out of your ears. Take my hand."

After a final moment of indecision, I took another breath and did just that.

As soon as his fingers closed around mine, he gave me a little tug, pulling me off balance and onto my knees on the bed. He tugged once more and I fell softly onto my side. Without a chance to think, he had me up against him, my head on his shoulder, my hand on his belly, my left leg tangled with his. "Oh," I said in surprise, not only because he had me off balance, but in surprise to how he felt.

His skin was so warm, surprisingly soft, the little hairs on his stomach crisp and springy. His ridged muscles flexed and tightened when my fingers moved. I wasn't used to touching people like this, and definitely not without their clothes on. Sure, I made contact with my karate classmates, but it was clinical, like going to the doctor's. It was *nothing* like this. Who needed an electric blanket in the winter when you had a man to warm you? This was something I could easily get used to. Or easily long for once it was gone.

Nick gently brushed my hair back from my brow. It was a calming gesture, and I liked it. I couldn't see his face to know if we were doing it right, but I didn't have to, because I was in his arms. He tugged the sheet back so I could climb beneath, then settled against his full length, only his boxers and my pajamas separating us. He was relaxed; his muscles—except where my fingers roamed—were lax. His breathing was slow and steady. His heartbeat beneath my palm was strong and even. "Okay?" he asked, his voice soft.

I nodded against his shoulder. It was more than okay. It was…perfect.

13

rif

I STAYED STILL, JUST LETTING MY HAND LIGHTLY RUN UP AND DOWN ANNA'S BACK, hoping to soothe her. It sure as hell soothed me. Feeling her heartbeat against my side, knowing she was in my arms, safe, made me feel better. All week, I'd wondered if Moretti would change his mind about giving me this little *assignment* and send someone else to finish her before I got to her. I'd wondered if she was off doing another job for Frank Carmichael. But in this moment, with her in my arms, it was just the two of us. The rest of the world, the Morettis and Carmichaels out there, didn't exist.

She might have been soothing to my stressful week, but having her pressed head to toe against me was a kind of torture I'd never experienced before. I should be given a fucking medal. She was soft in the right places. Her hair was silky against my shoulder, a wayward strand or two tickled my cheek. Full breasts were pillowed against my chest. I'd felt her nipples tighten when I pulled her against me, even through her pajama top. She definitely wasn't wearing a bra. Now, in sleep, her whole body had softened, her wariness gone. I watched the bedside clock, afraid to move, afraid to break the spell of the moment.

It was one hell of a moment—even with Anna sound asleep. When she'd come out of the bathroom in her little pajama set, *shit*. I figured she'd worn it because it was plain, modest. She probably picked it to cover as much of herself as possible, just like the dress from the wedding reception, the skirt and blouse at the police station. It had done a good job, it wasn't the least bit provocative, but I'd filled in the blanks by myself. Nothing she'd worn so far kept me from imagining what was beneath. Her breasts would be a handful, soft, heavy globes with pale pink tips. Her belly would be flat and firm, her legs long and lean. And in between...

It was sexy as hell. *She* was sexy as hell.

That wasn't what destroyed me, though. Anna had never been held. What the fuck was that about? What person hadn't been held? What kind of man was her husband? Parents? High school sweethearts? Girlfriends? Lovers? Anything? From my experience, everyone lied to get something. Why would she lie about this when being held was freely given by pretty much everyone? A hug between friends was a simple gift. Acquaintances even. When she came out of the bathroom and stood next to the bed, unsure, nervous—panicked even—it ripped to shreds any defense I had against her. Screw her job, her past. Her resume. I wanted to go out and beat the shit out of her ex. She hadn't been lying. No fucking way.

Her body, God, her body felt like heaven. Warm, supple, small. She was so small, her head tucked perfectly into my shoulder. Once settled, we didn't say anything, just...lay there, together, listening to the big city quiet. Her scent, citrusy and light, floated over me like a cloud, mixed with the summer air through the open window. She lived on a quiet street, so the hectic sounds of the city were distant, lulled. Anna had fallen asleep within minutes, her deep, even breathing against my chest the giveaway. The tenseness left her body. Her fingers had stopped roaming over my belly so I just continued to caress her back.

Eventually, I carefully slid from beneath her, pulled the sheet over her and watched as she curled into her pillow before finding my cell in my jeans pocket. I glanced at her one more time. Her hair was wild about her face, her mouth open, her breathing quiet. She wasn't going to wake, but I closed the bedroom door behind me and went into her living room to make my call.

"Got anything for me?" Peters asked. No preliminaries. It was late, even in Denver, but he wanted in. Wanted to help me figure out this mess. He had a soft spot for Anna, ever since she'd walked out of the police station last week. The guy didn't believe her involved with Moretti or Carmichael—or any bad guys for that matter—with much more conviction than I felt. Either way, the more we dug, the more we wanted to know. She was a mystery he wanted to solve, maybe even to prove someone innocent for once. Beneath my jaded experiences, the evidence building against her, I wanted her to be innocent, too.

"Military prep schools. She went to one for five years. Check yearbooks from the late nineties," I told him, my voice quiet.

"Military school? Anna Scott? Why the hell was she in a place like that?" Peters asked. I could hear the surprise in his voice.

"I have no idea, but I'm pretty sure her father was an asshole," I muttered. Since her mother supposedly died when she was really young, I wanted to track her dad down and beat the shit out of him for neglect. Who they hell didn't hold their kids? Even my parents, who were never going to win Parents Of The Year awards because of their less than amicable divorce, never let any of my sisters or me doubt their love. There were plenty of hugs, even when, as a teenager, I wasn't interested.

No way was I sharing her secrets with Peters. What we did in bed, what she told me—*me*, the real me—wasn't for Peters or anyone else. "She knows her weapons, saw my police issue and asked after it. Recognized it as a .38."

"A .38's not the same thing as the .22 that killed Bobby Lane."

"No, but they teach more than just French at a fancy military prep school."

"You're thinking she really does work for Frank Carmichael with that kind of background?" Peters asked, his voice laced with doubt. "That she was groomed for the job from what…eighth grade?"

"I have no fucking clue, but it's not looking good," I replied, my voice low. "I asked her outright if she'd done some bad things and she admitted it." I hadn't turned on a light in her living room, but I could see well enough from the street lights through the large front window. I ran a hand over a plant, touched the cool leaves.

"She admitted killing Bobby Lane?" Peters was stunned.

"No, dammit. Not that. Just admitted she'd done some stuff."

"Maybe she stole a pack of gum when she was a kid and her conscience is finally catching up to her."

"Maybe that's why she got shipped to military school. Too many youthful transgressions." I walked across the room, paced, trying not to trip over the crap on the floor.

"Well, a little tough love from military school seemed to have paid off. Her record—Anna Scott's—what we have of it, is completely clean."

"She might not do the petty stuff anymore, but we haven't ruled out Carmichael yet." Even as I said the words, I was doubtful. I had to know for sure, though.

"You're there in New York with her. You've made contact, seen her place, right?"

"Yeah," I answered, looking at her space, how perfectly *her* it was. Now that I had a tiny little crack open into the doorway to her secrets, I could see why she chose to keep her apartment a total mess. She needed control and this was something she had complete dominion over. No one—not Daddy, not a drill sergeant or ex-husband—could dictate this. It was a small thing, but it screamed a hard-fought battle. The only person she'd probably ever let in was...me.

"What's your gut telling you?"

My gut. *Shit*. I sighed. "My gut says she's innocent." I thought of her standing next to her bed, unsure of herself. "But there's a lot stacked against her. Bobby Lane, false identity, Carmichael, military school, familiarity with guns. Look, we're just making wild guesses here. Do the search, look at the yearbook photos because we know her name wasn't Anna Scott back then."

"That's going to take time. How many military schools do you think there are?" Peters wondered.

"It would have to be coed, so that narrows down the field considerably. Start with the private ones. The most expensive. You said she had money hidden somewhere, so maybe Daddy's got some, too. If he's looking to rehabilitate a wayward daughter, he probably wouldn't skimp."

"Right. I'll get a pot of coffee going and get on it. Werbler's on it, too."

I smiled, reminded that there really were some good guys out there. Anna had more people on her side than she knew. "Thanks. Text me when you learn more."

I sat down on the edge of her couch, elbows on my knees, and thought about how I was getting deeper and deeper into this shit. Into Anna. I was digging for the truth about her, even using Peters and Werbler to help. She'd shared some things about herself, maybe not intentionally, but she'd shared the truth. A tiny, tiny sliver, but definitely the truth. Then there was me.

May God not strike me dead. The truth...the truth? Everything about me was a lie. The only thing that I shared with Anna that was truthful was my attraction to her. I couldn't fake something like that. But would that be enough?

Anna

I slowly woke, warm and comfortable. I'd slept amazingly well, dreamless in fact. Something was different, something *felt* different. Opening my eyes, I looked down. Nick's arm was wrapped around my waist, my pajama shirt lifted enough so that his palm rested against my exposed skin. His hard length was fitted against my back. We were spooned together snugly. My pillow was Nick's shoulder.

This wasn't right! I shouldn't be molded to him, pressed against some almost-stranger like this. What did I know about Nick other than his kisses made my brain mush? His arms about me last night had knocked me out faster than any sleeping pill. And now—now! Being in his arms felt so right that it was *wrong*. I didn't do these kinds of things. I didn't *do* anything—this was completely over my head.

Grabbing his wrist, I tried to lift his hand away from my bare belly, but Nick just pulled me in closer and I felt him hard against my back.

"Shh," he soothed, his fingers making the skin tingle just a few inches below my breasts. "I've got you."

"That's the problem," I muttered. "You shouldn't be here like this."

Nick loosened his grip, but only a little. I was able to roll over to face him, both of us on our sides. He looked good in the morning. His eyes were sleepy and relaxed, his hair messy in a way only a guy could do; I had no doubt mine looked styled by a scarecrow. I didn't even want to drop my gaze below his neck because I knew how appealing the view would be. I'd felt every inch of it just a moment ago.

"Why not?" he asked, his brow creased with confusion.

Nick didn't have a problem looking his fill. His eyes took a lazy trip over my body.

"Because..." I couldn't think of a good reason to tell him. Why should I turn away from a hot man in my bed? I knew exactly why. Because I was terrible at sex. What if, once we started, Nick found me lacking? It would be crushing.

God, you're body's so tight. Such a fuckable little piece you are. Too bad you're frigid. Who wants to fuck a woman who just lies there? Doesn't respond? If you can't even get wet enough for me to stick my dick in, it's actually a good thing. Wouldn't want to get you pregnant with a brat anyway. You've got other places that will get me off. Open up—

I could justify Todd's cruel words with all of the other things I hated about him, pushed it all into a little vault I locked in the back corner of my mind. With Nick, though, I'd be devastated. I wasn't sexy. I wasn't alluring or any of those other words to describe ladies who knew what it took to get a guy revved up, and keep him that way. I felt tears prick the back of my eyes. I *never* cried. What was Nick doing to me? I had to—

"Hey, don't." He ran a knuckle down my cheek, startling me from my thoughts.

I looked up at him, his eyes dark, his face full of concern. I cleared my throat. "Don't what?"

"Think so much. This thing between us, I don't have to think to know it's real. I can just feel it."

He was right. Oh, how could he be right? This need I had for Nick just *was*. I didn't have to question it, wonder why it had been so instantaneous, so immediate. It just was. And that petrified me. I had no control over these emotions, or my body, and I needed control over everything. Like I needed to breathe. It was the only way I could function. With Nick, I couldn't keep up, couldn't process everything that was coming at me. Last weekend's insanity, his surprise appearance in New York, what he did for a living, and now, him in my bed. It was too much, too fast.

"No." I shook my head vehemently, as if that could keep the tears from falling. "I can't handle this. Let me up."

He must have seen the panic on my face because he let me go. My body felt cold where I'd been pressed against him, goose bumps rising on my skin even though the room was warm. Once standing, I looked down at him in my bed, completely relaxed as if he belonged there. The sheet rode low on his hips, his lean body...*stop!*

"I need to get dressed." I ran my fingers through my wayward hair, tucked it back behind my ears. Flustered, I went to my dresser, pulled out random clothes without really even looking at them. "You need to get out of my bed." When he just smiled at me, that wicked, enticing smile, I added, "Please."

I didn't wait to see if he did. I closed the bathroom door behind me with trembling fingers, knowing my resolve was at war with my control. Control was obviously winning, but I couldn't say for how long.

14

nna

Thirty minutes later I'd showered, straightened my hair, put on my usual eyeliner, mascara and lip gloss. After peeking to make sure he wasn't in the bedroom, I tiptoed to my closet wearing my robe and found an outfit that I could actually wear. In my mad dash to escape, I'd picked up two shirts, both a little dressier than I'd wear working from home, and that was it. No shorts, no skirt, no underwear. The man was making me insane. Once dressed and finally ready to face Nick, I went to the kitchen in search of coffee.

Nick looked up from my couch. He was—thankfully—fully dressed and had his phone in his hand. The way his heated male gaze raked over my body made me question the simple cotton skirt and blouse I wore. The skirt was gray, the blouse sleeveless with tiny buttons down the front. I had sandals to wear, but hadn't found them yet in my mess. Why did just his eyes on me heat my skin and make me question everything I thought I'd known about men?

Sure, they wanted one thing and Nick was no exception. But he seemed to want more, otherwise he would have taken me by now. He didn't have to stop with a kiss and just hold me all night. He kept me questioning, wondering what would come next, what kinds of ways he'd make me feel, how much more

I might ache. My nipples were hard constantly, the soft fabric of my bra a torture to the now sensitive tips.

And that was just my body. I needed caffeine to analyze why I wasn't running screaming from a guy who worked for the mob.

"Um...coffee. Want some?" I asked. Was I ever going to act normally around Nick or was I doomed to sound like a thirteen-year-old with her first crush? Make that a thirty-year-old and that was me. *Ugh.*

"Sure. Thanks."

I fiddled with the filters, dumping in the coffee grounds and water, then pushed the button, delaying the need to face Nick, to apologize. He hadn't done anything wrong. In fact, he'd done everything right. I bet I was the only woman who had ever fled from his bed. I was so stupid! So naïve and silly. He'd probably realized that and changed his mind about me. I couldn't blame him if he had. No guy wanted a woman with issues, especially ones like mine.

Other than standing in my kitchen like an idiot watching the dark brew slowly fill the pot, I had no other options but to face Nick. He didn't seem to be going anywhere. I went to the doorway, leaned against it and watched him. His fingers flew over his phone, then once done, he stood and put it in his pocket. "Sorry. Work," he said, causing me to remember what he really was, who he'd probably texted. Was he putting a hit out on someone? Ordering guns to be sent by UPS? Organizing a money laundering scheme?

"Right." I licked my lower lip, tilted my head back to look him in the eye. "Nick, I'm, um...I'm sorry about earlier."

He shrugged. "It's okay. I understand."

I shook my head. How could he understand? He didn't even know what I'd been through. Everything about me was a lie. I'd *told* him the truth when asked, but I didn't offer up who I really was. He hadn't said he knew my old name, but how could he have known about David otherwise? "You can't. Understand, that is. You can't understand what makes me act so...so silly. I mean, look at you!"

I pointed at him and he dropped his head to glance at himself, then back at me. Grinned. "Day-old clothes, no razor, and I could use a haircut." He ran his hands through his mussed hair. "I didn't realize I was such a catch."

It all made him even more appealing. He looked rumpled, as if he'd just come from someone's bed—which he had. The scruff on his jaw and mussed hair totally did it for me. And there was the dimple again.

"You're not. I mean...you are." I closed my eyes, took a deep breath, hoping it would slow my racing heart, my runaway brain. "It's not you, it's me."

Nick quirked a brow. "We're going with that line, are we?"

I was such an idiot. "See, this is what I'm talking about. I can't do this. I don't know *how* to do this." I pushed off the doorframe to move into the living room. "You're so great, except for the whole bad-guy thing, but when you touch me and I feel things, I just don't know how to respond."

"You don't have to know." He took a step closer, but I held my ground. "You just go with it. See where it takes you. Us."

Shaking my head, I continued. "I don't do 'just go with it'. Ever. The idea of that freaks me out."

His dark gaze flicked over me. "You have to be in control, you mean."

I turned back to the kitchen, went to the cabinet, pulled down two mugs, stalling. "Exactly," I finally said. "My apartment is a mess because I want it to be that way. I work for myself because I choose who I work for and when I work. I need that control."

"Okay, take a breath."

I'd started to pour coffee into a mug, but I shoved the pot back onto the coffeemaker and whirled on him. Spilled coffee sizzled on the warmer. "Stop telling me to breathe, dammit! I've been breathing just fine my whole life."

Nick ran a hand through his hair, perhaps employing his own stalling tactics. He didn't look fazed. Completely unruffled by my nervous breakdown —or at least that's what this little freak-out felt like. And wasn't that annoying? He pushed my buttons, riled me up and made me feel out of control. I wanted to scream in frustration.

"You're right. I'm sorry. You've been doing just fine on your own. But is that what you want?" He tilted his head. "To be *just fine*? It's okay to be out of control sometimes, especially with someone you trust to keep you safe. Take last night. Once you realized you were safe in my arms, you conked out. Think you can trust me?"

I looked at my granite countertop, slid my finger over a swirl in the hard surface. "I don't know," I said honestly. "I think...I think my body trusts you."

He groaned and I turned my head sideways to look at him. His eyes were so heated, so dark as to be almost black. His brow was furrowed as if he were in pain.

"Let's try something. Leave the coffee and come over here." Nick leaned back against the counter, crooked his finger at me, before putting his hands on the lip behind him.

I did as he asked, closing the few feet between us.

"Your body trusts me, so kiss me. Touch me. Do what you want. I'll keep my hands right here." I glanced at his big hands, the knuckles white as he gripped the granite. "You're in control."

I stared at him, testing the weight of his words. He might look relaxed, but I was beginning to recognize he was always this way. At ease. Calm. Except for the eyes. That was his tell. Nick was aroused. He wanted me. Wanted me to touch him, but was giving me the control. He knew I wasn't ready to let go of it, so he let me keep it. To run with it. With a tightness in my chest, I realized the little gift he was offering me. In that moment, I think I lost a little bit of my heart to him. I didn't think it was possible to do, or that I even had it to give away, but it happened.

Even with this ridiculous revelation, could I kiss him? Could I close the small space between us and take what I wanted? It was only about two feet, but it felt like a mile. He was right. I had to trust him, at least in this. The rest…it could wait.

I closed what was left of the space between us. He casually shifted one leg to the side so he stood with his feet shoulder width apart. I looked down at our bare feet. His were big, tan and surprisingly sexy. My fuchsia toenail polish stood out in contrast. Inching forward, I moved into the space between his legs, my belly brushing against his. Fortunately, leaning back as he was, he wasn't quite as tall and I didn't have to do more than lift up on the balls of my feet just a little bit and I was able to look directly into his eyes, to feel my breath mingle with his. He smelled of toothpaste and my soap.

Still, he held on to the counter, didn't lean his head in to kiss me, didn't move. He watched me with his dark gaze, searched my eyes, practically looked into my soul while he waited. Waited for me to trust him. As I closed the last inch between our mouths, my breasts pressed against his chest, hard planes aligned with my soft curves and I heard him groan softly. But it wasn't his abs I was thinking about. It was his mouth; soft, warm and still against mine. I was kissing him softly, but he wasn't kissing me back. Just letting me feel him, learn him with my lips alone. I feathered kisses over one corner of his mouth, then the other, slid over his rough stubble along his strong jaw. Just this simple contact made my nipples tighten, and lower, the ache grew.

He watched me as I kissed him, affected, yet passive. It was a strange, yet heady feeling, to be able to touch him like this. To do what I wanted with a man—yet still have control. Feeling bold, I moved back to his mouth and kissed him again, this time my tongue brushing out to taste his lips. A shudder ran through him, but he remained still. Strangely, it wasn't enough.

I pulled back, looked up at him. "Aren't you going to kiss me?" I asked, my voice breathless, as if kissing him were hard work.

He shook his head. "No." The one word came out deep. Rough like sandpaper.

"Why not?" I pouted. I felt like a kid with a toy, getting just what I wanted but realizing it wasn't enough.

"Because I won't stop. God, Anna, you drive me crazy." He lifted a hand, ran it over his jaw as if trying to wipe my kisses away. "Look, I have to go."

I looked down at the floor, my arousal fizzling out like a used match. I was a terrible kisser! I hadn't done it right or else he would have liked it. That's why he didn't respond. Tears clogged my throat.

A finger gently lifted my chin. "You being in control is pretty damn hot," Nick murmured.

I looked up at him from beneath my lashes, doubtful. "Seriously?" I whispered.

"Want to know what I want to do to you?" His voice had gone dark and rich, like the coffee brewing.

Did I? Yes, yes I did. I nodded.

He smiled and his dimple appeared. "I want to unwrap you slowly, like a present. I've been picturing what you look like beneath those prim clothes you wear. Don't panic," he said, probably witnessing the flare of hurt in my eyes as he spoke of my wardrobe. "I love your clothes. Know why?"

I cleared my throat. "No." My voice was a scratchy whisper.

"Once I undo those buttons on your shirt, unzip your skirt, I'll see things no one else has. At least for a long time. Right?"

His voice was almost hypnotic, soothing. I could only nod.

"Those clothes that cover you up so well means no other man can see. You'll only share with me." He leaned in close. "No one else."

I shivered as his warm breath fanned my ear.

"I wonder what color your nipples are. I wonder if they're as sensitive as I imagine. I bet I could make you come just by sucking on them. And lower, I want to spread your thighs and—"

It was my turn to put a finger to Nick's lips, silencing him. If I heard any more, I'd spontaneously combust. Nick's eyes lit up, little crinkles at the corner showing his amusement.

I felt warm all over. My body instinctually softened at his words, as if readying itself for him. My nipples tingled, as if his hands, his mouth really were working them. I swallowed, trying to return saliva to my dry mouth.

"Why say this and tell me you're leaving?"

"I think I've pushed you enough. For now. I want to do those things to you, but if I don't leave, my self-control is going to disappear and that's not what I want. You're not ready yet. You'll come to me when it's time. I'll even let you seduce me." He winked. "Until then, I'll show you how it will be between us, but you'll say when we finally come together." Nick ran his knuckles down my cheek.

My mouth fell open in surprise. "You're going to wait for me to be ready?" Was that ever going to happen? I panicked at the idea of being held, let alone have sex.

"I'll help you get there. For now, you need some space, time to yourself." He pushed off the counter, walked around me to the mug I'd put down, filled it. "My sister, she lives in Brooklyn and I dropped my bag at her place on the way from the airport." Stayed there for the first few days as I learned Anna's movements, but didn't need to tell her that. "I need to stop in there, get my stuff. Visit with her for a while. Can I come back later?"

"You have a sister?" I asked, surprised.

Nick chuckled. "You sound as if I were born in a cabbage patch." He handed me the mug full of steaming coffee, poured another. "I have three sisters, actually. Only one lives here."

I didn't really think about Nick having a family, being young and growing up with sisters. I wondered what it had been like for him; it must have been chaos. I felt a twinge of jealousy at the picture.

"I have some sketches I have to finish for a client. That should take most of the day." Half of the time I'd probably be daydreaming about Nick.

"Then I'll come back later, take you out to dinner. We'll talk about your friend that needs help." He took a sip of coffee, placed the mug back on the counter, grabbed his gun where he'd left it the night before and tucked it once again beneath his shirt. "And, Anna, tonight, when I come back?"

I nodded, remembering there was more to him than just a good kisser.

"I'm going to ask you to undo those top two buttons on your blouse so I can peek and see what color bra you're wearing. So make sure it's lacy and sexy as hell."

I felt hot at his directive. I hadn't considered my sleeveless top to be anything but modest. Nick had just blown that idea out of the water. Oh yeah, I was going to be daydreaming all day.

15

rif

Anna needed some space, some room to breathe. Acting as I had at the bar had scared her. She'd thought I was going to kill her. Hell, I couldn't blame her with the minimal amount of information she had on me. I'd given my word I wasn't there to hurt her, and my word wasn't much. She'd still believed me, or she wouldn't have let me into her bed. If she stopped to think about it now, the only thing she'd actually learned about me was that I had sisters.

I hadn't been subtle with her, blatantly telling her—and showing her—how much I wanted her. I didn't fuck her though. Some guys would have seduced her into pliancy, but I knew that wasn't going to work with her. I didn't want to just "work" with her. There was something between us, something intense and confusing and a whole lot crazy. I'd heard of guys on the force who'd come in on a Monday morning and share they'd met the love of their life. One guy even said he'd found the woman he was going to marry. They had no doubts. I doubted plenty for them, a lightning strike of love at just the sight of a woman had been unfathomable to me. I was just beginning to see where those guys—now happily married—were coming from.

It was as if, in the blink of an eye, Anna had become important to me. Her happiness came first. *She* came first. Wasn't that a kick in the pants?

Peters texted while I waited for a light to change, saying they'd worked through the military schools on the East Coast and the Deep South. Nothing yet.

Space was something I needed, too. My sister, Carrie, really did live in Brooklyn, and I really had dropped my bag at her house. I just had no intention of staying there. Fortunately, out of all my sisters, this one was a lawyer. I had a feeling I'd be needing her expert opinion very soon. I headed in the direction of the subway to meet her for lunch.

My short-term plan was to give Anna some room. Not a lot, just enough for her to decompress, get her control back around her again. She didn't *do* people. I wasn't a psychologist, but it wasn't hard to recognize an introvert when I saw one. She'd spend the day rebuilding her defenses as best she could. As I walked down the steps to the subway, I knew it would be harder and harder for her to rebuild them. Soon enough, I'd knock them down entirely.

"What do you mean you don't know her name?" my sister, Carrie, asked. "You spent last night with her, didn't you?" She was even more no-nonsense than I was. Tactful, straightforward and very deliberate. She had less tolerance for BS than even I did, which made her a fantastic lawyer.

We sat at a Midtown restaurant's outdoor seating, the street and pedestrian traffic made for a chaotic backdrop. The area was shaded by the towering buildings, but it was still muggy and warm. Denver's dry heat was not something I'd ever take for granted. The waitress put down our meals, Carrie a salad with seared salmon, a hamburger for me.

"Her real name. She took on a new persona when she was eighteen." I picked up the ketchup, lifted the top of the bun and poured some on my burger. "Some guys on the force are helping me look into why she did it and who she was before."

"If she committed a crime when she was a minor, most likely her record is sealed." She added sugar from a little white packet to her tea. "That gives you a very small window. A few months at most."

I took a bite of a dill pickle, pointed the tip at her. "A lot can happen in that time."

Carrie looked at me with her pale blue eyes. Somehow, she'd gotten lucky with the gorgeous Black Irish features of our father. Her dark hair was pulled back in a simple twist to complement the business suit she needed for a day in court. Only a year younger, she was my favorite sister. And she knew it. We didn't keep many secrets, but distance—living in two different parts of the country and both of us married to our jobs—made it hard to keep up.

"What do you think it might be?"

She knew I was undercover, but I filled her in about last weekend, Bobby Lane's body in the trunk, the wedding reception, Anna's appearance at Scorch, Moretti's idea that she worked for Carmichael. All of it. I left out the kissing and instant attraction part. There were some things we both agreed not to share. I didn't even want to think about Carrie's latest boyfriend.

I shrugged. "She admitted she'd done something bad. I was referring to killing Bobby Lane when I brought it up, but now that I talk about it, with you and with a buddy on the force, maybe she was referring to something else."

We both ate for a minute, considering the implications.

"Let's run a scenario," Carrie said after taking a sip of her iced tea. "She had nothing to do with that dead body. She's not tied in with Carmichael. She got involved, completely randomly, in last week's mess in Denver. She admitted to doing something *really* bad. Something bad enough that she had to change her identity."

The waitress topped off our drinks and left.

"People don't get a new identify easily. It would have to be big." Carrie put down her fork. "The only people I know who help someone with a new identity are...well, bad guys like you—"

I grinned at the implication and cut in. "The FBI for those people who are in Witness Protection."

"—and organizations that help women hide from abusive husbands."

My hand holding my burger stopped halfway to my mouth. "Oh, crap. She said she'd been married for six months. Had to have been her former self because Anna Scott has never been married."

My gut clenched. The burger didn't look as appealing as it had a minute ago. Had someone hurt Anna enough to send her underground, to create an entirely new identity? Her own husband? It happened, but to Anna? From what I'd seen of her, there wasn't a mark on her. No scars, not even a blemish. Some scars didn't show, however. She hadn't been held. That had definitely left a mark on her psyche. What else had that bastard done? *Shit.*

"She came to me asking for my help with a friend of hers, who, in Anna's own words, was in trouble with a very bad man." I bit into a fry.

Carrie glanced at me like an eagle-eyed lawyer, emotions on the side, critically considering every aspect of the situation. "The other option is that she really is working for Carmichael and killed Bobby Lane to get back at Moretti somehow. She duped everyone in Denver last week, slipped in and out even after a meet and greet at the police station. She's right now laughing over lunch of corned beef sandwiches with Uncle Frankie at how they'd both duped you. How does that scenario suit you?"

"Corned beef sandwiches?" I asked, chuckling. I picked up my burger once again. "Uncle Frankie?" I took a big bite.

Carrie rolled her eyes. "You're playing for the wrong team here, buddy. This is New York and Carmichael's turf, not Denver. What's Moretti's favorite meal?"

"Open-faced turkey sandwich and fries drowned in brown gravy." I cringed at the image.

She pointed at me with a forkful of salad, her eyebrows arched in a look that screamed, *See?*

"Right. Corned beef. Sandwich men," I grumbled, mouth full. I swallowed. "Do I want to know how *you* know what Uncle Frankie's favorite food is?" I looked at her in what I hoped was my bossy older brother face.

Carrie only grinned at me. Damn, the imp. "Probably not." She pointed her fork at herself. "I'm not working for him, if that's what you're thinking."

"Fine. Your second scenario is sounding less and less likely." I didn't like the direction my thoughts were turning. "If that's the case, Christ, she walked into Scorch on her own, knowing I was working for Moretti, to ask for help. Not for herself, but for a friend."

Pride flared for the woman who'd done that, taken that asshole out with a wrist lock. Worse things, deadly things, could have happened to her. She'd gone, into the proverbial lion's den, to see me. Because Moretti *owed* her. Jesus, she could have been killed. If I hadn't been there, if I'd gone home from the reception instead of to the bar, if she'd talked to one of the other guys, her body still wouldn't be found. I wanted to strangle her and kiss her at the same time. The woman was making me fucking insane!

"Let's go talk to her. Find out what's going on with her, with her friend," Carrie offered, making it sound so simple. Little did she know my relationship, or friendship, or acquaintance—whatever—with Anna, was far from that. How did I keep the sexiest woman I'd ever met safe when she was the person I was sent to kill? And if I didn't do it, then someone would come to kill both of us. This situation was a total shit storm.

Carrie glanced at her cell on the wood table. "I'll be done with court by three. I can meet you."

I took a second to calm down, knowing there was nothing to do about Anna's brave and stupid stunt—except maybe lock her in her apartment and never let her out, ever. But dragging my sister into this mess, more than just talking with her about it, might not be the best idea. I didn't hurt women, nor knowingly put them in danger.

"I don't want you mixed up in all of this," I told her. "I'm still undercover and Moretti's a wildcard."

Carrie shrugged my words off. "So? You need help. I'll be done by three," she repeated.

I sighed. What was it with stubborn women? But I was low on options, low on help. Carrie had connections here, with police, the justice system, and from the sound of it, Frank Carmichael. Her network was pretty vast and I had a feeling I was going to need some heavy hitters on my side. I'd just keep Carrie to the sidelines, out of danger, where it was safe. I doubted that would be possible—she owned a gun or two of her own—but it was worth a brotherly shot.

Then there was Anna. She seemed to be fairly thin on the friend front. Carrie could work that angle and wheedle something out of her I couldn't. If seducing it out of her wasn't an option—and it wasn't, I'd get her in bed for the right reasons—then a girlfriend for her might be the next best thing.

"Fine, but if things get the least bit dangerous, you're gone," I said.

The waitress dropped off our check and I grabbed it before Carrie could.

"Sure, whatever. Then how are we going to do this?" she asked, completely ignoring my worries.

"I was thinking good cop, bad cop." We had a bunch of scenarios we'd used as kids to get out of trouble, some that worked well enough to be used in our professional lives.

Carrie nodded. "Sounds good. Text me her address and give me a fifteen minute head start."

I threw some cash on the table.

As we left the restaurant, Carrie turned to me. "Oh, by the way, what's your name this week?"

16

nna

I SPENT THE DAY TRYING TO FOCUS ON MY WORK. *TRYING* WAS THE OPTIMAL WORD. The sketches for my client's new kitchen were due and I struggled all afternoon to finish. Not because there were problems, the renovation was going to be lovely, but because I couldn't focus. I found my mind wandering and wasted several hours staring aimlessly out the window. Nick, in just one night, had ruined me. I was tired and the only reason I could think of was that I had *too* good a night's sleep. I'd practically passed out in Nick's arms, not waking, not really even moving.

I was on my third cup of coffee and that wasn't helping. I just wanted to climb back in bed with Nick's arms around me. I was kidding myself it was just to sleep since that wouldn't be completely true.

I craved his touch, the warmth his body provided, the comfort and safety I felt when he was holding me. And more. Oh, yes. I wanted more. Kissing him had been like waking up. Silly, I know. Like a fairy tale and a princess waking from a long sleep. But it was true. His kisses woke up something in me that had been dormant for so long I barely remembered, or never knew.

I had no idea my body could react so violently to someone. My arousal was instant when he came in the room, at the sound of his voice. My nipples hardened by instinct, my core clenched, my body heating as if preparing for its basest needs, recognizing its mate. A frisson of apprehension ran down my spine. Nick called to me on some elemental level I couldn't understand. I was trying, but it was hard. This cellular-level craving I had for him went against my every honed instinct, the years of practiced survival.

If there were to be a study on nurture vs. nature, I'd be the perfect example. I'd been nurtured by institutions, been put in situations that required no friendly ties, no close relationships of any kind. When that happened, when someone became dear to me, I was whisked away, to another school, another life. Marriage, I thought, would be different. A man for myself, a bond of matrimony that tied me to someone else. Forge love between us solely because it was legal. But no. Wedded bliss did not exist, and I learned from the horrid experience that people still couldn't be trusted, that if you let someone in, they'd yank the world right out from under your feet. No nurturing for me.

I hadn't recognized any hint of nature in me either—that innate, instinctual guide that helped the caveman survive—until I'd run into Nick at the wedding reception. That attraction, arousal, lust even, had bubbled up like a hot spring from the ground. It just happened.

The question that kept popping up: Why did Nick want me? *Me*, the clueless one when it came to sex. I wasn't the least bit provocative or alluring. My clothes, while stylish, were unrevealing. I hid behind layers of fabric. It was my shield against the world.

Nick had seen through that, like Superman and x-ray vision, and desired me. He'd been the first man to kiss me, to touch me besides a platonic hug or handshake for over ten years. He knew, *knew,* something was wrong with me. What thirty-year-old woman would be petrified of him? Wary of his touch, afraid to lie in bed with him? He was unbelievably attractive if I used my friend Stephanie as a judge. He wanted sex. I might be naïve, but I wasn't an idiot. I could speak three languages and it was the same in all of them. He was a man and a man wanted sex. That was nature talking. Pure and simple.

Could I let my guard down to give it to him? Could I be everything he wanted? I considered this as I got a call from downstairs. *Nick.* My heartbeat sped up, excitement shot through me. I was doomed. Doomed for hurt with him since he'd either learn I wasn't worth the effort, or he'd get what he wanted—whatever that really was—from me and toss me aside. Or maybe he'd learn the sheer extent of my secrets and realize getting even with Todd wasn't worth the risk. I didn't want to push him away by telling him the truth. I wanted to see what happened with Nick, to give it a try, as he'd said.

"Yes?" I asked the doorman into the intercom on the wall.

"A woman named Carrie is here to see you. She says she's Nick Malone's sister."

Confused for a moment, then quickly surprised. His sister was here? Alone? Where was Nick? "Send her up. Thanks."

I stared at the door. I felt sick. Nick really did have a sister. She wasn't just someone Nick mentioned in passing. She was a real, live, breathing person. She made Nick real. Not just some sexy guy of my fantasies who'd spent the night in my bed. Not the man who made me reconsider getting close with someone. I knew nothing about Nick other than that he carried a gun and worked for Moretti. He could be a number cruncher or just a bartender for all I knew of him.

Using him for sex was one thing, revenge was another. Saving Elizabeth meant I could exact my revenge on Todd and that wasn't going to be easy, or safe. It most likely wouldn't be legal and would be potentially deadly. Could I ask that of Nick? To have him risk his life, his very soul—because that's what he'd give up if he had to kill someone—to help me?

At first, it had been simple. Get his help, then walk away. That was before he'd wheedled himself into my life, getting me to trust him with my body. Could I trust him with all of my secrets, too? Would he want to take on that burden? Would he still want me after he learned the truth? Was I even worth it?

I jumped at the knock at the door. Two people in two days in my apartment was a record. Glancing around, there were still clothes strewn about and I'd never found those sandals I wanted to wear.

The woman I let in looked exactly like Nick. Dark hair, olive skin, strong features. Her eyes were lighter though. She was strikingly pretty, tall and willowy. She wore a conservative suit, slim black skirt with a trim jacket, a little ruffle at the collar of her white shirt peeked through and ruthless high heels.

"I'm sorry for barging in like this, a complete stranger." She smiled and she looked...nice.

"Is Nick okay?" I asked, realizing maybe he'd been hurt or killed or shot in the head and left in the trunk of a car. I held on to the door in a fierce grip, afraid I might fall over if I let go. Why else would she be here? Oh, God.

Carrie's smile slipped and held up a hand. "Whoa. Nick's fine. Really."

I took a deep breath and my stomach moved back down out of my throat. "Sorry, I just couldn't think of why else you'd be here." My heartbeat was frantic, but I was starting to calm down. My visceral response to Nick being hurt took me by surprise. I feared for his safety, worried about him. The idea of him being hurt made me completely irrational. Maybe having him help Elizabeth—and bringing down Todd—wasn't such a good idea after all.

"I saw Nick for lunch and we thought we'd surprise you by taking you out to dinner. We were going to meet here, but I guess he's a little late." Carrie gave my arm a quick squeeze. "Which is perfect because we'll have time for a little girl talk. Mind if I sit down?"

She was like a whirling dervish. I couldn't keep up. "Sure, sorry." I led her to the sofa.

"I guess your reaction answers my first question."

"Oh?" I asked, not sure what she meant.

"How you feel about Nick." Carrie picked up a little glass paperweight on my coffee table, fiddled with it. Did she know what her brother did for a living? Was it a secret I just fell into last weekend like everything else? I didn't want to ask and find out. Somehow tossing out there—*So, Carrie, did you know your brother is a member of a large crime syndicate and is most likely considered armed and dangerous by law enforcement?*—wasn't going to work.

I dropped to the couch next to her. "Feel about Nick?" I repeated. Was I that obvious?

"You care a lot about him." She watched me closely, gauging my response.

I did care about him, and that was scary. God, everything was scary! I was such a wimp to hide from *everything* just because it was scary. Sure, I'd had good reason to do so, but now, Nick was becoming something more important than staying safe, and the irony was, he might be the one putting me in danger—and my heart didn't seem to care!

I had to let go a little bit of control to be with him and that was risky. But I was handing that control to Nick, not just tossing it into the wind. He'd said he'd keep it safe. Keep me safe. Could I do the same for him?

"Yes, I care about him." It was time to change the subject. "You look so much like your brother."

Carrie patted her hair. "Yeah, well, that's genetics for you. Do you have any brothers or sisters?"

I watched her put the paperweight back. "No. Only child."

"That must have been so nice. No bathrooms to share. Having two sisters was a pain. I can only imagine what Nick had to go through growing up sharing the bathroom with the three of us. Talk about estrogen overload."

The only comparison I had was sharing a dorm bathroom with seven other girls. It probably wasn't remotely the same thing. "Oh, sorry, bad hostess. Would you like a drink?" I'd gotten pretty darn good at diverting questions I didn't wish to answer. "Water, iced tea, soda?"

"Soda sounds great. Thanks." Carrie stood and followed me into the kitchen. I busied myself with a glass, added ice, got a can from the fridge. I placed both on the counter next to her.

"Did you like your trip to Denver? Wedding, right?"

"A friend's sister got married."

"Sounds like fun. Was it a fancy affair? Garden party? Cocktails? Formal? I love a man in a tux," Carrie said, dreamily.

I couldn't keep up with how fast she talked. "Um...black tie."

"I think we're at the age where we have several weddings a year. Lots of friends getting hitched. It's great to see everyone fall in love, and it's a good excuse to get a new dress. I've already been to three. How about you?"

She was really overwhelming. I could see how Nick had gotten the laid-back thing down pat. Having to live with Carrie growing up forced him to do so at a young age. It was like having a verbal steamroller in my kitchen. To keep busy, I got my own can from the fridge.

"This year? Just one."

"Huh." She poured her drink into the glass, let the bubbles rise, then filled the glass again after they receded. "Listen, I have to admit something."

I raised an eyebrow in question.

"I'm a little curious about the woman who's got my brother flying halfway across the country after meeting her only last week."

I ran my damp hands over my skirt. "There's not much to tell. I'm really boring, actually."

From the look on her face, I could tell she didn't believe me. "Come on, seriously? You met a guy over the weekend and he's here, with you, two time zones away. That is *not* boring. I wish I had a guy do that for me."

She took a drink from her glass. No ring on her finger. A definite romantic.

I smiled at her. "I guess I am pretty cool, aren't I?"

Carrie grinned. "Totally."

I took a bag of chips down from the cabinet, opened it and placed it on the counter between us.

"My new best friend. God, I love salt." Carrie crunched on a chip while I watched her, confident in herself, even her flaws. She just seemed so...normal. I wanted to be her when I grew up.

"Fine, what do you want to know? Although, I've heard, a girl's got to have some secrets," I warned.

Carrie pointed a chip at me. "That's with men, not best friends. Since you pulled out the chips at three on a Friday, you're stuck with me. You can keep secrets from Nick, but not from girlfriends."

I eyed her suspiciously, not sure if she was kidding or not. "Okay. Shoot."

Carrie chewed and swallowed, licked her finger. Made me realize we needed napkins.

"Twenty questions!" she declared.

I looked at her as I opened a cabinet. "Don't we have to be drunk or at a sleepover for that?"

"No," she said grumpily. "Bra size."

I paused from pulling out napkins, looked down at my chest. "Seriously? That's what you want to know?"

"I'm starting off easy," she countered, grinning. "Bra size."

17

nna

I shook my head, questioning her questions, but answered, "34C."

Her eyes darted to my chest. "Now I'm totally jealous of you. I wish I was a C," she grumbled. "I need another chip to get over it." After eating another, she continued. "Name of pet growing up."

"Didn't have one. Next." I wasn't a big pet fan.

"Um... Name of prom date."

"Didn't have one. Next."

"Didn't have...? Okay. Next. Um...favorite color."

I relaxed at the lighter direction of the questions. "Orange."

Carrie gave me a surprised look. "Really? I figured you for a pink girl."

I tilted my chin down to get a good look at her. Seriously? A *pink* girl?

"What number am I up to?"

"Five, and that was a question, so six."

"Smart ass." She grinned.

This was fun. I really liked Carrie, except when she thought I was a pink girl. She was easygoing, lighthearted and had the hottest brother on the planet.

"Are you from New York?"

"No."

"You're going to make me use another question for this?"

"Yes, and that was a question, so eight."

Carrie rolled her eyes. "Fine. Where are you from?"

I didn't respond right away. I wasn't exactly sure how to, so I stalled as I took a sip of soda. "I grew up all over actually. Moved a lot."

"Army brat?"

I gave a dry laugh. As if my father would serve anyone but himself. "No."

The intercom rang.

"That must be Nick," Carrie said, snagged another chip.

Nick's timing was perfect; Carrie couldn't grill me anymore. I could only imagine what questions she'd come up with by the time she got to twenty. I talked with the front desk and Nick came in the door a minute later. He found us in the kitchen, the bag of chips between us. He'd changed his clothes; he wore khaki cargo shorts and a white button-up, sleeves rolled up and left untucked. On his feet, he wore the same pair of beat-up sneakers.

Seeing the bag of chips, he reached in and grabbed one as he ruffled his sister's hair in a way only brothers could do. Turning to me, he leaned down and gave me a quick, salty kiss.

"I see you two have met and are bonding over snacks."

"She's my new best friend," I said, my voice full of confidence. Although, once the words left my mouth I wondered if I'd overstepped my bounds. The look on Carrie's face—a big grin—said I wasn't mistaken.

Nick looked at me, smiled. It felt good to be part of something, part of a family, even momentarily. Nick and Carrie seemed to have an easy sibling bond and having them include me, even for right now, felt...special. Simple, yet special. "So, what did I miss?"

Carrie eyed me, but said to Nick, "Girl stuff, only girl stuff. Do you really want to know?"

Nick held up his hands. "Absolutely not."

I couldn't help but laugh.

Smiling at me, Nick took my hand, kissed the knuckles. "We were going to take you to dinner. You told her our plans, right?" He looked to his sister, who nodded. "Great. It's pretty early, so what do you say we kick back with these chips and you tell me what kind of help you need. You've been pretty patient with me, so if you give me a soda of my own, you can tell me about it."

I took a deep breath, pasted on my bland face that hid my emotions. How did I get him to help without getting him in so deep he might get hurt? I'd asked him for his help, and now that he was giving it, I questioned myself. The revenge I sought wasn't going to be pretty. All this was going to lead to exposure and I had to figure out how many secrets I wanted to dole out.

"Sure. Have a seat and I'll bring it out."

Nick snagged the bag of chips and winked at me as he escaped the kitchen.

"Hey!" his sister yelled, following him. "Those aren't your chips, those are girl chips."

"There's no such thing as girl chips," Nick complained. I couldn't see either of them from where I stood at the fridge, but I could easily hear their bickering.

I brought Nick a glass with ice and his own can, my glass tucked between my arm and my side, and placed them on the coffee table. The siblings sat on the couch, so I took my comfortable armchair perpendicular to them.

"This is a great apartment," Carrie said, looking around. "I'm jealous of your location."

"Thanks. I've been here for twelve years." I took in my cluttered chaos. "And no, I'm not as much of a slob as it looks."

"You should see my place. This is nothing," Carrie replied.

Nick nodded his head in agreement, but when he saw his sister looking his way, he stopped and smiled innocently.

"You don't have to stay with me, you know," she added, sounding put out, but it was obviously fake.

"Good, because I'm staying here," Nick said as he stared at me, his left arm going up along the back of the couch, as if he was settling in.

I caught my breath at his heated glance, stared back. He was staying here? I liked—no, loved—how it felt to be in his arms but his staying with me officially changed the entire dynamic.

Carrie looked between us, grinned. "Did you two want me to leave?"

Nick flicked his gaze to his sister. "Yes, that would be great, but I know it's not going to happen."

Carrie shook her head.

"If you're staying, then stop being annoying. Did you have enough time to get your work done?"

The last, he asked me. Enough time, yes. Did I get anything accomplished? *No.* No way was I telling Nick I daydreamed about him, so I just nodded.

"Great, then do you want to tell me what's going on with your friend?"

"Now?" He'd just walked in the door. I was happy he asked, but surprised.

He shrugged. "Sure."

I took a sip of my drink to wet my suddenly parched mouth. I'd wanted help, needed Nick to save Elizabeth from Todd, but now that he was ready to do so, I was at a loss. "Um, okay. Sorry, I don't know where to start." I flicked my gaze to Carrie. It was one thing to talk with Nick, another to bring his sister into it, too.

"How about her name?" Nick prodded.

I ran my fingers over the glass nervously, realized what I was doing, then clenched them tightly in my lap. I'd only talk about Elizabeth. Nothing else. Only general specifics when it came to her. Nothing more. When Nick and I were alone, maybe I'd share something more.

"Elizabeth. Her name is Elizabeth and she's engaged to marry a very bad man. I need your help getting her away from him."

"Why don't you tell her the guy's bad for her? She'd believe a friend," Carrie said. She pulled the bag of chips closer to her on the table, took one.

"I'm not really her friend. She's actually never met me."

Nick crossed a leg over a knee. "You know her fiancé, then."

"Yes."

Nick was a quick thinker. "He hurt you?" His voice had dropped to a deeper timbre.

I flicked my gaze between Nick and Carrie. They looked back at me with identical expressions, the only difference was the eye color.

"Yes." The word dropped like a bomb, so I hurried on. "She can't marry him. He'll hurt her, in ways she probably never imagined."

Nick looked grim; a muscle ticked in his jaw. He looked to Carrie.

"Why don't you just tell her what happened to you? Don't you think she might believe you?" Carrie asked, her voice soft, concerned.

I shook my head. "Like I said, we've never met and I doubt she even knows who I am. Would you listen to a strange woman telling you bad things about your fiancé?" I questioned Carrie.

She thought for a moment. "If I really loved him, it would be hard to believe a stranger. I'd wonder her motive."

Nick listened intently, but every line of his body was tense, every look he gave me dark and very brooding. "Police then. Tell them what he's done."

I shook my head. "I can't. They wouldn't believe me."

"Why?" he asked, as if *he* didn't believe I'd said that was possible, or that I could mean it.

"Because—" I stopped there. I looked between Nick and Carrie. My heartbeat quickened, I could feel the throbbing at the base of my neck. Nerves plucked at the very thought of revealing things I'd held as secret for so long. "You've pushed your way into my life, into my apartment and it's a little overwhelming. But you're here, listening, and I can't do it." I'd been insane to think Nick would help me without having to reveal anything. "I'm sorry, Carrie, but I just met you and I can barely trust Nick." I tucked my hair behind my ear.

They glanced at each other, then back at me.

"Is it because you work for Frank Carmichael?" Nick asked, his voice sharp, harsh.

I turned to stare at Nick. Confused. What did this have to do with Elizabeth? "Who's Frank Carmichael?" I glanced at Carrie, then back.

"I've got to ask." Nick ran a hand over his face, heard the rasp of his stubble. "Did you kill Bobby Lane?"

If he'd hit me in the head with a bat I would have been less surprised. He thought...*holy shit*. He—I stood up, paced the space. After this, he still thought...? Really? We were back to this again? I was royally pissed off. "You think I killed Bobby Lane? That's why you're here?"

I waved my arm in the air, indicating my apartment. God, he wasn't here to help me. Sure, he wanted sex, but that was just a typical guy. Sleep with me, then what? He was such an asshat he was willing to sleep with me thinking I killed Bobby Lane. I'd wasted my time worrying over sharing the truth about myself with him. I'd wasted my time, period.

"No," Carrie said, shaking her head. "Nick does *not* think you killed Bobby Lane." She looked at him as if she could shoot lasers out of her eyes.

"I don't think you killed Bobby Lane," Nick repeated.

"Then why did you ask?" I shouted, completely fed up. "Look, never mind. I think it's time you both left. God, I'm such an idiot! You're not here to help me. I know who *you* work for. That's why I went to Scorch that night. I need your expertise in...whatever the hell you bad guys do. Your connections."

Carrie looked at her brother in a way I couldn't decipher.

"I even let you spend the night knowing what you do. At the same time, you thought...wow." I shook my head in disbelief. "You...you think I'm a murderer."

"No. I don't," Nick replied.

"You do. You just don't think I killed Bobby Lane. There's a difference. What are you going to do, take me to the police? Kill *me*? Fine, but at least do it knowing the truth instead of wondering. You know what? You're right. I did kill someone. Just not Bobby Lane. Now get out."

My blood was pumping. I was so mad I couldn't think straight. I'd said it. Out loud, and someone had heard. It felt good, like leaching poison from a festering wound, but it didn't matter. Nick didn't care about helping me. About the truth. About anything. He especially didn't care about me.

Carrie and Nick just sat there, stared. Nick had shifted positions so he leaned forward, his elbows on his knees as if he hadn't heard me clearly and had to get closer. He looked ready to pounce, his look almost feral.

"Give me a dollar," Carrie said, holding her hand out. She was the calm one of the two.

"What?" I asked, staring at her. My mouth had fallen open, but I didn't care. "Are you insane?" I put my hands on my hips. "Get out of here. Both of you. I was stupid to involve you." I pointed at the door.

"Just give me a damn dollar. Do it."

Rolling my eyes, I stomped over to my bag, pulled out a bill from my wallet, not even seeing what kind it was, walked over to Carrie and slapped it into her palm.

"Good. Now, I'm your lawyer. Everything you say is privileged."

I glanced at Nick, because I couldn't figure him out.

"Don't worry," Carrie said. "If he does anything with what you share, I'll shoot him."

I laughed dryly, shook my head. "No wonder the twenty questions earlier. Professional hazard of a lawyer." I was a dupe. A patsy. An *idiot*. She just waltzed right in to my apartment and I shared potato chips with the woman. All under the guise of getting me to talk. I'd been so careful for so long and now, a stupid bag of chips and I turned into an open book.

"Seriously, Anna. You wanted help. You wanted Nick, now you've got me, too."

"Do you think I killed Bobby Lane? Do you even know who he was?" I asked Carrie. If she was my lawyer, I had to know if she was on my side.

She gave a little shrug. "I know what Nick told me about him, and no, it doesn't matter whether I think you did it or not."

"It matters to me," I responded.

Carrie looked at me with her light blue eyes for a moment, then nodded. "No. I don't think you killed him."

Could I trust them both? These siblings who looked at me in the same way. Guarded, questioning, concerned. I'd been kidding myself, thinking I could tell someone about Elizabeth, get her away from Todd without anyone discovering who I was, what I'd done. These two were going to yank every last secret out of me. Everything intertwined, which meant my entire life had to unravel.

Trust. Nick wanted me to trust him, but right now, I didn't even *like* him. I closed my eyes. I'd told him my body already trusted him. That had been easy. Elemental. If I shared my secrets, I'd have to trust him with my very soul. Because that would be what I'd expose.

A thought came to me, so blatantly obvious and yet scary. It blew the issue of trust away like a hurricane, ripping it from me with a painful quickness. "Why did you come to New York?" I asked Nick, putting my hand over my eyes for a moment. "God, I'm blind and stupid. I can speak three languages, went to Harvard, for Christ's sake, and it took me this long to figure it out. You didn't come here to help me."

I saw Nick's mouth thin into a line.

"You still think I work for Moretti. No, that's not right because we'd be working for the same guy. As Moretti's lackey, you'd have heard of me."

Nick winced.

"You think I work for this guy, Carmichael. As a hit man. Right?"

Carrie looked to her brother, surprise etched on her face. "Are you fucking kidding me?" she asked him.

I shook my head. "After you pretty much told me to fuck off that night in your office, you *still* came here, *still* think I'm a murderer. Then you got in my bed." I looked into Nick's dark eyes, held his stare. He'd used my attraction against me and that hurt in a way I'd never experienced before. "Tell me Nick, the truth for once. Why are you really here?"

He looked at me with his brooding intensity and said, "Moretti sent me here to kill you."

18

rif

ANNA LOOKED AT ME WITH SUCH LOATHING, SUCH HATRED, I WINCED. SHIT. SHIT, *shit*. I'd blown it. I didn't think she'd killed Bobby Lane, didn't think she worked for Carmichael, but I had to hear it from her. It was the detective in me. I couldn't take it on faith alone. She hadn't seen it that way, hell, she didn't even know I was a cop. But it was true, all of it.

The worst was, she thought what we'd done together—kissing, holding each other as we slept—was done as part of an agenda. I'd told her last night that the chemistry between us was the only truth we shared. I hadn't been wrong. It had been me, Jake Griffin, in bed with her. I just couldn't tell her. Everything I felt for her was true, pure.

I ran both hands through my hair. It didn't matter anymore. She'd never trust me again. This whole situation was fucked up.

I glanced over at my sister. She hauled back her hand and wailed me in the arm. "You little shit." Carrie turned to Anna. "He's not going to kill you. Why would he bring his sister to meet you if he was going to kill you?"

Anna's eyes looked just as they had back at the police station in Denver. Shuttered, flat, empty.

"Finish your sentence, *Nick*," Carrie continued, accenting my fake name.

"What the hell are you talking about?" I had two pissed-off women in front of me. I'd grown up with three older sisters, so I could handle emotional women. But this? I had no idea how to handle damage control of this magnitude. I just stared at Carrie and rubbed my arm. She had a strong right. In a different situation, I'd be really proud of it.

She rolled her eyes, tossed up her hands. "Fine, I'll start it, you finish. Anna, Moretti sent me here to kill you, but...?"

Ah, okay. Carrie was helping. Thank God, because two homicidally justified women could make a man disappear forever. "—but I never was going to do it," I finished, glancing at Anna. She was still shutdown, but her eyes darted to look at me.

Carrie nodded as if to prod me along even further.

I took a deep breath. "Moretti sent me here to kill you," I repeated. "He sees you as a loose end since you drove the car that had Lane's body in it. I told you in Denver, I don't hurt women. I told you I'd keep you safe." I ran my hands through my hair. "I'm here because if I didn't come, he'd send someone else. Moretti thinks I'm here to kill you, but I'm really here to save you."

Carrie smiled. "Now that's a lot better. You're a complete idiot for the way you handled this whole thing, but a lot better."

"What happens when you don't kill me?" Anna asked, her voice soft.

"That's the problem. I figure I have a week to come up with a plan before Moretti sends someone else. To kill you, and probably me, for not following through on his order. I do want to help your friend. The reason I didn't bring her up sooner is because my first priority is you. I just have to figure out how to get us out of this mess. I can help your friend while I come up with a plan."

Anna relaxed, her eyes became watery. Oh shit, she wasn't going to cry, was she? She had me by the balls already. I didn't know if I could handle her tears, too.

"Really?" She moved close and loomed over me. "Wait. Moretti is going to kill you, too? You can't be here! You have to leave, get away from me. I'm nothing but trouble for you."

"Say that again," I replied, my voice rough, very dark. She wanted me to leave to save myself? I slowly stood up so we were about a foot apart, but I towered over her. I tried to keep calm and remember I didn't hurt women.

"I can't let anyone get hurt because of me. I'm not worth the chance that Moretti's going to shoot you and dump your body in the trunk of a car."

"What about you?" God, she was a beautiful, *stupid* woman!

"I'll get a new identity. I did it once, I can do it again. I can just disappear. I have a go bag I can grab and be gone."

I knew what a go bag was. Military, Special Forces and anyone undercover had them. A packed bag with everything needed to go on the run. Cash, clothes, forged documents.

I moved just a few inches closer. "You're going to go into hiding, change your name...again, just to protect me?"

She nodded. I heard Carrie sigh.

"My brother's an idiot, but he's not an asshole," Carrie shared.

"Thanks, sis," I said, but didn't take my gaze off of Anna's as I took her hand and tugged her back down into her chair. Her fathomless brown eyes held mine, and I could see so much. She was so brave, protecting others while sacrificing herself. "The last thing I'm going to do is walk away. We do this together. *We're* together. Those kisses, Anna? What we did last night in bed?"

"Your sister is sitting right here!" Carrie practically yelled, pointing at herself. "I don't want to know about your sex life. I'll be scarred for life."

I sighed and shot her a look. Carrie was not helping anymore. At all. She was supposed to have gotten some girl time with Anna before I arrived, to learn something about her, but from what Carrie had said, it really had been just that, girl talk. Now, I wanted her to go away. "We didn't have sex. Jesus." I picked up my glass. "Here, go get me another drink. Pretend you can't find the soda in the fridge for about two minutes."

With a little huff, she took my glass and went into the kitchen. I could hear her opening and closing cabinets with a little extra aggression than necessary.

I shifted so I faced Anna in her chair straight on. Our knees bumped, her eyes darted up to mine. She felt the little zing then, too. We were close enough I could smell her shampoo. Floral and feminine. "This chemistry we have is the most honest thing between us. When I kiss you, it's me. The real me. I'm not faking. I'm not fucking walking away just so you can save me from Moretti. That's bullshit. Not going to happen, so I don't want to hear anything more about it. I want you so bad, I ache, too. That's why we didn't do anything last night, no matter how much I wanted—want—to. I don't want just to fuck. Sorry, but that's the only word for it. There's more to it, to us, than that."

A smile broke the corner of Anna's mouth. Her color was better; she wasn't quite so angry. I reached out, took her small hand. She was so tiny, so fragile in comparison to me, to the big, bad world. Her fingers closed around mine and I knew, with that quick squeeze, that she'd forgiven me. I exhaled a deep breath. My eyes dropped to her mouth. "I'm going to kiss you," I whispered, giving her warning like I had the night before.

Anna's eyes flicked toward her kitchen, then back to me. I may have given her warning, but I wasn't asking her permission. I leaned forward, ran my hand through her hair, cupped her nape in my palm and brushed my lips over hers. Gently, softly.

Kissing Anna was like coming home. It felt right, as if it was the most perfect thing to do.

"Can I come back in now?" Carrie called from the kitchen.

I felt Anna's smile on my mouth before she pulled back. "Yes."

I wasn't quite ready, but there was no putting off my sister. Once I got rid of her, however—

Carrie came back with a can of soda. "Here." She shoved it at me, grumpily.

"Your brother has redeemed himself," Anna said.

"That's good to hear. Better than hearing about you two having sex." She cringed. "But we have bigger problems to deal with than how to burn that image from my brain. How are we going to keep the two of you alive?"

I'd given it a lot of thought, but hadn't had too many good ideas. I hadn't known exactly what I'd been up against. I still didn't. We were short on information only Anna could share.

"I had to ask if you killed Bobby Lane because you made me doubt. Last night, you admitted you'd done something bad. Jesus, woman! I assumed it was killing Bobby because I couldn't imagine what else it could be." I cracked the top on my new soda, took a big swig, wishing it was a beer. "I need to know what the real story is. If that asshole who hurt you is still out there, is involved with whatever you did, I'll help you. I'll protect you, Anna." *I'll kill him.* I wouldn't let the bastard within ten feet of her. Hell, no man was going to touch her from now on but me.

Ten days ago, my life had been simple. It had totally sucked, but it had been simple. Now, I had a woman—yes, she was mine. She wasn't simple. Far from it. She had more issues than anyone I'd ever met, and she'd accomplished that while rarely leaving her apartment. What she'd already shared with me was like a tip of an iceberg. There was more, so much more than what she'd said, but it was beneath the surface. Hidden, yet so overwhelmingly big. And deadly.

"What I did has nothing to do with what happened in Denver. It's not relevant," Anna replied, picking up her glass, taking a sip.

"We'll deal with Moretti in minute. Tell me what you did."

Whatever she had to say wasn't going to be good. Of that, I had no doubt, since the little bit we'd heard included the phrase *I killed someone*. Solving the problem wasn't going to be easy. Or safe. Or *simple*. That didn't even include dealing with Moretti. Carrie had been smart making Anna a client. God bless her career choice. Lawyer or not, I didn't need her involved in this. It was going to be dangerous, I felt it in my gut, and I wanted Carrie nowhere near the fallout.

My top priority was to protect Anna. My instincts to do so, regardless of that unseen portion of the iceberg, was overwhelming. Some guy had hurt her. I was going to find him and kill him. Like a fucking caveman, I'd rip him limb from limb.

She ran her finger over the condensation on her glass. She'd heard me. I couldn't tell if she was ignoring me or thinking. I'd hoped for the latter. My impatience had me repeating myself, although this time not as gently.

"God dammit, Anna." I ran my hands through my hair. It was that or reach over and strangle her. "You think I'm going find out you killed someone and just let it go? Tell me what happened."

She looked up at me, glanced at my sister, then shared. "Fine. For the record, I didn't kill Bobby Lane." Anna pulled her shoulders back, clasped my hand in her lap, stared me dead in the eye. I, of course, noticed how her breasts thrust out with her actions. It wasn't the best time to notice this, but hell, I was a man and I wasn't dead. "I don't work for that guy, Carmichael, whoever he is. Nor Moretti. I really did get the wrong rental car."

"Go on," I urged, thinking about the statistics behind her getting *that* specific car from an idiot valet. What were the chances? A billion to one?

She looked down at her lap for a moment. "I did kill someone a long time ago, but it was self-defense. His name was David."

"Since he's dead, I can safely say he's not the man your friend is marrying, right?

"No. This was his brother," Anna replied. "I know it's confusing."

"Wait," Carrie cut it. We both turned to look at her. "Something you said earlier doesn't make sense and I should have picked up on it before now." She pointed to Anna. "How can this woman be your *friend* if you've never met? If she doesn't even know who you are?"

I hadn't thought of that. I turned to Anna.

She put her fingers over her lips for a moment, as if afraid the words would fall out. "I've kept all this to myself since I was eighteen. This isn't easy to do." She took a swig of her soda, placed the glass back on the table. She ran her hand through her hair and I noticed it shake. She gave the impression of cool and collected, just like at the police station, but now that I knew her better, I recognized when she was struggling. "She's not a friend, she's...God, um...okay. She's my half-sister. I've never met her before because I was twelve when she was born and I was living in Switzerland at the time. The guy she's marrying is my ex-husband. The man I killed...was my brother-in-law."

I just sat there and stared at Anna, processing her words. Carrie was, too. For once, my sister was surprisingly quiet. "You killed your brother-in-law," I said, breaking it down.

"Yes," she admitted.

"Your ex-husband is engaged to your half-sister."

"Yes."

"Your half-sister doesn't know you exist because you were in Switzerland when she was born."

"Yes."

"Anna Scott isn't your real name, is it?"

Her eyes widened at my question and she pinched her lips together into a thin line. Shit. I'd pushed her too far. She wasn't going to answer.

Surprisingly, she shook her head.

"I figured as much. You told me you'd hurt someone, but you have no record. You said last night you went to military school. Anna Scott didn't go to military school."

"Oh? How do you know that?" she asked, arching a brow.

Crap. I was in trouble here. It was my turn to stall for time with my drink, taking a big, long swig.

"I did some research for him," Carrie piped up as I was putting the can down.

Thankfully, she covered for me, because I hadn't thought of an answer. If I told Anna about Peters—a police officer—digging into her past, I'd either have to tell her I was a cop, or she'd think I had Moretti doing it for me. Either way, I couldn't tell her.

"You have to admit, the evidence against you was pretty damning," Carrie added. "Dead body in the trunk of your car, showing up at that night club of Nick's, military school, gun knowledge." She ticked each one off on her fingers.

"Yeah, Nick filled me in on everything," she added when Anna looked at her questioningly.

"What's your real name, Anna?" I asked.

With this question, she paused, looked at me. *Really* looked at me. This was the Big One. She was giving up her well-controlled life once she answered. I'd know her real name, could look into her past. It would *all* be out there. She swallowed, cleared her throat. "My real name is Olivia Edwards."

Olivia Edwards. I gave her a small smile. I couldn't imagine how hard that must have been because everything about her was one big secret. I thought I was undercover. Up until this moment, she'd been undercover, more like underground, for some reason since she was eighteen. And doing it alone with no obvious backup of any kind. I had Peters and the entire police department to back me up if things got sticky. She could probably give me a few pointers.

"Good girl," I murmured as I took her hand in mine, gave it a quick squeeze.

"What else did you find out about me?" Anna asked Carrie, who shifted on the couch, a subtle squirm knowing she could easily be caught in her own lie.

I had my head down, so I briefly glanced at my sister out of the corner of my eye. She didn't actually *have* the answers. She knew just as much as I did, which was only what Anna had told us. This was the opportunity for me to come clean. Tell Anna I was a cop, that I had the police investigating her. I knew how well that would go over, and she'd most likely flee right after she kicked us out of her apartment. Literally. Then she'd disappear and I couldn't protect her. It was a total cluster fuck. I was damned if I told her, damned if I didn't.

"I'd rather you tell me," I answered, choosing the keeping-her-safe option instead of telling her the truth. "Us. Tell us everything—which I have a feeling is a lot. I want to know about what this guy David did to you." It had to be pretty shitty if she killed him because of it. "I want to know about the guy who hurt you. I want to know it all. Over beers. I need a drink. This is too heavy for soda."

Carrie grinned and stood, taking her glass into the kitchen, no doubt relieved we had time to regroup. By helping me protect my source, she'd lied for me and pulled herself into this mess. She was officially an accomplice in my deception. "Definitely beer. Let's go."

Anna looked surprised at the idea, but shrugged her shoulders and stood up. "If I can just find my sandals."

19

nna

I HADN'T HEARD MY REAL NAME ALOUD IN OVER TEN YEARS. I HAD IT SET UP AS A web search on my news feeds that got sent to my email, but nothing had popped up—at least as it related to me and not an Olivia Edwards from Oklahoma—in about eight years. Even the media had given up on me. It was rusty sounding, as if the name were of an old friend. *Olivia Edwards.* I was born Olivia, but I'd left her behind when I was just a guileless teenager, like shedding a coat after a long winter, to be Anna Scott.

In the past week, since meeting Nick, I'd molted once again, becoming something more. Something even better than what I'd been doing—living—for a decade. I wanted Nick to be here. I wanted him to keep me safe. I wanted to know I could give some of my troubles to someone else, but it wouldn't be easy. Old ways were hard to change. And...the *and* was huge...and he worked for Moretti who was ruthless enough to want me dead. Nick's presence was proof of that.

Nick had said he wasn't a killer, but that didn't mean he didn't deal drugs, run a sex slavery ring, pimp out girls on the streets, launder money...

I turned to look at Nick, who sat wedged in the middle of the backseat of a taxi. We were headed to some obscure Italian restaurant Carrie liked. He met my gaze, gave my hand a little squeeze. He was *bad*. He worked for a *bad* guy. I'd seen firsthand what bad guys did. Shoot people, execution style, and dump them in the trunk of a car. If I hadn't gotten myself taken off the short list of suspects at the police station, if I'd been officially accused of the crime, Moretti wouldn't have come to the rescue, saying I'd had the worst case of bad luck *ever*. He would have let me take the fall for the crime and rot in jail. Why wouldn't he? The only other option was that he'd put out a hit on me behind bars, so instead of a bullet to the brain, I'd have a shiv to the gut instead. Dead was dead, either way.

The windows were down and the wind blew my hair into my face. Pushing it back, I tucked it behind my ears only to have it whip around all over again. The bother only ratcheted up my frustration.

What was my deal falling for bad guys? Sure, most women liked the whole *bad boy* thing, but I doubt their definition was the same. I'd blindly fallen for Todd because he'd been the first man to pay any kind of attention on me. Sure, he'd been doting and attentive until the ring was on my finger, but that had been extremely short term until the reading of my mother's will's codicil on my eighteenth birthday. Nick was equally attentive, equally charming when he wanted to be, yet his past was equally sinister. What made Nick any different than Todd? Why did I flee and go into hiding for twelve years because of Todd and seemingly fall into Nick's arms without any trepidation?

What was *wrong* with me?

Questions. Endless questions. I trusted Nick, but why? Was it because he'd brought his sister over? Included her in his little investigation into my past? I might question whether she really was related, that they were just some Bonnie and Clyde act, but genetics like theirs couldn't be feigned. I still couldn't rule out *who* Carrie worked for. Was she Moretti's lawyer, too?

As I looked out the window, I considered all of this. I couldn't have just run into a simple accountant whose biggest problem was an April fifteenth tax deadline who made my heart go pitter pat. No. I had to stumble into Nick, the mafioso underling, that night at the reception who practically made my heart stop every time he smiled.

I internally rolled my eyes.

The bottom line was that I needed Nick's help to save Elizabeth. I really did. I couldn't do it on my own, especially remaining hidden. I'd made the decision, made the deal with the devil, when I walked into Scorch that night. I knew then what Nick was, what he did for a living, and I'd been okay with it.

Elizabeth was worth the *complication* of Nick's background. Even now, she still was. The difference between that night and right now in the backseat of a dang taxi was that I was falling for him. I'd planned to use his help and then walk away. That hadn't changed, except now I'd probably walk away with a broken heart.

Our table was inside the restaurant, but next to the open windows that led to outdoor seating. Nick held out my chair, then sat next to me, Carrie across. A chunky red candle sat on top of a crisp white cloth next to the sugar packets, the scents of garlic and cheese mixed with the fresh summer air coming in through the window.

The table was situated where we could talk about my past openly—albeit quietly. Nick hadn't run away screaming, he hadn't shook his head at me in disgust. Neither had Carrie. They'd had opportunity and reason.

The fact that the two of them didn't look at me with revulsion on their faces meant they were used to hearing people admit to heinous crimes of various kinds. We were getting drinks together, not booking photos. They wouldn't run from little-old-me killing in self-defense. In their world, this was *normal*.

Which, sitting here as the waiter dropped off a basket of bread sticks and a small plate of olive oil and herbs, it made me realize it wouldn't be as hard as I thought unburdening my secrets. If Nick were that accountant I was supposed to fall in love with, it would be impossible. There would be judging, disgust and possibly fear at learning the truth. Nick and Carrie would probably just shrug their shoulders and say it was another day at the office. If they turned me in, they'd be exposing themselves. I was *safe* in the most ridiculous, backward of ways.

"Why were you in Switzerland?" Carrie asked once the waiter left us with beers for them, Chianti for me.

"You didn't ask about what I did to David first thing. I'm surprised." I shrugged, but added, "I should probably start at the beginning so it makes the most sense."

Nick's leg brushed up against me beneath the table. His right hand was on top of mine, which was on my thigh. With his fingers much larger than mine, they rested directly on my skin above my knee. His warmth seeped into me and it felt reassuring. Comforting.

I took a sip of my wine. "This isn't easy for me, to share like this. You're the first to know the truth." I took another sip of wine. Maybe if I got drunk, it would numb my nerves, dull my fear of sharing.

"You can't stop now, love," Nick said. "Just rip that Band-Aid off."

Carrie nodded.

I looked out the window, watched people walking by, heading home from work, going to the gym. Simple life stuff. Their lives were so simple, carefree. Would I ever have that? I was stalling. God, okay. I could do this. I didn't have a choice. With just my real name, Nick could find out everything on his own, just from his phone. Read the skewed stories the media had written. He'd learn about what happened, but it wouldn't be the complete truth. No one knew that but me.

Until now.

"My mother died when I was six. Car accident. I don't remember much of that time, I was too little to really understand, just that she didn't die right away. I wasn't allowed to see her once she was in the hospital. My nanny told me she'd died, gone to heaven." I paused, remembering that time. I fiddled with my fork. "I remember her, although not that well. Bits and pieces really. She was really nice. I remember doing fun things together, putting on her perfume and makeup before she went out to a function, watching movies together. The hugs." I looked over at Nick. "The hugs stopped when my mother died."

He squeezed my hand beneath the table.

"I never saw my father. He always worked. Always." I swirled the wine in my glass absently. "I'm not sure what my mother saw in him, why she married him, but he wanted her for her money. I have no doubt I was a mistake."

Carrie and Nick were both quiet, listening closely. The restaurant was busy, a waiter carried a large tray of food past, delicious smells followed. The sound of rustic music drifted over the bustle. We ignored it.

"For about six months, I was raised by a nanny and went to a local private school. My mother died in September, I remember because it was just a few weeks after my birthday and she had given me a pretty charm bracelet. The following April, my father remarried. A woman named Victoria. She was young, twenty-nine at the time if I remember correctly."

"A trophy wife?" Carrie asked.

I shrugged. "She fit the profile. Beautiful and smart. Fake. I was really young, so I didn't know at the time. Now that I'm older, perhaps. For a trophy wife, she had a lot of influence on my father. By June, I was packed off to a girls' camp in Washington State for the summer. After eight weeks of camp, I was taken directly to my first boarding school."

"You were what…six?" Carrie wondered.

"I was almost seven."

Nick shifted in his chair, said something under his breath, but I didn't catch it. He released my hand, took a big sip of his beer, then put his arm across the back of my chair, his fingers brushing against my shoulder.

"At first I didn't understand where I was, or why I was there. The school said that I should be thankful for parents who cared enough to send me to the best school."

Carrie waved over the waiter with efficiency. "We're going to need another round of beers. Bring another glass of Chianti as well, please." The waiter nodded, left.

"I hated it," I continued. "Hated everything about it. I missed my nanny, missed my room, missed my mother. I thought if I misbehaved, they'd send me home. So I could have it all back. I got in trouble the first month. They kicked me out and sent me home. But not for long. My father found a different boarding school and I was there a year. This one had a summer program so I was a year-round student."

"Holy shit." Nick wasn't happy. He put his beer down on the table a little harder than necessary.

"What about Christmas?" Carrie interrupted.

"I was sent home with the headmistress for the breaks. I have no doubt my father gave her nice Christmas bonuses. Let's see, that was in Virginia, so I was nine by the time I got myself kicked out of that school, too."

The waiter brought the beers, the wine. Nick finished off his first and handed the empty pint glass to the waiter. He drank about a third of the next one in one gulp.

"Switzerland?" he asked, remembering what I'd told him.

I gave him a little smile. "Very good. Yes. Father shipped me to Switzerland next. There, to fill my time and keep from plotting ways to get kicked out, I was put in the bilingual program, so I was immersed in French for two years." That had been miserable, I remembered, not being allowed to speak English at all. "Then he added the request of German to the mix."

"You said you spoke three languages, but wow," Carrie murmured.

"What, you thought one might be Pig Latin?" I said, although it wasn't all that funny.

God, my life was not very happy and I was making Carrie and Nick feel sorry for me. I could see it in the way they looked at me. I took a sip of wine. At this rate, we were all going to be plastered in an hour. "This is like a big pity party," I laughed weakly. "I'm sorry. You really don't need to hear this."

"Yes, we do," Nick said, his voice rough, like tumbled stones.

Carrie nodded her agreement.

I shrugged again. "Well, I'll move it along a little faster then. When I was twelve, I learned Victoria had a baby. Elizabeth. I was very excited to have a half-sister, thinking they'd want me to join them in their little family. I actually figured out how to buy a plane ticket back to the US, got a taxi to the airport in Geneva and to the gate before I was finally stopped. The good news of the story is that I didn't have to study French and German anymore."

"Military school?" Nick interjected.

I nodded. "Kansas." That transition hadn't been smooth. Europe to the Great Plains was vastly different. Assimilating to the strict rules of pseudo-military life had been rough. Total understatement of the year.

"Have some more wine," Carrie urged, lifting her chin as if pointing to me.

"You're trying to get me drunk."

"Yes," they said in unison.

20

nna

I LAUGHED AND SURPRISED MYSELF. TELLING THE SORRY DETAILS OF MY LIFE wasn't as hard as I thought. Maybe the wine was loosening me up. Or knowing they might have worse skeletons in their closets than I did made it easier.

"Five years of military school. I then realized getting kicked out wouldn't bring me home, so I gave up. Settled into school. It wasn't so bad once I accepted it. After graduation, my father sent for me. I was surprised as I hadn't seen him in eleven years. I was thrilled. He wanted me back! He told me I was marrying his business partner, Todd Lawton. I turned eighteen the following month and I was married the day before my birthday."

The waiter stopped by the table to take our orders but Nick shooed him away with a simple wave of his fingers.

"The day before?" Carrie wondered.

"I could be underage since my father blessed the union and I'll explain why they did that in a minute." I picked up my wine. "At first, I was so happy. My father wanted me home, he'd found someone he thought special for me to marry. I was just so excited about that alone I was blinded to the *why* of the whole thing. Turns out, my mother left me money for when I turned eighteen. Money becomes mixed property with marriage so my father and Todd had plans to control it. To answer your question..." I glanced at Carrie. "I think they wanted to ensure I was married to Todd *before* I got the money so there weren't any chances of the things falling through."

"This is like a soap opera," Carrie said, ripping up a bread stick into a pile on her little plate. "It would be really good if you weren't the main character. I think I can guess, but what happened next?"

"My mother's will indicated the money would come to me. It listed the amount, millions of dollars." Carrie's eyes went up at the amount, but didn't say anything. Nick didn't even blink. "Her will didn't mention that there was a note to give me when I turned eighteen. When the money became mine. I never knew about the money, nor the letter, before then. Never. Sitting in the lawyer's office with my brand new husband, I'm given a letter from my dead mother. She told me the money was mine outright, no one could touch it, but me. I guess my mother learned the hard way what a husband could do and wanted to protect me from a similar fate."

The waiter came to our table to get our orders once again.

"Do you want me to order for you?" Nick whispered in my ear.

I nodded. I'd completely forgotten about the menu and didn't think I could focus on it now.

After the waiter took our dinner choices, he left.

Nick prompted me to continue.

"Todd was furious. I remember he broke a vase in the office." I picked up a bread stick, swirled the tip in the plate of oil. "When my father found out, he was livid. Todd was legally bound to me, not my money. I'd just turned eighteen and was stuck. Stuck with a husband I'd only known for a month, who, it turns out, didn't even like me. I couldn't have our marriage annulled." I blushed at the thought, even now. I didn't dwell on my wedding night. Ever. It wasn't something I wanted to remember. Lots of girls hated their first time, and I wasn't an exception. That was before Todd learned about the money. He'd been rough, uncaring toward my needs even with the expectation of my millions in bed with us. "Todd wouldn't get a divorce. Both would have been scandalous in their circle, especially immediately after the wedding. Two months later, he gave me to his brother."

Two months of enduring all kinds of hell, I thought as I put my uneaten breadstick down on a little plate.

You're worthless. I can hardly get it up around you. When I do, you don't even know what to do. My secretary fucks better than you and she's dumber than a box of rocks. Maybe I'll have her give you a few pointers. Now roll over, ass in the air. I don't want to see your face.

There had been no escape, no way to get expelled. Military school had actually looked appealing.

Nick slammed his beer down on the table. I jumped, lost in the past.

"Gave you?" Carrie asked, sounding stunned.

We were getting to the part of the story where I'd done things I couldn't take back, that would surely drive Nick and Carrie away.

I licked my lips, took a sip of wine. "He drove me to David's house and told me to do whatever his brother said."

The waiter brought our salads, twisted fresh cracked pepper on each one while we sat there silently. I had no doubt Nick and Carrie weren't thinking about their food. I wasn't even hungry.

"Short version so we can eat—David tried to rape me, I got away from him, found a gun, killed him. I was arrested, accused of murder, denied bail and sat in jail for forty-two days. It was finally ruled self-defense and I was free to go. A woman gave me a way out, I took it, and became Anna."

I picked up my fork and pierced a cherry tomato, but Nick and Carrie just stared.

Nick pushed back his chair, the legs scraping against the black and white tile. "Will you excuse us for a moment?" he asked his sister without even glancing her way. He stood, held out his hand to me. I just looked up at him, at his unreadable expression, and took it.

He pulled me through the restaurant and into the hallway that led to the restrooms. At the very back, he turned us both so my back was to the wall with him blocking me in, sheltering me from the world. I couldn't see around his broad shoulders. I could only see him.

"Nick, I—"

"You said attempted rape." He looked tormented, concerned, yet lethal. "Did he do other things to you?" Just because Nick worked for Moretti didn't mean he condoned rape. It was like child molesters in jail. They didn't last long. There was a code, even among criminals. I hadn't had people worry about me before so this strange new feeling, something akin to being cherished, took root. I liked it. Because he made me feel that way, I wanted to put his mind at ease.

I put my hand up to his cheek, rough with stubble. "No. He tried, but I got away before he did anything." When Nick just looked at me skeptically, I continued. "Really. He just ripped my shirt. I got some scratches, a black eye, but that was it."

"That was it? A black eye?" He looked at me carefully for a moment. His eyes dropped to my mouth, stayed there. "So if I kiss you, and I don't mean like I did before, I mean *really* kiss you, it won't dredge anything up? Freak you out?"

I shook my head. "No. At least I don't—"

He shut me up with a kiss and there was nothing gentle about it. He was demanding as he angled his head to take it deeper all at once. His mouth opened and his tongue licked out over my lips. I gasped at the erotic touch, and he took full advantage and plundered into my mouth. It wasn't just a kiss, but a full onslaught to my senses. I picked up Nick's scent—soap and a hint of male. His shirt was soft, the material cool beneath my fingers on his chest. He tasted of beer, but his mouth was hot against mine.

"I don't want to hurt you," he whispered against my lips.

"You won't," I promised. *Not right now.*

With one hand at my nape, the other at my waist, I couldn't move. He held me right where he wanted me. The world didn't exist but for this kiss, this man, this moment.

He pulled away suddenly, a second before I heard footsteps coming down the hall. Nick stepped back slightly, to let a little bit of space come between us, but he didn't break his dark gaze from mine.

Once the hallway was quiet again, I asked, "Why did you kiss me like that?" My breath came out in little pants, heat pooled low in my belly.

"I had to. Had to feel you, taste you. Your story, Jesus." He tilted his head back, looked up at the ceiling for a moment. "I'm so...bent out of shape. I don't pity you, don't think that. But I feel bad, that's not the right word, but I don't know if I can explain what your words do to me." His fingers dove into my hair at the back of my neck, cupped my nape. "I feel like shit, sorry, because it's my job to protect you and I wasn't there for you."

I tilted my head, gave him a little smile. It thrilled me to my toes to hear his possessiveness of me. Good possessiveness, not the creepy kind. A week ago I didn't need anyone. Or at least I thought I didn't. I'd been doing fine on my own. Now, I *needed* Nick. It was hard to justify, to come to terms with needing someone who was *bad*, but he was just so *good*. "You didn't even know me then."

"I know that. Deep down, I know," he continued. "That doesn't make it any easier. I want to keep you safe and it practically kills me to know what you went through. I can't take it away, but I can make it better. Now, I can."

He lowered his head so our noses bumped, rubbed his back and forth Eskimo style, our breaths mingled.

"You do make it better," I reassured him. "Your kisses, they're like a drug. I want more. I can't stop."

Nick grinned and lifted an eyebrow at my words. "You want more? Then you can have more. Later. We should get back to my sister. But first, I want you to undo the top two buttons of your blouse."

I just stared at him for a moment, processing his words. Yes, I'd heard him correctly. "Um..."

He looked at me now, so brooding and dark, his eyes heated. I'd made him that way, aroused and curious. It was a very heady sensation, this power I had over him. This little request, it was a game between lovers. Or almost-lovers.

"Just for me, Anna," he murmured.

Reaching up, I undid the first button, my fingers fumbling a little, then the next, Nick's eyes eagerly following the motions. Once undone, I dropped my hands to my sides.

He leaned in, placing one forearm on the wall above my head. He was so close, close enough where if I tilted my head up I could nip his jaw.

I was frozen in place, waiting for him, taking tiny little breaths, like prey caught in the sights of a wild animal. Using just one finger, he slid the fabric of my shirt to the side, opening the V at my neck. The very tip of his finger brushed my sensitive skin and the back of my neck rose. With the two buttons undone, my shirt still wasn't revealing. Some ladies in the restaurant right now were exposing more cleavage than I was. But I used my clothes as a barrier, separating myself from others. Like my secrets, Nick was revealing all of me, one little button at a time. He nudged the cotton over about two inches, exposing the very top curve of my breast. From his vantage, I had no doubt he had a decent view down my top.

"Is that pale pink?" he whispered, his head tipped down, overly intrigued with a scrap of lace.

I felt like melting into the wall. How did just showing Nick a tiny hint of my bra turn me on like never before? He was taunting me, teasing me, while doing the same to himself. This was foreplay at its finest. If I could feel like this being completely clothed in a restaurant full of people, what would happen when he got me naked?

I licked my dry lips. "Yes."

"Pretty," he said. His finger slid lower, over the top of my shirt, to run a small circle around my hardened nipple.

The searing touch, even though the layers of my shirt and lace bra, was so intense I felt my legs buckle. I pushed against the wall to hold myself up. I couldn't see anything else but Nick, his dark, intense eyes focusing solely on me. I was lost, completely lost in him.

"Feel that?" he asked.

I could only nod. I bit my lip to keep from crying out.

"I feel it, too. Later," he murmured, full of promise. "Later we'll explore this thing between us. For now, I'll think about pink lace."

21

rif

MY HEAD WAS ABOUT TO EXPLODE. IT WAS BORDERLINE IMPOSSIBLE TO KEEP CALM after hearing Anna's story. I now knew what the Hulk felt like when his anger had made him transform into a big, green scary guy. I was ready to morph right then. Jesus, what she'd survived.

I thought my childhood had been shitty, with my parents getting divorced. That had been nothing. I'd had my sisters go through it with me, together. The Griffin family looked like a fucking Norman Rockwell painting in comparison to Anna's.

Olivia's. I couldn't picture her with that name. To me, she was Anna.

And shit, to her, I was Nick. Not Jake.

I had to yank her out of her seat, lead her to the only private spot in the restaurant. It was like my inner caveman took over. No one would get to her, have her like I would. I had to kiss her. Touch her, know she was real, that she was in front of me, and that from now on, she was going to be okay. I was going to make sure of it.

Just the feel of her, God, she was incredible. So small, so soft, so special, yet had survived things that would have broken a lesser person. And she'd been six—*six*—when she'd been shipped off to boarding school. Her father had literally gotten rid of her, only to yank her back into his life when it was time to claim her money for himself and his asshole "business partner".

Anna had been a pawn. Just that. Nothing more. Not any longer. I'd only known her for ten days, but that was enough. The physical attraction I had for her had been a problem since Moretti wanted me to use it like a weapon. No longer. Now it was a distraction, a completely different kind of problem entirely. One I liked immensely, especially if it involved a pink lacy bra.

Anna was mine and I was going to slay those fucking dragons of hers. The way Carrie looked when we returned to the table, lawyerly and laser focused, I knew she would help.

I didn't want to push Anna further; she'd told us so much we needed to process it. I needed to talk to Peters, get other details that might be useful. Things Anna might not remember or reports she didn't know about. We didn't talk much for the remainder of the meal, lost in our own thoughts.

Carrie, bless her fucking heart, saved the day when we walked out of the restaurant. "I feel like some ice cream. There's a great place up the block. Anna. Olivia. Crap." Carrie laughed. "What do you want me to call you?"

"Anna. I like being Anna."

"Good, because I'm terrible with names. I'll get all confused and sound like my grandmother rattling off a bunch before she gets to the right one."

Nana Addie never called one of her four children by the right name. By the time grandchildren came into the mix, sometimes she called out the dog's name.

"Walk ahead with me because I want to ask your advice about my boyfriend and Nick doesn't want to hear it." Carrie gave me a sisterly look that screamed *payback* for making her go into Anna's kitchen earlier.

Anna looked to me, then to my sister. Shrugged. "Sure, but I'm not sure I could be much help."

"You're my new best friend, remember?" Carrie linked arms and pulled her ahead. "And we're getting ice cream. The world's problems can be solved with both."

The minute they were far enough away, I whipped out my cell, called Peters.

"Holy shit, man. We were going in the right direction last night, but this? I couldn't have come up with this," Peters told me.

I remembered Carrie's soap opera reference and ground my teeth together.

"She told me," I replied. "I know what happened."

The street noise was loud. It was Friday rush hour and everyone was leaving work, beginning their weekend. Taxis whizzed by, horns blared, the sea of pedestrians fast moving. I stepped out of the main stream of people so I could focus, stood by a parking meter.

"All of it?"

"I got the main idea, but we didn't go into the details." I glanced out into the street when a taxi honked at a wrong-way biker. "Yet."

"I'll email you some links to read if you don't want to ask Anna—Olivia, herself. It's pretty rough."

Shit. I'd wanted her secrets, but they were bigger, darker than I ever imagined. Now, I didn't want her to tell me more, to have her dredge it up. I could see why she built up those walls, to separate herself from one fucked-up thing after another.

"Give me the worst," I said, dreading it. "The two-minute version."

I could give the girls a head start, but not much.

"You know about the money."

"Yeah." I kicked at a pebble on the ground, watched it arc off the curb into the gutter.

"When it didn't pan out for her ex, Todd—" he said the name with complete scorn, "—decided to share her with his brother. That's some weird shit. One account is that she went to his house and murdered him in cold blood. She'd just graduated from military school and knew her way around a gun. Eighteen years old and a Prep champion sharpshooter, three years running. Won state, too. The military was wooing her right alongside of Todd Lawton."

I ran a hand through my hair, paced between the parking meter and the light pole. I wanted to kick the shit out of something.

"She was arrested for murder. Her side of the story was self-defense, attempted rape. Her husband at the time didn't take her side. Said that he'd married a psychopath whose skills were groomed at an elite military academy and the crazy bitch killed his beloved brother. Hubby pushed for murder. So did her dad."

The fucker.

"Bail was denied," Peters continued. "She spent forty-some days in jail because her due process was slowed down to a crawl."

"Forty days? Let me guess, her husband and father got to the cops. The judge. Left her there to rot. Where the hell was *her* lawyer? She had buckets of money, she could have afforded the best out there."

"The money was frozen. She was considered a flight risk since she'd lived overseas."

"Lived overseas? It was fucking boarding school and she'd been, what, twelve?"

"Like I said, no due process," Peters grumbled. He was as pissed off as I was about the corruption she'd faced with law enforcement.

"She learned interrogation procedure firsthand. That's how she was able to work over Werbler and Gossing. She'd been interrogated before, probably frequently, trying to get her to confess to something she didn't do. I bet they used every trick on her, too, especially if they were crooked. Nothing worked since she was innocent."

If I had to spend forty-two days in jail for something I didn't do because men in blue were on the take, I wouldn't be quick to forgive either. Hell, I was one, which made it like a stab in the back, that there were men out there who had hurt Anna that way. Cops were supposed to protect, but she'd only met corruption, greed and manipulation.

"No wonder she's not a fan of the police," I muttered. Great. Just *great*. The more I learned the more of a total fucker I was. A hypocrite. I wasn't planning on holding her in jail against her will, but I was guilty of deception.

I should tell her the truth, that I was a cop, not a *bad guy* working for Moretti, but I couldn't. I had to keep her safe and doing that meant to remain undercover. If Moretti found out I wore a badge, I'd lose my leverage, my underground contacts. I might need those resources to help her. She couldn't learn the truth, not until she was out of danger.

I'd lose her over this, I had zero doubt, knowing how she'd been so cruelly used by cops in the past, but I'd rather have her walk away than be buried in the ground. It was worth the risk.

"After all that time, she finally got in front of a judge who wasn't being, shall we say, swayed," Peters continued, unaware of the direction of my thoughts. "Ruled self-defense and she was free to go. Assets unfrozen. The papers say she left the courthouse in a taxi and was never seen again. It was a big deal in San Francisco. Headlines read *Where Did the Heiress Go?* and *From Murder to Missing*."

Anna hadn't said where she was from. Scratch that, where her father lived.

Where she lived until she was six. Shit. I clenched my free hand into a fist, ready to beat the shit out of her father. Her ex.

"Hubby didn't put out a missing person's report?"

"He served her divorce papers in jail."

"You're fucking kidding me."

"Nope. His lawyer was good and it was done fast. Really fast. By the time she was released, they weren't married anymore."

"In less than eight weeks?" The ex had to have some cash of his own to grease so many palms.

"Less than eight weeks," Peters repeated. "He'd washed his hands of her and didn't care that she'd disappeared. Even with her money—which he couldn't touch. One report said good riddance."

Good riddance was right. Anna was better off without that asshole. It just made her escape, however she did it, that much more clean of a break. Over ten years later, she didn't have to worry about being legally married to the guy, to have that looming over her.

"He was probably thrilled she disappeared. Was there any thought he might have had something to do with it? Something truly criminal? He had motive," I pointed out. "She killed his brother."

"Seriously, man, the guy had enough connections to keep his wife illegally imprisoned. In the United States. This isn't some third world country we're talking about. Even if he'd killed her in front of the police station with dozens of witnesses, the slimy bastard still probably would have gotten off."

I ran a hand over my face, squeezed my eyes shut, trying to cool my anger. It wasn't helping. Neither was this conversation. "Yeah, you're right."

"The real story, when you look at the files, see the pictures, is that this guy David Lawton, attacked her. She wasn't raped, she'd gotten lucky with just bruises, a cut on her arm."

A black eye, Anna had said.

"He had a gun cabinet and she found it. Shot him, center of the chest."

"Bull's eye," I murmured. It was the first moment of satisfaction I'd felt since I dialed Peters. Good thing the bastard was already dead.

"Military school paid off," Peters replied, his voice bitter, yet I could hear some admiration in there, too.

I didn't wish military school on anyone. Marching in lines, hospital corners on the beds, zero privacy. For years. She never went home. Hell, military school *was* her home. It sounded horrendous for a young girl who was alone in the world, who got put there only because she'd wanted attention from her father, but I had to agree with Peters. If she hadn't been there, hadn't learned how to shoot, her life would have turned out much different.

"No question dear old Dad and business partner had this planned for years, probably since she was six. No matter what boarding school she was shipped to, she would have been called home to marry," I pointed out. "I'd say Daddy made a mistake when he put her in military school."

"Big time," Peters agreed.

22

rif

AN HOUR LATER, WITH MY SISTER ON HER WAY HOME IN A CAB, I HELD ANNA'S hand as we walked a few blocks to grab one of our own. I kept her on my right away from traffic. It was a simple thing, walking with a woman, holding her hand, but it was a novelty for me. In our marriage, Nadine and I hadn't been ones for PDA of any kind. Perhaps that had been an early indication we were doomed, one that I only now saw in hindsight.

Because I was so caught up in the mundane, enjoying a walk and holding hands, I missed the obvious, at least to me—a former military man and cop. Anna stiffened next to me, her fingers squeezing mine. By the time I glanced over at her in question, a guy had changed our little walk from a duo to a trio.

"Keep walking," he muttered, offering a fake smile as people passed us on the sidewalk.

Mid-forties, salt-and-pepper hair, a little under six feet. Tan. Thin scar in his left eyebrow. Smoker, based on the rasp in his voice. I memorized him for later, when I would make him pay for this. Anna glanced up at me and I could see fear in her eyes, watched as she darted them down and behind her, and I knew the guy held something against her back.

A gun? A knife?

It didn't matter. All that mattered was getting Anna away from that weapon.

"What do you want?" I asked, my voice deceptively smooth, guiding us around a group of teenagers staring at a person's tablet, laughing at whatever was on the screen. A biker careened past down the narrow bike lane. A man paid a parking meter. I took in everything, processed it, rejected it as an option for escape. I couldn't do much with the weapon on Anna. On me, the guy'd be dead by now.

"This is just an introduction from Moretti."

Shit. Moretti. Some common street thug wouldn't meander with us down a busy street at rush hour all *la-di-da*; they'd shake and take. A back alley, nighttime was more their MO.

I knew what the guy looked like, could identify him to a sketch artist, pick him from a lineup, even after only a second's glance. It's what I'd been trained to do. No way was he going to pull something now. He didn't have a clean getaway. The subway wasn't near, taxis were scarce. From what I saw of him, which was only from the chest up since Anna blocked him, he wasn't a desperate drug addict willing to risk everything for a score. I slowed my breathing, calmed myself so I could respond better.

"Oh?" I asked as I slowly pulled Anna in to my side, ready to push her out of harm. My girl had a gun or knife in her back. I wanted her away from here and somewhere safe so I could beat the shit out of him.

My alpha instincts were being honed on a daily basis these days. I hadn't needed them much until now. Until Anna.

"Moretti wanted me to introduce myself before Monday." The stench of cigarettes clouded around the guy like he was Pigpen from Charlie Brown. "I'll see you both then. Monday's going to be fun. At least for me." He sneered, then blended into the crowd, letting us walk on.

My senses were at heightened awareness like I was back in Afghanistan under attack. The enemy was the enemy, no matter where I was. Every sound, every smell, every person was scrutinized. He'd slipped in because my guard had been lulled, underestimating how ruthless Moretti really was, but not now.

The guy was gone. I pulled Anna around and into my other side, my left arm wrapped around her, my right arm free and ready to pull the gun from my back. It wouldn't have served any purpose before; the bastard's weapon was already on its target. If he'd meant to kill her here on the street, he could have —would have—done it. Moretti was toying with me, sending me a message. It didn't matter how far up in the ranks you were, he always had a backup plan in place.

We were safe until Monday. I'd figured we had a few more days than that, but at least now I knew. That didn't mean I didn't assess everyone we passed as a danger, a threat to Anna. The jogger, the mom with the two kids, a businessman in a suit talking on his cell. I gauged them as dangerous, ruled them out one by one.

We didn't speak until we reached the corner, turned. We both looked back to verify he was gone, I also scoped the new street, then moved to stand in front of an electronics store. The window held a flat screen TV with a blockbuster movie playing. It was shady, cooler with a breeze coming down the street, but I was still sweating.

"Are you okay?" I asked, looking Anna over for any injuries. She could have been shot or stabbed in the back. Dead either way. The tension I'd ratcheted down was back. Shit.

I was pissed at myself, knowing there was nothing I could have done to prevent it, for not keeping her out of harm's way. I willed my heartbeat to slowly return to normal since she was in one piece. Not a hair out of place, not a wrinkle on her clothes. Her pupils were dilated, her pulse frantic in her neck, but otherwise she seemed fine.

At least one of us was.

Adrenaline was still pumping and I wanted to go chase after the bastard, even though I knew he was long gone. I also wanted to grab Anna, yank her in my arms and kiss the hell out of her, confirm she was alive and breathing. What I had in mind wasn't legal on a city street, unfortunately.

"Was it a gun?"

She nodded. "I felt it before I knew he was there. I'm sorry I didn't do more, but I didn't want to set him off, have him pull the trigger."

I saw red, tried to breathe through it, to hide my anger from her. "Smart. Glad you know when to fight" —I was thinking of the asshole at the bar in Denver— "and when to play along with an attacker." The fact we were having this talk made me feel grim. "He was here for me, not you."

That pissed me off. Moretti didn't trust me. Hell, he didn't trust anybody, so I should have expected this. I considered my cover and if there was anything left of it. If it had been blown, I'd be dead in a trunk of my own by now. Like the guy said, it was a message.

I had two days to save us both.

"You're wrong, he's not here for you. Don't you see?" Anna held her hands out in front of her in the way that said *Really?* "If Moretti wanted you dead, he'd have killed you in Denver. If he hadn't sent you, he'd have sent this guy first and I'd be dead. I know karate, but I don't have Wonder Woman bracelets that deflect bullets."

She didn't have to remind me how vulnerable she was.

Anna took a step back, then another. Her gaze shifted left and right, then back at me. "I've got to get out of here. If I don't, he's going to kill you, too. Collateral damage. I warned you this would happen. This way, you can go home and avoid a car trunk of your own. If I disappear, then no one kills me and you don't have to die. I've got to hurry." Anna scoped the street again as if she was formulating a plan. I saw no fear, just conviction.

Oh crap. I didn't want to be sexist and think that once a woman made up her mind there was no changing it, but Anna had been on her own for her entire life. She didn't run ideas by anyone. Talk them through. Once she made a decision, she ran with it, because she'd only had herself. In this case, she was going to do exactly that. *Run.*

I leaned in so we were eye to eye, placed my hands on her upper arms. I wanted to shake some sense into her, plus I wanted to make sure she didn't bolt. "What the hell are you talking about?" In the past five minutes, I'd lost control of everything.

"Just leave me alone." She shrugged my hands off, stepped back again. "Go, Nick. Tell your boss you killed me, or I just disappeared into thin air. By the time you get back to Denver, Anna Scott will be gone. She won't exist anymore."

I didn't like the sound of that. Her disappearing, letting me save myself. Whatever. I didn't know if I should strangle her or kiss her. My adrenaline made me feel several things at once. Her cheeks were flushed with determination, and I couldn't stop seeing her pink bra in my mind. I shook it off. I couldn't be distracted by attraction because she wasn't making any sense. "Won't exist anymore?"

She took another step back, almost off the curb, looked up at me with her dark eyes and I saw it. The wall was back. Her look was the same as in the interrogation room in Denver.

"'Bye, Nick," she murmured.

With that, she turned and walked off, head held high, moving quickly, stretching the space between us with long strides, leaving me standing there. It took me about two seconds of just watching her to realize she wasn't coming back. Had no intention of even looking back. I knew, right then, if she got out of my sight, I'd never see her again. She had the money, millions from what she said. She had the means, she had the motive and the contacts, to disappear. To change her identity again. She'd done it once, she could easily do it again. Hell, she could even leave the country, go somewhere that spoke French or German and she'd blend right in.

Shit. If I was smart, I'd just let her go. She was right, she'd be safe. But at a very high cost. Starting over again would isolate her even more, would ruin everything she'd spent the past ten years trying to achieve.

I was also very greedy. I wanted her for myself and she couldn't disappear on me. I'd only seen a hint of her bra. No way in hell was that enough.

I jogged to catch up with her. I grabbed her arm, spun her around.

"Don't! Just go. I told you before, this is stupid. That guy," she pointed behind her. "He's proof. This isn't a game. He's here for *me*. You need to get away from me." She pushed at my chest with both hands, shoving me back, her hair falling forward over her face. Anger, annoyance and frustration pulsed off her in waves. "I don't want your help."

I knew she could karate chop the shit out of me, so I pulled my hands back. Didn't mean I wouldn't push her. "You're lying."

She narrowed her gaze. "I don't need you." She shook her head roughly as she spoke, pushed her hair back behind her ears.

Her cool control was slipping. Her words were becoming louder, more emotional. A few heads turned as people walked past.

"You're lying," I repeated, standing my ground, hands on my hips. "At least tell me the truth, Anna. I deserve at least that, don't I?"

"I don't want you to die, all right?" Her voice broke a little. "Now go."

She gave me a bigger shove, but I didn't move. Couldn't. I just stood there, my feet rooted to the ground, stunned. No way could I let her push me out of her life after those words. They slayed me. Ripped me open. She practically pulled my heart out, still beating, and held it in her hands. That's what it felt like, at least. She was pushing me away to save me. *Me.* While sacrificing herself. What she'd become in the past decade on her own. Without any family. Without her ex. Scared of everyone and everything. Anna Scott. She was willing to walk away from being Anna Scott for what she knew me to be...a bartender, a two-bit enforcer for a loser like Moretti.

I wanted to grab her, pull her into my arms and never let go. But that wasn't what she needed right now. She was too raw, too exposed. Hell, so was I. I darted a glance left and right down the busy street. "People are starting to stare. We can't talk about this here in the street. Let's head back to your apartment."

"Then you'll go?" she asked, eyeing me suspiciously, her breaths coming out short and fast. "We'll talk, but then you'll go."

Anna was begging me to leave her, but she wasn't going to win this fight. I ignored her question, her ultimatum, grabbed her arm again and hailed a taxi, which was, miraculously, passing by.

Climbing in, we made it two blocks before we got caught in traffic—an impressive feat for Manhattan. Before I had a chance to stop her, Anna was out of the taxi in a flash, bolting down the sidewalk.

What the fuck was she doing?

It took me a few seconds of looking out the open door to realize what she'd done, as the taxi driver yelled at me in some foreign language I assumed was Eastern European in origin. Fumbling, I pulled out my wallet and tossed a few bills at him, leapt out and ran after her.

She was fast and she had a solid head start. It took me a block to catch up with her. I grabbed her shoulder, pulled her back toward me, slowed her down. Stopped. She froze, but reacted in a way I hadn't anticipated by pivoting on her heel and throwing a wicked straight punch. It would have popped me in the nose if I hadn't deflected the strike with my hand. Using my own self-defense skills, I grabbed her wrist and pulled her into me, tightly. She was breathing hard, winded from her hundred-meter dash across the streets of New York.

"Shit, Anna. What the hell was that for?" I asked, trying to catch my breath. Sweat poured down my face, made my shirt cling to my body. No way was I letting her go, even with her struggling in my grasp.

"You grabbed my shoulder. I warned you not to do that!"

I'd forgotten that was a trigger for her. Why, I didn't know, but I should've remembered. "Right, sorry. You ran off. Jesus, are you insane?"

"I told you," she gasped against my shirt, her breaths coming short and fast. "You'll be safer away from me."

"If you keep trying to deck me like that, you're right." My heart rate was coming down, but I had to make time to get back into the gym. I was too old for this shit. I forced her chin up to look at me. Her face was sweaty, her damp hair stuck to her forehead and cheeks. Her eyes were bright, her pupils dilated fully from the rush of adrenaline. "I'm not letting you go. No matter where you go, or how fast you run, I'll find you," I said fiercely.

"Hey, lady. Is he messing with you?" A thirty-something man walked by, stopped. Figured, the one chivalrous guy left in the world had to be on the same street.

I loosened my hold on Anna just enough for her to turn her head toward him. I couldn't do what I wanted and drag her by the hair back to her apartment caveman-style. This guy, and a few others, would probably do more than ask if she was okay.

Anna shook her head against my sweaty shirt, replied, "No. I'm fine. Thanks for checking."

Mr. Chivalry gave me the once over, then nodded and went on his way.

"We're going back to your apartment. We'll talk about this there, without any straight punches or interfering bystanders." I just held her for a minute until we'd both recovered. This time, I took her hand in mine, held it tight. As I searched for another taxi, I knew I wasn't going to let go until we were safely back at her place.

23

rif

Twenty minutes later, we walked into her apartment. We hadn't spoken on the ride; Anna kept her gaze diverted out her window, with her hand still in mine. I'd been surprised she'd given in, but I'd proven my point. She couldn't get away. I'd keep following her, keep finding her. This didn't mean she wasn't scheming, making plans in that genius brain of hers. Most likely, she was biding her time, which only meant I'd have to be extra vigilant. She was an exceptional opponent. If it weren't life-or-death we were dealing with, I'd enjoy this battle of wills.

As I closed the apartment door behind us, flipped the lock, I looked around the small space, considering it with a completely different mindset. No wonder she kept it a mess. Boarding school, especially military academies, didn't condone messiness. Her ex, the fucker, no doubt had a tight rein on her, even for the short time they'd been married. Being in charge of her own life, finally, she got to do what she wanted. In her own space, not shared with a roommate or two. Even all these years later, if she wanted to leave her dirty laundry scattered across the floor, what was the harm? No one was going to give her detention or make her do pushups or have her arrested.

Her personal appearance was a different story. She was always neat and tidy, her garments pressed with the precision of an expert dry cleaner. No hair out of place, makeup pristine.

She dropped her keys in a little dish on a table by the door, then moved into the kitchen and pulled a glass down from the cabinet.

There was a different Anna hidden away beneath all the layers of her façade she'd so carefully built. I'd seen a few quick glimpses of her. Enough to know I wanted to see more. Every time I kissed her, she participated a little more, became less wary. When I'd let her have control of our it, right here in her kitchen, it had been pure torture not touching her, keeping my hands tightly gripped against her counter. I'd wanted to grab her close, hold her right where I wanted her so I could kiss her in a way that imprinted her on my DNA. And vice versa.

She'd been tentative at first, skittish even, kissing and exploring my mouth, learning what she liked, what made me groan. She recognized the power she had over me, how she could take me to my knees with just a brush of her lips against my skin. I saw the flare of awareness of that fact in her eyes.

She wasn't in control right now. She didn't know it, but when she willingly sacrificed herself, her identity, to save me, I took it from her. Running off had shown me how serious she was. Sure, yelling at me made her point clear, but that hadn't solidified it as much as watching her sprint down the sidewalk.

It was an invisible thing, something she didn't even realize yet, but there was nothing I wouldn't do to protect her. She'd crossed the line and there was no going back. I wanted her, in every way.

When she undid those two modest little buttons on her blouse in the restaurant, I almost lost it. The look on her face, nervousness and arousal combined, had me shaking. I'd hoped to bank my eagerness for her, my instinctual need to rip the blouse open, not caring if buttons flew across the hallway, to see her, to take her. It had been damn hard. Just nudging the edge of the delicate fabric over a few inches exposed a tantalizing glimpse of her collarbone, the very top soft swell of her full breast, a tiny glimpse of her lacy bra.

Standing here now, watching her simply drink a glass of water, made me rock hard. I knew what she wore beneath. Pale pink lace and satin. Would her panties match the bra? Knowing Anna, I had no doubt. Everything she had matched.

I had to go slowly, carefully. She wasn't thinking clearly. Her first option—

flight—was what she could see, could focus on. It wasn't the answer. I had to come up with an alternative, a better way to save both of us. I had until Monday to do so. In the meantime, I had to prove to her that staying and fighting for what we had was the right thing.

The only thing.

Pushing her up against the counter, lifting her skirts and thrusting quickly and deeply into her from behind, wasn't going to work. I couldn't be rough. At least not now. I'd show her the pleasure to be had in that, too, but first, she needed to know I'd take care of her, treasure her like no one ever had. That what we had couldn't be thrown away. I would teach her the chemistry between us was not common, that the feelings we had for each other didn't just go away with a new identity. She couldn't shed me like a skin and grow a new one, tougher and stronger.

We were weaker apart and I was going to prove it to her. Right now.

"You've been seducing me all night." I couldn't let my anger or frustration show. Couldn't scold her for running off. That tact wouldn't work. Somehow, I needed to play it cool. Calm. Now that we were back in the apartment, I could let my guard down—a little—and focus solely on Anna once again.

She looked at me, eyes big. "I have? How?"

"I know the color of your bra. Just that scrap of lace has me thinking thoughts. Things I want to do to you," I murmured.

The way her eyes flared, I knew she could see the intensity on my face. I felt it, my gaze had her pinned like a butterfly on a display board. Her pulse fluttered at her neck, her tongue darted out to lick her lips. I groaned at the sight. "You just have to be in the same room and I want you. I don't care what your name is, what you've done. I want *you*."

She glanced down at her glass, her dark lashes shielding her thoughts from me. "If you walk away, we'll both stay alive," she said, her voice wilted and wounded.

Did she really think Moretti would let me live if I went back to Denver without killing her? That having her disappear would save me from ruthless repercussions? Moretti would see me as weak, being bested by a woman. Too weak to be useful to him, which meant I'd have a car trunk with my name on it. Telling her this would only make things worse.

"Walk away? For what, love? Will it be worth it? You'll have a new identity but you'll be alone. I can't think about being without you."

Saying those words surprised me. I'd never imagined I'd feel enough for a woman to utter them, let alone really mean it.

Her gaze flicked to mine as if she debated the truth of my words. She shook her head as she denied it. "No. No! You have to go. Please, Nick," she pleaded.

"No."

She rubbed her hand over her face. "This is happening too fast."

"You want time?" I narrowed my gaze at her, assessing. "You can have time to figure out what this is between us. But I'm not leaving you and I'm damn well not going to keep my hands off you."

She just closed her eyes, as if to block me out, and shook her head.

Stubborn woman! So fucking determined. "You don't believe me when I say there's something between us? Fine. I'll show you instead." I closed the space between us before she could react, pulled her into me roughly. Her eyes opened wide as my mouth claimed hers in a searing kiss. A kiss made to forget everything.

Anna tasted of red wine and vanilla ice cream, decadent and rich. How could I walk away from this? I angled my head, adjusting the kiss, letting myself sink even deeper and deeper until I felt her fingers grip the front of my shirt, as a sigh slipped from her lips. I took advantage, my tongue plunging deep. The warmth from her body seeped into my belly, her scent swirled around us, making me dizzy with need.

I was being ruthless, I knew. Words weren't working. I had to show her, make her *feel* what we had, what could be. From what I knew of her, she had no comparison, no idea the depth of our connection. What I felt for her wasn't like anything I'd ever felt for any other woman, even Nadine. I'd been married to her and I'd felt less with her than I did just kissing Anna. It only proved how wrong Nadine and I had been for each other. I thought I'd never want a woman again, after Nadine's cheating, but this, now, with Anna, was like a drug. I was addicted.

I walked her backwards out of the small kitchen, into her living room, never breaking the kiss. Her calves bumped the front of her couch. We lowered as one down its length, Anna on her back, our lips still fused. I propped myself up on my forearm with one knee wedged between hers, spreading her legs open, my other foot resting on the floor. I settled perfectly into the cradle of her hips, and when she moaned, I knew then she'd felt me, hard and thick with arousal, against her core. Shifting my hips ever so slightly, I rocked against her. Anna broke the kiss and tilted her head back, a cry of pleasure escaping.

Intense male satisfaction at the look on her face coursed through me. Her eyes were closed, her mouth open in surprise, her cheeks flushed a rosy red. Her breath escaped her swollen lips in little pants. I'd done this to her, made her lose control, forget everything but my touch and what it could do to her.

"Like that?" I asked, shifting my hips again to rub against her clit.

She licked her lips and nodded her head, but didn't open her eyes, as if it were a dream and she didn't want to wake up. I smiled to myself, knowing I could make it even better. Make her realize she couldn't walk away.

"This is what you do to me, Anna. What I can do to you. Do you really want to leave *this*? Leave *us*?" My voice was rough like gravel, my words harsh. My body was gentle, but my intent wasn't. She had to learn. Now.

Anna shook her head with abandon. I couldn't be sure if she was fighting me or lost in her own pleasure. Both, perhaps. I was pushed now to show her, not for my own desire, but Anna's. I had to make her come, to take her over the edge and watch her as I did. In this moment, it was only about her.

I ground against her, very slowly, very lightly. I was so hard for her, I knew I'd have a zipper imprint on my cock. Using my free arm, I undid the buttons on her blouse. It was slow going one handed, but I was enjoying the view, like unwrapping a present very, very carefully. Parting the two sides, I revealed her flat, toned belly, the rounded curve of her ribs, her pink lace bra. I ran the tip of my finger from the indent at the base of her neck, down over the soft skin between her collarbones, lower through the valley of her breasts, lower still to her belly button, ending at the top of her skirt. So warm, so smooth, so reactive. Her breath caught, her stomach sucked in as I brushed over it. I swear my hands could span her waist if I tried.

I was rough, hairy and angular. Anna was sweet curves and hidden delights. I wanted to know each spot on her body that made her gasp, that made a slight sheen of sweat break out across her fragrant skin, that made her forget.

Working my way back up the same path, I stopped at the front clasp of her bra, flicked it open. I lowered my head and used my teeth to push the lace aside, licked my way up the slope of one breast to the pert nipple. Sweet baby Jesus, it was just the shade of pink I'd imagined. Small, the tight little bud was very sensitive beneath my tongue. Just the slightest touch against the tip made her cry out. I closed my mouth over it, laved it, then sucked. Her back bowed as if I were pulling all of her body up with my mouth, a harsh cry escaping her lips.

I wasn't going to let up on my assault on her senses. Not until she came.

I switched sides, nudging the rest of her bra aside, licking, nibbling. Fingers of my free hand worked a tip, wet from my mouth, gave it a gentle tug, as my hips continued their slow movement, mimicking how I'd move once I got inside her. Anna's hands lifted to my head, sifted into my hair and on occasion, gave a little tug. I bet she had no idea she was holding my head to her breast. I loved that she was instinctively guiding me to where she found the most pleasure.

"Have you ever come this way before?" I asked, my voice soft as I moved up to her ear, nipped it, then soothed it with a lick.

She shook her head, licked her lips. "No. God, no...don't stop."

I smiled into her neck, sucked there gently, tasting her.

"What, this?" I asked, rocking my hips. Anna lifted up into me, our bodies rubbing together in a way that had my eyes practically rolling back in my head.

She nodded, her hair a shifting curtain around her.

"You're so sensitive, so responsive." I never stopped thrusting up over her. "Are you ready to come? Because I bet you can just by having your nipples played with. I'm going to watch you. You're going to be so beautiful." I plumped a breast, almost a handful, then rubbed my palm over the tip in a circle. She sucked in a deep breath, which pushed her more fully into me.

"I've never...I can't—" She started to thrash beneath me, bucking me up, which only had us pressing together with more fervor than I'd intended. "It's too much."

"Shh. You can," I insisted, driving her on, my breath ragged as much as hers. "I've got you. I'll keep you safe. Just let go."

I lowered my mouth back to one nipple and gave a long, deep pull.

Like plucking a bow, Anna's body went taut. She cried out her pleasure as I looked up from her breast and watched her face, the sheer bliss of letting go moving through every fiber of her being. I continued to draw from her, rub over her mound until she finally slumped down, sated, content. Satisfied.

She was as stunning in her pleasure as I'd imagined. And that had been with most of our clothes on. The fact that she was so responsive made me ache to be buried deep. I gave her this pleasure, but at the same time, she'd given me something as well. When I settled in between her legs, setting her off like that, felt like coming home.

It was perfect, it was right.

She was mine, and I wasn't going to let her walk away.

24

nna

ALL THE BONES IN MY BODY DISSOLVED. I WAS PANTING FOR BREATH, MY SKIN SLICK with sweat, Nick pinning me into place. I couldn't move, even if I wanted to. Minutes ago, all I'd needed was to get as far away from Nick as possible. Now, with him on top of me, even with his solid weight pinning me in place, he was still too far away. I wanted him in me, a part of me. *One.*

I'd never felt anything like that orgasm. It was light years better than any I'd given myself with my trusty vibrator. I had no idea a male-induced orgasm could be so unbelievably amazing. I couldn't help but grin. The endorphin rush was better than any exercise class. Holy shit, that had been incredible.

"You want to walk away from that?" Nick asked, his voice almost a taunt. I slowly opened my eyes, looked up at him. His gaze was heavy lidded, his brow furrowed. His cheeks had bright flags of color on them, a slight sheen of sweat coated his brow. He was tense, angry, aroused. I couldn't miss his erection pressing hard against me. He'd made me forget. Forget that I shouldn't want him. That I should just say goodbye.

"Nick, it's not about sex." I had to be reasonable. One of us did. When the lust faded, what would be left?

I was lying; the lust wouldn't fade. Deep down, I knew this. This *thing* between us wasn't normal.

"The hell it's not." He got a firm grip on my hair, gently tugged. Made me look into his dark eyes, where I was afraid I'd get lost forever. "It's about sex, and chemistry, and everything else that draws you to me, like I'm drawn to you, yet you want to walk away from all of it."

I wasn't scared of him, of his intensity. His passion ruled him now and I had to be strong enough to fight it. He swallowed and I watched the movement.

He lowered his head to my breast, pulled one nipple, now soft and pliant from my release into his mouth, gave a hard pull that had me crying out. Lifting his head, he watched me once more, those dark eyes gleaming.

"You can't use sex to prove your point." I was breathing hard once again, arching into him. The little wire that ran from the tips of my breasts to my very core pulled tight, reawakened my need for Nick.

"I'm not going to have sex with you," he told me, although I knew that's exactly what he wanted to do. "Not tonight. And I'm not doing this to prove a point. I'm showing you what we have, what we can be. We'll figure out what to do about Moretti together. Your half-sister, too. No running away."

He was so stubborn! Yes, God, yes what we had was incredible. Could we survive it? Could we survive Moretti? Nick's life wasn't a risk I was willing to take. "Moretti is dangerous. Nick, please—"

"So am I," he said, his voice decisive. "And I won't take no for an answer."

He sat up, one foot still on the floor, and slid his hands slowly up my thighs, catching the cotton of my skirt in his fingers as he went.

I reached down to push at his hands, but he wasn't to be deterred. "Nick, what are you doing?"

His thumbs brushed over my inner thighs, leaving a path of tingling skin only to stop inches away from exposing my panties. Everything about Nick, how he touched, how he pushed me, how he said he wanted me, was too much. What he was doing was working. I'd had an orgasm only minutes before, but I wanted another one. I wanted another Nick Malone-made orgasm. It was likely I always would. Was this what he was telling me?

"I would *never* use your body to prove a point, love. Know that. I'm making you come because words aren't working. You need to *feel* to know there's too much at stake just to run away." As he spoke, his hands worked their way up to my hips, my skirt now bunched up. I felt the cool air on my legs, knew by the flare of heat in his eyes he could see my panties, see they were wet from my orgasm.

This, oh...this was what he was trying to get across to me, but I wouldn't relent. The man was ruthless. But gentle. His thumbs slid back and forth over the lacy edge of my panties and I arched my hips—I couldn't help it—up into his touch. My skin was hot, almost feverish, every nerve ending awake and responsive to Nick's hands. The way he made me feel, the way he looked at me only enhanced...everything.

"I'm going to make you come until you agree with me."

Oh God, he was going to kill me with orgasms. He wasn't giving me a choice, actually ripped my control from me. Nick shifted back on the couch and slowly shimmied my panties down my legs, raising goose bumps in his wake. I was completely exposed to him, my blouse parted, my skirt at my waist. I was too aroused to be embarrassed.

Nick's gaze raked over me as he tucked my panties into his shirt pocket, the cocky bastard, then lowered himself down between my spread thighs. He nudged my leg wide, my foot falling to the floor, opening me up to him. Now, I was embarrassed. I tried to bring my knees together, but he was having none of it, his hand stopping me.

"So pretty," he said, his eyes almost black, every line of his body taut as he looked his fill. "So fucking pretty." As if I didn't feel vulnerable and open enough, he moved my other leg, lifted it up over his shoulder and I cried out his name in surprise. Modesty didn't matter to him, or he was ignoring me, because he lowered his head and I felt his hot breath over my very center. *Oh my God.* He was going to... Embarrassment was gone, driving need took over. I was close...so, so close. He only had to touch me and I'd go off like a firecracker. *Please.*

"I've dreamed about doing this to you. Get ready, you're going to come. Again. And again until you agree to stay."

I AWOKE SPRAWLED ACROSS MY BED, OPENING MY EYES TO THE SOFT MORNING light. The muted sounds of the city filtered in, and I could tell just by listening that it was still very early. My arm reached out to touch the space where Nick had slept. The only indication of his being there was a dent in the pillow and the sheet pulled back. His scent lingered, but the man was missing.

A quick flare of panic jolted me upright. I looked around. The clock read a little after six. Had he left? Had he done what I'd asked—no demanded—him to do? Was he now on his way back to Denver? The white sheet pooled about my waist and I was naked beneath, my nipples tightening in the cool air. Or maybe it was the memory of what he did to me the night before. His clothes weren't on the floor, no cell phone on the bedside table. No shoes. Listening closely, no sound came from the other room. He'd left and he hadn't even said goodbye!

Wait. Had he done the things to me last night as a way of saying goodbye? Who was I kidding? He'd pushed me to three orgasms before I gave in and agreed that he should stay, that I didn't want him to leave. My body tingled at the thoughts of what he'd done to me. But where was the man that went with the skill?

I was being completely irrational. Emotions were overwhelming common sense. Take a deep breath and think.

I smelled coffee.

He was still here. Butterflies fluttered in my belly and something akin to... happiness swept through me. Made me feel giddy. It was a strange sensation, definitely something very unfamiliar. Nick hadn't left. *He was here.*

I dashed to the bathroom, brushed my teeth before throwing on some fresh clothes. After last night and what he'd done to me, I shouldn't be modest anymore, but I was. Perhaps even more so now. I wasn't prepared to face him naked in the daylight and would probably be some time before I was able to do so.

As I opened the door to the living room, trepidation swept through me. Would he mean what he'd said last night? Had he changed his mind? Was he just getting some coffee before he left? I inwardly rolled my eyes at my wayward thoughts, took another deep breath, and sucked it up.

Nick sat on the couch, hair askew, wearing only—oh man, only his jeans. No shirt. He was confident in his body. No modesty issues with him.

I came around the couch and saw he was on his cell. He looked up at me, talking quietly to the person on the line and I gave him a little smile. He held out his hand and I took it, relieved. Giddy, once again. As I sat down, he pulled me in close to his side, his arm wrapped around me.

As he listened to the person talk, he kissed the top of my head. Soft, gentle. Tender, even. His skin was warm and I could see every cut line of his muscles. The crisp hair on his chest tapered into a V and then into a line that disappeared behind the unbuttoned waistband of his jeans. I tried not to drool at the first sight of him without his shirt. He smelled like my soap and something I was coming to recognize as Nick's own scent. I liked it, oh…I liked it a lot.

"Okay, let me know what time," he said, then disconnected. "Hi. Sleep okay?"

"Mmm," I murmured, reveling in just being held and the very fact that he hadn't left. Yes, I was dwelling on that, but I expected him to leave, no matter how much he'd been against it the night before.

Everyone left.

It was really only a matter of time. Even knowing that, it was hard to keep from feeling for him. Wanting him. Lusting after him. What we did last night, definitely lust. It hadn't been enough. The way my body warmed at my wayward thoughts meant it was learning to react to Nick. Warning bells should be going off, but who wanted to heed them when I knew what pleasure he could bring me? "I want coffee, but I don't want to get up."

I felt Nick smile against my forehead. "We could just stay here on the couch all day, continue where we left off last night."

I groaned. Literally groaned. The very idea of having Nick touch me again… made it slip out.

Nick shifted, turning his large body into me so I had to lean back. I was once again on my back on my couch and beginning to really like this position. Running his hand over my hair, he brushed it off my forehead. "Make sounds like that and see what happens."

The idea was very enticing. After I'd given in to Nick's demands last night, agreed I wouldn't go and get a new identity…again, I barely remembered he'd carried me to bed, held me all night.

I ran my fingers over his rough cheek, then back to hook behind his neck, feeling the silky texture of his short hair.

"We need to talk," Nick said, his eyes searching over my face, as if memorizing it. His breath was minty, with a hint of coffee. It made me wonder how long he'd been up.

"I like this position for talking," I replied.

Shifting, I bent a knee and slid my leg up next to his hip, allowing him to settle against my sex. It was his turn to groan. I felt him, hard and thick through our clothes. In my haste to dress, I'd put on a pair of cut-off shorts and a white tank top, not considering the easy access he had last night with my skirt.

Nick grinned, that wicked dimple forming and I was a goner. Melted, softened, *let go* all at once. He lowered his head to nuzzle first his nose, then his lips at my neck. Instinctively, I tilted my head to the side to give him better access. "I do, too. I can't think when you have me like this. I figured out how to deal with Moretti"—he shifted his hips like he did last night—"but we can save it for later."

"What? You came up with an idea?" I pushed up against his chest, the crisp hair springy against my palms. Nick nipped the spot where my neck and shoulder met and pleasure zinged through me. "God, Nick. I can't think...we need—"

"I love the way your skin tastes, how your body comes alive beneath my hands, my mouth."

A little moan of pleasure escaped my lips. "Moretti," I gasped.

"That's not the name I want to hear right now," Nick murmured against my neck. With one last little lick, he sat back.

Looking up at him, he was pure, virile male. His chest was broad, tanned and toned with slabs of muscle. He looked down at me with eyes almost black like midnight, dark and dangerous. His hair swept over his brow, tousled from sleep and my fingers. It was blatantly obvious his need for me was as strong as mine for him.

"I want to hear your idea. He's always going to be between us otherwise."

Nick's look softened. "Nothing will come between us." As he spoke, he ran a finger in lazy circles around my nipple through my tank top. His eyes followed his finger's ministrations. "He's just a distraction, love, but you're right. Once we get him off our backs, then I can take you to bed. For days."

The very idea had me rethinking why I pushed him away to begin with. I wanted Nick with such intensity it stunned me. I wanted to solve the Moretti problem so we could fulfill Nick's fantasy...again and again.

Oh no. I'd done it.

When had Nick become a forever kind of guy? He'd slipped in so easily, so quickly. I'd tried to avoid him, held him away. Even pushed him away. Literally. But he'd gotten over those stupid walls I constantly built and maintained and into my heart. Now what was I going to do?

First, we had to survive Moretti's hit man on Monday. Then, I could think about it. Figure it out, decide what I was going to do about Nick, and how I felt about the whole *thing*. Did I really even want to love a man? I'd been doing just fine without one until now. My traitorous body got a few orgasms and offered up my heart for the chance of more. After what I experienced last night, I wanted more. He made me wet just by a roaming finger over my nipple, and I was panting with desire for him. Hell, yeah.

Nick sighed, pulled his hand away, then swung his large frame off me and sat at the far edge of the couch. My mouth watered, watching his back muscles ripple and flex as he shifted. He looked over at me and pointed to the kitchen. "You can't lie there like that with your nipples hard and not expect me to do things to you. Don't give me that look, you know what I'm talking about. If you really want to talk, go get some coffee and stay away from me."

I didn't want to mention he was the one who'd made my nipples that way so I just did as I was told—perhaps for the first time with him—and got up and poured myself of cup of coffee. Instead of sitting on the couch next to him, I moved to the armchair, sank in and waited.

"You actually gave me part of the idea last night."

I just raised my eyebrows in surprise and let him talk. Took a sip of my black coffee.

"You said getting a new identity would protect you. But Moretti's going to want proof you're dead. A body, photos, a news report of a murder. Something. He won't just let me, or that guy last night, return to Denver and report you disappeared. You'd still be a loose end."

I nodded, following him so far. "Even though all I did was get the wrong rental car?" The next time I got a rental car—if ever—I'd pop the trunk before I drove off the lot.

"Unfortunately, yes." He sighed. "So, we do what *you* want while giving Moretti what *he* wants."

"Okaaay," I said. My stomach plummeted. He wanted me to leave him?

"We stage your murder, then you, instead of getting a new identity, go back to your old one."

I almost spilled my coffee in my lap. I felt the blood drain from my head. Nick must have seen it because he grabbed my mug, placed it on the table and pushed my head between my legs. "Jesus, don't pass out on me."

Staring at the light fabric of my chair from between my legs, I said, "Go back to being Olivia? Why? I can get a perfectly new name and life."

"Because it's time to stop running, to stop hiding and take your life back."

I sat up slowly, took a deep breath. "I've spent over ten years hiding from my father and Todd. Why would I want to expose myself to them now?"

"Why wouldn't you?" He looked at me with concern, a deep V marring in his forehead. "What do they have over you?"

"They kept me in jail, wanted me to rot there. The entire justice system was against me. Who knows what they could do if I came back."

Nick took my hand in his. "Like you said, it's been over ten years. They have nothing on you. You have your money. They can't touch it. They can't touch you."

"They could try me for David's murder."

"With what? There's no evidence, no witnesses. It's been a decade."

"There's no statute of limitations on murder. I wasn't tried, so no acquittal, no double jeopardy." The coffee burned in my stomach. "It's not that simple."

"You walked into Scorch as if the world couldn't touch you because Moretti *owed* you. Owed you to help with your half-sister. If you were a guy, I'd say that took balls. You are so strong. So brave. You're not eighteen anymore." His gaze roved my face as if searching for something. "You can't help your half-sister if you aren't Olivia. She'll only trust the real you."

I laughed dryly, stood up. Looked down at Nick. "What makes you think she'll trust Olivia? You realize, I've never actually met her. I don't know what she's been told about me, if she's been brainwashed or raised to be a total bitch like her mother. She may even *want* to marry Todd."

Nick reached for his cell sitting on the table, ran his fingers over it, stood as well and held it out so I could see the screen. I closed my eyes, blocking out the picture it showed. Blocking out the memory. It was my engagement photo with Todd. He was behind me, his hand resting on my shoulder, both of us sharing our joy with the camera. My smile had been honest, showing my happiness at being wanted. Needed. But it was only short-term happiness. I had no doubt Todd was smiling because he was going to get his hands on my money. At least that's what he'd thought at the time.

"If she's a total psycho bitch, then it won't make a difference. But if she's in trouble like you think—perhaps hope, since that means she's a good person—she'll trust Olivia—you—because you've been in her shoes." Softly, Nick ran a finger down my cheek, and I opened my eyes. "You know what she's going through, what she'll go through if you don't help her. What I don't know is why. Why is your ex now marrying your step-sister?"

"It's pretty gross," I pointed out.

"Uh, yeah," Nick countered.

"Elizabeth's mom is an heiress. My dad wouldn't have married for love. My mom hadn't even been dead a year before their wedding. Drain parts."

"Huh?" Nick asked, looking confused.

"Her family invented some kind of drain part that's an industry standard. Let's just say there's a lot of money in plumbing." I grabbed my coffee off the table took a sip. Went to the kitchen and topped it off. "She's got early onset Alzheimer's. That's not public knowledge, but I dug it up online. My father wouldn't want that kind of information made public. Neither would Todd. Elizabeth's the sole heir."

"Holy shit," Nick murmured from the living room.

"Right. Holy shit. Elizabeth's mom is in her early fifties—"

"—so her life expectancy went from about thirty more years to just a few," Nick finished for me. He was working through it, could now see why Todd was ruthless. "Your ex needs to marry her now before the mother dies and someone else snatches her up. What if that money's all tied to your sister like your money was?"

"Maybe he's running out of options." I shrugged. "He's getting older so being a kept man with that kind of money might not be too bad. Besides, being an heiress to a plumbing supply empire is much more substantial than my inheritance from my mother." I stepped over to my desk, messed with my papers, unseeing. "It's really ironic. Like you said, I was fearless going into Scorch that night. I was so daring, just walking through that door, because I needed help to save Elizabeth. That was easy. I did that as *Anna*, and envisioned helping Elizabeth while staying as Anna. Period. Now, you're the one who's trying to push me to help my half-sister." Turning to face Nick, I added, "I'm the one that's balking. I just can't be Olivia again. People don't give up a new identity and return to the old one. That's insane."

Nick held up his hands. "Fine. Let's forget about that for a minute because that's not what we need to deal with first anyway. We can't help her unless we stay alive."

"Right, you're going to stage my murder." I was a little skeptical and it came out in my voice. Any idea with the word *murder* in it couldn't be good. "How are we going to pull that off?"

Nick grinned, his dimple winking at me. Like a little boy plotting an adventure. "With a little help from Uncle Frank."

25

rif

ANNA WASN'T TELLING ME SOMETHING. I COULD SEE IT IN HER EYES. I COULDN'T even imagine how hard this was for her, reliving the one time she'd let someone in, let her emotions rule, and she was tossed aside, left to rot in jail. She hadn't just been dumped, she was kept in jail by those she cared about, the men she believed cared about her. They'd just left her there. She'd been betrayed at a level even I couldn't fathom. Nadine had betrayed me, left me for another man. It had bothered me for years. Perspective changed quite a bit. Nadine's actions were nothing compared to Todd Lawton, to Grayson Edwards.

If Anna became Olivia again, she could be tried for killing her brother-in-law, just like she'd said. She hadn't gone to trial. Double jeopardy couldn't save her. To be released like she had, evidence had to be solid in her favor. Proof that she'd shot David Lawton in self-defense. How could it change after all this time?

Was this the only reason she was still in hiding, or was there more? As I peeled back the layers that made up Anna, I recognized there was more she wasn't sharing, something big, something that kept her fearful, paranoid even,

even years later. I had to find out what it was. I'd texted Peters to look into it, carefully, without drawing attention to his search.

In the meantime, we had a day to set my plan in motion. I had a few key players I needed to pull in to accomplish it and—

Anna's intercom rang.

"That's going to be Carrie," I told her as she walked over to answer it.

Anna tucked her hair behind her ears as she arched a brow in question. "Anything else you've got planned I should know about?" she asked before talking with the desk downstairs.

Not only had I moved into her place, I'd invited people over. If she liked her solitude, tough. She'd just have to deal. I was in her life now and it was something she'd have to get used to.

A minute later, Anna let Carrie in. My sister wore tan cargo shorts, a T-shirt with the Rangers logo on it and flip-flops. After a quick hug with Anna, who appeared completely surprised by the spontaneous gesture, Carrie turned to me, hand on hip. "Since when do you want to know about my boyfriend?"

"Since your latest just happens to be related to Frank Carmichael."

Carrie's mouth dropped open, and I reveled in the moment as I'd clearly figured out a secret of hers. Dating the nephew of a major crime boss would definitely be something she'd want to keep from her cop brother. "How...?"

Anna just looked between the two of us.

"At lunch the other day, you told me what *Uncle* Frankie likes for lunch. Is the nephew named Huey, Dewey or Louie?"

Carrie rolled her eyes. "Ha, ha," she said, her voice snarky as she slumped down on to my couch, propped her feet up on the coffee table. "His name is Adam and he's very nice."

"Nice. Nice?" I asked, full of brotherly exasperation. "Does he work for his uncle?"

Carrie shook her head. "No, he's a lawyer."

"A lawyer in the *family* who's not in the *family*?" I wondered. "No way." Not a chance little Adam Carmichael didn't work for his uncle.

"He's an ADA with the city, so fuck off," Carrie grumbled.

"That's one way to stay out of jail—well-placed relatives," I scoffed.

"You're one to talk," she countered.

"It's true, Nick. You work for Moretti and I seem to want you around," Anna admitted. She moved to sit in the armchair.

I clenched my teeth. I was undercover, for Christ's sake, not a blood relative of an East Coast crime boss. "Fine. We'll stay off that topic."

I still couldn't tell Anna I was a cop. She'd be pissed—understatement of the year—and probably run off and take on that new identity. At the moment, it was critical I made connections with the likes of Frank Carmichael and I couldn't do that if I was a cop. He wouldn't take a meeting from me then if I held up the last corned beef sandwich on the planet.

"You dragged me over here on a Saturday morning to talk about my dates?" Carrie wanted to know.

"You have more than one?"

I wanted her to line them all up so I could check them out. Carrie might be thirty-two years old, but it didn't mean I wouldn't shoot any asshole who treated her poorly.

"Save your alpha personality for Anna," Carrie grumbled, letting her head fall back against the couch cushion.

Anna just arched a brow and her gaze flicked down my body. Just a look like that had me getting hard, which wasn't good in front of my sister. Alpha with Anna was definitely working—for both of us.

To hide my *eagerness* for Anna, I walked to the kitchen to get a drink. My dick was running the show now and I needed that to stop. It wasn't going to see any action until I saved Anna, so I needed to get my brain in gear and focus on the dangerous shit. "I need you to set up a meeting for me with Uncle Frank," I called out.

Carrie sat up. I couldn't see her, but I knew this because her feet hit the floor. "Why would you want me to do that?"

"Because he's going to help me kill Anna."

I rested my forearms on the counter that looked out into the main room. Anna's eyes practically popped out of her head. I hadn't told her about that. Yet.

"What?" Carrie screeched. "How is Frank Carmichael going to help you? Do you really think he's going to actually keep you alive? And I mean *really* alive?"

I figured it out in the middle of the night. Sleep wouldn't come, not with the weight of trying to save Anna's life on me, nor her naked body pressed against me. I had to get us out of the shit storm we were now in. Fast. I could kill the other guy Moretti sent, but that would make me just like him. Evil and dirty. Even if it was in self-defense, I couldn't guarantee Anna wouldn't get hurt in the process.

If it came down to that man's life or Anna's, there was no choice. Just as the sky started to lighten with dawn, it came to me. It was perfect. I could take down Moretti—get him put in jail for good—finish my stint undercover, and save Anna's neck. Pulling it off would be something else entirely.

"Carmichael hates Moretti as much as we do." Thoughts of Moretti and Carmichael made my hard-on go away and I was able to come out from behind the counter. "We're going to offer Uncle Frank a deal that will make him very happy, keep us alive and put Moretti behind bars," I told them.

"You work for Moretti. Don't your loyalties lie with him?" Anna asked.

God, she was so pretty. Even in cutoffs and a tank top, she was perfect. I knew how soft her skin was, how good she tasted, how she looked when she came. She had no idea of her effect on me. How desirable she was. On the direction of my thoughts, which seemed to divert off of what was going to save us to the feel of her beneath me. I was whipped. Big time.

Focus. No, my loyalties didn't lie with Moretti. I'd taken an oath to protect and serve, not shoot and kill. He'd ordered a man to finish both of us. Moretti didn't do loyalty.

"He sent a guy to kill you—and I'm not talking about me. Why would I side with that asshole when I have you?"

She also didn't have any sense of her own worth. After everything I'd said, everything I'd done to her, Anna still didn't see how important she was. I'd tried words, I'd tried actions. It seemed time and trust would be pivotal for her to realize this once and for all. "Don't you get it, woman? My loyalties lie with you." I moved and knelt down in front of her, tilted her chin up with my finger. Forced her to look at me. "Nothing else matters but you."

Carrie cleared her throat.

"Set up a meeting with Carmichael," I said to Carrie, but kept my eyes on Anna. "Today. Dangle Moretti in front of him if you need to."

26

rif

CARRIE HAD DONE HER JOB. WE WERE ON THE SUBWAY HEADED TO CARMICHAEL'S Brooklyn home for a meeting at two. I sat between both women on the row of seats, only a few other people in the car with us. The clatter of the wheels was loud, the car cooler than the summer air above ground. Once we had word of the meeting time, Anna and I took showers—separately, intentionally, but not what I really wanted—and dressed for our roles.

It was important—crucial—we got Carmichael's help. I hadn't come up with any other way to get Moretti to believe our deaths. He didn't take people's word. The second guy he sent to kill Anna, and me, was proof of that. She might be brave. She might be strong, but Anna didn't have the experience or ruthless know-how—thank God—to deal with Moretti.

There she sat, wearing another little skirt, flowing as if a stiff wind could kick it up. It wasn't overly sexy; not skintight or revealing, but it did a number on my desire for her, continuing to ratchet it up a notch to the point where once I had her beneath me, I worried I wouldn't be gentle. I'd lifted her skirt once and driven her to multiple orgasms. Once we had Moretti taken care of, I planned on doing it again.

I had blue balls from hell and only a time, or ten, with Anna was going to make it better. Would I always think like this from now on? Would my mind be perpetually distracted by a glimpse of her smooth thigh or remembering the taste of her?

This distraction would get me killed while undercover, so Carmichael had to pan out. Then Moretti would be behind bars, I'd be back on the beat and I could continue my pussy-whipped daydreaming without the chance of a hit on our heads.

"I figured your boyfriend would be riding with us. Thought he wouldn't want to miss out," I told my sister. I wanted to poke at her for her choice in boyfriends, but I didn't have much fight in my words. No matter what I felt, I couldn't leave Carrie out of this. She was our connection, our introduction to Carmichael. Without it, we wouldn't make it through the front door, so I didn't need to piss her off. Hell, I didn't even know where the front door was.

"He's meeting us there," Carrie replied, equally civilly. She probably didn't want to mess with me either, ensuring she was in the meeting with Carmichael. No way would she want to miss out on it.

I felt Anna's hand on my biceps, turned to her.

"I can't be Olivia again, Nick," Anna said, her voice quiet.

This is what had kept her quiet all morning? Worrying about taking her old life back?

"Let's get you dead first, then we can figure out who you're going to be."

"No." Anna shook her head as she spoke. "We need to figure this out now."

"What's the matter?" Carrie asked.

Anna stood, leaned against the pole in front of us to brace herself against the sway of the car. "Nick wants me to go back to being Olivia."

Carrie looked between the two of us. "What's wrong with that?"

"People don't just ditch a new identity. They take one for a really good, really dangerous reason. I can't go back. That wasn't a life, that was existing," Anna said.

I noticed her fingers were white holding on to the bar.

Carrie cocked her head to the side. "Isn't that what you've been doing for the past twelve years, *just existing*?"

Anna looked away, down the length of the car, her cheeks flushing pink with what I imagined was shame. She shrugged casually. "Yes, but I don't like the person I used to be. Waiting for years and years for a father to claim me.

Embarrassed just thinking about how gullible I was when Todd said he wanted to marry me. Naïve. Clueless. Stupid."

The last she spat out, bitterness lacing her words.

I pictured her as a child, wild hair and gangly limbs, waiting anxiously for any word, any kernel of love to come from her father. To watch as other kids went home for holidays and summer breaks to their families, knowing that she wasn't loved. She'd had a cruel childhood, but she'd endured, survived. Until she was duped—used—by her ex. I clenched my fists in my lap, wishing the bastard was here so I could kill the fucker.

"You weren't stupid. You were tricked," I told her.

I could see it. Carrie could, too. That's because we were on the outside, seeing her life as one long timeline. Anna saw it as failure on her part. She believed something was wrong with *her* for people to treat her like they had.

"You were strong and brave and just eighteen," Carrie shared. "Don't let Nick tell you about the stupid crap I did when I was that age."

I couldn't help rolling my eyes at the memories. "Who wasn't stupid and naïve and clueless at eighteen? Most people weren't attacked and then tossed in jail. Divorced even. You never gave that girl a chance to prove herself besides becoming Anna."

"Are you worried about your ex?" Carrie put her hand on the seat next to her at a sudden lurch.

Anna considered Carrie's question as we pulled into a station, watched as people came on the train: a family with tired children, a runner with earbuds in, an elderly couple.

"I'm scared of him. Of what I remember him to be like. What he did to me. He's toxic and I don't want to be anywhere near him again," she confessed.

"How did you think you'd help Elizabeth?" No way she could help her half-sister without running into Todd or her father. No question they'd have that poor girl on lockdown.

"I wanted you to do it for me." She ran her fingers over the cotton of her skirt. "I'd just be in the background and able to stay safely hidden behind my new identity. I just knew I had—have—to keep her from marrying Todd."

"What ammunition do you have against him? I know you have something."

She lifted her chin. I was starting to recognize that as her tell. She had a secret and she didn't want to share.

"I do. I have something you can use against him." She glanced around the subway car. "I don't want to get into it here. Now."

"Okay, love. It's time, don't you think? Reappearing after all these years is going to throw him off, on top of whatever you have against him. Don't you just want to fuck him over?" I wanted to do more than fuck with the guy. I wanted to kill him. One thing at a time.

"What my brother is trying to say in his crude way is: Get back at Todd. Show him you can handle him, then make him pay. Keep Elizabeth from him. Keep him from getting what he wants. Again. Revenge is going to be awesome."

Carrie's words coaxed a smile from Anna, a small nod. "You're right. I want revenge, more than you can even imagine. But first, Nick, kill me. Let's get rid of Moretti so we can move on. So I can move on. It's time."

The evil glint in Anna's eye made me rock hard. God, what about her didn't? She was plotting. I could see it. In the short time I'd known her, she'd recognized she was stronger, braver and more powerful than she ever imagined. Having someone on your side, rooting for you, supporting you, did that.

I'd showed this to her, showed her she was strong, but *we,* the two of us together, were even stronger. Through more than just words, through actions. Getting her beneath me, getting her to respond to my touch, was powerful business. It wasn't just about sex. It was about recognizing there was more to life than just *living*. She just didn't know that it was a two-way street. Her newfound strength came from trusting me, but I found my own strength in knowing that I held that trust, protected it. Cherished it. It made me feel like a super hero: powerful, invincible, whole.

27

nna

Instead of taking twenty minutes to get to a quiet street in Brooklyn from Manhattan, it took forty-five. We stayed on the subway an extra stop, backtracking via a coffee shop, a Jewish delicatessen and merging in with a group of Japanese tourists for a block before Nick felt confident we weren't being tailed by Moretti's man. Nick didn't want the guy to know we were visiting Carmichael, which seemed like a good idea.

A very attractive man answered Carmichael's door. It was obvious this guy was Adam since Carrie stepped up off the stoop and was pulled into his arms for a hug while Nick looked ready to clock him. The guy, over six feet and built like a football linebacker, gave her a soft kiss on the forehead before turning to Nick. The way they sized each other up, I had no doubt if his girlfriend's brother wasn't standing there watching, Adam would give Carrie a wholly different kind of kiss. Adam had sandy-blond hair, very blue eyes and a soft smile. The last was for Carrie, but when he looked to Nick, his expression changed. Guarded, assessing.

Nick glared at Adam with what I recognized now as the Look of Death. "Hurt my sister and I'll kill you and bury you in a place even your uncle won't be able to find," he said, his voice dark and cold. It was the voice he saved for strangers and those who pissed him off. I remembered it from his office at Scorch when he thought I'd killed Bobby Lane. It was difficult to tell whether Nick was joking or not. From his expression, I was leaning more toward him being completely serious. Since he had an inside track with the underworld of society, his words were also very plausible. Adam pulled Carrie in even closer, I'd even consider a taunt, as she rolled her eyes at her brother. Her arms went around Adam's waist and Nick's eyes narrowed into slits following the movement.

"Good. You're watching out for her as a brother should," Adam told Nick, with a nod of approval. "But now…you're not the only one taking care of her."

Another moment passed, then Nick somewhat grudgingly held out his hand. They shook and the tension dissolved.

"Men," Carrie grumbled. "Seriously, you guys are a bunch of Neanderthals."

I was a little wistful at the exchange. Carrie had no idea what she had. A brother who cared enough about her to grill and potentially kill a boyfriend to protect her. A boyfriend who knew his role wasn't just to fuck her and take her money. Adam seemed really to want Carrie, cared about her wellbeing, to the point of overbearing, alpha male. After spending my entire life on my own, overbearing and Neanderthal sounded pretty darn good.

"You must be Anna." Adam smiled as he shook my hand, his large one dwarfing mine. He had a firm grip, but gentle.

"Be nice to her, Adam," Carrie warned.

"I'm always nice to women. I would never hurt a lady, you know that." Adam kissed the top of her head, then winked at me.

"Hello," I said, taken in by his smile. He didn't have a dimple like Nick, but he did have that appeal that I had no doubt made women fall at his feet. Carrie hadn't quite done that, but she was definitely smitten. The way Adam held her, possessively, it was obvious he felt the same. I darted a glance at Nick, his jaw clenched tightly. Nick might have shaken the guy's hand, but he didn't have to like him.

"Come inside, please." Adam stepped back, keeping Carrie snug against his side, a place where she seemed perfectly content. I entered first, Nick following behind after taking one last look down the street. His hand was on my waist, which was reassuring, and remarkably arousing in its simplicity. I inwardly groaned; I was turning into a nympho, thinking about Nick and sex at a time like this. He'd said he'd have me begging for it. I was getting close.

We were in the main foyer, a staircase was on the right, to the left a formal living room decorated with fine antiques, a hallway down the middle. It was cooler inside, but not air conditioned. "My uncle's in the family room."

Adam led us to the back of the house and the family room, clearly an addition on the old structure, with large windows and skylights. It was bright, sunny and comfortable. I was a little surprised by the Carmichael home, expecting a shady storefront with a bunch of oversized thugs manning the door. Frank Carmichael would be a man with large gold chains about his neck, an equally gold tooth winking when he smiled. I'd seen too many movies. That was film, and my overextending imagination.

Instead, a man in his mid-sixties stood when we entered. There wasn't much of a family resemblance to Adam. Carmichael's hair was blond mixed with threads of gray. Laugh lines formed at the corners of his eyes and his mouth, making him appear kind and gentle. He wore khakis and a pressed polo shirt as if we were keeping him from a day on the links. This was the man who ruthlessly cornered the drug market in the US? This was the man who handled a bunch of Ukrainian ruffians like they were kindergartners? Where was his gun? The dead bodies?

"Carrie, my love, how are you?" He held out his hand for her.

Adam released his hold on Carrie and she leaned up to give Frank Carmichael a peck on the cheek. "Hi, Uncle Frank. Thanks for seeing us on such short notice."

"Anything for you," he replied, his voice almost tender.

Carrie turned to us. "This is my brother, Nick, and Anna Scott."

Frank smiled at both of us, shook our hands and had us sit down. There was a large, cream sofa with two matching chairs, one on each of three sides of a coffee table. Nick and I sat on the sofa, facing a stone fireplace with French doors flanking it on either side. There was no fire because it was close to ninety, but the doors were open to the warm sunshine.

"So, you work for Moretti," Frank Carmichael said. He sat in one of the armchairs, Carrie in the other across from him.

"My uncle doesn't like small talk," Adam told us as he sat on the armrest next to Carrie.

I wasn't really interested in small talk anyway. The sooner we were out of here, the better. My nerves were starting to fray. Not knowing the details of Nick's plan made me feel vulnerable, exposed, with no real way to protect myself. It was like walking into the lion's den with dangling pieces of meat attached to me. Frank could decide to kill us, not just *pretend* to do so. I just had to trust—which wasn't easy for me—that Nick knew what he was doing.

I looked to Nick, waiting, just as Frank did, to learn the details of this meeting. He'd just walked us both into the lair of the enemy, which was a very dangerous feat. I knew that firsthand. It was similar to walking into Scorch, knowing I'd be dealing with Moretti or someone who worked for him. Well aware the place was more than a simple nightclub. Just like Frank Carmichael was more than a sixty-something golfer.

Attraction didn't differentiate between good or bad. As Nick said, we had chemistry. I'd known he wasn't *good* when I sought him out at Scorch, but I'd gone anyway. Wanted him anyway. Felt that pull between us. Now, Nick had worked his way into my heart. Deep enough to even say I loved him. I'd never loved someone before, so I didn't know what it felt like. Had nothing to compare to this feeling. Was love when you wanted him with such a desperation you were afraid to let him out of your sight, out of your grasp? Was love when you'd rather push him away and go on without him so he wouldn't be killed? Or was love knowing he lived on the wrong side of the law and trusted him anyway?

If those were indicators, then I was officially in love. It had happened fast; I'd known him only ten days. It was enough. Perhaps I'd only needed that first moment, when I ran into him at the wedding reception, for him to change my life. One meeting and my heart had been captured.

That love, the need for Nick, didn't really seem to care what he did for a living. He may have killed people, hurt them, ruined their lives. How could I condemn him for that when I'd done the same, albeit for a very different reason, but a killer was a killer. How he treated me, how he made me feel, were what counted. Walking into Frank's home, asking Nick's boss' enemy—by proxy, his—to help save us, showed *his* depth of feeling.

I wanted Nick to leave Moretti, leave that lifestyle behind. But when Moretti had sent that man to kill us, Nick made up his own mind, masterminding a way to save us both. He'd done so much, changed so much for me. I hadn't been quite as flexible, adjusting so easily to this...relationship we had. Once we worked through this plan—whatever Nick had devised—we could both be free of Moretti once and for all.

"Small talk isn't necessary, Mr. Carmichael. To answer your question, yes, I work for Moretti. I run one of his nightclubs in Denver."

I remembered the place, the crowds, how Nick took control. How he'd been so angry with me. So intense.

Frank rested his elbows on the armrests of his chair, steepled his fingers together. "Don't let the fact that you're in my home keep you from remembering who I am. What I do for a living," Frank warned.

I shifted in my chair, ready to bolt if things fell apart. This was insane! I knew exactly what happened when you got involved with crime bosses firsthand, and with Moretti, that had been accidental. This, this was intentional.

I didn't doubt for a moment that Frank was intelligent, calculating and ruthless. He didn't get to be where he was in his business without a little cunning. Maybe that was what Bobby Lane had lacked. A person didn't get fired in this line of work.

"I have to admit, you look like a smart guy," Frank continued. "This stunt... and it is a stunt, is just plain stupid."

Adam took Carrie's hand, kissed her knuckles. He didn't seem bothered by his uncle's choice of professions, nor how he talked to Nick. Were men always so forthright in their conversations? Carrie didn't seem worried either, although she'd met the man before, more than once it seemed. Was I the only one freaking out here?

"No, sir. I'm well aware of who you are," Nick countered. "That's actually why I asked my sister for this meeting with you. I have something you might want."

I noticed Nick didn't comment on Frank's opinion of his intelligence.

Frank arched a brow. "In trade for..."

"Killing us," Nick said, pointing his finger between the two of us.

I gulped. *Fake* killing us. He'd forgotten the most important word.

"Now you have my attention," Frank said, crossing a foot over a knee.

"Moretti sent a guy here to kill Anna. Tomorrow. I want you to kill her first."

Nick paused, taking his time.

"Go on," Frank said. Not only did he have the older man's attention, but Carrie and Adam were listening, too.

"Moretti will want proof she's dead. If you were the witness, called Moretti to tell him you saw her body, then he'll believe you."

"Why should I get involved in this?" Frank shrugged. "This is a problem between you and your boss."

"He thinks I work for you," I said, speaking for the first time. I didn't want to be in the spotlight, but Nick was trying to save me, and I owed it to him to help.

Frank turned his gaze to me, cocked his head. "And why is that?"

"Because Bobby Lane was in the trunk of the car I was driving."

Frank just stared at me for a moment, his blue eyes penetrating and a little unnerving, then threw his head back and laughed. "Moretti thinks I put out the hit on Bobby Lane?"

I glanced at Nick, then nodded. I was used to making business arrangements with contractors and plumbers and interior decorators, not a regional crime lord.

Frank laughed some more. "And used you to do it."

I wasn't sure if I should be insulted or not. I'd killed David in the same way as Bobby Lane. I knew what it took. I could've killed Bobby Lane; shooting a gun was second nature to me. I wouldn't want to, but I *could* do it.

"I heard about that, but there was never any news that he was found in your car." His blue eyes met mine, held. "No news of *you*."

I smoothed out nonexistent wrinkles from my skirt. "That's because I was given the wrong car at my hotel."

Frank's smile slipped, froze in place as he thought about my words. "You're telling me you got the wrong car and got pinned with Bobby Lane's murder?"

His stare was a little unnerving, but I refused to back down. When Nick took my hand and gave it a squeeze, I took a deep breath to calm my nerves. "Not by the police, but Moretti, yes."

"That stupid son of a—" Frank ran a hand over his mouth.

"Now you see why we're here," Nick concluded.

"Uncle Frankie, you've got to help them out," Adam added.

Frank held up a hand. "Now hold on. I didn't say I wouldn't help. I just needed to hear about the whole mess, and it is a mess."

I couldn't agree more.

"There's nothing more I'd like to do than fuck over...excuse me, ladies, Moretti." Frank actually rubbed his hands together.

Nick gave a tentative smile, although probably remaining careful with his words. "Here's my idea. We let Moretti continue to believe Anna works for you. When you find out Anna is *consorting* with me, one of Moretti's men, you kill her. Perhaps you find us together and kill me, too. The man Moretti sent plans to kill both of us, so if you kill me first, you'll do Moretti a favor."

"Very Romeo and Juliet," Frank said.

"With a crime family twist," Adam added.

"You said you have something I might want." Frank wasn't a guy that would do something for nothing. He wanted to know what was in it for him. What would he receive in return for helping us? I had money, but he seemed to have enough of it already.

"As a thank you for your help, you can help put Moretti away for life."

Frank's eyes lit up like a kid in a candy shop. "How so?"

Nick leaned forward, bracing his elbows on his knees. "After you kill us, you call Moretti and tell him what you did. You'll follow a script and get Moretti to cop to sending a man after Anna, that he'd planned her murder, planned mine. Moretti killed Bobby Lane. No one else has claimed it and he hasn't sought retribution. I can't prove it, nor say who pulled the trigger, but you can probably coax that out of him as well. Accessory. Conspiracy. Principal in a murder. With that on tape, he'll go down for life."

"How do you plan to keep these fake murders from putting me in jail?"

Carrie answered this question. "This is where Adam and I come in. I'll get the wiretap on your phone from the police, get them in on this. Adam will help make the murders look real so it's believable."

I didn't want to know how Adam had experience with that, nor did I want to consider what *real* meant in this case.

"What happens to both of you once you're dead?" Frank wondered.

Nick glanced at me. "There aren't many ways out of a group like Moretti's. Being dead's one of them." He paused, no doubt wondering if Frank had a similar arrangement with his business. "If you kill me, I don't have to work for Moretti anymore."

"You don't want to stay in the life?" Frank asked.

Nick looked at me, his gaze soft, warm. "With all due respect, sir, to you and your line of work, but hell no."

"What about you, Anna?" Frank looked to me. "It could end up on the news. What about your family?"

"I don't have any family, so that's not an issue." I gave him a small smile to let him know it didn't matter.

"Your life as you know it will be over. Are you prepared for that?" he added.

I listened to Frank, but looked at Nick. Read from his expression that things were going to be okay. "Yes. I have another life waiting for me."

Nick arched a brow, no doubt wondering if this new life was as Olivia Edwards or as some new identity.

Frank was quiet, and thankfully didn't push.

"So, Nick"—Frank paused, waiting for Nick to look at him—"this took balls...guts coming here like this." He waved his hand in the air. "You could've come here for Moretti, to shoot me in my own home. Your plan, it's pretty big. Enlisting me to help, even bigger. You could've just bought two tickets to Paris to avoid the hit man Monday. Instead, you come up with this scheme so Moretti's off both your backs. Permanently." He shifted forward in his chair so his elbows rested on his knees, his fingers steepled together. "The way I figure it, you're either in love with Anna or you're a cop."

Nick froze. I froze. Out of the corner of my eye, I saw Carrie whip her head around to look at her brother.

Nick pivoted his body to face me, his back to Frank. He looked at me with his dark eyes, searched my face. His lip curved up, his dimple appearing. "You're right, Mr. Carmichael." Nick's gaze dropped to my mouth. "I'm in love with Anna—"

I smiled, instantly and brilliantly, tears pricking my eyes. I'd never heard anyone tell me that before. The words were new, rusty to my ears, but the swell of emotion, the overwhelming feeling of joy pumped through my body with every beat of my heart. He loved me. *Nick loved me!* How had that happened? I'd tried and tried to push him away, keep my distance, to protect myself, my heart from him.

Reaching out, he grabbed my hand and pulled me to him for a quick, rough kiss. It was filled with a tenderness and need I'd never felt before. His hand at the nape of my neck held me in place, even after he pulled back and stared into my eyes. He was breathing hard, his eyes dark.

"—and I'm also a cop."

What? What had he said? My smile fell, but the tears remained, slid down my cheeks. Now they fell out of something other than happiness. "You're a..." I swallowed past the lump in my throat as I pulled back out of his grip.

"Cop." Nick took my hand as if he needed a lifeline, but I yanked it away.

What had he said?

"Anna, love, I'm undercover."

Undercover? He didn't work for Moretti? He hadn't come to kill me? I'd been waging an internal battle about falling for a guy who had hired hit man and goon on his resume when he was really a police officer? I was smarter than this. The saying *love makes you blind* was certainly true. Thinking back, the clues were there. Probing questions, knowing where to find me, his *friend* who had investigated me. Nick had been a cop with me all along.

I stood on shaky legs, looked down at the man who'd just made my life complete in one moment, then ripped it to shreds the next. "I...I've got to...I—"

I couldn't stay here. Embarrassed, shamed and afraid at the same time. Had Carrie known? I flicked my gaze to her. Of course, she had. She sat there looking guilty. She knew her brother didn't work for Moretti. Knew he was a cop. I thought she was my friend, that she really actually cared about me. No, she just wanted to help her brother.

And Nick... God! All this time, spouting how much I should trust him, how often he'd pushed me to tell him the truth, had been keeping this a secret. He'd lied. *Lied.* I'd been right, thinking it safer to keep people at a distance. I was right to be wary, paranoid even, of people's intentions. No one wanted me for just me. They always wanted something.

Nick needed a way out just as much as I did. If Moretti found out he was a cop, he'd hunt Nick forever. So much for protecting me. Nick needed this to save his own skin. Nothing, and no one, else.

Men were all the same. And I'd just spent the last few minutes thinking about how much I loved this one. How honest and true, how freaking trustworthy he was. I was still that stupid eighteen-year-old craving love, needing to feel wanted.

No more.

Doing the only thing I could to protect myself, even though my heart had been ripped from my chest and stomped on, I fled. Instead of having another person leave me, use me and then abandon me, this time, I escaped.

28

rif

SHIT. *SHIT*. I WATCHED ANNA DASH OUT OF THE FAMILY ROOM, WINCED WHEN THE front door slammed behind her. Her reaction didn't come as much of a surprise. I knew she'd hate me when she found out I was a cop. Not because I didn't actually work for Moretti, that I figured she'd be happy about, once she stopped being angry. It was the fact that I'd lied to her. Or lied by omission. I had opportunity the entire time we'd known each other, starting as early as the wedding reception to avoid deception.

At first, I'd kept it secret because I thought *she* worked for Moretti, then the bastard himself had set me clear on that and redirected me to consider her a contract killer for Carmichael. I'd been a complete idiot to even think that. Sitting here with the man, no way would he put Anna in any kind of danger his work might create. I'd let my anger at being tricked, being deceived by a woman to blind me to what I knew deep down.

Anna was innocent. Of everything.

Nadine had done a number on me when we were married. Scarred my emotions to the point where I didn't trust a woman to get close, to always question her motives. She was in my past and I'd let her control my present. Ruin it. No, Nadine hadn't done that; I hadn't seen or heard from her in years.

I'd done it to myself.

Once I realized how foolish I'd been, I knew the only way to protect Anna from Moretti was to keep Moretti thinking I was his employee. If Moretti knew I was undercover, retribution against me would have been swift. Then who would have protected Anna?

No one. She had no one to watch over her. I ran my hand through my hair, frustration and desperation burning a hole in my gut.

I was torn between chasing her down and working out the details of the plan with Carmichael. I put my hands on my knees, rested my face in my palm. Jesus, what a mess. Right now, it was more important to keep Anna alive than to have her love me back. She couldn't die on me now. I'd never said the words *I love you* and meant them before. I intended to keep Anna around so she could hear it again and prove myself worthy.

"Christ, I fucked up," I muttered toward the floor.

"You kept her alive," Adam said. Turning my head, I looked at him. The guy wasn't an asshole, but I wanted him to be. I wanted to redirect my anger onto him instead of myself. "Yeah, Carrie filled me in. If Moretti found out you were undercover, you'd be dead, and so would Anna. No question."

"If...and I'm using the word *if* here—" Carmichael said, his voice dark, his look menacing, "—I found out someone was undercover on my team, they'd be deader than Bobby Lane."

"She hates me, and that's my fault," I told him. "I have to protect her, regardless. Are you in, Mr. Carmichael? I've got my girl out there on her own so I need to know right now if I'm wasting my time." I cocked my head toward the front door.

"I don't like your tone," he replied coldly.

"Like I said, I love her. No one fucks with my woman, so I need to bring Moretti down. Today, before that bastard finds her and finishes her. How would you feel if you found out someone wanted to harm your wife?"

Carmichael went calm, still. A lethal gleam came into his eyes.

"I can speak for my uncle when I say we respect your motivation," Adam said, his words diffusing the tension. He pulled Carrie up from her seat with a gasp from her lips, slid into her spot and pulled her down on to his lap. The hold about her waist was tight enough to indicate he never planned on letting her go.

That's how I felt about Anna; I wanted to grab hold of her and never let go. Carmichael murmured something under his breath.

"Uncle Frank, tell him you'll help him," Carrie pleaded.

"I don't like having a cop sitting in my family room on a Saturday under false pretenses," Uncle Frank said, his voice indicated that I'd fucked up. Big time. "It's not only your fault, but Carrie's and Adam's as well, since they both knew you were undercover." He looked to the couple for confirmation. Their uncomfortable silence was agreement enough. "But if Moretti thinks you work for him, then you work for him. Undercover or not. Your plan is sound."

"Uncle Frank," Carrie repeated, sounding a tad contrite for her deception.

"I'll help. It will be my pleasure," Carmichael told me as he cracked his knuckles. "Like you said, no one fucks with our women."

Carrie nodded, smiled her relief. "Great. Let's get this done," she told him. She turned to look at Adam. "Get the stuff we need to make these murders look legit. I'll tackle the wire tap angle with my contacts on the force. Grif...thank God I can call you that again, go get your girl. Once Uncle Frank has it set, I'll text you where to meet. Shall we agree to eight tonight?"

I looked to Carmichael and Adam. They both nodded, so I did as well. Only five hours to find Anna.

"What are you waiting for, young man? You heard your sister. If you love that girl, go get her," Carmichael told me as he stood.

I got up as well, shook his hand.

"Go get her so I can kill her," Carmichael added with a chuckle.

I nodded toward Carrie and Adam, and left the house as fast as I could to catch up with Anna.

THE HEAT WAS LIKE A WET BLANKET WHEN I STEPPED OUT ONTO THE SIDEWALK. I looked both ways down the street having no idea which direction Anna took. A horn blared and I turned my head. Of course, she wasn't there. Where would she go? Could she get a new identity right away and disappear? I'd never see her again if she did. The very thought was crushing.

I'd told Nadine I loved her, but the words had been empty, something she'd wanted to hear. I'd thought it was love, but now, only now after knowing Anna, caring for her, protecting her, did I know what love felt like. The look on Anna's face had been telling. She'd smiled, grinned—beamed, even—at hearing those three words. The joy there was a miracle to see. Who else had said those words to her? Definitely not her father, nor her bastard ex-husband. Probably no one since her mom died. I had no doubt the first man to tell them to her had been me.

An incredible first. I grinned at the thought, but sobered instantly.

I completely blew it because with the love came a great big lie. A lie that had, until that point, kept her safe. A lie that proved how much I felt for her. If I hadn't been in love with her, I wouldn't have kept my job a secret. Looking back, I think I'd loved her ever since I bumped into her at the wedding reception. It had been instantaneous, like a lightning strike. I just hadn't been ready for her then. Now, I wanted Anna more than my next breath. I just had to find her, then I'd never let her go.

With a city the size of New York, she was going to be almost impossible to find. That boded well for avoiding Moretti's hit man. If I couldn't find her, then hopefully he couldn't either. I just had to track her down first, before Moretti's hit man. My fists clenched at the thought.

Her apartment was my first stop. She'd mentioned her go bag before and it most likely was stored there. She'd need that cash, papers and clothes before she did anything rash. She was smart, though. Smart enough to hide millions of dollars from Peters and his digging. If she could do that, then she must have an escape plan if discovered. No one ran from an old life without Plan B in place. I dashed for the subway, knowing it would be faster than taking a taxi, even on a Saturday.

By the time I reached her apartment, my T-shirt clung to my skin in the heat. To the doorman, I must have looked a little wild because he stopped me before I could get near the elevator. Taking a deep breath, I forced myself to calm down, to relax and even try to smile as if nothing were wrong. "Hey, sorry," I told the guy, whose name I remembered as Hank. He'd been working when I'd come in with Anna before. "Almost got run over by a crazy taxi. Do you need to call or can I just go up?"

Hank relaxed at my story. Every New Yorker had been involved in some kind of altercation with a taxi and could relate. "Haven't seen Miss Scott since I came on shift."

I nodded. "Okay. I'll just try her cell then. We were supposed to meet up but I guess she's behind." I shrugged. "Women."

Hank offered that man-to-man slap on the back. "Tell me about it. My wife is late for everything."

"I'll just go get a cup of coffee and come back. See you around, Hank."

I left the building, went around the corner and stopped to consider where to go next. Anna wasn't at home. She worked for herself. She had no family. When I was really mad at someone, I wanted to beat the shit out of them. When Anna was mad, she'd want the same thing, but took the civilized route. Since I was the target of her anger, she had to release her angst somewhere else. Wearing a skirt and sandals, she wouldn't just go for a run to work off her anger. She'd need to go somewhere where she could—

Yes! I took off down the street in a sprint, hoping the excess energy would be burned off on my way to her karate school.

Ten minutes later, I pulled open the door to the dojo, my eyes adjusting to the darker interior. There weren't any classes this late on a Saturday so Anna was alone. I stood just inside the doorway looking at her. She wore a pair of running shorts and a white tank top, feet bare. Sparring gloves covered her hands and she was beating the crap out of a heavy bag hanging from the ceiling. Jab, hook, uppercut. I had no doubt she was imagining my face on the leather as she followed all that with a backhand and a solid reverse punch.

Relief had me exhaling. I'd found her. She hadn't left. Hadn't disappeared. She looked so good, pissed off and full of angst. Her skin was flushed, her stance aggressive. She was breathing as hard as I was.

"You keep running away," I called out from across the open space.

Her head whipped around at my words, her ponytail flipping over her shoulder. She stood ready to spar, one foot in front of the other, hands up, blocking her body and face. It would be a one-sided fight; she could hit me all she wanted, but I wouldn't hit back.

I didn't need anyone coming in to interrupt us so I turned the dead bolt on the door. I didn't intend for her to escape...again. "You should know by now I'll always find you."

She shrugged casually, lowered her hands as if she weren't upset. Every line of her body screamed otherwise. "Why would you care?"

This wasn't going to be easy. Shit. I'd hurt her, probably as bad as every other guy in her life. Maybe worse. "I wanted to tell you," I said, recognizing the words were pretty empty. It wasn't much, but it was a start.

"Which time? At the reception when you told me you worked at Scorch? Was it when we were in your office and you accused me of working for Moretti?" She turned and round-house kicked the bag with enough force to make me wince. "I'm surprised you didn't just arrest me right then and there."

Jab. Jab, cross.

"What was I to think when you showed up at the bar?" I asked. "Why would you show up there if you weren't corrupt?"

She turned her head, her ponytail whipping around behind her once again. "I needed help to save Elizabeth from Todd."

"Your record was so clean it looked sanitized. Only criminals or people with something to hide have records that look like yours. What was I supposed to think?" I slowly worked my way across the room.

"That I had something to hide?" she asked, her voice bitter. The heavy bag rocked behind her. "Wait a minute." She held up her gloved hand as she narrowed her eyes. "You knew. You *knew* when I walked into that bar about my record. How?"

I ran my hand through my sweaty hair. "I was there when you were being questioned by the police."

Her mouth fell open and I swear I saw the gears working in her brain figuring everything out. "Our little run-in at the wedding reception wasn't an accident."

I shook my head as I stopped just out of reach of her fighting weapons—her arms and legs. "The way you maneuvered Werbler and Gossing through their interrogation was really impressive. We'd never seen anything like it before. It had me wanting to learn more about you. Then Moretti wanted me to check you out."

Anna crossed her arms over her chest, cocked a hip. "So, when you held my hand at the reception, leaned in and whispered that you felt something for me, it was part of an act to get close to me." She rolled her eyes and turned back to the bag. Punched it once, twice. "You must've been laughing at me. The naïve woman who melted at the first man who touched her in a decade."

Jab. Hook, uppercut.

I closed the space between us, grabbed her tense shoulders and spun her around. Anna's training kicked in. Crying out her frustration, she let her punch fly, clocking me right in the eye, making me stumble back a step.

Shit, that hurt. The sting, the jarring wallop made me feel like a cartoon character with little birdies circling my head. Thankfully, she wore her sparring gloves. I had no doubt I'd have either a broken nose or a ruptured eye ball from that hit otherwise. Wincing, I rubbed my hand over my face. "You can hit me. Yell at me. Hell, I deserve it. But I won't stand here letting you bad mouth yourself."

Anger flared in her eyes, what I could see of it through my one good one. She brought a knee up, but this time I was prepared. I turned my hips so her strike hit mid-thigh. Stepping around her, I moved one of my legs behind hers and buckled her, taking her to the soft red karate mat. I went down with her, knowing her longest weapons—her legs—could kick the shit out of me.

I moved so my body covered hers, pinned her hands up by her head.

"Get off me!" She was spitting mad. Wiggling her hips, she tried to buck me off. I countered by shifting my hips to maneuver one of my legs between hers.

"You are going to listen to me," I told her, my breath coming out in heavy pants. My one eye was still blurry, but seemed to be working.

"Like I have any choice!" She bucked her hips up, trying to get me off. It wasn't working, only made me realize—and Anna, too, by the hint of surprise on her face—that I wasn't immune to her shifting.

I loved this woman. What man in their right mind would let a woman clock him in the eye and practically unman him otherwise? She was feisty, sweaty and aggressive and it was turning me on. The feel of her beneath me was heaven and hell; she was alive and I had her right where I wanted her, but I couldn't do what I wanted until she understood, until she forgave me.

"I told Peters, my old partner, that I thought you were innocent. Right from the start in the police station. You blew me away in your little flowered skirt and white blouse."

Her mouth fell open when I told her what she'd been wearing that day, proof I really had been there. I covered her lips with my finger to keep her from talking.

"The way you handled Werbler and Gossing—you were incredible. You can ask them. Then, only hours later, Moretti wanted to know who you were, sent me to that wedding reception to fuck the answers out of you." She fought against my hold with those words. "I'd gone there with that in mind. When you ran into me and I shook your hand, it was all over for me. I fell in love with you right then."

"Please," she said, her voice belligerent. "You hated my guts two hours later. That's not love."

"Fine, we'll table the talk about love for now. I'll even skip the instant attraction I had for you. How I couldn't, wouldn't, fuck you for information. I wanted to *know* you. Be with you. *You.* But I was undercover and I had to know if you worked for Moretti. If I got you to cop to killing Bobby Lane, I could bring down Moretti. After six months of working for that asshole, I still had nothing solid to pin on him, not even when he directed me to kill you. I didn't record it, so it didn't happen. If you were in on it, it was a way to bring him down. I couldn't stop being undercover. No matter the connection between us, I had to be sure. So I told you I worked at Scorch, knowing Werbler let it slip during the police interview."

"You set me up," she said, her dark eyes narrowed to slits.

"If you were innocent, you would have gotten on that plane with your fake, gay boyfriend and that would have been it. But you took the bait. You showed up at Scorch. When I saw you, even kicking that guy's ass at the bar, I took you for working for Moretti."

She stopped fighting me, finally lying still beneath me. I could feel the rise and fall of her chest against mine, the beating of her heart. "You were mad at me because you thought I tricked you."

"I thought you were faking it at the reception. Using your feminine prowess like a weapon. It totally worked, too. I was pissed because I'd fallen for that same trap with my ex-wife a long time ago. A guy doesn't like being led around by the balls and then having them stomped on."

Anna threw her head back and laughed at that. "Feminine prowess? Are you kidding? I have no clue how to draw a guy in. Remember, I had an arranged marriage."

I ran my hand over her brow, pushing loose strands of hair back from her face. "Like I said, you hooked me right away." I snapped my fingers. "That's not something that's ever happened to me before. I've seen so many bad things. Death, betrayal, cruelty. I'm jaded and think the worst."

"Then why did you come to New York?" she wondered. "I was gone, nothing to worry about."

"Moretti confirmed you didn't work for him, but he wondered who you *did* work for. He figured Carmichael since you live here. He knew you came to the bar that night. No innocent woman would show up there."

"I did."

"Yes, you did," I repeated. "For your half-sister. But your appearance made him nervous. You were a loose end, and working for his enemy, Moretti wanted —wants—you dead. He sent me to do it."

Searching Anna's face, I looked for something, anything, that showed she wasn't mad anymore. Understood what I'd done and why.

"All of this because I went to Scorch that night?"

I shrugged. "Yes. Moretti would have forgotten about you if you hadn't shown up there. Really though, everything happened because of the rental car switch."

Anna groaned. "God, I want to go back and kill that valet."

I personally wanted to kiss the man. If he hadn't sucked at his job, I never would have met Anna.

"Because I went to Scorch, Moretti sent you?" she continued.

"Yes, he wanted me to kill you. I couldn't say no. If I did, he'd send someone else and my cover would have been blown. I came to New York because I couldn't let Moretti kill you. Jesus, I'm a cop, not a killer."

"But he sent another guy to make sure."

"I don't know if he thought I was soft on you, if he found out I am really a cop, or what. If I'd told you who I really am, you'd be dead now. I love you, Anna." I searched her face to see if she was truly hearing me. "I do, and I'd lie all over again if needed to keep you alive."

29

nna

My mind was trying to keep up with everything Nick said. With his hard body pressing me into the workout mats on the floor, it was difficult to concentrate on anything but what he'd done to me the last time he was above me like this. I felt every lean, hard inch of him. His thigh was between mine and he rubbed against me, making me sweat in a completely different way than my workout on the hanging bag.

I'd been so mad at him. So furious that I needed an outlet. Karate had always helped me release tension, forget about the bad things that crept into my life, that popped up from the vault of bad memories. From Frank Carmichael's house, I came directly to the dojo, changing into the workout clothes I had in my locker. Fortunately, I had a key to the front door since I helped teach classes, allowing me to get in and beat the crap out of something without having to explain myself to anyone. I'd used mental pictures of Nick when I punched and kicked and it had helped. By the time he'd appeared, I'd worked off some of my mad, but I had plenty left for the man himself.

I hadn't wanted to listen to his story, to find out why he lied, but he'd given me no choice. Lying beneath him, pinned to the mat, had forced me to listen. Once I heard, I understood.

"We're both really good at pretending to be someone we're not," I told him, looking up into his face. He'd put everything on the line. Everything. Tension left his body and he gazed at me with unguarded tenderness, yet a fierceness of someone who would do anything to protect the one they loved. He loved me. He did. I knew it, I could see it. I felt it deep inside.

At the soft tone of my voice—I'd given up on anger—he smiled. "We've both had quite a bit of practice."

Nick climbed off me, stood and helped me to my feet. He held out his hand and I stared at it. "Hi, I'm Jake Griffin, but everyone calls me Grif. It's nice to meet you."

I just stared at his hand. Big, with long fingers that could wield a gun, mix a drink, kill a man, yet bring me to pleasure in the most gentle and sweet way. He was offering me the chance to be with him, as himself. Not Nick. Not Moretti's goon. As himself. *Grif.* The name suited him.

This was the moment. Did I put my hand in his, bridging the huge gap that stood between us? Did I put my trust in him, want to be with him because he was the man who'd done those things for me? Protected me, saved me? Loved me?

I swallowed down a swift case of nerves, knowing this moment would be etched in my brain forever. Slowly, I put my small hand in his, even with my sparring gloves on. "I'm Olivia Edwards, but everyone calls me Anna."

Nick—Grif—pulled me into him, his arms circling like bands around my back, lowered his head and kissed me. It wasn't gentle. It was demanding, searing. Possessive. His tongue swooped in, tangled with mine. One hand held me about the waist, the other slid up my back to my nape, anchoring me as if afraid I'd disappear if he didn't hold on. He walked me backward until I was pressed firmly against the wall.

I lifted my hands to cup his face but my sparring gloves were in the way. I pulled back from Grif's mouth and yanked at the Velcro straps, tugging the gloves free and tossing them onto the floor. Placing my palms against his jaw, I felt the rasp of his stubble beneath my palms, tasted the familiar flavor that was all Jake, engulfed in his heady male scent.

Rough hands moved underneath the hem of my T-shirt to cover my breasts through my sports bra as one of Grif's legs moved to wedge between mine, making me ride his hard, muscled thigh. I moaned into his mouth, the assault on my senses too much. Breaking the kiss with a gasp, he lowered to his knees, aligning his face directly with my breasts. He pushed my shirt up, getting it caught beneath my arms. I grabbed hold and tossed it over my head. Roughly, he worked my sports bra up and latched on to a nipple that had me arching my back into him, wanting more. I ran my fingers through his damp hair, holding him in place. I cried out as the intense pleasure overwhelmed me, sent heat coursing through me, my core aching and ready for him.

"I love you," Grif whispered against my breast, laving a path to the other one before licking it, pulling it into his mouth. I was close, so close to coming, his mouth—and his words—taking me there quickly.

"Please, Grif, hurry," I panted. I wanted it all. Now. I needed him deep inside me, filling me, making me whole. "Don't stop."

"God, I love hearing you say my name. No. I won't stop," he murmured. Slipping his fingers into the waistband of my shorts, he tugged them down along with my panties. I stepped out of them while he undid the zipper on his shorts, pushed them down, along with his boxers, enough so his cock sprang free. It was thick and hard, pulsed upward by his navel. It was the first time I saw it, and I had a flash of panic, wondering if it would fit. I hadn't had sex since I was eighteen, so long I considered myself an almost-virgin.

My fingers touched it tentatively, bobbing in place while he hissed through his teeth. "I've never... God, Grif, are you sure—"

"Shh, love." He reassured me with his soft words, as he lifted my thigh with one hand, pulling it to his hip, the other slid to my core, running gently over me, feeling the wetness there. Sliding one finger, then two deep inside, I forgot about being scared, about everything but what he was doing to me. Curling one finger, he rubbed a spot deep within that had me arching into him, crying out with pleasure. It wasn't quite enough to tip me over the edge, to push me to that place only Grif had ever taken me.

Slipping his fingers free, I felt empty. But when he lifted them to his mouth, sucked on them, I was done for. Reaching into his back pocket, he pulled out a condom, ripped the package open with his teeth and rolled it on. "Wrap your legs around me."

I didn't know what he meant, but when he grabbed on to my thighs and tugged, I hooked my legs around his waist. Between the wall and his rock-hard body, I was pinned, his cock positioned at my very center. My eyes fluttered closed at the pressure, the slight push of his broad tip into me. I could feel myself opening, stretching as I was slowly filled. I shifted my hips, trying to adjust to him. He was so big and I was so full, even with just the very head inside.

"Look at me, Anna." His words were rough, tinged with a dark growl of possession.

I couldn't help but stare into his eyes, deep and fathomless and filled with lust, a need so powerful he slipped another inch into me. This is why he'd waited before, why he said it wasn't yet time. He wanted me to know who he really was when we came together. Wanted to be Grif when we did.

"Mine. You're mine."

With those words, he shifted his hips and thrust deep. The exquisite pressure, the fullness had me wrapping my arms about his back, my nails digging into his skin through his T-shirt. My sensitive nipples were abraded by the cotton.

"It's too much," I said, trying to lift myself up, but Jake's hands held firmly on to my hips. He wasn't moving, just filling me, letting me adjust. He hadn't taken me before because he didn't want anything to come between us. It really was just the two of us. Grif and Anna.

"Yes, it's too much. Being with you is too much." He licked at my neck, nuzzled down to nip at the spot at the juncture with my shoulder. My inner muscles clenched around him from the hint of pain and Jake groaned. "It'll always be like this with us. No, don't fight it. Accept it. Accept us. Say it, Anna."

I was adjusting to him, my core softening, accepting, but I still fought against his hold, his possession. My eyes were squeezed shut, my head thrown back. "Say what?" I asked, frustrated with the feelings, the need that was overwhelming me. Jake was consuming me, us, in this *thing* I didn't understand.

"What you feel. How it feels to have me inside you, part of you." Grif demanded, pushed me to give in, to give over to *us*.

"I love it."

He slid out a fraction of an inch, shifted to fill me once again.

"Oh God, I...Grif, I don't understand," I cried out. The feelings of pleasure, the pressure, Grif's all-consuming presence was too much. Tears rolled down my cheeks and I fought, pushing now at his chest, trying to push him, the feelings, the need back just a little. I didn't know how to handle it, didn't know what to do with the emotions washing over me like a tidal wave.

Even with my struggles, Grif didn't relent. He pulled out of me, almost completely, then surged in. It was so intense I wanted to scream. "I'll help you. Do you want me?" he asked, his hips starting a slow rhythm.

"Yes," I said, feeling my legs clench tightly around his waist.

"Can you feel what's between us?"

In. Out.

"Yes," I panted.

"This is love, Anna. I love you. You love me."

In. Out.

I shook my head. Did I? I didn't know what love was. Couldn't let myself give in to it.

With a deep thrust he said, "Yes, you do. Say it."

"I can't!" I cried. My orgasm was right there, just out of reach. I needed—

"Yes, you can. You do. Just let the words out."

A sheen of sweat slicked my skin, our bodies wet where we were joined. I never wanted him to stop, to be parted from me. I needed this. Needed him. This wasn't just sex. This was possession, and not just on Grif's part. I did this to him, made him lose control. He *loved* me and it showed in everything he'd done for me. I felt it with every stroke of his cock inside me.

"I—" I licked my dry lips. "I love you."

Grif lowered his forehead to mine, paused. Just breathed me in. Took a moment to revel in what I'd said. He had to be, because I was. I'd said it. Felt it. Meant it.

"Good girl," he whispered, bringing one hand between us to my cleft, his thumb finding my clit and moved in slow circles.

I cried out, arched my back, my fingers digging into his shoulders.

He circled his hips, moving now within me without the same precision, as if he'd lost his control, driving us both to the brink...then over.

I came hard, crying out his name as my inner muscles milked him, holding him deep within me. Grif drove into me deeply one last time and shuddered against my neck as he came. I could feel his seed pulsing within me, even through the barrier of the condom. I held him tightly, never wanting to let go.

30

nna

Somehow, we made it back to my apartment. My body was sated, softened, relaxed. Pleasured. I was in a daze, overwhelmed by what we'd done. Not just the fact that we'd had sex; that was enough for almost any near-virgin to handle. What we did wasn't *just* sex, it wasn't making love, it was bonding at an elemental level and in a way where there was no going back. I was his and he was mine.

Grif—it was strange to call him that—led me directly to my bathroom, turned on the shower, adjusted the temperature. We didn't speak; words weren't needed. He took off my clothes slowly, exposing my body to him one bit at a time. In return, I lifted his T-shirt. He helped me, drawing it up and over his head. I pushed his shorts and boxers down over his hips and to the floor. He was fully erect once again and I stared at it in awe, wondering how it had fit. I was sore—God, I'd been stretched so fully—but my body was ready for him once again. My core clenched in need at the sight of him completely naked. Broad shoulders, tapered waist, muscular thighs, heavenly butt. I could officially say that his dark skin was not from being out in the sun. He tested the water and pulled me into the glass enclosure with him.

Leisurely, he soaped my body, paying special attention to my breasts, between my legs. Once rinsed, he continued to touch me, learning my body, recognizing what made me hotter, wetter for him. Dropping to his knees, he was right there.

Oh. My head fell back, knowing what he could do to me with his mouth. "Put your foot up on the bench," he murmured darkly, looking up at me through wet lashes.

I did as instructed, never before imagining the shower seat would be used for anything so carnal. Parting me with his fingers, he licked into me, his tongue moving from my opening, which clenched around its tip, to my clit. He pushed me, higher and higher, his skill at oral pleasure impressive. But it wasn't enough. "I need you inside me. Please, Grif."

I felt him grin against my inner thigh. "Greedy now, are we?"

Putting my hands in his wet hair, I tugged him up. "Yes. Now give it to me."

He stood, looked down at me, quirked a brow. "Give it to you? With pleasure, but I don't have any more condoms."

"It doesn't matter," I said, my words coming out in a rush as I ran my hands over his muscled abs, the crisp hairs tickling my palms. "I'm on the Pill."

Grif's brows went up, searched my face, considering. I lifted up on my tiptoes, kissed him, licking into him. "Please."

Taking my hips, he turned me to face the wall, pressed me against it. I hissed from the chilled tile against my belly, my breasts. Grif slowly slid my palms up the slick surface to place them by my head. He bent his knees, nudged himself against my opening, already swollen and slick for him, then thrust deep in one stroke.

I cried out, surprisingly sore from before, but the pleasure of having him fill me completely, pressing into me so deeply, made sure that I didn't care. I arched my hips back and into him, letting him slide in to the hilt.

"God, Anna. You feel so good." With those words, Grif drove into me, took us up and over, pounding into me without mercy, but I didn't want slow or soft. I just wanted him to possess me, consume me. He did. When he came with a growl against my neck I felt his come spurt deeply within me and I knew he'd given me everything. I was his. Marked. Taken.

Grif

. . .

ANNA WAS GOING TO KILL ME. SEX WITH HER WAS ONE OF THE MOST PLEASURABLE things I'd ever experienced. When she said I could come in her without a condom, the sensation, the connection was unlike anything I'd ever experienced. I'd never had sex without a condom. Never. Not even when married to Nadine. She'd made me wear them, saying the Pill made her sick. Since neither of us wanted kids, condoms were our go-to option. I hadn't been too excited about it at the time, but now, I was glad. Glad I could experience this connection first—and only—with Anna.

As she turned around, I saw the satisfied look on her face. She looked well used, very well fucked. Her nipples were full and soft again, her cheeks pink from her pleasure.

"That was the first time for me without protection." I glanced down, ran a finger through my seed coating her thighs. I'd filled her, all but branded her as mine. "That...that's one of the hottest things I've ever seen. I had no idea."

Anna's eyes grew large as my cock filled with blood and hardened once again. Was it always going to be like this? This desperate need for her?

I reached for the scented soap and began to clean her once again, washing the evidence of our pleasure from her body. Gently, I cleaned her thighs, then between, her skin there swollen and hot. Anna's eyes slid closed at the contact.

I could have easily taken her again, but my cell chimed from the pile of clothes on the floor, signaling a text. "Later," I murmured, planting a soft kiss on her plush lips. Opening the glass door, I dried quickly, wrapped the towel around my waist and retrieved my cell from my jeans pocket. "We're on for eight," I said, reading Carrie's text.

The soft mood that languished was gone. Reality returned.

"Adam's meeting us at your building's back entrance." I looked the clock on my phone. "We'll need to hurry."

Anna stood in the shower, naked and flushed, dripping wet and perfect, her shoulders squaring, sadly slipping out of her arousal and into the present. The sated look morphed into determination. She nodded and reached for the shampoo.

"Before we do this...thing, maybe you can tell me something about yourself. The real you," she said, ready to pour the shampoo into her palm.

I hadn't yet closed the door. I could have let it click shut, let the steam swirl and fill the void between us, keep her at arm's length. Instead, I stepped in, took the bottle from her.

"You know my name. You know Carrie and that I have two other sisters."

I lathered her hair, reveling in how her head fell back, her eyes closed as I massaged her scalp.

"We grew up in Michigan, parents are still there. Doctor and school teacher. Just to clarify, my mom's the doctor, dad the teacher."

"That's a nice twist," Anna murmured. From the soft smile on her face, she seemed to be enjoying my hands in her long hair.

"I played baseball in high school, went to the state school on a scholarship for it. Ended up going into the Army after graduation."

"Why?" she asked.

"I always wanted to go but my parents pushed me to go to college first. Since I had the scholarship, it made sense. If I still wanted the military after, they said it wasn't going anywhere. They were right. Turn around."

She did and tilted her head back, letting the spray rinse the suds away.

"I did four years in the Army with two tours of Afghanistan. Someone in my platoon was from Denver and going into the police academy. I had no plans, so I joined him."

"Why undercover?" she asked, once she slicked the water from her hair and could open her eyes. We faced each other.

"I was married." Anna's mouth fell open but she didn't say anything. "I thought it was love, but when I found out she'd been cheating on me, I pulled my head out of my ass and noticed our marriage had been a sham. I might have worked too many shifts, handled too many cases late at night, but I was faithful and expected the same. If she wanted someone else, all she had to do was tell me, not go behind my back. She made me jaded. I didn't trust women after her. At all. With my marriage over, I took an undercover assignment no one else wanted. No family commitments. It was easy and I went under for six months. When that one was done, my life still sucked and along came another opportunity. I took it. My life didn't get better. I dealt with the wrong kind of people that only backed up my skewed view of life. Then, I went undercover to bring down Moretti, and you know the rest. You *are* the rest."

"So we both had sham marriages," she said. We were just standing there, letting the water fall around us. "Maybe it was good we lived through them. Made us learn what we were missing."

What we were missing. I hadn't known I missed Anna until I found her.

No matter how much I wanted to stay in the shower with her, to hide in the foggy bathroom forever, I had to focus, get my mind back in the game. Once I met her, it hadn't ever really been *in* the game. I had a feeling I'd never be back all the way ever again. Now, there would always be a part of my mind wondering, worrying and thinking about Anna. I'd had it all wrong, all this time. Those guys on the force who I'd thought were slackers because they were pussy whipped by their wives or girlfriends? They'd had it all right. They knew what had been missing, found it, and never let go.

I left Anna in the shower by herself, needing a little separation to focus on what was to come.

Twenty minutes later, Anna joined me in the kitchen in a white tank top and black cargo pants. Taking a sip from a can of soda, my hand stopped halfway to my mouth as I looked at her hair.

"Holy shit, Anna." It was mostly dry, but curly. Completely unlike the stick-straight hair I was used to. Full, thick ringlets went down over her shoulders, a few inches shorter than I was used to seeing. I placed the can on the counter and walked over to her, touching a curl, amazed how it twirled around my finger. "How?" I asked, mesmerized by the difference.

A pink blush rose to her cheeks, clearly little shy about the new look. "I straighten my hair every day. This," she tugged on a curl and I watched it spring back into place. "This is natural."

It was soft, like silk. Wild. I couldn't get enough of it.

"You straighten this away?" Her gazed flicked up to mine, wary. "It's hot as hell."

Anna's eyes cleared as she grinned. "Everything to you is hot as hell."

"When it's you, definitely. Why?" I asked, still enthralled by the amazing change. She looked different. More relaxed.

Anna arched a brow. "Why do I straighten it?"

I nodded, but watched a little twirl of dark hair spring back into place as I gave it a little tug.

"Because it's out of control. Unruly. I didn't straighten it now because we're in a rush. You had me a little too distracted to plan my time."

I ran a finger down her soft cheek. Leaving her hair curly, instead of ruthlessly attacking it with a straightening thingie—I knew nothing about women's hair care tools—was a big leap for her. "I don't want you straightening it anymore. I love it like this. I love it when you're out of control. I love it when you're unruly."

Taking a hair tie from her wrist, she pulled her hair up into a tail and tied it back.

"Don't," I said as I watched her fingers run through her curls expertly.

"It's too hot. Besides, for what's in store for us, I need it out of my face."

I conceded because she was right, but I thought about how it was going to look later spread across her pillow as I made love to her. Again and again.

31

nna

Just before eight, we took the back exit out of Anna's building. It led to an alley used by trash trucks and other service vehicles supporting the neighboring buildings. It was still hot, the temperature hovering near ninety. The smell of rotting garbage and exhaust wafted down the pavement.

Before I had a chance to scope my surroundings—if I was going to admit it, I was focused too much on Anna to recognize danger—it was too late. I didn't see the men waiting for us. Before I could react, a cloth bag was pushed down over my head, darkness overwhelming me. Before I could lift my arms to grab at it, my wrists were yanked behind my back. Flailing out, trying to avoid being tied up, I hit the guy in the midsection with my elbow. It didn't do enough damage to stop him and he was able to zip tie my wrists, tight enough where I couldn't pull them free.

"Grif!" Anna screamed, her voice panicked. I knew, she too, had been caught off guard. Turning my head, I tried to see something, anything. The fabric was rough, coarse, so some light filtered through. It was snug though and the mustiness of the material made it hard to breathe.

"Don't fucking hurt her," I shouted fiercely, continuing to struggle.

There had to be at least two men, perhaps more. One to cover our heads, another to zip tie the wrists. This had been a complete ambush; I'd been expecting Adam to take us somewhere to a staged shooting. It was hard to remember this was fake—at least I hoped it was—but I called out to Anna anyway. "Are you okay?"

When she didn't answer, I started to panic. "Anna! Answer me," I shouted.

I heard a guy's muffled grunt, then shuffling. "Grif, Grif!" Anna shouted.

Thank God. I heard a car approach, stop directly in front of us. I could feel the air stir on my arms. A door opened, I heard the trunk pop. I was shoved from behind. Without anything to stop me, I fell face first. There was no time to panic as my face smashed against rough carpeting inside of the car. The trunk. My legs were lifted and tossed in so I was folded in half, uncomfortable in the confined space.

"Get off me!" Anna shouted, then she was dropped in next to me, the lid slammed shut. Any light through the cloth hood was gone. Car doors closed, the engine revved and we were moving.

"Grif," Anna breathed. I could hear panic in her voice. "This sucks."

I couldn't help but chuckle. Instead of crying out in hysterics, she had to give her feelings on the situation.

"I don't like it either, love. Are you comfortable enough?" I wasn't. We were shoehorned in, Anna's head down by my feet. Her knee was pushed into my shoulder. It was tight, claustrophobic. Without any light and my hands tied behind my back, the space closed in around me. The temperature was rising quickly and I heard Anna taking big gulps of air. I was sweating now, the bag on my head clinging to my skin.

"Not really, but I'm okay. Where do you think we're going?"

"I have no idea. Just remain calm, try not to panic and remember this isn't real," I said into the darkness.

"Moretti's not here, so why do we have to go through this?"

"I've done this before. They have to make it look real. In this day and age, proof comes in the form of video. Not just pictures."

We didn't get a chance to talk longer because the car came to a stop and I heard a garage door opening. The car moved slowly, the garage door closing once again.

"Remember, no matter what happens, everything's going to be okay," I reminded her.

The trunk opened. Light filtered through my hood and I could feel the cool air pour in.

"I love you," I murmured.

Men laughed. "I love you," they mimicked together in a high-pitched voice. "Hey, Vince, he's so romantic."

"Up we go," another voice said, possibly Vince. I heard Anna being hoisted out just before a meaty hand grabbed me under my arm and pulled me to my feet. It was difficult to stand, to get my legs beneath me without being able to see. As if someone read my mind, the bag was yanked off.

Blinking, I looked for Anna. They'd pulled the bag from her head as well, her hair a wild mess about her face. Her hands were tied behind her back and she was sweaty and unnerved, but calm. Her white tank top was smudged with dirt in several places and her pants had a small rip in the thigh.

There were three men. They were large, beefy, wielding very realistic-looking guns and serious faces. They, too, were sweating in their long pants and shirts. No one could escape the heat.

We were in some kind of dingy warehouse, cavernously large and mostly empty. A few wooden shipping crates were stacked along one wall. Small windows, caked with dirt, were high up by the ceiling, letting in what was left of the daylight. The space was lit by old single-watt bulbs hanging sporadically through the space, casting eerie shadows and pockets of darkness.

"This way," Asshole One said, waving his gun in the direction he wanted us to go.

Anna watched me, unsure of what to do. I didn't move, and received a shove on the shoulder to get me going. As we walked deeper into the warehouse, I could see it was actually L-shaped, bright light coming from around the corner. We were led that way. Clenching my fists, I tried to get blood flow back, the tingles from ten minutes ago were gone and now my hands were completely numb.

A construction light on a bright yellow tripod, used to brighten indoor projects like hanging drywall or running electrical wire, spotlighted a large patch of the dirty concrete floor. An old metal chair, perhaps part of a dining set from the '50s sat in the center of the lit space. I was led to it, pushed down onto it so my arms were fitted over the seat back. My shoulders were wrenched painfully and I had to lean forward slightly to take the pressure off.

Beefy Guy leaned down so his face was in line with mine. "As you've probably figured out, we're planning on killing you." He grinned, like this was the highlight of his day. "Doesn't mean we can't have a little fun with the lady first."

What the fuck? No one said anything about rape. This was not how this was supposed to go down.

"No!" screamed Anna. I couldn't see much more than a sliver of her body around the fucker's face. But what I did see made me want to kill. The bastard shoved Anna down onto her knees in the filth. She resisted, so he slapped her. Hard.

These weren't Uncle Frank's boys. This wasn't a game. *Shit.* This was way too fucking real.

"Moretti." His name left my lips, half curse, half rage. Leaning forward, I tried to head-butt the man in front of me but he was just out of reach. All I got for my actions was intense pain in my shoulder and a laugh from Beefy Guy.

"I'll move out of the way so you can watch. Don't worry, you won't miss any of it. You've got a front-row seat."

Anna looked up at me through her lashes, bent forward so her head was on the ground, her knees tucked up underneath her. She was crying, her lip bleeding, her eyes pleading with me to help. Sheer terror blanketed her every breath. What could I do? Three men. Guns. This was supposed to be fake. Asshole Two sported a hard-on I couldn't miss through his pants. *That* was not fake. Shit. *Shit!*

The one who'd remained quiet up until now pushed Anna over and tried to maneuver her onto her back. Her arms were in the way so she only made it onto her side. Kneeling down in front of her, it was obvious Asshole Two was going to be the first, since his dick was hard. He even started working on his belt.

Anger and helplessness overwhelmed me. I tried to stand, actually got to my feet with the chair wedged beneath my arms, but I was bent over, the chair seat across the back of my thighs. I couldn't walk, couldn't get to her.

"Hey there. Can't have you going anywhere and missing the fun." Beefy Guy came over and knocked me down, forced me to fall sideways onto my shoulder and hip. The loud clang of the metal chair hitting the concrete echoed through the cavernous warehouse. My head whiplashed onto the concrete floor with a crack and I saw stars.

Blinking, I tried to stay conscious, the pain overwhelming and sharp like a knife to the skull. I couldn't do anything to help Anna if I was knocked out. Hell, I couldn't do anything for her trussed up like I was.

"Who the hell are you guys?" I asked, breathing heavily. My voice shot zings of pain across my scalp and I winced. Moretti's men were going to rape

Anna before they shot her. Jesus, this was completely fucked up. "Where's Moretti?"

Beefy Guy turned to look at me. "Who the hell's Moretti?"

Holy shit. Who were these men? Why had they grabbed us? Were they Moretti's guys? I didn't recognize any of them, but then again Moretti would contract out this hit. From the blank look on his face, he didn't have a clue who Moretti was. Carmichael's men would at least know the name. So, if they didn't work for Moretti, or Carmichael, who the hell were they? Jesus, we were in trouble. Where was Carmichael? Where the *fuck* were the police?

"No. Get away from me," Anna growled at Asshole Two who loomed over her, belt undone. She pulled her knees back and kicked the guy in the belly, an angry growl ripping from her throat, knocking him back on his ass. She turned onto her side completely, then onto her knees, facing away from me. Her hair was completely snarled, her tank top and arms black with grime and dirt. She struggled to stand, but with her arms behind her, it was futile.

Beefy Guy and Asshole One laughed at their friend, who was sucking wind and looking up at the ceiling. Pride washed over me, knowing Anna was going to give as good as it got.

"Oh, you want it this way instead?" Asshole One asked. This one was smarter, going in on her quickly, not giving her room to defend herself. "I like it from behind, too." He grabbed her around the middle and pulled her up onto her knees, pushed her head to the ground. He was fumbling between them and she squirmed and struggled.

Knowing Anna was going to be raped with nothing for me to do but watch it happen was ripping me open inside. My wrists pulled and tugged at the plastic restraint, but it wouldn't give. I felt wetness drip down my fingers. I'd cut my skin wide open, but I couldn't feel it. Couldn't feel anything but the pain in my skull and rage. Pure, uncut rage.

"No. I won't let you," Anna said, fighting for breath.

Sitting back on his haunches, the guy pulled a gun that he'd had tucked into the waistband at the back of his pants, this one with a silencer. Holy. Fucking. Shit. He brought it around behind Anna's head.

"No!" I shouted, struggling futilely even more against my bonds. I was dripping in sweat, some of it trickling into my eyes, making them sting. It was coming down to this moment. Right now. He held the weapon execution style. He was going to kill Anna. There was no question of his intent. I couldn't help her. Couldn't save her.

"Let her go! Shoot me instead," I called out. *Shoot me.* If they killed her, I was as good as dead anyway.

"No!" Anna screamed. "Don't hurt him."

"Ah, isn't that sweet. They both want to save each other," Asshole One said, waving his gun back and forth between us. At least he'd pulled it away from Anna's head, for the moment.

Beefy Guy squatted in front of me, his knees cracking on the way down. "Shut up."

I shook my head and nausea overwhelmed me. "No way, you fucker."

He pinched off my nose in a tight grip, making me open my mouth to suck in some air. He pulled a rag from his pocket and shoved it in my mouth, let me go.

My head fell against the hard ground as I breathed in through my nose. Panic flared at how hard it was to get in air. I wanted to focus on helping Anna but my survival instincts kicked in and I tried to calm my heart, my breath.

I just lay there and watched as Asshole One moved the gun away from the back of Anna's head. Her whole body shook. He wrapped his arm around her. He fiddled with her pants as she cried out and fought with him once again. She even got a head butt in, this time well placed because blood poured from his nose, dripping onto the back of her shirt.

"That's it, bitch. You're not worth it." With his gun arm still around Anna's waist, he fired. I recognized the muffled sound of the silencer.

Holy fuck! *No!* I cried out through my gag, squirming. Struggling against my bonds, I watched Anna fall to her side. Asshole One struggled to stand, one hand on his nose, trying to stop the bleeding, the other still holding the gun. Blood coated the side of his weapon and the sleeve of his shirt.

Anna's blood.

I cried out against my gag. Anna lay there on her side, unmoving. Her back was to me so I couldn't see her face, but her whole body was slack, her hair a tangled mess about her head. Her fingers weren't moving. She was no longer struggling.

Everything I did came down to this moment. Time in the military, the police department, undercover, even my marriage to Nadine. I'd learned what mattered, what was important in life by what I'd been missing. I hadn't realized what that was until Anna. She'd changed my focus on life. On what was important. The reason for doing all that stupid shit was to get to her. She'd been out there, moving through life, just like I had. Just coasting, as if in neutral gear. Then, in one moment at a wedding reception, when she'd placed her hand in mine, my life shifted into high gear. I wanted more. I wanted it all. I wanted *her*.

Her. Anna. Alive and breathing. Not motionless, lifeless.

Bucking, I tried to shimmy my body across the floor to her, but it was no use. Lying on my side, I couldn't get any traction and I couldn't get enough air to continue, my breaths coming in short pants. I was beginning to black out, the signs familiar. Darkness around the edges, little white spots floating and moving. Anna! *Fuck, Anna.*

Beefy Guy knelt down, laughed at me. He came in so close I could smell his cologne, see the salt-and-pepper color of his short hair. "Your turn," he said as he flashed me his gun. He leaned in closer, placed one hand on the ground in front of me for balance. "Any last requests?"

I made noises against my gag.

"What's that?" he asked, maneuvering in so he was by my ear. Subtly, he slid something against my belly, tucked it beneath my shirt. It felt cool, like plastic. Not too big. Directly after, he pulled the cloth from my mouth.

"Fuck. You," I told him, breathing deeply, gulping in the air for my burning lungs. I struggled again, trying to process what he'd placed against my belly.

He stood and stepped back. Laughed. "So be it."

Pointing his gun at me, I looked down the barrel. There was none. It was a fake.

Bang.

32

nna

I DIDN'T MOVE. I WAS TOO AFRAID TO EVEN BREATHE. ONE MINUTE I THOUGHT I was going to be raped, then killed, the next I knew—finally—I was part of an elaborate ruse. For a stretch there I questioned who these men were. Had we been found by Moretti? Had he moved up his death day to Sunday? The people who said your life flashes before your eyes right before you die were right. Lying in the trunk of the car, I imagined the things I hadn't done yet. Travelled, made friends, had a lover. Well, before today at least. Then anger boiled in my chest. I realized one day of having sex with Grif wasn't enough. I wanted a lifetime.

I wanted a damn life.

Grif was hurt, I'd seen it in his eyes before I was shoved onto my hands and knees. When they'd knocked over his chair, he'd hit his head. Hard. He hadn't been thinking of himself, he'd been thinking of me. Willing to die for me. Yet again. So I'd fought, as best I could with my hands tied behind my back. It hadn't been enough, wouldn't have done any good to save either of us if it really had been Moretti. It made me realize how close we'd come to dying if Grif hadn't come up with this plan. I had no doubt Moretti's man had similarly gruesome plans made for us.

Too bad. We were already dead.

So I just lay there, listening as the men shut off the industrial light, walked away, opened the garage door and left. Even after the garage door slid back in place and it was quiet, I still didn't move. My hands were numb, my shoulder scraped raw. The fake blood oozed thickly down my belly, seeped into my shirt. The concrete was cool against my cheek.

All at once, chaos reigned. The garage door reopened, footfall came our way. The overhead lights came on.

"Hang on and I'll have your arms free," someone said over my shoulder. Adam? The plastic restraints were cut and my arms were free, my shoulders screaming in protest. I cried out at the return of blood. I was helped upright. It really was Adam and he was rubbing down my arms. God, he looked good. Anyone looked good right about now.

"Anna!" Grif yelled, his voice frantic.

I whipped around, watched as a man I didn't recognize helped him to stand. The stranger had a badge attached to a chain around his neck. The cavalry was here.

Men fanned out around the room, pulling tiny things...they were, um... remote cameras from hidden locations. On top of a stack of wood pallets, the top of a doorframe, beneath a pile of soiled rags in a corner.

"Careful, he hit his head," I told the man as I shook out my arms, rubbed my wrists.

The adrenaline wore off like air leaking out of a punctured balloon. I slumped against Adam, smearing fake blood on him. "Sorry," I murmured, pulling back.

"No worries, doll," he murmured, smiling at me. "Okay?"

I nodded. My arms prickled with pins and needles and my knees were bruised from smacking them against the rock-hard floor.

Grif dropped to his knees beside me and pulled me roughly into his arms. His breath fanned against my ear. As the blood packet was pressed between us, a final gush came from the bag, running down our chests. He reached in, pulled it out from under my tank top and dropped it on the floor.

Pulling back, he palmed my face with his hands, forced me to tilt my head up at him. We were both filthy, Grif's face streaked with grime, a bruise forming on his right temple. He looked amazing. "I'm okay. I'm okay," I repeated.

"I know you are, love. You were amazing," he told me, lowering his head for a gentle kiss. Oh, his lips. This was what I fought for, desperately wanted. Needed.

"I know that was fake, but, Grif, God. I love you," I said, pouring my heart into my words. I meant it. With my entire being. I didn't need to be coaxed, fucked into saying it. This was where I belonged. I didn't care who I was...Anna or Olivia or even some other name. I didn't care if he was Nick or Grif, as long as I was with him. He made me whole. "I was so scared."

He wrapped his arms about me, so tightly I almost couldn't breathe, but I didn't care. I didn't want him to ever let go.

"Hey, guys, I'm Carmody with NYPD. No hard feelings?" We both turned and looked up at the man who'd been messing with Grif. All fierceness, all asshole-ish bravado was gone, replaced with...normal guy. He held one of the small cameras in his hand.

My heart leapt up into my throat for a second at the sight of him, but instantly relaxed knowing he'd been acting.

The other men who were part of the scene came up behind him. It was hard not to cringe away.

Grif released me and stood, winced, then helped me to my feet. "You," he pointed to the guy I'd kicked, his voice a dark threat. The softness left his face, now a hard mask. Before anyone had a chance to blink, Grif punched him in the face.

Several plainclothes officers ran over and grabbed Grif's arms, holding him back. "That was for touching Anna like that. For having a fucking hard-on during all this. Jesus, what the fuck?"

The guy held his hand up to his nose, only a trickle of blood sliding down to his lip. "I deserved that," he said as he held up his free hand to hold off the other guys who restrained Grif. "We're good."

The men released Grif and he rolled his shoulders.

"Ma'am, I'm sorry, but I had to make it believable for the cameras."

"A believable hard-on?" Grif questioned, eyebrows disappearing beneath his tousled hair.

"I understand you've been to war. You know what it's like," the man said, looking contrite.

Looking to Grif, I waited. He didn't push, just gave a small nod of acceptance. I had no idea what he was talking about, but Grif did. Guys must get hard in stressful and dangerous situations.

"I'm sorry, ma'am," he repeated.

"It's okay," I murmured.

"You have a real good kick there. I swear for a minute I didn't think I was going to breathe again. I'm Bob, one of Carmichael's men," he finished as he held out his hand to me to shake, then offered the same courtesy to Grif. The way he enunciated Bob I had a feeling it wasn't his real name.

Grudgingly, Grif took it. Then he glared at the second guy whose nose was bent at a funny angle.

"My nose is already broken," the man said, his voice all nasally and thick, as he faced me. "I'd say we're even."

Grif just grunted.

"Special Agent Graves, FBI." He held out the hand he wasn't holding up to his nose to shake next.

"What about Carmichael? Where's he?" Grif asked as he slipped an arm gently around my side. "I thought he would be the one to kill us, or at least be here to witness it."

Carmody said, "He wouldn't get his hands dirty with this kind of thing. We had to make it real, and we've got the video footage for him to watch."

Oh, it had been unbelievably real. A shudder ran through me at how *real* it had been. Grif ran his hand up and down my back.

"It's his turn now," Graves replied.

Carmody held up the little camera before handing it off to someone, who I assumed was going to use it to send to Moretti. "That's the last one. The video is being pulled together as we speak. Carmichael's calling Moretti from one of his personal lines to make it legit. We just need to keep you hidden for the next day or two, then you can return to being Jake Griffin again. We're working on your paperwork now, Olivia. We'll have an ID for you soon and you can take your old life back."

It really was happening. "I might be Olivia Edwards again, but I'll still go by Anna."

The man nodded his understanding.

"That's it?" I shook my head. "I just have a hard time believing that the FBI, local police and Mr. Carmichael are going to work together on this. Wouldn't they want to arrest him, too?"

Bob and Agent Graves glanced at each other. Agent Graves answered me. "We don't usually play on the same team, but in this case, the opportunity to bring down a guy like Moretti, it's worth it to all of us," he circled his finger in the air, "to work together."

"We've done stuff like this before and will probably again. It happens more than you think," Bob added.

"We can't go back to her apartment," Grif said, ready to change the subject. It wasn't a question.

Carmody spoke up as he absently rubbed his stomach, his eye starting to swell shut. "We have a hotel reservation in your name, Detective Griffin. If you need anything from the FBI, you can contact me. Otherwise, just lay low until you hear from us."

Detective? Grif was a *detective*. I liked it a lot better than murderer, extortionist, money launderer, pimp, thug or any other role he might have played for Moretti. Grif looked down at me and he grinned, that dang dimple popping out. "That should not be a problem."

Turns out, we were only a few blocks from my apartment. When shoehorned in the trunk, it had seemed farther, but perhaps we were just driven around long enough for it to seem that way. We skipped it entirely and rode in the back of an unmarked police car to a nearby hotel. Led through the service entrance and elevator, we made it to our suite without running into any guests. With the authentic dirt, scratches and bruises, combined with the fake blood, it would have drawn plenty of unwanted attention.

Once the door closed behind us, deadbolt flipped, Grif pulled me back into his arms for a hug. "Are you okay?"

I nodded into his chest, soothed by the loud thump of his heart against my ear. He was so strong, so brave. How had I made it through life without him?

"Let's take a look at you." He stepped back, gently pulled the hem of my tank top up. Raising my arms, I let him pull it over my head. Grif's eyes dropped to my flat belly. It was covered in dry, caked fake blood. It pulled my skin taut, made it itch. I longed to have it washed off, but I basked in his attentiveness.

It was my turn. I wanted to see his body as well, to make sure there were no marks, no injuries. I pushed up his shirt now, collecting the fabric in my palms before Grif ripped it over his head. I ran my fingers through the sprinkling of hair on his torso, feeling his warmth, feeling his heartbeat. Watching his breath go in and out. We didn't talk, just slowly removed each other's clothes, one item at a time until we stood there naked. Marked, stained, bruised. Marred. *Alive.*

He led me to the shower, turned on the water, adjusted it to be just right. He climbed in, held out his hand for me to join him, slid the shower curtain closed behind us, enveloping us.

"Your head," I said, touching the tips of my fingers gently to his brow where I could see swelling and a hint of a bruise starting.

"I'll put ice on it later. Let's get clean first." He reached for the soap and began to run it over my skin. Softly, slowly, almost reverently. "My touch. Does it bother you?"

My stomach clenched as I took Jake's wrist, looked up at him. "No. I love your touch," I murmured. The steam from the shower filled the bathroom with white fog, closing us off from the rest of the world.

"But those men touched you," he bit out.

I shook my head hard. "No. No, they didn't touch me. It was pretend." I soothed him with my soft voice, the featherlight brush of my fingers against his skin.

Okay, it hadn't seemed like pretend at the time. I really had thought the guy was going to rape me. The look in his eye, that evil gleam, I'd seen before. David had intended to rape me—and not pretend—that night long ago. He hadn't cared if I fought, hadn't cared if I struggled. It actually seemed to turn him on when I did. I hadn't fought back then, just been lucky enough to get away. This time...

When Grif's jaw clenched even tighter, thinking he might snap from the images filling his mind, I added, "Really. He did a really good acting job. He leaned over me and gave me the blood packet, whispered in my ear that he wasn't going to hurt me and to play along."

I felt the corded muscles in Jake's forearm relax so I let go. He continued to clean me, the dirt and grime and darkness from earlier swirling down the drain. "No one whispered in my ear," he grumbled. "No one gave me a warning about what the fuck they were doing. I thought he was going to rape you. He had his gun up to the back of your head."

His voice was bleak, his hands on me almost reverent as he continued to clean my body. There wasn't anything I could do to ease his mind, to wipe away those memories that would stick with him forever. Perhaps once Moretti was behind bars he would see our actions had been worth the price, but not yet. Not now, standing here together with the memories and emotions still too raw. But I could make him forget.

I lowered myself down to my sore knees, Grif's body blocking the hot spray, and my hands slid down his solid thighs, his impressive erection only a few inches from my face. I wanted to taste him, to learn what got him hot, just like he had to me. He didn't move, stayed as still as a statue. His body was like one, all rigid planes, hard angles and impressive proportions.

"Jesus, Anna," he groaned. "What are you doing?"

Glancing up at him through my lashes, I answered him. "Making you forget the bad stuff."

He tangled his fingers in my wet hair leisurely, as if he savored my position. "You do. Hell, woman, you do."

"Then let me make you feel good. Show me how."

Grif's eyes slid shut, his whole body tense. "You've never done this before?" His voice was a desperate thread, barely audible, barely controlled.

I shook my head.

"Jesus." He took a deep breath, then tugged gently on my hair, holding me in place. "All right, love," he said, and fed me his cock.

33

rif

It wasn't difficult to do as the police wanted. Staying in a hotel room with Anna for two days, with nothing to do but make love to her, was far from a burden. After the blow job she'd given me in the shower, we'd moved to the bed where I took over. It was enchanting to watch as she discovered her innate sexuality, and it was a heady experience for me. I'd never been one to want someone naïve when it came to sex, always avoiding the concept outright, but I'd been wrong.

The first time I rolled her on top of me, positioned her so I thrust deep, her firm thighs clenching against my hips, she hadn't known what to do. Her need was desperate, tears sliding down her cheeks in frustration with a need to come, her sex pulsing around me. Guiding her hips, I showed her how to move, then watched as she learned what felt good, watched her nipples tighten beneath my fingers, her hair wild and curly over her shoulders, following her own path to pleasure and pushed me over the edge right along with her.

Anna was a voracious lover, greedy in her need for my hands on her, my body. We didn't talk about the past, nor the future, just spent our time entwined in the now. Room service, bad TV and making love. It was a reprieve from what was to come. Only when a delivery of new clothes arrived on Wednesday afternoon did we even think about the outside world.

Adam, Carrie and Frank Carmichael came to our suite, bringing takeout deli sandwiches and the latest news. Fortunately, Carrie had called first so we weren't indisposed when they showed up. I didn't really care who knew that Anna and I had sex, but she'd be mortified if caught in the act. Besides, I was becoming a tad overprotective where she was concerned and didn't want any man thinking about her in that way.

The suite had two rooms, and we sat around a seating arrangement of couch and chairs, a glass-topped table in the middle. Carrie raved about Anna's curly hair, nattering on about wishing hers did that as the sandwiches were handed out. It was corned beef for everyone. Drinks were poured then Adam shared the news. He wore a suite and tie—coming directly from work—and sat next to Carrie on the sofa. "Moretti's been arrested."

Anna stopped chewing, her sandwich halfway to her mouth.

"Attempted murder, attempted murder on a police officer, hiring of mercenaries, aiding and abetting a felon across state lines—which pulled in the FBI—as well as first degree murder."

"First degree murder?" I asked, taking a big swig from my water bottle.

"He took the rap for Bobby Lane, the idiot," Carmichael said. He was one happy man right now, relaxed, smiling and very pleased with himself. "I got him to talk, with the FBI listening in, recording it all. Shop talk, if you know what I mean. I told him Anna—he knows you as Anna, not Olivia—did work for me and that I killed her because I didn't appreciate *fraternization* across organizations. That was the word I used. Moretti understood this, and didn't blame me when I killed Nick, too. So the score was even. One of mine for one of his."

I followed Carmichael's recap. It was amazing how people in the "business" had a completely different set of rules than everyone else. An eye for an eye and all that.

"He was grateful to me because I saved him a couple G's for the hit man he sent. No body, no payment."

"The FBI had him then," Adam added. "Hired gun across state lines."

Carmichael held up his hand. "But wait, there's more."

He was on a roll, loving every minute of this.

"I was going to end the call there, but he kept running his mouth. The FBI agent did that hand sign thing telling me to let him keep talking. Stupid fucker with all his swagger. He threatened me. Me! Said he'd killed Bobby Lane and could do it to me easy enough, proving that his balls were bigger than mine. Whatever. As if I couldn't pop a guy and toss him in a trunk," Carmichael grumbled, as if Moretti was weakening the system with his actions. "If he'd kept his trap shut, he wouldn't be going down for murder one. Dumb-ass."

Yeah, a real dumb-ass. Fortunately, with my boss going to prison, I was officially out of a job. Which meant I was no longer undercover. Usually, I went from one role right into the next, volunteering to do the shit work no one else wanted. Who wanted to be an asshole minion for a guy like Moretti for months on end, living in a shitty apartment and dealing with scum on a daily basis? I had. Why? Because I had no life. No one to come home to. No one missed me.

Until now. I glanced at Anna who sat there, listening intently to every word, hopeful, but almost afraid to believe she was really safe from Moretti. I loved her, quirks, compulsiveness and all. No more undercover work for me.

"To make the phone recording legit and hold up in court, we tracked down the man he hired to kill you," Adam added. "He was pretty easy to find. He rolled on Moretti once we put the pressure on him. He'll be out in a few years because he didn't kill you, but he's small time. Moretti's going down and the recording will hold with the man's corroboration of events."

Not only was Moretti off the streets but the bastard that had threatened us as well. I figured that to be a bonus.

Carrie popped the top on her can of soda, realized she'd distracted her man and grinned.

"The men who were supposed to have your car"—Carmichael pointed to Anna with his sandwich—"were supposed to pick it up from the hotel lot where Moretti left it."

"He left the car with Bobby Lane's dead body in the trunk with the valet?" I asked. Like Carmichael said, the guy had balls.

"Smug little bastard," Adam added, with a slow shake of his head.

I wasn't as surprised as I should be. Moretti was bad to the core.

"He really thinks we're dead?" Anna asked, licking a little mustard off her finger.

I shifted in my seat, my cock hardening at the dart of her tongue.

"The video was freaking scary," Carrie replied, giving a little shudder. Adam ran his hand down her back in a soothing gesture. "It completely freaked me out when I saw it. Geez, you guys, that was some rough stuff."

Rough stuff? If that had been pretend, I didn't even want to consider what Carmichael did when someone really did cross him.

Anna and I both looked to Carmichael, who sat there eating his sandwich as if he'd planned a trip for us to the Statue of Liberty instead of staging fake murders.

"What?" he asked, shrugged. "It had to be realistic, and the FBI was involved. It wasn't that bad."

"Oh, it was," Carrie grumbled, picking up a chip. "I'm going to have nightmares."

No fucking kidding. I woke up in a cold sweat in the middle of the night, envisioning Anna at the hands of those men. Fake or not, it was haunting. With Anna tucked into the front of me, I was able to settle back to sleep, knowing she was safe.

"I'm sorry, Anna, if that was too much for you. It had to be rough. That's the way it goes down in my world."

I didn't give a shit about Carmichael's reputation, which wasn't the best anyway, but I did relate to the need for realism. Moretti wouldn't have believed anything less than a nightmare-inducing murder.

"What now?" Anna asked. She wasn't eating. Her sandwich sat on her plate, only a corner nibbled.

"I continue to be the upstanding citizen that I am, helping the police and FBI get common criminals off the streets," Carmichael said before taking a huge bite of corned beef.

The four of us just stared at him. He was far from an upstanding citizen, but in this particular case, no one was going to argue. He'd done what we needed, and done it well. The FBI wasn't going to condone his work, nor was he going to receive a Citizen Of The Year award, but he definitely was in the good graces of the law. At least for the moment.

"Nick Malone and Anna Scott are dead. It's not in the news because really, what's two more murders? You're done with your undercover work and your captain is expecting you back at the station next week, Detective," Adam told Jake. "As for Anna Scott, there's a death certificate for her. Her social security number has been terminated. She is officially—and legally—dead."

I narrowed my eyes, considering the scenario. "Legally? How can that be?" I wondered.

Carrie shrugged. "Her identity was solid. She paid taxes, had a credit card, was a homeowner."

"What about her apartment? Her things?" I asked as I glanced at Anna. I'd pushed her into this, and now it was reality. She couldn't go back to her apartment. She couldn't get her things. Anna had the clothes on her back and a bank account. Millions of dollars would go a long way to kickstarting her former life, but it wouldn't make her happy. That fell to me.

"For now, it will sit there as is," Adam replied.

"My will is in the top drawer of my desk," Anna said, sipping her soda. "My beneficiary is the women's shelter that helped with my new identity. I'd like to get a few of my things, I can give you a list if that's okay, but everything, including the apartment, should be sold. The proceeds go to the shelter."

I didn't think I could love Anna more, but I'd been wrong.

"I'll take care of it for you," Adam said, giving her a wink.

Anna smiled, almost relieved to know her wishes would be met.

"As for you, Olivia Edwards, the FBI will be issuing you a passport and will fix everything so that you can return to the living," Carrie said, picking up her pickle. "You were never declared dead, just missing, so it should be fairly easy for them."

"I'm not much of a fan of the FBI, but they're in a generous mood with Moretti being a new resident in one of their cells," Carmichael added. "He's been denied bail, so he won't see the light of day before trial, nor after, with all you've done. If you ever need anything, you two, you let me know," Carmichael said, his tone serious. "Anyone messes with you, you're under my protection."

"Uncle Frank, he's a cop," Carrie countered.

Carmichael pinned me with a look. "Cop or not, it's important to know who your friends are. Who has your back."

I stood, went over to Carmichael, held out my hand in thanks, in respect. The man hadn't had to help us, could've just left us to fend for ourselves with Moretti. Sure, he'd had a personal stake in the man's downfall, but even Carmichael had a sense of right and wrong. He might have blurred lines when it came to the law, but he protected the weak, he took care of his friends. He chose good over bad, at least for us.

Carmichael stood, looked me in the eye—man to man—and took my hand. We shook, but he pulled me into a hug, solid and strapping. Adam and Carrie laughed at the surprise on my face. I couldn't hide it. I was being hugged by the most powerful businessman on the East Coast. The man didn't hug everyone, so I took it for what it was, a sign of respect, of belonging.

"Let me know if you're looking for a job," he said as he sat back down, picked up his sandwich once again.

I eyed him. Was he serious? "Me?"

"No, Anna." He was serious.

Her mouth fell open as she pointed at herself. "*Me?*"

Over my dead body.

Carmichael grinned. "I saw the video. You broke that guy's nose with a damn head butt. Plus, I swear you launched the other guy across the room. You're one tough little lady. And boys will be boys. Most of the time, they don't suspect a woman until it's too late."

From a guy like Carmichael, tough was a huge compliment.

Anna paused. I could tell she was thinking about what to say to that. "Wow. Um...thanks, Mr. Carmichael, that's really sweet. I'll keep that in mind."

Carmichael just shrugged. "And you, Griffin. You've got a pretty decent resume. You were a big shot in Moretti's group, you know the ins and outs of the underworld. Military man. Years on the force. I could use a man like you."

I may have worked my way up the ranks with Moretti pretty fast, but I didn't fall for the flash and sizzle that went along with it. I'd stuck to my crappy apartment the force had arranged. I didn't go in for the expensive clothes, the women. The money. The power. That's what brought men down. That was Moretti's downfall in the end. It wouldn't be mine.

I glanced at Adam and Carrie, who'd been quiet. "I've never seen him offer a job to anyone before," Adam replied.

"You'd live nearby," Carrie added with a shrug.

I resisted the urge to roll my eyes. I wouldn't show the man who'd just saved my life such disrespect. Still, I was a cop, not a criminal. It was one thing to work *with* him, another to work *for* him. "Like Anna said, I'll keep it in mind."

My days of working undercover, with working for guys like Moretti and Carmichael were over. There was no way in hell I'd accept another assignment like that. I was too old for that shit. Too in love. That kind of work was for loners, loners who were bitter and had no one loving them, no woman waiting for them to come home every night.

Anna and I had a future together. Neither knew what it might be, but that was okay. As long as she was with me, we could do anything.

"What about your ex?" Carrie asked Anna, changing topics.

"I've got some ideas," she replied, glancing my way. "I can help my half-sister and deal with Todd at the same time."

"Don't you want to tell your dad to fuck off, too?" Carrie asked. Adam and Carmichael looked at Carrie with curiosity. "I haven't told them. Privileged information, remember?"

I didn't doubt Carrie would keep her word. It went beyond legal responsibility with her.

"It's fine. You can tell them. Over drinks. Lots and lots of drinks."

"This is going to be interesting," Adam murmured.

"To answer your question, no." She looked at Adam. "My father didn't want me. Plain and simple. He got rid of me when I was six, then handed me off to Todd, my ex, at almost eighteen. I don't want anything to do with him."

Anna glanced at me and I could see a little hurt in her eyes. Her dad had dented her, but hadn't done damage. He'd pretty much abandoned her to boarding school, but Anna seemed to be recognizing it was probably for the best. The guy was an asshole. She was better away from him.

Todd Lawton, on the other hand, was going down.

34

nna

Two days later, I looked out at the spectacular view from our hotel room in San Francisco. I hadn't been back since the day I was released from jail and disappeared almost twelve years ago, but San Francisco looked the same. Same tourists, same famous skyline. The only thing that seemed to have changed was me. I was older, definitely wiser, and accompanied by the sexiest man on earth. *Who loved me.* I sighed, wistful and surprisingly sappy at the very idea.

Grif—I still had a tough time calling him that—had talked a few times before we left New York with his colleague Peters. I'd heard one side of many phone calls with the man and they both agreed that steering clear of Moretti's turf would be safer and smarter than trying to get help from the Denver PD. It would be just our luck to bump into one of Moretti's men that held a grudge. Instead, Peters offered to reach out to fellow men in blue in San Francisco if we needed them.

It was a nice gesture, but that wasn't going to happen. No way. I knew everyone on the force wasn't bad; I was in love with one of them, but past experiences clouded my judgment. I spent forty-two days in jail because they'd either looked the other way or were in Todd's pockets. Some were most likely still on the force. Still on the take. If we reached out to them for help, would my return get back to Todd? Most likely. Could I end up back in jail on the same trumped-up charge? Definitely.

Grif seemed more tied to me than Denver. It could be the sex marathon we seemed to be on. From the relaxed, just-fucked male look on Grif's face, he was more than fine with the pace. I fell under the feast-or-famine arrangement. None for a decade and then almost more sex than I could handle in less than a week.

When we weren't in bed—okay, when we weren't having sex, because we didn't always use a bed when a perfectly good wall or chair was available—we talked through our options for making Todd pay. My long-term wariness, outright fear, at confronting him was wearing off. It was well past time I confronted my real, living, breathing demons so I could move on with my life.

Olivia Edwards was back, for better or worse. Proof of that was my plane ticket, purchased under my real name. That made it official, especially in the eyes of the FBI, who'd helped arrange my long overdue return.

I'd watched the news, online and TV, for any kind of mention about our faux deaths, but I had yet to find anything. New York had moved on as if nothing had happened. I'd isolated myself so well that even my neighbors had barely talked to me. No one would miss Anna Scott other than my few karate friends, and that was pretty pathetic. In hindsight, it was obvious how depressing my life had been. Grif had been right; I'd been not only alone, but desperately lonely as well. I'd been so fearful of being found by Todd and my father that I hadn't even known how much of life I'd been missing. Two weeks with Grif and I never wanted to go back. Never wanted to be alone again.

Worried my karate friends would hear about my demise and dig into my not-real murder—which the police and FBI didn't want—everyone agreed it was best to tell them a washed-down version of the truth.

Under police protection, Grif and I had gone to the karate dojo together and told Paul, the owner, and Zach—I owed it to him especially—that I'd been abused by my husband years ago and taken a new name to hide from him. It was the truth, minimally, which made it easy to tell. Grif had picked up the story from there and told them he was a cop who had helped me get my old identity back. Before we left, we told them not to believe any stories they might hear, as the media's spin could be inaccurate. The men didn't like any of it, but they had little choice in the matter. They'd been wary of Grif the sole time they met him, but when they discovered he was a cop and was helping—and protecting me—they let us leave reassured.

My goal all along had been to keep Elizabeth from marrying Todd. I'd had it backwards. I had to keep *Todd* from marrying *Elizabeth*. If Todd was willing to try and marry Elizabeth in such a similar fashion to me, Victoria's illness must be more advanced than they were sharing, which wasn't anything at all. I'd had to dig for the information about her early onset Alzheimer's since they wouldn't share that *weakness* with the press. An Edwards was never weak.

"Tired?" Grif asked, nuzzling against my neck, distracting me. It was only four, but with the time difference, it had been a long day. I never tired of his affection, his singular focus he had on me. His scent swirled around me and I was intoxicated. By his smell, by his touch, by his very presence.

My skin tingled as his hands moved from my waist and up to cup my breasts. "Not anymore," I murmured, followed by a moan. When he licked the spot where my shoulder met my neck, I didn't say anything else for quite some time.

THREE HOURS LATER, THERE WAS A KNOCK ON THE DOOR, WAKING ME FROM A post-orgasm nap. I was in bed, on my stomach, sprawled next to Grif. His hand, which had been resting on my thigh, clenched at the sound right before he jumped up. He'd brought me to orgasm in the shower, under the guise of getting clean after our long trip, before we wore each other out in bed directly after, beads of water still clinging to our skin. I tugged the sheet over my body as Grif moved quietly to grab his boxers that were strewn with our other clothes across the floor.

He'd checked his gun with the airline, but had put it within easy reach once we'd checked in to the hotel. Taking the weapon from the nightstand, he made his way barefoot to the door. I was instantly wide awake, my heart pounding at the sight. No one knew where we were staying except Grif's colleague Peters. We'd left the local police in the dark, for now, but his partner was our link to help if we needed it.

We hadn't called room service, so who was there? I climbed from the bed, grabbed Grif's white shirt off the floor and slipped my arms through the sleeves. Whoever it was, I didn't want to be completely naked when Grif opened the door. Or shot them through it.

With his gun by his ear, he looked through the peephole. I saw every muscle in Grif's body relax, tension seeping out as he sighed. He dropped his weapon, letting it rest against his muscular thigh. Set the safety. He ran his free hand over his face and glanced at me.

"Who is it?" I whispered, staring at his weapon.

Instead of answering, he opened the door.

"Oh." The sound escaped when I saw my half-sister for the first time. I stood there, like a statue, wearing nothing but Grif's unbuttoned shirt. It barely covered my thighs and my fingers gripped the front together. I flushed and tugged the hem down with my other hand. Grif held the door open in just his boxers, which hung low on his lean hips. Elizabeth's mouth dropped open and she just stared at the *just had sex* tableau we portrayed.

"Um...wow. You're so beautiful," I said, taking in her long blond hair, jeans and crisp white blouse. She had sandals on her feet and silver hoops in her ears. Her makeup was artfully applied and she was oh so young. She was taller than me by several inches, built more willowy and graceful like her mother. No one would take us for sisters.

She stared at me, too. Ugh. What a great first impression I made. I hadn't had sex in over ten years and now I looked the complete slut.

"Can I come in?" she asked, looking between the two of us. She was chewing gum and she wore a silver thumb ring, both helping me to remember she was just a teenager.

Taking a step forward, I shook my head to clear it. "Of course. This is my...um...Grif."

I didn't know what he was exactly. Lover, definitely, but I wasn't going to tell that to Elizabeth. She obviously knew that now, but I didn't have to reinforce it. Boyfriend was probably accurate, but it wasn't sufficient. He was more. So much more. I had to ask him about that. Sometime.

He closed the door behind her, then held out his hand with a smile. She took it as her gaze raked over his chest and arms.

"I'll just go and get dressed," he replied, offering me a quick wink as he moved past me. Was he blushing?

I know I was. "Let me get some clothes on, too." I started buttoning Grif's shirt as I went over to my suitcase, pulled out a pair of cargo shorts.

"I'm sorry if I...um...interrupted anything." Her voice was soft, cultured.

I glanced at her as I pulled up my shorts, buttoned them, let the large shirt fall. This wasn't how I envisioned this moment to go. Caught with post-sex hair, wearing just a man's shirt. Unbuttoned. With said man answering the door in just his plaid boxers. Seriously, it couldn't be worse.

"We were actually asleep." Like she was going to believe that. I tossed the bedspread back up over the pillows, sat on the edge.

"Please, sit." I pointed to the only chair in the room. She sat, crossed her long legs beneath her, popped her gum. She had freckles across the bridge of her nose, clear gloss shiny on her lips.

"I'm sorry I'm staring. I've known you your whole life but have never met you." I pinched my lips together, glanced down at my fingers in my lap. "It sounds ridiculous."

She shook her head, her straight hair slipping over her shoulder, then pushed it back with her hand. "Knowing our family, it's not ridiculous at all."

"I didn't think...did you even know about me?"

"My mother...you remember her?"

"Yes," I replied. I didn't need to go into details and alienate the girl before I knew anything about her.

"She has Alzheimer's. Early onset. I didn't know you existed until three years ago when her mind started to go. Before that, I thought I was an only child. She was cold. Distant. My mother and I never saw eye to eye on anything. Ever. When I was little, I'd pick out my clothes only for her to make me go change. Every day. After a while, I used to put on the ugliest outfit just to get her riled. I played piano. I didn't even like piano. I wanted to play the cello. I was forced to play until she couldn't remember I took lessons anymore. When I got older, she took control of everything I did, everywhere I went. Who I got to see. My father...I mean, *our* father, was never around. Never. When he was, he went along with whatever Mother said."

She wasn't like Victoria. Relief washed through me to know she hadn't been brainwashed or turned into an obnoxious brat. She was even completely disinterested in our father.

"When Mother first had problems with her memory, she'd talk about the past like she was in it. She'd talk about you. At first, I didn't know who you were, but over time, she'd share more and more. I'd pretend to understand, to ask her questions and I soon realized you existed. I was stunned to know I had a sister. A sister that she hated so much. I'm sorry, but it's true."

She paused, looked at me to see if I'd become upset by her words. I just ran a hand through the air. It had been so long ago, I didn't care anymore what Victoria had thought of me. I'd known the first time I met her. She may have been the impetus to send me away, but perhaps being at boarding school, away from her and her nastiness, may have been to my advantage. It sounded as if being stuck with her would have been far worse.

"You were like, six, when she married our father?" Elizabeth cocked her head and considered. "I don't know how she could hate a small child like that, but she did. When her mind started to slip, she'd talk about how you killed Todd's brother, how you were a murderer."

My stomach bottomed out. She thought I'd killed David. So I had to be careful what I said. "You were twelve when that happened. You didn't know? What about the press? There was so much in the news about what I did. It was impossible to miss. Magazines, newspapers, TV."

Grif came out of the bathroom wearing shorts and a T-shirt, eyed us both, probably wondering how it was going. He knew how important meeting Elizabeth was to me, important enough to enlist his help, even when I'd thought he worked for Moretti at the time. When he sat down next to me, he shifted the mattress with his weight and I tipped into him. He kissed me on my temple.

"I remember being in France with her and saying we were going to have a French tutor for a few months. That was when you went to jail?"

I nodded.

"We eventually came home and I was home schooled. Sheltered would be an understatement," she muttered, rolled her eyes. "A convent would have been more exciting. But, I didn't know anything different. Didn't realize I'd been kept in the dark about so much."

"Until your mom got sick," Grif commented. He'd either been listening in from the bathroom with super-power hearing or he remembered when I told him about Victoria's illness.

Elizabeth looked to Grif, nodded. "Then I went online, read up about what happened. I didn't tell anyone because the reason had to be pretty big never to talk about you. So I kept it a secret. Tried to find out as much information as I could about what you did. God, I'm sorry," she said, her voice rough.

I reached out, took her hand. "Don't be. Really."

Wiping at the corner of her eye, she pulled her shoulders back. "I hired a private investigator to find you."

"What?" I felt sucker punched. I'd hidden to keep Todd from finding me. It kind of freaked me out to know there were other people on a similar hunt. "When?"

"After I read the stories about what happened."

"You were what, fifteen?" Grif asked. His hand stroked up and down my back.

She'd hired an investigator at fifteen?

"I was given an allowance. Money wasn't an issue. No one paid attention to me as long as I did what was expected. Mother was off on tangents then, my father never home. They never knew about it. I was careful and the man was only supposed to contact me if he found something. Anything, even a trail you'd left behind. Unfortunately, the man never found you."

"Why were you trying to find me? For Todd?"

Elizabeth looked as if I slapped her. She stood abruptly. "For Todd? I hate Todd. Look, I've got to go."

She walked to the door.

She hated Todd? Did that mean—

I jumped up. "Wait!"

She took her hand off the doorknob, turned. When I looked at her, I saw myself, just a few weeks ago. So sad, so alone.

"Please, tell me. Why did you want to find me?"

"So I could know the truth. Whether you were alive or dead. Why you ran away. What you were like." She paused. "What they did to you."

Tears filled my eyes, rolled down my cheeks. A huge lump formed in my throat and I couldn't get any words past. I just walked over to her, pulled her into my arms, hugged her. At first, she stood there, arms at her sides, stiff. I felt her shudder. Then, slowly, she lifted hers to wrap around my waist, her head on my shoulder.

We stayed like that long enough for me to get my emotions under control. It was difficult when I felt her breathe, felt her warmth, knew she was real, flesh-and-blood real and had come to me.

I let her go, stepped back. "Will you come and sit with me? Please."

She looked so forlorn when she lifted her head, looked me in the eye.

"Come. Sit."

I didn't wait for her to answer, just moved back to the bed. Grif was where we'd left him, although now he leaned forward, elbows on his knees. Just quietly watching.

Elizabeth returned to the chair.

"Okay, you wanted the truth," I said, my voice strong once again. I told her about my mother dying, being sent to boarding school. About her birth and trying to get home from Switzerland. About Todd, our wedding. What happened to David, jail. Escaping. Everything I'd told Grif and Carrie and maybe a little more since she knew the people involved. To Grif, they weren't real. Yet.

By the time I'd finished, the sun had set and the room had grown dark. If there ever was a mood killer, it was my life story. We sat there quietly. Grif just stared at Elizabeth, probably doing his usual "people reading". Elizabeth was pretty good at hiding emotion, like I was and I didn't know what she was thinking. What she'd say. If she'd run off.

"I understand why you left because there are days when I wish I could just disappear, but...why did you come back?" she finally asked.

I glanced at Grif for a moment, but focused on Elizabeth's eager eyes. "I came back for you."

35

rif

THE PAST THIRTY MINUTES WERE LIKE A HALLMARK MOVIE. TWO GROWN SISTERS, never meeting before, crying in each other's arms. A sob story told of a life lost. One giving up the safety of anonymity to save the other. Screenwriters would kill for a plot like that.

Reality, however, was heartbreaking. Anna's bleak, lonely childhood, her life derailed by a sociopath. She'd just shared things with Elizabeth I hadn't heard before. Additional details that her half-sister could recognize from her own sad experiences like forgotten birthdays. Watching Elizabeth closely, she knew what Anna shared was the truth. Could finally understand *why* she'd left and never come back. Anna hadn't just been tossed aside, she'd been assaulted then accused of murder. I pictured Elizabeth a little like Anna: strong, brave, wise beyond her years, yet so unbelievably young.

It was hard to imagine Anna at eighteen, like Elizabeth now, falling for all the shit Todd had shoveled her, yearning for attention and affection, instead being given to his brother like a whore, getting arrested for murder. I never wanted to hurt someone more than I did that sack of shit. If I could take the heartbreak from her, I would. I just had to help her find closure on her past, then just look forward to a life with me.

"You know why he's marrying you?" Anna asked Elizabeth cautiously.

"Of course. Money's the only thing he wants from me." Her chin drooped, the tough woman replaced by the vulnerable teenager. "There was this guy." She shyly looked down at her lap but I couldn't miss her schoolgirl blush. "I...I liked him." Her smile slipped, fell away entirely. "Somehow Todd found out about him and the next day he'd transferred to some state school in Texas. Todd's afraid of competition, but he wants to keep me happy. At least temporarily."

Temporarily, all right. As soon as Todd married her, who knew what he had planned? Based on what he'd done to Anna, and the lessons he'd learned from that experience, he would tie up loose ends, be more precise and deliberate to either keep under his thumb, devise a plan to get Elizabeth in jail, or ensure her death. Her father would stand behind him, whatever his plans, just like he had with Anna. Her mother didn't even know who her daughter was anymore, it sounded like. She wouldn't be of any help at all. Todd didn't have any more siblings left to kill off, so this time he had to do it right. There were no third chances for him.

Elizabeth looked calm and pulled together, but I could tell she'd really cared for the guy that Todd had shipped away. I'd seen my sisters mope through crush after crush in their teens. With three of them, there'd been a lot. At least they'd had each other to console and commiserate. Burn photos in an old coffee can together, but Elizabeth, from what I'd heard, had no one.

This was why Anna had been so desperate to help Elizabeth that she'd come to Scorch that night. She'd been willing to deal with the devil—Moretti and ultimately me—to save her half-sister. It had meant that much to her. Sitting here, meeting the girl, she was barely a woman, had me thinking similar thoughts. I'd do anything in my power to help her. Not just for Anna, but because this girl deserved more than what she'd been given. What she was going to get if we didn't help. Money didn't buy love. Safety. Security. You couldn't buy your way out of her kind of misery and heartache.

"You don't really think I'm going to marry him, do you?" she glared, eyebrows raised.

"I didn't know anything about you before today. I didn't know if you'd grown up just as...cruel as your mother or not. For all I knew, you wanted to marry Todd."

"Please don't make me vomit," Elizabeth replied.

"Why don't you just say no?" I wondered. It was rather simple. He could sink his claws into someone else's millions instead. She wasn't the only heiress out there. "Tell the guy to fuck off."

Both Anna and Elizabeth froze, stared at me. They looked at me as if I asked them both to marry *me*.

"What?" I asked. The question wasn't that strange.

"The only way out is to disappear like I did, or be dead," Anna told me.

Elizabeth agreed. "I could run away, but they'd find me. My father and Todd. I don't know how Olivia did it, hiding like she did, so I wouldn't get far."

She didn't know her sister's other identity. Didn't know she wanted to be called Anna, not Olivia.

"I always figured he married my mom for her money, but she died so young. He knew it was all tied up waiting for me to turn eighteen. He wanted it, wanted it enough to pull in Todd, who he'd been grooming to take over."

Elizabeth considered Anna's words before she spoke. "Could be. Then. Now, he's got gambling debts. Big ones. He's used money from the business to pay them off, but the Board is getting suspicious. Todd's obviously in on it, so they need quick cash."

"You," I said.

Elizabeth pursed her lips. "Yes, me. I'm the quick—and long term—cash they need to solve their problems. So if I ran away, like I said, I wouldn't get far. All that would happen to me would be a commuter flight to Vegas and a quickie wedding. My father's off in Asia on some new deal or trying to get extensions on his debts, so Todd could do whatever he wanted. My father wouldn't do anything to stop him since he needs the marriage even more than Todd."

"You've thought about this and have some ideas on how to get out of it," I said, watching Elizabeth closely. She was good at hiding her emotions, but I saw that quick flare of spark in her blue eyes.

"It's all about the money. Which means Father can keep on gambling and Todd can keep on living the high life." My inheritance when my mother dies, which is sooner rather than later. It's not like Todd has to wait until she's old and gray to keel over anymore. Alzheimer's is taking care of that."

The fact that Elizabeth talked about her mother so bluntly, so clinically, depicted how much she disliked the woman. How there wasn't any type of mother/daughter relationship at all.

"I'm eighteen, so I drew up a will without either of them knowing. If something happens to me, I put *you* as my sole beneficiary." She pointed at Anna.

"Me?" Anna looked stunned. "You didn't even know if I was alive!"

The contrast between the two were remarkable. Anna was dark, her hair and eyes just shy of black, while Elizabeth was all California blond and blue eyed. Where Elizabeth was tall and slim, a model's build like her mother's, Anna was sleek curves and lean muscle. Personalities, however, were much similar. Equal toughness, wariness, eagerness to please and be loved. Whomever Elizabeth finally fell for would be lucky to have her—right after I ran a background check and had a little chat with him and my service pistol.

"What I do know is that the will would have gone into probate, which would take years, most likely driving Todd crazy and pissing him off. Besides, the company is large enough where my death would make news. I'd hoped you would hear about it, come forward."

"Missing half-sister sole beneficiary of dead heiress," I muttered. It made sense. For a teenager, it was smart reasoning.

"Something like that. It didn't really matter. I figured Todd wouldn't be able to touch the money if all of it was in probate and when you did show up to claim it you'd get to tell him to fuck off."

Anna's mouth fell open, probably because Elizabeth had said fuck. "Oh."

"That would only happen if you were dead," I countered, and that idea didn't sit well with me. What eighteen-year-old thought about wills, probate and planned for their death? Anna's little half-sister, that's who. Smart enough to come up with a solid plan to give Todd the finger. But only after she was dead. They were one seriously fucked-up family. "Once you were married, he could live the life he wanted. With you alive."

"I had a plan for that, as well. But so do you." Elizabeth looked to Anna. "You have something on Todd. You know his secrets. You wouldn't have come back without something really good."

"I came back because I couldn't let you marry Todd. I've saved the information I have as insurance. For a rainy day."

This was news to me. She'd never had the chance to tell me what dirt she had on her ex. It couldn't be damning enough to bring her out of hiding because she would have used it like a weapon by now.

"I'm not sure if it's enough though. He wants your money and nothing's going to stop him, especially with our father's backing. Not you, and definitely not me. He can easily accuse me again of murdering David."

Elizabeth stood, moved to lean against the wall, arms across her chest like a defiant teenager. "Then let's disappear. Like I said, I can't just run away. That won't work. But I can disappear. Like you did. No one will miss me. My mother doesn't even know who I am anymore."

Oh shit. They were just alike. What I didn't need was for this girl to talk Anna back into hiding again. The only thing that stood between Anna and being free—truly free—and getting on with her life was Todd.

"We could do that—" Anna started.

My head whipped around to look at her. Had she lost her ever-loving mind?

"—but it won't solve anything. Todd will still be out there, perhaps preying on some other girl."

I exhaled a deep breath, surprised at myself. I'd actually thought for a moment there, a split second, that Anna would change her mind and do her little disappearing routine and take her sister with her. For that very short moment, I'd let my vulnerability take over and thought Anna would leave me. Just like Nadine. I trusted Anna, but I obviously needed to work on my issues. She'd done nothing to prove her not worthy of the trust, and I had to remember that.

"It doesn't matter. We'll be free!" Elizabeth said, with all the naivety of youth.

Anna shook her head. "No. When you disappear like I did, you're not free. In fact, I pretty much lived in my own little prison. Elizabeth, I was afraid of Todd finding me up until a few weeks ago. I didn't know if he'd toss me back in jail or kill me. I had no real life. No friends. No experiences. I was scared of *everything*."

I took Anna's hand, knowing all that was hard to admit. That she had to recognize a big chunk of her life had been flawed. She wasn't leaving, she was *joining* me. Joining life. We both chose to leave all the dark shit behind.

Elizabeth looked at me. "But you've got Grif. Look at you two together. It can't be all that bad."

Anna's gaze met mine, held. She smiled and it reached her eyes. I saw the love there, the confidence in *us*.

"I just met Grif last month and that's a whole other story."

I couldn't help but grin. One crazy story.

"A month? But you're in—"

"Love?" I cut in. "Oh yeah. Listen to your sister, Elizabeth. Disappearing isn't going to do anything to Todd except let him get away with being a complete asshole. Let's work together and give him what he deserves."

"What?" she asked. "Bankruptcy? That won't solve anything. He'll just find a dumb blond—I'm blond so I can say that—to take care of him."

"How about public humiliation?"

"Jail time," Anna added.

"How about humiliation in jail? That would work for me," Elizabeth offered, eyes alighting with downright glee.

"We should work together, merge ideas and fuck Todd over," I said, although I had no idea what either woman had in mind.

"And stay alive," Anna added.

That was the best idea yet. No way would I let anything happen to either sister.

Elizabeth grinned. "Works for me."

I was pleased to see them as allies, working together against a common cause, which was to fuck Todd. There should be bumper stickers made that said that. *Fuck Todd.*

I paused, let the sisters chat while I cleared my head. Thought about Elizabeth showing up at the hotel. This whole feel-good-moment had distracted us all. The sappy reunion made us forget something crucial. *Shit.* "Wait a sec." I held up my hand. They stopped talking and turned to me. "How did you find us?"

Elizabeth looked at me, blinked. "Here, at the hotel?"

I nodded.

"I have the private investigator on retainer. He couldn't find anything on you, but I told him not to give up. If he ever found anything, he'd let me know. Out of the blue, he called me this morning. Said your name came up on a flight manifest out of LaGuardia. Same birthdate listed with TSA. Your tickets were on the same confirmation number and the hotel is under your name." She pointed to me.

"The airline ticket put you on everyone's radar," I replied as I met Anna's surprised glance. "Which means Todd knows you're here, too."

"What?" Anna asked, her face turning pale.

"You're a loose end. A threat to him. He'd want to find you, just like you thought, but you hid really well. Elizabeth's PI couldn't find you. Todd wouldn't dirty his hands with a search himself, so I'm sure he's had somebody searching for you as well. Waiting for you to mess up. If Elizabeth's PI found you, then Todd's man has, too. The press won't catch wind of it. You're literally old news. No one's watching for you. Except Todd."

"Shit. He's right." Elizabeth started pacing. "We have to assume he knows you're back."

Anna moved to sit in the empty chair across from me so she could look at me easier. "It's not like he's going to show up here himself."

"No." Elizabeth shook her head. "He wouldn't get his hands dirty like that."

"He'd send someone else," I replied. "Time to pack. We're switching hotels."

36

nna

WE PACKED QUICKLY—WE'D BARELY HAD A CHANCE TO UNPACK—TOSSING THE few items of clothing into the suitcases and zipping them up. Grif refused to let Elizabeth leave us, not at this late time of night and not by herself. She wasn't in danger of Todd—he wanted her alive and marriageable—but it was a big city and Grif's big brother instincts had taken over. She'd spend the night with us. End of story. Elizabeth was surprised by Grif's soft side, ready to argue with him that she'd been out on her own before. Obviously, she hadn't ever had someone worry about her or care about her safety without an ulterior motive. After he gave her that glare I recognized as his don't-fuck-with-me-on-this look and mumbled something about being only eighteen, not thirty, she'd just nodded her head and followed us out of the room.

We didn't check out, just went out a side entrance and walked a block before hailing a cab. We couldn't be sure we weren't followed, so we switched taxis twice before finding another hotel, this one in Oakland. Grif chose a suite, a main room with a pull-out sofa and a separate bedroom. By the time we were settled in, it was late. We made Elizabeth's bed up and I gave her my pajamas to wear.

Ten minutes later, I was settled into the crook of Grif's arm, safe, secure and very comfortable.

"I'm really glad you gave your pajamas to your sister," Grif whispered. The room was dark, only a hint of city lights peeking through the blackout curtains. The air conditioner was loud, but Elizabeth was just a closed door away.

"That's because now I'm not wearing anything."

I felt Grif's chuckle more than heard it. "Damn straight. I think you can forgo pajamas from now on anyway."

His hand ran idly up and down my arm.

"Grif, we can't—"

"Of course, we can't. I just want to hold you. Your being naked is just an added perk."

I responded by giving him a kiss on his chest, the crisp hairs tickling my nose. I settled in, expecting to have my mind think about Elizabeth and Todd and returning to California, but I must have fallen asleep.

If I can't have your money, then you can at least be of some use. I don't want you. I've got women who know how to fuck, unlike you. David can have you. He'll teach you how to fuck like a good wife. In the morning, David will have you show me all the things you've learned.

I bolted upright, my skin slicked with sweat, gulping in air. I didn't know where I was. The room was dark and unfamiliar. When I felt someone stir, I stifled a scream.

"Shh. Anna, it's okay."

I pulled the sheet up to cover myself, moved back away from the voice. The cool air raised goose bumps on my damp skin.

"It's Grif. Jesus, you had a nightmare," he whispered in the darkness.

I felt the bed shift as he sat up, his dark shape in front of me. I was breathing deeply, trying to calm my racing heart.

"I'm going to reach out, so take my hand, okay?"

I saw it, the tentative motion of his arm, and I grasped it like a lifeline. "Oh God, Grif. It was awful."

He pulled me into him and we both tipped back on the bed so I rested on top of him, my head on his chest, our legs entwining. I could hear the steady beat of his heart, feel him breathing. His warmth seeped into me as I inhaled his familiar scent. It soothed me, the panic of the dream seeping away.

He pushed my damp hair back from my face, just let me rest.

"Better?" he asked, a few minutes later.

"Yeah." I gave his waist a squeeze.

"Want to tell me about it?" he asked, his voice quiet. Elizabeth was asleep in the next room.

I just stared into the darkness, feeling safe with his arms around me. "In the two months we were married, David had us over for dinner a few times. He was an okay guy. A few years younger than Todd, he was a lawyer. He was nice to me."

Grif continued to stroke his hand up and down my spine as I talked.

"One night, Todd showed me David's gun collection since I was on the shooting team. I'd only been out of military school about two months at that point. Just won state championship so he said I might be interested in seeing all of the guns David had. The guy was an avid hunter and also collected antique weapons. He had one whole wall in his den covered in guns. Rifles. There was one from the 1700s, another from the Civil War, others equally historic and valuable. Many modern ones. Pistols, high-powered rifles, shotguns. He had it all.

"I hadn't thought about it at the time, but looking back, Todd was setting me up. He made it a point to tell me which ones David kept loaded, what David killed with each one."

Grif's hands stopped moving, but held me close.

"The night Todd dropped me off, literally dropped me on his doorstep, he expected me to have sex with him. He'd told me David would *show* me some things."

I took a deep breath, let it out. Even though it was dark, I could see the past clearly.

"When David took me inside, he'd said Todd had called him. Told David I'd had my eye on him and wanted to sleep with him. With both of them. I was so surprised that I just stood there. I think he took that as a sign and started kissing me. Touching me.

"I panicked. Pushed him away. He grabbed me again, thought I liked it rough. I fought him off. He got mad and hit me. I knew what he'd do if I didn't get away. He chased me into his den where the gun collection was. I didn't think, just went to the wall and grabbed his nine millimeter. I don't remember much after that, but I shot him. I remember pulling the trigger."

"What are you saying? That Todd *wanted* you to kill his brother?"

"A few years ago, I dug up online Todd took out a life insurance policy on David the month before we were married. While I was still at school. I think at first he planned to have someone else do it, a hired hit man, but when he learned he couldn't touch any of my money, he wanted rid of me, too. It was really smart actually. Todd set me up by showing off his brother's gun collection. He set up his brother by telling him I wanted to sleep with him. He only came on to me because of whatever lies Todd told him. David wouldn't have done it otherwise. Todd killed his brother for the insurance money by using me to pull the trigger."

Grif rolled us both so I was pinned beneath him, his weight resting on his forearms by my head. He ran his thumbs over my temples. "It's really good. Jesus, that's one twisted man. You had no idea, did you?"

"I knew he was the one who accused me of murder. I knew he had the cops and the judge in his pocket and that I was going to rot in jail until someone outside of his reach caught on. I knew I had to disappear in order to stay alive. When the woman from the battered women's shelter approached me with an escape, I took it."

"When did you figure it out?"

"I watched the news, kept up with what was going on with Todd and my father through the Internet. It wasn't until years later that I found out about the insurance policy. I was then able to put it all together. I couldn't do anything with it. Don't you see? Even now, he can have me arrested again for David's murder. I wouldn't put it past him to fabricate new evidence against me. He had friends in very high places and probably even more now. An insurance policy is nothing."

"The grand jury might not see it that way," he replied, his voice dark. "They wouldn't take it to trial."

"I had no one backing me up. I wasn't willing to take that chance," I replied softly. "Until now. Don't get me wrong, I don't want to go head to head with him again, but this time, I have people on my side." I leaned my head into his caress. I could barely see him, but I knew his eyes were pinned to mine. "I have you."

"He won't fucking touch you again. I swear, Anna. I'll kill him first."

He lowered his head, kissed me with a fervency that was different. A little desperate, a lot demanding. I wanted his touch, his possessiveness as much as he wanted to give it to me. I needed to erase the nightmare, to replace Todd's evil with Grif's love.

"I need you," I breathed. I needed to be reassured he was there. That he could make it all go away.

"I'm right here, love."

We were quiet, touching each other slowly, taking our time in the darkness, in the quiet of the night. With Elizabeth just a door away, we pleasured each other in whispers and by taking in my sounds of pleasure with his mouth. We finally fell asleep, entwined.

Grif

I'd stayed awake, thinking about what Anna had shared. It had been so much more than the glossed-over story I'd heard with Carrie back in New York. The fact that she'd had to go through with that, let alone relive it through nightmares made me hold her tightly, listening to her breathe, knowing she was safe, and at the same time wanting to drive through the dark night to Lawton's door and kill him. I had my gun. It would take one shot. Anna wasn't the only expert marksman.

I spent the early morning hours planning more than just making Lawton pay. It was my turn to keep secrets. I'd let Anna and Elizabeth get their revenge, then I'd get mine. Lawton was a dead man. I fell asleep as the sun came up repeating that over and over, like counting sheep. *Lawton was a dead man.*

My face was tucked into the crook of Anna's neck when my cell rang, her curly hair tickling my face. I was on my belly, one arm thrown over her breasts, my right knee wedged between her thighs. She didn't stir at the second ring.

I carefully turned, trying not to wake her and grabbed my cell, whispered a quick, "Yeah."

"Someone's knocking on your door in five minutes. Open it. He's one of mine," Carmichael said, his voice clear, but intense. It was a voice I'd never forget.

I looked at the clock. Six thirty. With a three-hour time difference in New York, he'd been at work for hours.

I sat up, naked, slung my legs over the side of the bed as I wiped my face, rubbing the sleep away. What was it with people waking us up? "Yeah. Okay."

He hung up.

I looked over my shoulder at Anna, who shifted in her sleep, her arms now wrapped around her pillow, hugging it close. It was damn early and I hated to wake her after her nightmare. She needed her rest, an orgasm had helped her drop into a deep sleep, but Carmichael wouldn't have sent someone out of the blue if it wasn't important. Besides, she'd kill me if I left her out. "Anna, love, wake up." I put one knee on the bed to reach her and ran my hand down her arm. It was warm and soft and I wanted to just climb back in and wrap her in my arms. Instead, I nudged her gently. "Anna."

She made those morning snuffling noises, groaned. "What?"

"Carmichael sent a guy. He'll be here any minute to talk to us."

That perked her up as if I stuck a cup of coffee under her nose. She looked around, trying to get her bearings. "What time is it?"

"Early," I replied as I dug some clothes out of my suitcase, threw them on.

"Okay. Just give me a minute." She climbed out of bed and I enjoyed the view of her perfect ass as she walked to the bathroom. She'd either lost her modesty or wasn't awake to realize she was naked.

Once dressed, I grabbed my gun and went out into the main room, pulled back the curtain and woke Elizabeth. "Hey, kiddo. Rise and shine."

She made similar grumbling noises as Anna, but threw her pillow over her head. "Just a few more minutes," she mumbled.

"That's fine. The guy that's stopping by probably won't mind watching you sleep. Better wipe that drool off your chin." I stood and waited for that to sink in, the gun hidden behind my back.

One, two, three, four...she sat upright, her hair sticking every which way and wiped the back of her hand over her chin. "I do *not* drool."

I shrugged. "Maybe not, but there really is a guy coming—"

There was a knock at the door.

"There he is."

Elizabeth's head twisted to the door, realized her situation. "Holy shit, why didn't you tell me?" she squealed, dashed for the bedroom and shut the door behind her.

I grinned, having fun pushing her buttons. She might be going through all kinds of crap with her life, but she was a typical teenage girl and reminded me of my sisters.

At the second knock, my smile dropped, my gun raised, I looked through the peephole. If Carmichael hadn't called first, I would have shot the guy through the door and asked questions later.

I opened the door, eyed the man. He was my height but had thirty, maybe forty pounds on me. All muscle. He had the neck of a rugby player, shoulders like a linebacker with the bearing of Special Forces. He wore jeans and a pale blue dress shirt, sleeves rolled up to show Popeye forearms. Age was somewhere between thirty and forty with a military high and tight haircut and a strong jaw. He was the kind of guy who sprinkled nails on his cereal in the morning.

"Griffin? I'm Anders. Since you opened the door, I assume Carmichael gave you advanced warning."

He eyed the gun but did nothing.

I shook his hand, tilted my head toward the couch to sit, but remembered it was turned into a bed.

"Sorry, hang on." I tossed the pillow onto the floor, lifted the frame and folded it back into itself, jamming it in place with the blankets and sheets all crumpled. The seat cushions were next. "Sleepover."

Anders took a seat but stood again when Anna came in from the bedroom. "Ma'am. I'm Anders."

Anna had tamed her hair into a ponytail, put on a pair of jeans and a plain pink T-shirt. Her face was scrubbed free of makeup, which made the purple smudges beneath her eyes stand out.

Anders returned to the couch. Anna sat on the edge of the coffee table so I could sit in the desk chair.

"Know a man by the name of Todd Lawton?" Anders asked. No reason for chitchat. He certainly wasn't here for that, especially not at dawn.

Anna might be tired, but she was alert. Her eyebrows went up at the name, although neither of us knew this man's connection. Whatever it was, it couldn't be good. The triangular relationship—Carmichael, Lawton and Anders—wasn't based on fun and games.

I gave a quick nod.

"I got a call from him yesterday to do a little job. Wanted me to take out a woman named Olivia Edwards. I assume that's you?"

37

rif

I STOOD, GRABBED ANNA'S SHOULDER AND PULLED HER UP BY THE ARM AND shoved her behind me. With my right hand, I aimed the gun at Anders, who hadn't moved, hadn't even breathed. "What the hell do you want?"

My body was honed from my time in the Army to be instantly ready for Defcon One situations like this. My heart rate, although through the roof, didn't impact the steadiness of my hand. Everything was in sharper focus. I could smell Anna's shampoo, hear the low hum of the air conditioner, see the coffee stain on Anders' shirt.

I wanted to glance into the bedroom where Elizabeth had fled at the knock, but didn't want to give her away. I prayed she remained in there with Anders unaware of her presence. It was hard enough to protect Anna from a fellow military guy like him. It took one to know one. He'd been Special Forces, Rangers, SEALs, someone trained to do stuff you couldn't ever talk about.

Anders didn't blink, only slowly and deliberately lifted his hands in front of him. "I work for Carmichael. A few days ago, he put out a notice on Olivia Edwards and you, Griffin. You're under his protection."

That may be all fine and good but I wanted to hear it from the source.

"Anna, pull my cell from my pocket and hit redial. Put it on speaker."

She didn't hesitate. She pulled the phone from my pants, did as I said, as I kept my eyes—and my gun—on Anders.

"Carmichael."

"What's your friend's name?" I asked, my voice even, although I was ready to pull the trigger if needed.

"Anders. Looks like Paul Bunyan joined the Marines. You can trust him. He's there to help."

"You have a long reach." What were the odds of Lawton hiring a hit man that belonged to Carmichael? We were three thousand miles from New York. Millions of people, yet Lawton, the fucker, pulls out his Rolodex and dials one of Carmichael's men?

"You have no idea," Carmichael replied, his voice loud in the room.

He was right. I had no idea, but I was catching on. I wasn't going to ask any more questions. I took the phone from Anna, pushed disconnect and shoved it back in my pocket. I gave Anders one last hard look, then lowered my gun.

"Go get Elizabeth," I told Anna as I pulled her in to my side to brush my lips against her brow in reassurance. My tone was rough, but it couldn't be helped.

She looked at Anders, then nodded, disappearing into the bedroom.

"Tell me quickly. What did he want you to do?" I said quietly.

Anders darted a glance at the bedroom door. "I understand she disappeared for a number of years." At my nod, he continued. "I'm supposed to make her disappear again. This time, permanently."

My jaw clenched. "How?"

"His father-in-law had some Asian clients seeking willing women to leave the country with them."

Willing, my ass. He meant sex slaves. Jesus, what kind of sick fuck was her father, dealing in the flesh trade? I heard the sisters stirring. "Go on. Be quick."

"Heroin, deliver her to their private plane by six. She wouldn't be coming back." He, too, kept his voice down.

Heroin meant addiction. Addiction meant they held power. Anna would have done anything, anything, to get the drug. Including whatever fucked-up sex shit they wanted. When tired of her, they'd give her enough heroin to OD. It was a one-way trip.

"This is between you and me," I murmured to the man as they came out.

"This is my sister Elizabeth. Mr. Anders," Anna said by way of introduction.

He stood, towering over both women. Elizabeth's mouth fell open, but she quickly shut it, took the offered hand.

I gave Anders a pointed look and he nodded imperceptibly. Neither woman needed to know her father and Todd's plans. No way in hell. Since it wasn't going to happen, ever, it wasn't worth sharing. Anna didn't need any more nightmares. Shit, I was going to have them thinking about Lawton's fucked-up plan.

Taking a deep breath, I tried to calm myself. I needed to direct my anger in the right direction. *Lawton was a dead man.* I repeated in my mind my thoughts from the middle of the night. "Okay. Let's make sure we have this correct. Lawton contacted you about killing Anna." I gave it a little spin, but it was the truth.

"I'm Olivia, but I go by Anna."

Anders nodded his understanding. "Ladies, please sit." He offered them the couch by moving to lean against the wall.

I felt like I had three shots of espresso. I was too keyed up to sit. "You also work for Carmichael who has both Anna and me under his protection," I continued. "This means what, exactly?"

"Anyone who works for Carmichael knows not to touch either of you. He's not a man to cross."

"What about Lawton? Is he a man to cross?" I asked, weighing Lawton's power in comparison to Carmichael's.

"Hardly."

He didn't seem impressed by Todd Lawton, although Anders was a linebacker with military combat skills. He also wasn't eighteen like Elizabeth, and at one time, Anna.

"I called Carmichael and told him about the hit. Instead of killing you, it's my job now to keep you safe."

"Todd doesn't know you work for Carmichael?" Anna asked.

The big man shook his head. "It's not like we have business cards. I work for a number of people, as a consultant."

Consultant. Without all the sugar coating, he was a hit man.

"Does he...Lawton, think you're still on the job?" Grif asked.

"He does, but if Carmichael wants my mark to have protection, that trumps Lawton. Besides, if Lawton thinks I'm still on the job, that's the easiest way for me to help keep you safe. If I'm supposed to be killing you, no one else is."

Anna glanced at me and I knew she was thinking I'd done the same thing for her back in New York.

"So what's that mean?" Elizabeth asked. Anna must have given her clothes to wear because she wore a blouse I recognized along with a pair of shorts. Her hair was long down her back, slightly damp as if she'd run wet fingers through it to tame it. Without the expensive clothes and makeup, she looked her age.

"Lawton will go on thinking I'm working for him when in fact no one touches anyone under Carmichael's protection. If Lawton bothers you, I take *him* out."

That would be tidy. We could just sit back, play cards and watch reality TV while Anders tracked down Lawton and killed him for us. Neither Anna or Elizabeth would have to worry about that sick fuck anymore. I didn't think Elizabeth cared one way or the other how Lawton left her alone, but Anna wouldn't have closure. I couldn't have her waking up, night after night, with nightmares about her past.

"Anna has to deal with him first. On our terms. Safely. Then he's all yours," I told him.

"Mind telling me what the bad blood is between you?" Anders asked. "Some background here would be good."

Anna glanced at me before she began. It took about five minutes, but she'd given Anders the basics of what had happened to her. "I don't want him dead. He needs to rot in jail." She glanced at me, then at Elizabeth. "I know that's cruel, but he does."

She had a kind heart, but very misplaced. Cruel was giving Anna to his father's clients as an unwilling, drugged sex slave. Prison was too good for him. If something happened to him in prison, like a shiv to the gut, it would ease my mind. I looked at Anders briefly, but said nothing. I had no doubt he could read my mind—and get it done.

"We just have to catch him doing something that we can use against him. He's smart and very slick, which means that's not easy to do," Anna said.

"No, it's not," Elizabeth countered. "It's fairly easy actually. I just couldn't do it on my own. With all of you, my idea could work."

I stared at her. Blinked. So did Anders and Anna. This teenager had the magic answer? Why hadn't she piped up sooner?

"Well? What is it?" I asked, when she didn't say more. Drama. Teenage girls and fucking drama. When I had kids, I was having boys. All boys.

"Todd has an escort meet him at a hotel every week. Obviously, I wasn't supposed to know, but my PI keeps me posted. I needed ammunition against the man who's marrying me solely for my money. I mean, really, who wants to marry a guy named Todd, anyway? Oh, sorry Anna."

Anna's lip quirked up, but she said nothing.

Elizabeth was so young, should be getting ready for college, not using a PI to dig up call girls on her sociopath fiancé.

"Okay, um...hunh." Anders cleared his throat. "You're marrying Lawton?"

Elizabeth rolled her eyes. "I'm engaged to him, but I have no intention of marrying the guy. I've known about the escorts for a while and hoped to expose him to the press, but it wouldn't be enough. My mother's...out of the picture and my father's playing for Todd's team. He's too ruthless to fight alone."

"Damn straight," Anders said, his voice angry. If Lawton planned on giving Anna to some Asian assholes, no doubt he had a similar fate in mind for Elizabeth. The way Anders skin flushed red and the tone of his voice, he knew this, too. "How old are you? Nineteen?"

"Eighteen," Elizabeth replied.

"Oh, this man's going down." Anders focused his intensity toward me. It felt good to have a little manpower—literally—on our side. Anna could definitely take care of herself, but I couldn't protect her and let her go after Todd without someone else joining our team. If Elizabeth was going to enter the fray, which was most likely considering her gene pool, Anders was going to be a huge help. "When's his next little rendezvous?"

"Tonight."

I pulled out my cell, hit redial one more time. "I need a call girl. Tonight," I told Carmichael.

He paused only briefly. "I'll send Stormy Dawn."

38

nna

ANDERS LEFT US TO DO HIS THING. I REALLY HAD NO IDEA WHAT IT WAS. IF HIS JOB was to protect us now, it wasn't going to be too hard if we stayed in the hotel room. Which was the men's plan. Both Grif and Anders decided—it was pointed out this was not a democracy—we would lay low until tonight. I gave Grif the evil eye for not including me in the decision making, but they were actually right. We didn't want to blow it at the last hour by seeing the sights and either having Todd find us and do something else, or have the press get wind of my return. So Anders went off, promising to pick up Stormy Dawn, whoever she was, from the airport.

It was only seven thirty and none of us had had coffee. Once we returned the sofa to a bed, tossed Elizabeth her pillow, we all went back to sleep. Grif, usually frisky any time of the day when I was anywhere near a bed, fell onto the mattress like a Redwood, clothes and all, and didn't stir when I woke at noon.

I took a shower, put on makeup and a pair of jeans, white T-shirt and a pink hoodie sweatshirt. I left my hair to dry naturally, something I enjoyed now that I didn't straighten my hair. When Grif tugged on a curl, I knew how much he liked it and wouldn't go back to using an iron on it ever again. Not when he gave me *that* look. I found Elizabeth watching TV, sitting cross-legged with her pillow on her lap. The sofa was back to its original form so I sat down next to her.

"Did you sleep at all?" I asked.

She shrugged. "Some. I'm a morning person though."

"I wouldn't have known that from earlier."

Glaring at me, she replied, "Yeah, well, I'm not used to being woken up by a guy."

"I hope not," I muttered. Lots of kids had sex even younger than eighteen, but I could see Elizabeth finding some willing guy to sleep with because she'd grown up so sheltered.

"You're having sex." It wasn't a question.

"Yeah, well, I'm thirty. When you're my age, you can have sex, too."

"You were married to Todd when you were my age," Elizabeth countered.

I picked at a fray in my jeans. "That was a different kind of sex."

She raised an eyebrow.

"Being in love, lust even, is a requirement for sex. If you don't have that, don't do it. Take my word for it."

Oh, how I wished Grif had been my first. I was both in love and in lust with him. The first time would have been painful, but he would have made it good, made it special.

"I have no intention of marrying Todd, so I'll keep your words in mind." She tucked her long hair behind her ear. "Does Grif have any younger brothers?"

I tugged the pillow off her lap and smacked her with it. "No, annoying sisters, just like you."

She grabbed the pillow, tucked it back in her lap.

"You better be careful. I think Grif's going to be very particular about the guys who are interested in you."

"He is? Why?"

Why? God, she was just like I'd been just a short time ago, questioning why people were nice to me, completely wary of any kindness. She was just as jaded and that broke my heart.

"Look at you," I waved my hand in her direction. She still wore my clothes she'd thrown on earlier, all wrinkled and slept in. "You're gorgeous. All that blond hair and crazy-long legs. Grif's going to be interrogating every date you have because he cares about you. It's his job to keep the women in his life safe. That includes me, his sisters, *you*."

"So I get an older brother, too." I watched her as she considered this. I knew how hard it was to transition from being self-reliant to depending on people overnight. She fiddled with a thin silver bracelet on her wrist I hadn't noticed before. "Cool," she said, as her mouth tipped up into a sly smile.

"Since you're not marrying Todd—" over my dead body, "—then what are you going to do with yourself. College?"

She bit her lip, glanced sideways at me with her gaze on the TV.

"I know you have secrets. We all do. Grif, too. We're all really good at keeping them, and for good reason, but it's time to share. So, college?"

"College. Definitely." She looked at me. Her eyes were so blue, so completely different from mine. "I want to be an interior designer."

"Really?" I was surprised at that. The way she finagled and cajoled I pegged her for a lawyer.

"I applied to schools. That's my secret."

"And?"

"And...I got in. Being home schooled made getting good grades easy."

I didn't believe that. She got in to schools because she was really, really smart.

"Yale, Rhode Island School Of Design, Duke."

"Wow. Amazing schools. All on the other side of the country. Just like me."

She drew her eyebrows together. "Just like you?"

I shifted so I leaned against the arm of the couch, facing her. "After I disappeared, I bought my apartment in New York, then went to Harvard. It took a little time, but the people who made my new identity gave me the fake transcript needed to go to college. That had been one of their demands on me. I could have the new identity as long as I went to college. Looking back, the woman was looking out for me. So I rented in Boston close to school, but kept my apartment as home. Went back on breaks, summer. It's being sold now since I'm Olivia again."

"Won't you miss it?"

That was a good question. Would I miss my little bolt hole? It had been my world, and it had been safe. I zoned out at the TV as I answered her. "Looking back, I was lonely. Really, really lonely. Being afraid is hard work, Elizabeth. But do I miss it? No. Home is where Grif is."

"When this is all over, where's that?"

Another good question. One I couldn't answer on my own. "That's something Grif and I have to decide together."

She stared at the TV for so long, I thought we were done. "Can I come visit you?"

My mouth fell open. I grabbed her hand, forced her to look at me. "You're my sister. The only family I've got. Maybe we can all decide where to go from here. Together."

The smile she gave me was brilliant and I could literally see her shoulders lift. The weight of being alone was gone from her as well. "Wow, I feel like Sloth from the *Goonies* when Chunk tells him he's going to live with him now."

Okay. I got stalled for a minute on the eighties movie trivia. "I don't have a Baby Ruth bar like Chunk did, but we can order room service." I loved that movie. I remembered seeing it Switzerland on movie night, which meant a group of girls in the lounge with a VCR and popcorn. I longed for adventure like the kids in the movie had, where One Eyed Willy would help them save the day.

"Oh my God, you know that movie! I'm such a movie geek," Elizabeth squealed.

She was eighteen going on thirty going on twelve. I grabbed the menu by the phone.

Grif came out of the bedroom, hair mussed and a crinkle down the length of his cheek. He rubbed his eyes blearily. "I swear I haven't heard a girl squeal like that since Carrie was seventeen and Tommy Landecker asked her to the prom." His voice was rough like tumbled rocks.

I stood, went over to him and wrapped my arms around him. He was warm from the bed and his T-shirt was soft against my cheek.

"Sorry," Elizabeth murmured.

"As long as it's not for a stupid spider or something, I'm good. Listen, I got a text from Anders." He lifted his hand holding his cell. "The time and place has been arranged. We need to move hotels one more time. We're reserved down the hall from Lawton's little get-together so we've got to get there before he does."

"Can we order room service before we go?" I asked, savoring his scent.

"Order me a cheeseburger and fries while I'm in the shower. You." He pointed to Elizabeth, eyed her warily. "You better not be one of those girls that eats like a bird."

"Make that a double, but I want a chocolate shake, too," she told him.
"That's what I like to hear."

39

rif

LAWTON, OF COURSE, WOULDN'T TAKE ANY OLD HOTEL ROOM FOR HIS FUCK session. He had to get a suite. Which meant we were in one of our own two doors down. It was twice the size of my apartment in Denver; two bedrooms, a kitchen, even a baby grand. I liked the finer things in life as much as the next guy, but this was over the top. For what Lawton was going to do with his escort, he might not even need a bed, let alone two of them. Thinking about the guy's sex life made me want to hurl.

Regardless of what happened, we weren't moving again, and the two bedrooms were going to come in handy. Elizabeth would be in her own room situated on the other side of the massive main living space, far enough away from us for privacy. And I needed privacy for what I planned to do to Anna. When she completely freaked out by the nightmare, I had not only to soothe her, but myself, too. I couldn't hold back, even knowing only a door separated us from her sister. Every time Lawton crept into her mind, I wanted to erase it all with my touch. I literally wanted to fuck her until she forgot. So far, it was working.

It was time. Lawton would get what was coming to him and Anna could get closure. Elizabeth could give the guy the bird, too, then be a perfectly normal, obnoxious teenager. Stormy Dawn turned out to be a woman closer to my age but with breasts that could be used as flotation devices and legs that never ended. I did a double take when she came into the suite, I couldn't help it. Anna gave me the evil eye, considering the woman looked like she just stepped out of a porn flick. And she was wearing jeans and a T-shirt. Okay, the T-shirt had a V neck showing a vast expanse of cleavage and a pierced navel with a jewel sparkling enough to draw a man's eye. Her hair was long, with side-swept bangs. The color couldn't be natural, although based on her profession I doubted she had any hair elsewhere on her body that could offer confirmation.

I stole a glance at Anna, who, along with Elizabeth, were openly staring at the woman. I had no interest in discovering Stormy Dawn's hair color. Although beautiful, she was all fake. Plastic surgery, tanning beds, a hair salon and tons of makeup made the overall effect. But Anna, she was natural. Real curves a man could grip, soft skin that was so pale in places a network of veins showed through. It reminded me she was real, flesh and blood. Breakable.

Stormy Dawn could easily distract Lawton. Hell, I was distracted. Any conscious male would be. That was obviously why Carmichael had sent her specifically. Anders wasn't paying her much attention, digging in a small bag and pulling out the paraphernalia for a wire, but he'd had an extra hour or two with her getting her from the airport.

"You're real name isn't Stormy Dawn, is it?" Elizabeth asked as they shook hands.

"No. I use that name when I work for Carmichael. And that means, no, I won't tell you my real name." She added the last when Elizabeth started to open her mouth. Her voice was soft, her words kind, but direct.

"I love your makeup. Do you think you can show me—"

"No," I cut in. Elizabeth was not getting tips to look like a hooker.

"Hi, Stormy Dawn. I'm Anna."

When Elizabeth realized she wasn't going to get anywhere, she flopped down on the couch with the TV remote.

"Anders filled me on the way from the airport. It's nice to meet you all." She gave a small smile, approachable, but clearly here for business.

Anders was turning out to be a decent guy, considering his profession. He had to know I was a cop, it took one in the industry to know one, but he didn't care. Clearly, he took the protection business seriously. Either that or the threat of being executed by Carmichael was his motivation. He'd been nothing but courteous to Anna, and even more so with Elizabeth. When he learned she was engaged to Lawton, I thought he was going to lose it, and he was one cool customer. He followed the code, killing only those evil enough to deserve it. He didn't mess with women or kids. Protected them when needed.

Between Anders and Stormy Dawn, we seemed well equipped for tonight. Somehow, Anders, even with his giant size, had slipped into Lawton's suite to bug the place. It would let us know when he arrived and when Stormy Dawn should arrive. All we had to do was prep and wait. Elizabeth watched a movie on satellite and Anna, giving up on any amount of patience just sitting around, went to take a bath in the suite's Jacuzzi tub. Now wasn't the time to join her— it was large enough for two—but I vowed to do so before we left.

"Are you going to sleep with him?" Elizabeth asked Stormy Dawn. The woman sat in a comfortable chair perpendicular to the sofa, her feet up on the ottoman in front of her, reading a book she'd pulled from her suitcase. I was setting up the computer that would record everything that happened in Lawton's suite: video and audio. Stormy Dawn would carry a bag with a hidden camera and mic. She'd be going in alone, relying solely on the wires for us to see her and help if needed. She wasn't nervous about the job she was about to do, in fact, she was downright relaxed. She'd obviously done this kind of thing before, so I had to let it go.

Stormy Dawn flipped over her book to hold the page, looked at Elizabeth, unfazed by the probing question. I pretended to fiddle with the machine as I watched and listened. Kids could ask questions grownups couldn't. "With your fiancé? No. I don't sleep with any of the marks."

"He might be my fiancé, but I'm not marrying him. Do you...um, do you kill them?" Elizabeth questioned, biting her lower lip as she did so.

Smiling, Stormy Dawn leaned forward and patted the ottoman. "Sit." When Elizabeth did, she continued. "I'm a lawyer. That's really what I do. This," she pointed to herself, "is all fake."

No kidding.

Stormy Dawn chuckled. "Yes, they're fake," she added when Elizabeth just gawked at the other woman's breasts. "What I mean is, Stormy Dawn isn't the real me. I don't normally dress like this. I bet you wouldn't recognize me if I wore my regular clothes, did my makeup and hair like normal. And that's the point. People see what they want and I use it to my advantage. You need me to be a call girl to frame your fiancé. So that's what I'll be. I don't need to have sex with him to do that."

This was a relief to me. Honestly, I had no idea the kind of woman Carmichael would send. I knew the plan, but didn't know how she was going to achieve it. Stormy Dawn, or whatever her real name was, was right. I had only looked at her *assets* and made immediate assumptions about her. She was a lawyer. She was no dummy.

"What kind of law do you practice?"

"Public defender. In New York."

There was the connection. Twenty bucks said she worked with Adam Carmichael.

"When you listen in tonight, remember, whatever you hear is not real. Okay?"

"She shouldn't be listening in, period," Anders said from across the room. He was still working with the electronics but gave Elizabeth a hard stare. "It's not appropriate for a kid."

Elizabeth's chin bumped up as she narrowed her eyes at the big man. "I'm not a kid. I'm eighteen."

I swore beneath my breath. "Hey, kiddo. He's trying to protect you. Lawton's not going to be a gentleman and we don't want you getting the wrong impression."

She cocked her head. "About what? Todd? I think I know more about him than you do."

"No. About sex." Jesus, I was having a sex talk with a kid. I was getting old. "This isn't how it's supposed to be."

"It's not all rainbows and sunshine," she countered. I smiled to myself, remembering I used those same words about my life undercover.

"No, but you need to find the right guy—"

"Todd's *not* the guy," she said as she stood, crossed her arms over her chest. Defiant.

"Thank Christ," I muttered. "You need to find the right guy and make it special. When you're thirty," I added.

"Like you and Anna?"

I thought for a moment. Thought about all the women I'd been with who'd meant nothing to me. I couldn't remember their faces, let alone their names. I thought about Anna and how she did something to me, filled something inside me that had been empty. That when I put my hands on her it was with reverence—and a whole lot of lust. The difference was, I needed Anna like I needed my next breath and that wasn't going to change. Ever. "Yeah, like me and Anna."

"Don't worry, you've both given me the same sex talk now. I'm good."

A door opening then closing came through the speaker of the laptop. We turned our attention to the machine, listened. Lawton had arrived.

"Listen, the deal needs to go through," he said. Then silence. "No, Edwards isn't involved. He's in Asia somewhere with a client." He was on the phone. "Look. I've got a meeting. Solve this problem and get back to me tomorrow."

His voice was clipped, cultured. Cranky. He sounded like a complete asshole. Hearing that Anna's father was in Asia only validated what Anders had said.

We heard a clatter, probably his cell being tossed onto a table, footsteps, nothing for about thirty seconds, then a toilet flushing.

Stormy Dawn stood, pushed her blond hair back over her shoulder. "Looks like I'm up."

I sent Elizabeth to get Anna. If I'd gone into the bathroom and seen her in the tub, bubbles on her slick skin, I wouldn't have cared what Stormy Dawn did. I'd have been too busy making Anna wet in other ways. Yup, I had it bad.

40

nna

This was it. I'd been waiting for over ten years to get back at Todd. We heard Stormy Dawn's knock through the hidden mic, the video feed from her large purse showed the hotel room door. Anders, Grif, Elizabeth and I pulled chairs from around the dining room table to sit in a semicircle around the laptop. We were quiet, eyes riveted to the screen.

Todd made her wait, which ratcheted up my nerves. What if he found the wire? This wasn't a simple game. I knew what he could do firsthand. He was dangerous.

Finally, the door opened and there stood Todd. He wore a white dress shirt and tie, the top button undone, but the camera only showed as high as his chin so I couldn't see his face.

"Hello," Stormy Dawn said, her voice softer, more sultry than normal.

She stepped into the room and the door clicked shut behind her.

"Wow. When the service said Mindy was sick and sending a replacement, I wasn't expecting sheer perfection."

Elizabeth didn't say anything, but stuck her finger in her mouth and rolled her eyes. Yeah, I wanted to gag, too.

"What's your name?"

"Stormy Dawn."

"Well, Stormy Dawn, you can call me John. Want a drink?" Todd asked.

John? Seriously?

Grif muttered something along the lines of *fucker*.

"Whatever you're having, John." Stormy Dawn followed Todd into the large room. From the fisheye lens of the camera, the suite appeared similar to ours with the layout reversed. Stormy Dawn kept the camera on Todd and he poured scotch into two glasses. I remembered that was his drink of choice. The smell of it even now was repulsive to me. He turned to face the camera as he handed one to her, then took a big gulp of his own. Set it down with a loud clink on a table.

I finally got a glimpse of his face. Even through the screen, I recognized him. I sucked in a deep breath at seeing him again after all this time. I'd seen pictures, but this was different. He was moving and talking. Breathing. Living his completely fucked-up life as if I never existed.

His hair was still cut parted to the side, neatly groomed. Clean shaven, I could see new lines around the corners of his eyes. Even though the screen only showed black and white, I could tell he still sported a healthy tan. He was grinning at Stormy Dawn, his white teeth almost sparkling. He was so fake, so two-faced. He really was a sociopath. Grif took my hand in his and I felt the warmth there, making me glance up.

"Can you do this?" he asked, his eyes serious.

I pinched my lips together, nodded. This wasn't easy to watch. It stirred up...everything. I glanced at Elizabeth.

"What?" She pointed at herself. "You think I have a problem with this? Hell, no."

Grif gave my hand a squeeze and we turned back to the screen.

"Let's fuck," Todd said.

"We have all night, don't we?" Stormy Dawn laughed.

He held out his hands in front of him, palms up. "Look, sweetheart, you're a sure thing. I don't want to chat. I want to fuck. So strip."

There was the Todd I remembered.

The camera moved, stilled. She'd angled it so that we could see the profiles of both of them. Her hands worked the buttons on her blouse. As she undid them, slowly, she said, "I'll give you a taste. What do you want that your wife doesn't give you?"

Pulling the hem of her blouse from her skirt, she slipped it from her shoulders and it fell to the floor. She stood before Todd in a lacy bra, her very ample breasts practically spilling over the top.

"Big tits." Todd's eyes were glued to them. "I'm engaged. She's young. Inexperienced. Once we're married, she'll come with me to learn from the best. Do you do girl on girl?"

Girl on— Oh my God, visions of being eighteen again popped into my head. No, he'd never made me be with another woman, but he'd said something like that once. *I'll teach you, baby.* I was going to be sick. I stood abruptly, knocking my chair back and dashed to the bathroom. As I heaved up my dinner, I felt hands pull my hair back, run down my spine.

"You're okay," Grif murmured, soothing me with his words, but his voice was rough.

Finally, when there was nothing left, he went and wet a washcloth, handed it to me. It felt cool on my clammy skin. A nasty taste filled my mouth. I wiped my face, my mouth, then took the toothbrush he offered. I leaned back against the wall, the marble floor chilly against my legs.

I brushed my teeth as he knelt down in front of me, met my gaze. His look was haunting. "I can't take it away, Anna. God, I wish I could take it away. What he did to you."

I pushed myself to my feet, went around him to the sink, spit and rinsed my mouth. Our gazes met in the mirror. "Every time you touch me, you make me forget," I told him. "Every time I think about sex, I think about you. I just can't handle the thought of him touching Elizabeth."

Grif's shoulders went back and a dangerous glint came to his eyes. "He won't touch her. Ever."

"Okay." I didn't know what else to say. "Later. Later, with your hands on me, you can make it go away."

He ran a hand over my hair, brushed his knuckles across my cheek. "Yeah. I can do that." He dipped his head, looked at me carefully. "Can you go back out there?"

I took his hand. "Let's go."

Both Anders and Elizabeth looked at us as we came back, concern mixed with anger on their faces. I held up my hand so they didn't have to say anything. Grif and I sat back down, but he kept my hand in his as if he refused to break the connection between us.

"What did we miss? he asked.

"Not much," Elizabeth commented, eyes glued to the monitor. "Stormy Dawn talked about girl on girl for most of it. It was pretty educational."

Anders glared at her. A vein in his temple stood out.

"What? It's not like I want to do it or anything. I was only giving a recap." Elizabeth rolled her eyes.

I think I heard Anders growl.

"Now, I need to freshen up first, so get more comfortable in the bedroom while you're waiting," Stormy Dawn told Todd. If she hadn't taken off her shirt, Todd probably wouldn't have liked being told what to do.

Without waiting for an answer, she picked up her purse and we watched as she walked into a dark room, turned on a light. The screen brightened on bathroom fixtures and we could briefly see Stormy Dawn's reflection in a large mirror. Closing the door behind her, she set the purse down on the vanity with the camera aimed at a glass-enclosed shower.

Nothing happened for two, maybe three minute before we were on the move again—a hallway, a low-lit room.

There was the bed, with Todd sitting on it. He'd removed his tie, kicked off his shoes. The bag was expertly placed across the room so we could clearly see the bed.

"I forgot my drink," Stormy Dawn said outside camera range. "I'll bring you a refill."

We watched as Todd stood, removed things from his pants pockets, placed them on the end table next to the bed. A few coins, a cell phone, wallet. Muttering to himself, we couldn't make out the words.

Stormy Dawn came back in the room, handed Todd his drink, stood in front of him so her breasts were directly at eye level. "You want to fuck?"

Todd nodded, his eyes on cleavage.

"Drink up," she said. "You're going to need it with what I have planned for you."

We all watched as Todd emptied his glass. If his eyes hadn't been glued to Stormy Dawn's breasts, he'd have seen her faking a sip before placing it on the table next to Todd's things.

Returning to face him again, she reached behind her and unzipped her skirt, let it slip over her hips and down her legs to pool at her feet. She pushed Todd onto his back, his legs off the side of the bed. If I didn't like her, I'd hate her for her body alone. She had long legs that went on forever with those stilettos and a to-die-for ass that looked great in her lacy panties. Climbing up on top of Todd, she straddled him.

"Ooh, you feel so big."

"This is so gross," Elizabeth murmured.

I couldn't disagree. I think Anders growled again.

Stormy Dawn was an exceptional actress. I'd had sex with this guy. I knew how big he really was, and Stormy Dawn was lying through her teeth. It wasn't all that big and unless he'd improved with age, he didn't really know what to do with it.

She leaned forward so her breasts almost spilled over the top of her bra as she unbuttoned Todd's shirt. Slowly, she undid one after another, letting him ogle her chest, making him forget he was in a rush. She had to stall for five to ten minutes. With Todd, he could have fucked her and been done in that timeframe.

Parting the shirt, she ran her hands over his torso, taunting him, before she tugged at the shoulders, pulling the shirt down behind his back, pinning his arms in place. It was an expert move that looked seductive, but had a more practical purpose.

Todd tugged at his wrists, but with his expensive cufflinks holding the shirt tight, it wasn't going to give. His arms were pinned at his sides. Before he panicked or caught on to her moves, she spoke. "I've got you at my mercy. I like this. Now you can't touch me as we fuck." Her voice took on a soft, slow cadence, almost a purr.

She pinched one of his flat nipples and he hissed. "Like it rough?"

"Hell, yeah," Todd replied.

Her hands slipped to his belt and she started to undo it. The clanking of metal on metal as she did so was loud in our hotel room.

Anders broke the silence. "Elizabeth. Close your eyes."

"Don't worry. I'm not watching this. It's grossing me out. No way do I want to see Todd's shlong." She looked away.

Shlong? To be honest, I didn't want to see any naked parts of Todd either.

The tenting of Todd's pants was unavoidable, so instead of sliding down the zipper, Stormy Dawn rubbed her hand over him. That was a small mercy, but that act alone made us all shift uncomfortably.

"This is like a really bad porno," Grif commented.

"So, John, do you want my pussy or my mouth first?" Stormy Dawn asked.

Todd said something, but it was slurred, like he was drunk. I think he said pussy but it came out more like shush me.

Stormy Dawn grinned. "Let me get a condom."

Shimmying back, she slid off him and stood, walked over to her bag, her full body on display until she moved out of camera range.

We watched as Todd struggled for a minute with his shirt, then tried to prop himself up on his elbows, before he slumped back.

Stormy Dawn sauntered back to Todd, hips swaying as she held up a strip of condoms, tossed them on the bed next to him. "One's not going to be enough, is it, *John*?"

No response.

"John?" She leaned forward, one hand on the bed and nudged him. He muttered something too low to hear.

From her position, she turned her head and looked directly at her bag. At us. All slutty looks gone, she nodded her head.

Anders stood, towering over us. "Let's go."

41

nna

G RIF TURNED TO ME. "S TAY HERE. P LEASE."

This was hard for him, too. He wanted to keep me as far as possible from Todd, from anything that hurt me. I couldn't imagine how he had to fight with himself to even help organize something like this, but that's why I loved him so much. There were limits to what he could take, to things he wanted me involved in. Our relationship was a compromise. He was giving me this revenge. I had to give him the reassurance that I was safe when he couldn't be with me, but also sheltering me from the seedier side of life Grif worked in and Todd delved.

So I nodded my agreement and gave him a swift kiss. He ran his hand over Elizabeth's hair.

"Hey!" she muttered, but I could tell she was secretly pleased by the affection.

Anders didn't say anything, but got the gear bag he needed and held the door for Grif.

A minute later, we watched them come into camera view, joining Stormy Dawn. They stood staring down at Todd's prostrate body.

"Okay, what pose do you want first?" Anders asked.

Stormy Dawn walked over to Todd, undid the zipper on his pants. "Let's get him undressed."

Grif's head dropped in front of the camera, his image slightly distorted from the lens. "Anna, I'm turning the camera. No way can Elizabeth see this. Turn off the sound. If we need you, I've got my phone." He held it up for me to see. "Text me that you hear me."

I dashed for my phone, sent him a quick note back, watched the screen. I heard the beep and Grif looked down. Read my note. Grinned. "Yeah, later."

The camera turned into the wall.

I hit the button on the laptop enough times to drop off the sound.

"I want to hear that," Elizabeth said moodily.

"No, you don't." Grif and Anders were going to take pictures of Todd and Stormy Dawn together and it wasn't something for her to see. They had to talk each shot through, so their conversation was going to be XXX as well. I wasn't too keen on Grif seeing Stormy Dawn naked, but any interest he probably had would be ruined by her having fake sex with Todd. A naked Todd.

"What do we do while we're waiting?"

I hated waiting for other people, to be out of control, but I trusted the three of them to handle this part of the operation. My job was to keep my little sister safe and from being corrupted. "Cards?"

"Fine, but let me go to the bathroom first," Elizabeth said.

Once she'd closed the door behind her, I went to the laptop and nudged up the volume.

"—don't have to show it all the way in your mouth, just maybe put your tongue near his dick," Anders said.

My eyebrows shot up.

"That's better for me, like this?" Stormy Dawn asked. I could only imagine what she was doing.

"Good, now what if he fucked your tits?" Grif asked her.

My blood started to boil.

"Shit, I hate this," Grif mumbled.

"Let me get in position. Are you ready?"

"Yeah," Anders replied. "Tilt your head back so I make sure to keep it out of the shot. "Good. One more. Okay, done. What now?"

"Sixty-nine," Stormy Dawn said. "My hair will cover up—"

I heard the toilet flush, the sink turn on. I quickly hit the mute button and tracked down the cards.

After an hour, Elizabeth and I were settled on the couch playing Gin, a cushion between us with the discard pile on top. Grif and Stormy Dawn came back, both completely dressed as if they hadn't been involved in something shady, and naked. He came over to me and dropped a kiss on the top of my head before going to the big table and taking out the digital camera. Popping the memory card from it, he slipped it into the port in the side of the laptop.

"She's not going to ask, because she's too polite, but I'm not. How'd it go?" Elizabeth asked.

Stormy Dawn sat down in the comfortable chair where she'd read earlier, tugged off her stilettos and propped her feet up on the ottoman with a sigh. "Grif's putting the email together now. Give me the details behind what happens next. Anders filled me in a little, but this all somehow has to do with you."

She had her head turned toward me.

"And me," Elizabeth added.

Anders came into the suite, gave us a little wave of hello. "He's all set," he told Grif, who was focused on the laptop. "All tied up and waiting to be found."

"I killed Todd's brother for him. I hadn't realized I'd been set up until years later. You've heard this part?"

Stormy Dawn gave a little nod.

"Back when I was arrested, there'd been one reporter among the many who had believed my innocence. Her pen name was Jane Doe. She'd kept the media spin, the suppositions and plain lies out of her articles." I took the cards from Elizabeth and started stacking them. "When I disappeared, I followed the media frenzy. I followed everything, afraid he'd track me down. She was the only one who had even considered my disappearance was actually an escape. That exact word—escape—hadn't been in her articles, but the subtext was definitely there. I remember her specifically because of that. I looked her up this week and she's now an editor at one of the city papers, still using her pen name."

"This one?" Grif pointed to the screen. His brow was furrowed, his gaze serious as he talked with Anders.

"Yeah. That one, too."

The men were focused on their work, most likely culling the images to give to Jane Doe. I had no doubt they were also listening to me.

"I want to confront him. It's all I've wanted to do for years. Get him to tell me to my face that he used me to kill his brother. But that won't work. We can't get him to confess anything. Even if he was tied naked to that bed in his suite and video taped an admission. He's too smart for that. I could threaten violence, but he wouldn't believe me."

"I'll torture the guy for the fun of it, let alone get the truth out of him," Anders muttered as he cracked his beefy knuckles.

It felt good knowing the big giant would beat up Todd for me. "It would be coerced and nothing would be admissible in court. It'd be back to he-said-she-said and he could spin it so I'd be arrested for conspiracy to commit murder or something for what Anders would do. It would be a stronger case since I disappeared for twelve years, then held him hostage and threatened him. I'd be the one in jail, not him."

"He's squeaky clean," Elizabeth added. "The jury would side for him. Even if I were to testify on Anna's behalf, I have nothing on him. He's done nothing to me."

"It's not illegal to marry the eighteen-year-old sister of your in-hiding ex-wife," I said.

"There should be." Anders winked at Elizabeth.

Was that corner of his mouth curling up? Was that a smile? He'd kill Todd without thinking twice, but winked at a vulnerable girl. He was a softie.

"So you're going to share these pictures with this Jane Doe woman," Stormy Dawn said.

"Plus the information I collected about David's insurance policy. That's Todd's brother."

"Plus the asshole's room number and a keycard downstairs for her," Anders added. "He's trussed up like a Christmas turkey in there. By the time she shows up, he should be awake and in need of rescue."

"It's not punching him in the face, but it'll be closure."

"Insurance paperwork, illicit photos, naked in a hotel room, a press rescue and most likely a media scandal to follow. Not bad." Stormy Dawn seemed impressed.

"Done." Grif pushed back from the table, ran his hand over his face.

GRIF

. . .

WE SET AND BAITED THE TRAP. ALL WE COULD DO NOW WAS WAIT. ANDERS AND Stormy Dawn left, I assumed to hotel rooms of their own, but I didn't really care. The plan went off without a hitch. Stormy Dawn was impressive in dealing with Todd and her job was finished. Watching that asshole paw all over her was enough to make me want to go down the hall and beat the shit out of him, but the woman knew what she was doing. And it had worked. The GHB she'd slipped into his drink had knocked him out quickly enough. The rest—incriminating photos with Stormy Dawn—was easy.

One thing was for sure, I'd never look at another porno or *Playboy* the same way again. The whole photo shoot had been clinical and a little repulsive, aside from completely illegal. I'd done it all for Anna, but I felt dirty. Lawton lived in the borderlands, the space between civilized people and the underworld. Getting mixed up in it, even for the night, was like wading through shit. That was saying something with the undercover work I'd done.

"Are you okay?" Anna was in the bathroom, standing at the vanity. She'd put on the white hotel robe after her shower, her hair damp and her face scrubbed clean. I smelled toothpaste. She looked so sweet and clean and I wanted her. Needed her.

I moved to stand right behind her, pressing my cock into her back. There was no doubt she felt how hard I was; it was a permanent condition around her. We made love often enough, but I'd shown her the down-and-dirty fun of a good fuck too, which she enjoyed immensely if her breathy little moans were an indicator.

I wanted to take her to bed, savor every soft inch of her, but I couldn't. Not now. I was too over the edge. Lawton had riled me, amped up every protective instinct I had. Here she was, right in front of me, safe and whole. I needed to reassure myself she was with me in this, that this constant want was elemental for her, too.

Leaning forward, I nipped at her neck. "Now, Anna. It has to be now." Undoing the belt on her robe, I pushed the whole thing off her shoulders, let it drop to the floor. "Hang on to the counter."

She said nothing, just looked at me in the mirror. Her skin was a soft shade of pink from the shower. I ran my hands over the soft skin of her ass, looked my fill of her. I tugged at my belt, my zipper, then pulled myself free. With one thrust I drove deep with a groan, buried to the hilt. She was scalding hot and wet.

I watched Anna in the mirror, saw her skin flush red, her eyes slip shut. Her long hair—which she kept curly now because I demanded it—ran down her back in a thick, damp mass. "I can't get enough," I murmured in her ear, my hips bucking up and into Anna. We were slick and wet between us, her body primed for fucking just as much as mine. Just as often.

Anna arched her hips, pushing herself back into me, driving me that little bit deeper. "Please move," she pleaded, a little cry escaping as I slowly slid out, hitting that spot inside that lit her up.

Reaching around, I held her gently by the neck, my other hand on her hip, keeping her right where I wanted. Her inner muscles clenched me like a fist and I had to move. The instinctual need to mate, to bury my cock, empty my seed into her drove me. I was more animal than man and Anna loved it. Her body quivered with every thrust, a sign she was close to coming. Reaching down, I found her clit, ran my thumb over it in small, slippery circles, knowing I didn't have long. "Now, Anna. Come now," I demanded, watching her as she succumbed.

Intense pleasure built at the base of my spine, pulling my balls up and tight, readying for an all-consuming release. Sweat dripped from my brow as my hips pumped, one, two last times before I was engulfed in the deepest, most intense orgasm. I couldn't contain the shout as I emptied myself, all the while Anna's own pleasure had her pulling, gripping me within her. It was as if her body wanted to possess me. I know her heart already had.

I don't know how long it took for the aftershocks to wear off, for me to catch my breath. I released the tight grip on her hip, stepped back and slipped from her body. My seed slowly trickled down her thighs.

"What's the smirk for?" Anna asked, tucking her wayward hair behind her ear.

"Now we both need a shower before I take you again."

42

nna

Jane Doe's paper ran a front page spread on Todd's late-night activity. It showed a few very embarrassing images with Stormy Dawn, with strategically placed black bars over areas that were illegal to show in the press. Grif and Anders had done a good job to keep Stormy Dawn's face out of the picture, so only Todd was easily recognizable. It had gone on to describe how he'd been found tied up with alcohol in the room, but there was no mention of GHB or the insurance policy.

Neither could be confirmed in such a short time, but the damage had definitely been done. We were dressed and watching the local morning shows with their individual spins on Todd, his supposed philanthropic endeavors and the exposure of his secret side. Anders let himself in the suite. Although we looked up from the TV and greeted him, we didn't say more. He joined us by sitting in the chair Stormy Dawn used the night before.

Flipping through the channels, we spent an hour surfing the various newscasts, but they all said the same. In the eyes of the media, Todd Lawton was a fallen man.

"Is Stormy Dawn gone?" I asked Anders.

"She was on the first flight out this morning. Don't worry, she looks completely different when not dressed like a call girl. No one would connect her with the photos."

Good. She'd done her job, done it well and was safely out of the spotlight. I'd have to thank Frank Carmichael for having her help us.

"Now what? You didn't get a chance to confront him. He doesn't even know you were involved last night."

I shrugged.

"Is that going to be enough?"

I hadn't been able to face Todd like I wanted. Was what the media doing to him enough? Could I live with this attack on his character alone? Perhaps, once Jane Doe worked through the insurance angle, the police would look into his involvement in his brother's death. But it wasn't a guarantee.

"I don't know actually. Maybe. I think—"

There was a knock on the door. Anders stood, pulled his gun from a shoulder holster and went to see who was there. He turned to look at us, his face grim. Grif stood and the men did some kind of mental telepathy because Grif nodded and Anders beelined for our bedroom and shut the door behind him.

Grif looked through the peephole, opened the door.

"We're looking for Olivia Edwards. Is she here?"

I stood, moved to see who spoke. There were three men in the doorway. Police. Two plainclothes and one in uniform.

Grif stepped back, let them in.

They saw Elizabeth and me easily.

"Miss Edwards, it's been a long time," one of the plainclothes cops said to me. He held up a folded piece of paper, flipped it so I could see a black-and-white copy of an old photo of me.

"What do you want with her?" Grif asked.

"I'm Detective Roberts," he said instead of answering.

"Detective Hosanski," the other replied. Both men's badges were clipped to their belts at their hips. "This is Officer Gomez."

The men were all in their thirties, clean cut, conservative.

"You need to come with us, please."

"Is she under arrest?" Grif asked them.

"Can I see your IDs please?" Roberts asked of Elizabeth and Grif as he held out his hand.

Grif pulled his wallet from the back pocket of his jeans, handed it to the man.

"My wallet's in the other room," Elizabeth told him.

"Gomez, go with her."

Elizabeth looked to Grif who gave her a quick nod. She left, followed by Gomez.

Roberts looked up from Grif's ID. "Mr. Griffin, we—"

"*Detective* Griffin." Grif made his title very clear, that they couldn't walk all over us with their cop crap. Grif wouldn't stand for it, and neither would I.

Roberts eyebrows went up. "Detective? Out of where?"

"Denver."

"Well, Detective, we have some questions for Miss Edwards in relation to a murder."

"A murder? Who was killed?"

"David Lawton."

"I understand, *Detective,* that David Lawton was killed in self-defense. Not murder." They'd started already, insinuating murder.

Elizabeth returned, the officer giving her license to Detective Roberts. He looked down, read the ID, then looked back at Elizabeth. "Another Miss Edwards. Sisters?"

"Yes," said Elizabeth, her chin up as she looked at me. She wasn't going to say half-sister. To her—and to me—we were definitely real sisters.

"Aren't you engaged to Todd Lawton?" he asked, then looked to me. "You were married to him, weren't you? This is very interesting."

I tried not to roll my eyes. The man was an ass. "One thing is a constant in what you just said. Todd Lawton. Perhaps you're looking at the wrong people?"

"David Lawton was killed twelve years ago and Miss Edwards was found innocent of any crime. She moved on with her life. Is she under arrest?" Grif asked again, cutting into my war of words with Roberts. I wasn't going to win this one so I pinched my lips together.

"Not at this time," Hosanski replied. "Even though she moved on, went completely off the radar for all that time—"

"There's nothing illegal in walking away from the public eye," Grif cut in. He wasn't giving these men an inch. It came down to a battle of legalities, and I knew who was going to win.

"No, there's not. Since she's returned, we're within our rights to take her to answer some questions. This shouldn't take too long."

Yeah, right. Like forty-two days.

"You are, but I'm coming with her."

Hosanski shook his head. "Obviously, she's a flight risk, so she'll be riding with us. You can meet her there."

I was nervous. I didn't have butterflies in my stomach, but hornets instead, vicious and nasty. This was all Todd's doing. It had to be. He was twelve years older, but so was I. I wasn't that lost, alone teenager. I had people on my side. Todd couldn't do anything besides drag me to the station and make my life hell. This was payback. If he was going down, he wanted to take me with him. The difference between the two of us is that I'd been down for years.

"It's okay, Grif. I'll be fine." I walked over to him, went up on my tiptoes and gave him a kiss on his warm cheek. He hadn't shaved so his stubble was scratchy against my lips. I glanced at Elizabeth, gave her a small smile.

Grif didn't look too convinced. His hands were clenched as tightly as his jaw as if trying to keep himself from grabbing me. I knew the feeling. "You handled Gossing and Werbler in Denver. You can handle this," he whispered.

I HELD ON TO GRIF'S WORDS LIKE A LIFELINE, KNOWING I COULD TACKLE whatever Todd decided to throw at me. I was being brought in for questioning and accused of something new he'd made up. It didn't matter anymore. I had enough proof to prove reasonable doubt and I had Grif and Elizabeth on my side. Carmichael, too, although I wasn't sure how often he'd get mixed up with the police.

Once again, I sat in a sterile interrogation room. It was chilly with the air conditioner vent above the table blowing directly on me. The room had a heavy pine scent, as if the linoleum floor had been recently washed. Once again, they left me to sit. Stew. Worry. Another can of soda sat in front of me so I kept my hands folded in my lap. They knew who I was. My FBI-issued ID was proof of that. That wasn't needed in this town. They had enough old photos from when I disappeared to pull out.

Where was Grif? Was he with Elizabeth, shielding her from the media? Since her engagement photo with Todd was in the paper—that's how I'd learned about it—she'd be hounded by reporters about her fiancé's transgressions. Carrie was my lawyer, but she was in New York. Detective Roberts had wanted me for *questioning*, but that hadn't happened. Yet.

An hour after I sat down, the door opened. Instead of the detectives, in walked Todd. I was surprised, not expecting him. I had a moment of panic, but took a few deep breaths; he was the source of all my nightmares. He looked remarkably the same as the last time I'd seen him in person, almost twelve years ago. He had all his hair, but he had small lines at the corners of his eyes. His clothes were immaculate, pressed khakis and a white dress shirt. Beneath the façade of perfection, he looked gaunt, his skin pale, his eyes bloodshot, the after effects of GHB. I didn't feel sorry for him.

"Look who's back. And right where I left you the last time." He smiled, but it didn't reach his eyes.

"From the pictures in the paper this morning, you don't look like you did the last time I saw *you*. You should cut back on the sweets. That fat tire around your middle is an indicator of diabetes at your age," I countered.

His fake smile slipped. "Well, you're all grown up now." He eyed me in a way that made me feel dirty.

"What are you doing here, Todd?"

"That's my question for you."

"So you're the one who's going to interrogate me? Instead of your friends on the force? This isn't going to take forty-two days like last time, is it?"

He pulled out the chair across from me, the metal legs loud sliding across the floor, sat down. "This doesn't involve the police. It's between you and me."

I tilted my head toward the two-way mirror. "And everyone who's watching?"

"We have some things to work through." He tapped the tips of his manicured fingers on the table. "I'm not waiting another decade to have you resurface, fucking up my life."

I had to laugh. "God, are you serious? I fucked up your life?"

Todd leaned forward on his forearms. "That little stunt you pulled last night, it's not going to keep you from being charged with murder."

"It didn't stick the first time, it won't stick now. But that's not why I'm sitting here."

"Why'd you come back? I mean, it's not like I want you back."

"I came back for Elizabeth." It didn't matter that he knew. He had all the power at the moment, but that didn't mean I'd let him keep it. Just letting him think he had it was what was important right now.

His brows went up. "You, what, disappear for over a decade and you come back for a half-sister?"

"Don't you think it's a little sick, marrying another eighteen-year-old?"

Shrugging, he said, "She fits my requirements."

"Is that a double-D cup like the woman in the newspaper photos or a billion dollar bank account?"

A muscle in his jaw jumped.

"Elizabeth won't have you now, after the media spin that's going to go out of control after last night."

"You don't know what kind of public relations spin I can put on this whole thing. Ex-wife, in hiding for twelve years, distraught that he's moving on with her younger sister, pays a woman to drug and take pictures of him."

This was like a game of chess. One person moves, the game shifts. A good player plans a move far in advance, considers all the possibilities of the opponent and adapts. He might be smart, but I had more on my side. I was a woman scorned. And, I had the life insurance policy details—and so did Jane Doe.

"You want money? Fine. What's the price?" I leaned forward so our positions matched.

"For Elizabeth or for making you go away?"

I pretended to consider for a moment. "Elizabeth, but I'll go away for free. Life is so much better without you in it."

"Twenty million." He didn't bat an eyelash. Didn't have any qualms just swapping Elizabeth for cold, hard cash. She was worth more. Hundreds of millions, maybe a billion if the market held, but last night's fiasco had tarnished him. He'd put some spin on it to save himself, but only if he let Elizabeth go. The media wouldn't give up on them if they married. The speculation, the questions behind a marriage based on infidelity. With a call girl.

To go for only twenty million meant he was desperate. This money wasn't for my father. This was a side deal just for Todd. He could live easily on this arrangement for the rest of his life. "Done." I stood. "What about your crooked friends on the force?" I turned my gaze to the two-way mirror where I knew the cops who were loyal to Todd stood watching. "And Judge Nicholson, DA Saunders, Officer Reiman who initially arrested me." I started ticking off those who had a hand in my forty-two day stay in county jail. These weren't names I would forget.

Still glancing at the mirror, I continued. "There was that pretty ADA, what was her name, Todd? Melissa, something? Let me guess, the others might have been in bed with you to get me convicted, but ADA Melissa was literally *in your bed*." I turned back to Todd. "Isn't she running for mayor?"

Todd paled a little beneath his fake tan. "I'm not legally responsible for any of their involvement."

I raised an eyebrow. "Oh, so you admit they were involved."

"I'm not saying shit." Todd's eyes narrowed and he leaned even closer to me. "The twenty million, it's a payout, for those months we were married. Alimony. Yeah, alimony."

"I assume there's at least one civil servant watching our little discussion that wasn't involved twelve years ago. Probably taking notes right about now. I'd use the twenty million to pay them off to keep quiet too." I shrugged again, as if what happened to Todd and the corrupt cops, lawyers and judges didn't mean anything to me.

"Wire the money, then you're gone." He thumbed the air like a hitchhiker. "For good. My PI will keep tabs on you. If you so much as think about coming here again, think about me, he'll know and I'll have the murder charges stick."

Empty threats. Little did he know he'd be seeing murder charges in his own future. "Whatever. You're so vain, Todd. As if I'd ever think about you. Besides, that list I just gave, they're going to roll on you. Elections are coming up. They'll do damage control and take you down. Besides, the hit man you hired alone could put you behind bars."

He stood as well, the metal table all that separated us, his eyes narrowed. This was the man who'd destroyed my life. This was the man who'd made me scared of everything. This was the man who made me realize what love really was, because compared to the sham, miserable marriage I had with him, Grif was everything. *Everything.*

"What the fuck are you talking about?" he asked, looking at me as if I'd lost my mind. "Don't accuse me of crap I didn't do."

Oh, please. "What, buy off city employees? Or do you mean the hit man? If he'd really killed me, you would've gone down for murder. It was a stupid move. This," I waved my hand around the small room, "this is more your style. Using your friends on the force to protect you from one woman."

He tossed the chair out of his way, came around to stand directly in front of me. I tilted my head back to keep my eyes on his, refusing to retreat. "I admitted to wanting Elizabeth for her money. Hell, the next guy that hears her name will do the same. I'll even take your millions and admit I'm in it all just for the money. The judge is dead. The others," it was his turn to shrug, "they've taken money from others besides me. They'll go down all on their own. But don't, for one second, think I'd be stupid enough to put a hit out on you. Talk about vain." He backed up. "My people will call you. Have the cash ready."

He turned, opened the door. There stood Grif, blocking his exit.

43

rif

"I WANT TO KILL YOU," I GROWLED.

Lawton's eyes got as round as saucers as he looked up at me. I was several inches taller and a foot wider. He retreated as I stepped into the room. The guy really was a pussy. "Who the fuck are you?"

I continued as if he hadn't talked. "Inside a police station isn't the best place to do it, so consider yourself lucky."

"Oh yeah, why's that?" he asked, all false bravado and hot air.

"Because all I'm going to do to you is this." Before he even had a chance to blink, I clocked him. He went down, out cold, blood dripping from his nose. Yup, total pussy. I wanted to do more, to cool the raging anger I had in me.

I'd had to fucking stand with all the other officers, a public defender and Lawton's asshole lawyer in the tiny viewing room and watch Anna and Lawton *discuss* Elizabeth as if she were a car. Anna had let Lawton talk smack about her, let him have the upper hand. This whole fucked up *questioning* hadn't been about the police wanting to talk a decade-old death, it had been about fucking *Todd*. He'd needed the police to corral a woman into talking with him. Total. Fucking. Pussy.

I knew what she was doing and why she sat there, taunted the man, then let him have what he wanted. Or at least let him think he was getting everything he wanted. It was only a matter of time before Jane Doe got enough hard evidence to print a piece about Lawton's life insurance policy on his brother. At that point, Anna wouldn't have to say a word. Jane Doe would get the DA to look into his actions and a grand jury would find enough to bring him to trial. If he got off, which was highly likely, he'd be ruined.

If I had my way, and if Anders followed through, Lawton would only make it to a holding cell in the county jail before he got what was coming.

I stared down at Lawton, breathing hard.

"You got to have all the fun," Anna pouted.

I looked up, met her dark gaze, grinned. "Yeah, I did. That felt damn good." I held my hand out for her. "Let's get the hell out of here."

She took my hand and stepped over Lawton, not before kicking him in the crotch on the way. "Whoops, I slipped."

Roberts and Hosanski shouldered their way into the room, looked down at Lawton, hands on hips. I didn't wait for them to comment, not only because I didn't give a shit what they'd say, but I wanted Anna out of the building. Now. "You have nothing on her. The next time Lawton needs to deal with a woman, I recommend staying out of it. He's bad fucking news. Stick with him and your careers are over. Like McDonalds? That's where you'll be working by the end of the month if you don't get your noses out of this shit. Sounds like it's a good thing that judge—Saunders is dead, otherwise he'd be disbarred, arrested and put in jail with the men he put away. He'd wished he were dead about five minutes behind bars."

Both men shifted uncomfortably. They were young, too young to have been around twelve years ago, most likely playing junior varsity football at the time.

"If you have anything else for Miss Edwards, or the other Miss Edwards, talk to their lawyer."

I didn't let go of Anna's hand until we were out of the building and in the back of a taxi.

"You came for me," she said, looking up at me as if surprised.

My brows shot up. "I never left you. As soon as you walked out that door with the detectives, I grabbed a taxi to the station. Anders stayed with Elizabeth in the suite." I had to touch her, to know she was all right, so I ran my knuckles down her soft cheek "It took me an hour to clear the front desk; I needed Peters to vouch for me and talk to the captain before they'd let me stand in that small room and watch you and Lawton." I grimaced at the sight of the two of them squaring off. I couldn't do anything to protect her from the bastard, to stand with her as she battled her biggest fear, her worst enemy.

I pulled her into me and kissed her. Just the feel of her in my arms soothed the animal inside me. Those detectives took my woman and I had to get her back. I couldn't strike another officer, clearly on the way to turning bad, but luckily I had a chance to deck Lawton. Fuck, that felt good.

"You heard our conversation then?" She placed her palm against my jaw.

"Every word."

"I don't think Todd called Anders to have me killed."

"You don't think he was lying just to cover his ass?" I wouldn't put it past the asshole. I paid the driver and walked through the hotel lobby. Besides being a misogynistic sociopath, the guy was a total sleaze.

Anna thought for a moment, bit her lip as we waited for the elevator to take us up to our suite. "It's been so long, I didn't know what he'd be like. He was exactly the same. He had to get his friends to bring me in. He was only worried about himself. About the money."

"He came up with the plot to kill his brother. That says devious to me."

"He's gotten away with it. All these years and he's still free. No one's even considering him, at least until Jane Doe pulls it all together. It was the perfect crime. Why mess with it? Why would he want to go to jail now?"

"Desperation?"

We took the elevator to our floor.

Anna shook her head as we walked down the hall. "No. He didn't do it. I'm sure of it."

I pulled the keycard from his pocket. "Then who?"

We pushed open the door and found out.

ANNA

AS GRIF WOULD SAY, HOLY FUCK. "HELLO, FATHER." MY VOICE CAME OUT stronger than I expected, especially since I hadn't seen the man since my eighteenth birthday and never imagined it happening again.

Grif's hand tugged me so half my body was behind his. He slid his hand around to his back in an automatic reaction to grab his gun. It wasn't there.

My father stood with Elizabeth at his side, gun to her head. Anders was on the floor facedown, unconscious, with blood seeping from...somewhere. I couldn't tell where he'd been shot. God, I hoped he wasn't dead.

I wanted to go to him, to help him, but I couldn't.

I wanted to scream for help, but it would do no good.

I wanted to freak out, but it wouldn't help.

The only way I could help any of us now was to deal with my father. He wasn't *Dad*. He'd never been a dad.

"Olivia, you look...older." That voice. I remembered that voice. He was a handsome man, handsome in a way that millions of dollars could provide. Tanning beds, manicures, face lifts, a three–hundred-dollar haircut, bespoke suits. It did a good job hiding his gambling problems. I never would have known by looking at him that he was desperate for cash.

"You just look...old," I replied. He did. I did quick math. He was in his early sixties now and he hadn't aged gracefully. He seemed smaller. I hadn't grown since the last time I'd seen him, so perhaps he was shrinking. Or, over the years, my mind had made him into something more than he really was.

Elizabeth stood tall, her shoulders back. She looked nervous, but remained calm. I met her blue eyes and her chin went up. We were in this together. The man holding the gun to her head meant nothing to her either.

"Who's this? Your policeman friend?" A sheen of sweat coated his brow. His hand holding the gun to Elizabeth's head shook slightly. The calm, powerful demeanor I remembered was gone. Somehow, my return had made him snap.

"Grif, let me introduce you to my father, Grayson Edwards."

Grif didn't say anything. Didn't even blink.

My father laughed, the sound coming out a little hysterical. "Father," he replied. "Right."

He was losing his mind.

"Tie him up," Father lifted his chin toward Grif.

I held out my hands, palms up. "With what? It's not like I carry around a bunch of rope in my suitcase."

"I have a tie or two in my luggage. Will that work, sir?" Grif's voice was flat, even. Calm.

I glanced at Grif, surprised he was offering something that would incapacitate himself.

Father's eyes darted between us, indecision on his face. "Fine. But don't do anything stupid. I shot that big guy, I have no issue about doing the same to Elizabeth. Olivia, you go. *Grif*," he said it with such venom, "can stay right there."

I believed him when he said he'd shoot Elizabeth, probably Grif after. I darted a glance at Anders. No change. I looked to my father whose gray eyes showed how agitated he was and nodded.

I left Grif's side and went into our bedroom, dashed to his suitcase to look for something, anything, that I could use as a weapon. Flipping open the top, I grinned. Exhilaration washed through me at the sight of Grif's sidearm.

Of course. He couldn't take it into the police station; he'd have to leave it behind. I grabbed the cold steel, tucked it into the back waistband of my jeans, made sure my shirt covered it.

Remembering the ties as the ruse for me to get to the gun, I ransacked the clothes until I found two. Returning to the main room, I glanced at Grif. He just looked at me with that dark, brooding gaze, giving nothing away. I took a deep breath, slipped into that space in my mind where nothing could touch me. Where I was shielded from all emotion. If I was going to do this, I needed to take all feelings out of it. Pretend Grif was just another man, that Elizabeth wasn't my only sister. My father was here threatening our lives for a reason and I had to find out what it was, as well as try to save us.

"Over there," Father said with a tilt of his head. Grif walked slowly, deliberately, to the dining room chair. He sat and I moved to stand behind him.

"Make it tight," my father growled.

I wasn't a Boy Scout, but I tied it fairly snug, reassured by the quick squeeze of Grif's fingers around mine. He could free himself if he worked at it.

Father dragged Elizabeth around to see my handiwork and seemed satisfied when gave it a test tug. I breathed a quiet sigh of relief that I hadn't tried to fool him.

He pushed Elizabeth toward a chair, and she caught herself before she fell. "Sit. Both of you. Let's have a little chat."

I lowered myself across from Elizabeth, Grif next to me. I sat between him and my father, who chose to stand. Pace. He waved the gun around as he spoke.

"You had to fuck up my life, didn't you?"

I looked to Elizabeth who gave a negligible shrug.

"You!" Father pointed at me. "I'm talking about you!" Beads of sweat dripped down his temple. His gray hair was damp. Circles formed beneath the arms on his blue golf shirt.

"I haven't seen you since I was eighteen," I said carefully. "How did I fuck up your life?"

"By being born. Jesus, you don't know." He ran his hand through his receding hair. "Of course you don't know."

This family reunion couldn't go on forever. Anders lay on the floor, dying. I had to move this along.

"What is it I don't know?" I asked.

"Didn't you ever wonder why I shipped you away? Why I never wanted you back?" He paused and glared at me. "I never wanted *you*, because I'm not your father."

44

nna

MY MOUTH FELL OPEN AS I TRIED TO PROCESS. "YOU'RE...YOU'RE NOT MY FATHER," I whispered. My mind started spinning, processing what he'd said. If he wasn't my father, then...

"Your mother," he spat out the words like venom. "She got pregnant with you by the chauffeur. She said she loved him, wanted to leave me for him. *Him*. A chauffeur. Of course, I couldn't divorce her. So she had you."

My world as I knew it bottomed out. This man, this crazy, cruel man, wasn't my father. I wasn't sure if I should be numb, scared or relieved. I glanced at Grif, but he just stared at the man with an unleashed rage. Quiet, focused. Waiting.

"Are you *my* father?" Elizabeth asked, her voice soft.

My father...no, I was glad to say I couldn't call him that anymore, whipped his head around to look at Elizabeth. "Oh, you're mine all right. I kept *your* mother on a short leash."

I needed to keep his focus off Elizabeth. "Why did you marry my mother in the first place?"

Grayson looked surprised I even asked. "For money, of course. You're not very smart, are you? Before you ask, yes, obviously I married Victoria for her money, too."

It was all about the money. Everything. My father—Grayson. Todd. All they wanted was money. They were completely blinded, obsessed by it. Addicted even. It seemed it had even driven them slightly insane and completely corrupt.

"I've only seen you a few times since I was six years old. I still can't understand why I fucked up your life. You literally wiped me from it."

"Because you're going to dig into the past. I know you are. Todd's an idiot and you'll see through him and get to me."

"You were the one who arranged for Lawton's brother to die," Grif said, seeing through Grayson where I couldn't. I was too close to it, too muddled by all of his revelations. "To get Olivia out of your life. You waited all those years until she was eighteen to get a hold of her mother's money, but then it was all locked up in a trust, which neither you nor Lawton could touch."

Grif sat there, arms pulled behind him, as if we were talking about the stats of a baseball game. I knew him though, could tell every nuance of his emotions. He wasn't relaxed, he wasn't calm. He was coiled tight like a spring. Once the bindings at his wrist were undone, he'd release all that tension on Grayson.

"It didn't take much," Grayson told us. "A nudge here, a suggestion there. The man's a follower. A lemming. He'll do whatever I say and he has no idea." His voice was so smug. Spittle flew from his mouth and he wiped the back of his hand over his lips.

I glanced at Grif, trying to keep up. It was like wading through mud, understanding everything Grayson was sharing. Everything was murky and unclear. I kept getting stuck. Held up by the fact that he wasn't my father.

He was the one who'd arranged for me to kill David? Todd thought, after all this time, that he'd been the mastermind, when he was a mere puppet. It, this... everything, wasn't about Todd, it was about me. Making me go to jail, to make me pay for my inheritance being tied in a trust. For being born.

We'd set up Todd last night because I'd needed payback for all he'd done to me. For being *his* puppet to murder. I'd sought revenge on the wrong person.

When Todd told me earlier that I'd ruined his life by coming back, it was the truth. Once I disappeared, he probably hadn't even thought about me. Kept a PI, sure, to make sure I didn't return, but if he didn't get an update, I was as good as gone. He could go about his life, making plenty of money off his position as my father—no, Grayson's—right-hand man. Sure, he'd been disappointed at not getting my inheritance, but Grayson had kept him on the payroll so someone knew he skimmed money from the company for his debts. Todd wouldn't tell, he wanted the big paycheck. Besides, he just needed to wait for the next big score. Elizabeth.

For twelve years, I'd been looking over my shoulder in fear of Todd finding me. The irony was, he'd never been looking.

"Did you know where I was? All this time?"

Grayson shook his head. "No. Not until one of my men found your name on a flight. Then I knew I had to get rid of you. Once and for all."

"You put out a hit on your own daughter?" Elizabeth asked, her voice just shy of a squeal.

Grayson's eyes narrowed. "I told you, she's not my daughter!"

All at once, like in a movie, my brain went from super slo-mo to fast forward. "My mother. It wasn't just a simple car accident. You killed her, didn't you? That's what you've been trying to hide. Not your gambling problems, but murder." It was so obvious now. Oh my God, my mother was murdered. When he said nothing, just looked at me with those anger-filled eyes, I knew I was right. "Why?"

"She was going to leave me. Take you and leave. So I had to do it. I needed her money. I owed people. If we divorced, it would all go away."

"The driver. Was he—"

"Yes. Andrew Harris. Can you imagine?" he asked as he paced back and forth. "Grayson Edwards cuckolded by the chauffeur. Wife takes child and leaves to live a life slumming for love."

Tears filled my eyes, slid down my cheeks. I couldn't stop them. I could appreciate what my mother felt. Being trapped by a man who didn't love her—didn't even like her—who was using her for her money. Money that wouldn't be used on her or her child. To pay people off, to pay gambling debts. Then, finding a man who made her world come alive, who cherished her. Who loved her.

I glanced at Grif, reassuring myself that he was next to me. I felt all those things with him.

"Now, you all have to die. This is a secret that can't get out." He puffed up his chest. "I mean, I'm Grayson Edwards."

He walked over to Elizabeth, grabbed her arm and hauled her up, pulling her into his side. She cried out. I saw panic flare in her eyes right before they were covered by her whipping hair. I saw Grif's arms tense as if he was working at the knot.

Elizabeth and Grif were innocent in all of this. This wasn't about them. It hadn't been about anyone but me. I was Grayson's reminder of what his wife had done to him. While I was alive, her duplicity was, too. This was about me. Grayson had even said it. *I* was the one who fucked up his life. *I* was the one to die.

It was my job to end it. To end the horrible, crazy nightmare that had been Olivia Edwards' life. So I slowly stood, too. I wasn't handling him sitting down.

"You killed my mother, sent me away, gave me to Todd, then set me up to kill an innocent man. Now you hold a gun to my sister?" I narrowed my eyes, put my hands on my hips, closer to the gun.

The tears had dried and now I was pissed. I was thirty years old, but my entire life started a few short weeks ago. All because a stupid valet mixed up my rental car. If that hadn't happened, I wouldn't have met Grif. Grayson wouldn't have become paranoid. I would never have learned the truth.

I wasn't Anna Scott.

I wasn't Olivia Edwards.

I was Olivia Harris.

"She's not your sister," Grayson spat. "Didn't you learn anything in those boarding schools?" He lifted his gun, put it to Elizabeth's temple. "Say goodbye." Her eyes widened, but she held still.

"Actually, I learned quite a bit in boarding school," I countered. "Including how to shoot." I pulled the gun from the back of my jeans and fired. I didn't even have to aim. Military school had provided good training. Just like the SEALs, I shot Grayson Edwards with a double tap.

He fell backward to the floor, leaving Elizabeth standing there. It had happened so fast, she hadn't even blinked.

"State Champion," I added, but he couldn't hear. He was dead. The gun felt familiar in my grasp, from all the times I spent at the shooting range. Just in case.

I tried not to think about the fact that I'd killed two people. The first, David, hadn't deserved it. He—and myself—had been innocent in a twisted game. Grayson Edwards, on the other hand, deserved to die. He'd killed three innocent people, three I knew about at least, and ruined my life. Or my life so far. It wasn't over.

It was just beginning.

We stared at Grayson's body for a few seconds, then I came back to myself. So much had been answered. I wasn't Grayson Edwards' daughter. My mother had been murdered. My real father, who I never knew, had been murdered. Elizabeth wasn't my sister. Now wasn't the time to sort it all out.

"Elizabeth, call 9-1-1 and check on Anders." I dashed to Grif and slid to my knees behind him to fumble with the knot. He'd almost gotten it undone. Once free, he stood, pulled me up into a fierce hug, then tipped my face back to look at him.

"Jesus, Anna. Are you okay?"

"Yeah." I nodded and breathed in Grif's scent, comforted by it. By him.

"He's alive!" Elizabeth called out.

Grif's eyes flared with heat so intense I felt scorched. "Later," he promised as he pulled his cell from his pocket. "Call Carmody with the FBI. This is going to blow up in our faces. You need protection."

We dealt with getting Anders loaded with the paramedics and then the police. We were taken to the station for questioning, but this time, when I sat in the cold interrogation room, I had Grif by my side.

45

rif

I SWEAR I AGED TEN YEARS. I HADN'T LOOKED IN THE MIRROR YET, BUT I wouldn't be surprised if my hair had turned gray. Every alpha male, caveman instinct had screamed to protect Anna, but there had been nothing I could have done. Not when Lawton was working her over at the station, getting what he wanted from her. Not when Grayson Edwards held a gun to Elizabeth.

The hours we spent being questioned the FBI had been busy. They'd taken us from the police station and whisked us away to another hotel and away from the reporters. Watching the news on TV, they'd put a good spin on everything.

It was simple: Grayson Edwards had taken objection to his daughter, Elizabeth, ending the engagement to Todd Lawton because of the call girl escapade, which wasn't even a day old. Grayson had tracked Elizabeth to a downtown hotel where she'd been hiding from the press of her fiancé's infidelity, and forced his way into her hotel room with a gun, ready to kill her. Seeking protection from the media, she'd hired a bodyguard who had attempted to protect Elizabeth from her deranged father and had been injured in the process.

This spin left Anna out of it entirely. No one knew she had returned, other than her crazy family who'd had private investigators watching for her. The fact that Elizabeth, Lawton and Edwards had guys on retainer for just that purpose was alarming. The Griffin family, slightly dysfunctional, looked like the Cleavers from the '50s TV show in comparison.

Most importantly, Anna's photo had only popped up on the screen in passing, referencing her disappearance, but that was old news and the photo they used didn't look much like her. There was no chance Moretti could see her on the national news and learn she wasn't actually dead. He'd never met her, so I didn't even think he knew what she looked like. The name wasn't even the same. But it wasn't a guarantee. With Moretti in federal lock-up awaiting trial, the FBI could keep tabs on him. While they did that, I'd keep tabs on Anna. Which wouldn't be a hardship.

Elizabeth had been unable to visit us, since the media followed her every move. She'd stayed at Anders' hospital bedside, tending to the guy who had saved her life. In a way, he had. I didn't want to read much into the two of them. Elizabeth was just eighteen and Anders was a *consultant*. Once the media storm blew over, I'd be keeping tabs on them.

"This seems to be a trend," I told Anna, two days after the shooting. We were in another hotel room, another bed.

Naked, Anna rolled on top of me and kissed my chin. "Oh?"

I ran my hand over her silky curls. "Hiding out in a hotel room. For days." When her mouth moved lower to kiss my neck, I added, "Not that I mind."

"Yeah, I don't mind sex and room service either."

I smiled, rolled so she was on her back and I hovered over her. "Vixen. We can't stay here forever."

Anna pouted, her full lip plumping out. "I know. But where should we go?"

"Denver's out." I didn't need to go back there. My captain could give me a recommendation to work anywhere. Anywhere Moretti wasn't.

"New York's probably out, too. Unless I take Carmichael up on his job offer."

I reached down and pinched her very nice ass.

"Ow!" she squealed.

"Pick another job," I growled.

Anna's face relaxed as she smiled up at me. "I want to take Grayson's money and start an organization to help women and children."

Grayson Edwards hadn't left a will. Why, I had no idea. Perhaps he considered himself invincible. Regardless, Anna and Elizabeth were his beneficiaries. Most of his estate was tied up in stock with Edwards Enterprises, but the remainder was sizable. I didn't know the exact amount of money Anna's mother had left for her, but she wasn't hurting for cash. She didn't need Grayson's money. Or want it.

"I think that's a great idea," I replied, my voice soft. She amazed me constantly, this woman who had come into my life, completely by mistake. Completely randomly. "What about Boston?"

She considered for a moment. "Too cold."

"Hawaii?"

"Now you're talking," she replied, grinning. "Elizabeth has to pick which college she wants to go to in the fall, but she'll live with us over her breaks."

"You like that she wants to do that."

"I thought she'd be upset that we weren't really sisters, but I think it made her relieved. She'll need help dealing with her father, with Grayson. So will I. But we'll do it together. Sisters or not."

I lowered my head to kiss along her collarbone. It was a spot I loved to brush my lips over, a delicate bone covered with soft, warm skin. It reminded me of how fragile, how precious Anna was.

"She might want to be close to Anders," Anna added.

I growled at the idea. "He needs to find a new job, too."

Anna's fingers ran through my hair. I loved that feeling. "If you're going to treat her like a little sister, then you're going to have to come to terms with men being interested in her."

I looked up into Anna's eyes. "College. After she graduates from college Anders can have her. Until then, I'll be watching."

Anna was naked beneath me and we were talking about Anders and Elizabeth. It had only been a short time since I'd had her, but I wanted her again. I couldn't get enough. Now, with all the dangers of her past left there, we could think about the future.

"I HAVE TOO MANY NAMES," SHE SAID. ANOTHER TWO DAYS HAD PASSED.

We walked through Golden Gate State Park, enjoying the sunny weather. Anna wore a baseball hat and sunglasses as a precaution, but we were confident that the press wasn't focused on her.

I held her hand, keeping her close to my side. Neither had said it outright, but we were both afraid to be apart, that somehow the other would be taken away.

I smiled as I took in the view of the iconic bridge, the rugged shoreline in the distance. "Olivia Edwards."

"Olivia Harris," she added. "Anna Scott."

"How about one more?" I asked. It might not be the time, but I'd learned there never was a perfect moment.

Anna stopped, turned to look up at me. "One more name? Don't you think three is enough?"

I shrugged casually as I tucked a curl that had escaped from her hat back behind her ear. "I thought Anna Griffin had a nice ring to it. Speaking of rings..."

"Oh my God," Anna whispered as I pulled a black velvet box from my pocket.

Nerves got the better of me and my fingers fumbled as I opened the lid. She stared at the ring, a solitaire diamond with a simple platinum band.

"When—"

"It was my grandmother's. My mom had it. I called her, had her overnight it."

I couldn't see her eyes behind her dark glasses and couldn't tell if she liked it. It was modest, simple. "If you don't like it..."

She must have read my mind because she tugged off her sunglasses, let them fall to the grass at our feet. There, I saw it all. Love, longing, lust. "Don't like it? I love it, Grif. It's perfect."

I grinned. I couldn't help it. I'd never felt this way before, this overwhelming sense that all I'd been looking for stood directly in front of me. "Marry me?"

"Yes," Anna said, nodding her head. A tear slipping down my cheek and I wiped it away with my thumb. "I think Anna Griffin is the best one yet."

ABOUT THE AUTHOR

Vanessa Vale is the *USA Today* Bestselling author of over 50 books, sexy romance novels, including her popular Bridgewater historical romance series and hot contemporary romances featuring unapologetic bad boys who don't just fall in love, they fall hard. When she's not writing, Vanessa savors the insanity of raising two boys and figuring out how many meals she can make with a pressure cooker. While she's not as skilled at social media as her kids, she loves to interact with readers.

www.vanessavaleauthor.com
facebook.com/vanessavaleauthor
instagram.com/vanessa_vale_author

ALSO BY VANESSA VALE

Grade-A Beefcakes

Sir Loin Of Beef

T-Bone

Tri-Tip

Porterhouse

Skirt Steak

Small Town Romance

Montana Fire

Montana Ice

Montana Heat

Montana Wild

Montana Mine

Steele Ranch

Spurred

Wrangled

Tangled

Hitched

Lassoed

Bridgewater County Series

Ride Me Dirty

Claim Me Hard

Take Me Fast

Hold Me Close

Make Me Yours

Kiss Me Crazy

Mail Order Bride of Slate Springs Series

A Wanton Woman

A Wild Woman

A Wicked Woman

Bridgewater Ménage Series

Their Runaway Bride

Their Kidnapped Bride

Their Wayward Bride

Their Captivated Bride

Their Treasured Bride

Their Christmas Bride

Their Reluctant Bride

Their Stolen Bride

Their Brazen Bride

Their Bridgewater Brides- Books 1-3 Boxed Set

Outlaw Brides Series

Flirting With The Law

MMA Fighter Romance Series

Fight For Her

Wildflower Bride Series

Rose

Hyacinth

Dahlia

Daisy

Lily

Montana Men Series

The Lawman

The Cowboy

The Outlaw

Standalone Reads

Twice As Delicious

Western Widows

Sweet Justice

Mine To Take

Relentless

Sleepless Night

Man Candy - A Coloring Book

www.ingramcontent.com/pod-product-compliance
Lightning Source LLC
LaVergne TN
LVHW011802060526
838200LV00053B/3656